BED
S
4/7

Elizabe̲ ̲ ̲ ̲ ̲ ̲ ̲ ̲ ̲ ̲ ̲ ̲ ̲ she was thirty-four years old. During the war she worked as a bus conductress at Merton Garage. In 1956 she and her husband moved to Devon and bought their first guesthouse.

Now retired, they live in East Sussex.

Trouble and Strife

ELIZABETH WAITE

sphere
An imprint of
Little, Brown Book Group
100 Victoria Embankment
London EC4Y 0DY

An Hachette UK Company
www.hachette.co.uk

SPHERE

First published in Great Britain in 1997
by Little, Brown and Company and Warner Books
This paperback edition published in 2010 by Sphere

A CIP catalogue record for this book
is available from the British Library.

ISBN 978-0-7515-4494-7

Printed in Great Britain by
Clays Ltd, St Ives plc

Papers used by Sphere are natural, renewable and
recyclable products sourced from well-managed forests and certified
in accordance with the rules of the Forest Stewardship Council.

Mixed Sources

Part One

1950

Part One

1950

Chapter One

'I SWEAR THAT DAUGHTER of mine gets herself into more trouble than anyone else could imagine,' Ida Wilcox was muttering to herself as she replaced the telephone receiver.

It's unbelievable! Not to mention downright stupid, Ida thought. No sooner do we get our Ruby out of one mess than she gets herself into another. Yes, that was the truth an' there was no getting away from it.

Ida sighed heavily. Just lately she's taken me for a right old softie, and for the sake of keeping the peace I've let her get away with it. Well, a body can only stand so much.

She leant forward peering at her reflection in the mirror that hung on the wall of her narrow hallway. She looked tired and dishevelled, her cheeks hot, her hair a proper mess. God forgive her but there were times when the very thought of her daughter made her blood run cold.

She put the telephone back on the shelf and went into the living room. Now once again there was nothing she could do to stop herself from getting involved.

She would have to go and see for herself if Maggie Marshall's account of what had happened was true.

It was good of Maggie to phone her. After all, she was only a neighbour of Ruby's, but a kindly soul, not an old busybody like some she could name, and to be fair her reports to Ida were well meant.

'Ruby, what the hell am I going to do with you?' Ida cried out loud.

Somewhere something had gone wrong, she told herself wearily, and she supposed she would have to take a great deal of the blame on her own shoulders, although what she could have done differently was beyond her grasp.

As a little girl Ruby had looked like a china doll, tiny and so pretty, with a sweet nature to match. From her first day at school her teachers had stated that she was an intelligent child and each year her reports had been promising. Daft girl, she could have gone far if only she had put her mind to it, but, like most young girls, she had thought she knew it all. Boys and sex filled their heads as if it were a game. Well, Ruby had found out the hard way that if you partook of the sweets you had to pay the consequences.

Ida stared at the photograph of her husband which stood in a wooden frame on the mantelpiece. Ruby was the spitting image of her Dad. Short, small-boned, creamy complexion, fair hair that was as fine as spun silk and those blue eyes that at times could melt a heart made of stone.

'Poor Len,' she murmured, caressing the glass of the photograph frame with her forefinger. 'I honestly believe our Ruby would not have made such a mess of her life if only you had been here to help bring her up. It wasn't fair that you had to die so young.'

Where would Ruby go from here? Saddled with two babies and herself not yet eighteen. A wasted life, that's what it was and no mistake, and the galling thing is she'd brought it all on herself. If only she had used the brain God had given her, stayed on at school, there's no telling what she might have achieved.

Ida stood quietly looking at the photograph, wringing her hands, her face screwed up with worry. Her eyes that usually shone with brave determination were now clouded with tears. She was only five foot two inches tall and plump with it. No wonder she was always on her own with no one to talk matters over with. There were plenty of beautiful, well-dressed women about that men would look at twice, what chance did she stand of ever finding another loving partner? Half the time she didn't bother too much with her appearance and therefore could best be described as dowdy.

Ida ran her hands down over the brown twin-set and skirt she was wearing and vowed she would have to do something about herself. It wouldn't do to let herself become too frumpish. First things first, though. She would have to see what Ruby had been up to this time and do what she could to see her right. She certainly wasn't looking forward to it. But, as Maggie Marshall was fond of saying, every cloud has it's silver lining, and there was no denying that there was something pretty special about her only daughter, Ruby, when she was behaving herself.

She sighed again. Well, this time Ruby and her troubles would have to wait just a bit, she decided, as she sunk down into her deep familiar armchair, wallowing in the warmth of the fire-lit room.

She suddenly felt so tired and found that she was

filled with a longing she had not experienced for years. A longing for someone to share her worries with, someone to advise her, someone to comfort her, someone to laugh with, to be happy with. I'm always on my own when it comes down to it, she mused. Life could be so very different if only she had someone to share it with.

It was 1950 and she was almost forty years old. That thought alone was enough to sadden her. She, like a good many more, was a war widow, left with two sons and a daughter to bring up on her own.

During the war she had done her best. Month after month, year after year, trying to be optimistic, telling herself that it couldn't last for ever, that her husband would come home and from then on they would lead a marvellous life.

Leonard Wilcox and she, Ida Simmonds, had been childhood sweethearts. Married in 1929 when they were both nineteen, they had believed that the world was their oyster. Alan, their son, was born ten months after the wedding and Norman, their second, just one year later. What a year to have been born! 1931! Every newspaper and wireless programme had spelt out nothing but doom and gloom. The queues at the employment exchange grew by the day and by August the report was that two and three-quarter million men were now out of work.

She and Len had managed and were happy enough, even though Len was often put on short-time at the furniture factory where he had worked since he had left school at the age of fourteen. Ruby had been born in 1933 when everyone in their neighbourhood was finding it hard to make ends meet. By 1938 the dream that forming a League of Nations would prevent future wars was turning out to be an illusion. Britain was waking up to the fact that once again they had to prepare for war and many young men were joining the forces.

The summer that saw Ruby have her fifth birthday had been a scorcher and Len and herself had taken their children to the common and parks whenever possible. Ida sat back in her chair smiling softly to herself as she recalled those glorious days and the pleasure of getting Ruby's first school uniform together.

A fortnight before the German troops crossed the Polish frontier, the factory where Len worked closed down. Two days after Britain declared war Len joined the army.

Ida found herself wishing again, as she had so many many times, if only Len had waited to be called up, if only he'd had been sent to another regiment. Would it have made any difference? Who knows. The tragedy was that in May of 1940, Len, with the Royal West Kents, had only been in France for three weeks when the advancing German army swept through northern France. Thousands of British and French troops were safely evacuated by both small and large seagoing crafts from the beaches of Dunkirk. In all, over three hundred thousand men were landed safely back in England, in what Winston Churchill described as a 'miracle of deliverance'.

Over the years, Ida had lost count of the times she had said to herself, 'What a pity that the West Kents had been too far inland to make it to the coast'. Those men that weren't killed were captured by the Germans – Len amongst them. From June 1940 until his release in 1945, Len had remained a prisoner of war. Nothing could compensate for the heartache of those long five years.

Leonard Wilcox had returned home and with him had come hope. There had been days when Ida had felt that Len was gaining strength. Days when everything was bright, they were together again, tears and loneliness left behind. Each of them grateful for every smile, every touch of each other's hand, their heads resting on the pillow at night, in the same bed. Together. Other days she hadn't been able to bear to watch the pain that Len was suffering.

Within a year Len was dead. Dead too were their plans: the house they were going to buy, the trips to the seaside; seeing their two sons grow into men; watching their little girl grow into a young lady; thinking about the day she would get married, walking down the aisle on her father's arm. Well, that was only one of the dreams that hadn't come true. Len had been so ill that in the end he had been glad to die. She had been sad, so terribly sad and so very lonely.

For the umpteenth time Ida told herself that it was from the day that they had buried Len that the change in young Ruby had begun. It was only natural. Poor kid. She was thrilled to have her father back home. A father that thought the world of her and spoilt her at every opportunity that he got. Just coming up to being a teenager, Ruby had become embittered, jealous of her cousins and friends, resenting the fact that her father had died and theirs hadn't.

Then, as now, she felt helpless to know what to do for the best where Ruby was concerned. As her own two brothers often told her, no matter what you do for Ruby, she'll end up going her own way.

Aw well. Ida dragged herself to her feet and made for the kitchen. This was no time to be dwelling on the past. The sooner she got herself over to Ruby's and found out for herself what kind of trouble she'd landed herself in this time, the better.

Chapter Two

IT WAS A QUARTER to three on a Monday afternoon in late October and Ruby Brookshaw was well on the way to being drunk. She had only been at work for two hours when all the commotion had started and she'd been sacked.

The job at Morley's dress shop, not far from Morden Tube Station, had been a nice little number for her. It was only three days a week but at least it got her out of these two poxy rooms.

That Mrs Morley was a real bitch! 'She called me a lyin' slut!' Ruby shouted out loud. 'An' I wasn't gonna stand for that.'

As if in answer to her cry she heard the voice of Maggie Marshall calling from downstairs.

'The old bat must be down on her knees to be able to shout through that letter box.' Ruby muttered to herself as she steered clear of an overturned chair and made her way gingerly to the top of the stairs.

'Go away an' mind yer own bleedin' business,' Ruby yelled.

'Let me in,' answered Maggie, 'nothing's so bad that it can't be sorted.'

'Shut yer mouth an' go away,' said Ruby, and dragged herself down to sit on the floor.

She heard the bang as Maggie let the flap of the letter box drop and she grinned to herself. She shouldn't take her temper out on Maggie. Her life was bad enough as it was. Without Maggie living just across the street, God knows how she would cope. She'd never be able to get outside these four walls if it weren't for Maggie offering to have the babies. Nosey old thing that she was, she loved those two little ones and she took good care of them. And she kept a spotless home. Well, she should, shouldn't she? Ruddy whole house to herself.

You jumped at the chance to take a part-time job when she offered to have the twins, Ruby reminded herself. Yeah, well now you haven't even got a job to go to any more.

She'd have to have another drink. In the doorway of what served for a living room she gave a vicious kick to a bucket that contained baby clothes. She'd put them in to soak before she left for work that morning, intending to wash them and hang them out in the back yard when she came home. 'Sod 'em,' she said, as the water splashed over onto the worn linoleum, 'I don't give a monkey's if they never get washed.'

Life wasn't worth the struggle which ever way she looked at it. She picked up the bottle of Gordon's, splashed some gin into her glass and without bothering to add any tonic water she tossed most of it down her throat.

She'd never win! She'd done all right at school. 'Well, I did from time to time,' she muttered to herself. 'The

best part was when me dad came home. A lot of things
might have turned out different if only he had lived.'

The same went for Andy Morris. Only he wasn't dead.
Only on the other side of the blooming world. God!
Wasn't young love sweet? And blind.

She and Andy had been in love. No matter if all the
adults in the world told her it wasn't so, she knew
different. It had been true love. Andy had been four
years older than Ruby. Determined to make something
of his life he had been attending night-school three nights
a week, besides having a full-time job in an engineering
factory down in Bendon Valley.

A stray tear trickled from her eye and ran down her
cheek as she recalled meeting him up at Stockwell when
he finished classes.

'He used to give the fourpence for me tube fare,' she
mumbled. 'And he used to take me to the pictures every
Saturday night.'

She dashed the stupid tears away. 'Why did his family
have to go and emigrate to Australia?'

Be fair. When Andy had insisted that he wanted to stay
behind, both his mum and dad had offered her the chance
to go with them. Her mother was shocked. 'You've only
just left school, definitely No,' she'd said. Her mother's
brothers and their wives had all made a firm stand: she
was too young.

What had age got to do with it? Dear Jesus, she was
only seventeen now, married with twins! Andy had gone
to Australia. She'd not heard a word from him since.
She'd taken up with Brian Brookshaw. Or was the boot
on the other foot? He was five years older than her and
he'd made her pregnant before she'd known him five
minutes. If he'd had his way he'd have cleared off and

she wouldn't have seen his arse for dust. How many times had she wished that he had?

It hadn't been like that. Oh no. Her mother's two brothers had seen to that. The pair of them were great bruisers who no one argued with. Well, not if they knew what was good for them they didn't.

Ruby took another swig of her gin and grinned again. To be honest she loved her uncles, they both had a great sense of fun. If only they didn't always think they knew what was best for everyone else. The pair of them certainly were characters, outspoken, independent men, but hard drinking and hard fighting came easily to them when the occasion arose.

Her uncle Bert was the older of the two. Six foot four, with sandy hair, blue eyes and a ruddy complexion, he was married to Josephine. Ruby giggled and gin ran out of the corner of her mouth. Known as Jozy, her aunt was thin, even a bit frail-looking but no one who knew her was deceived by that. Jozy was lovely but her temper when she was put out would frighten the best of them.

Uncle Jeff was two years younger than Uncle Bert, still a great big tall man, very much alike in looks to his brother, but with a more cautious attitude to life. He looked before he leapt; Bert jumped in, feet first.

Jeff was married to Sheila. Do anything for anybody, would Sheila Simmonds, but woe betide anyone that crossed her. Ruby laughed happily at this thought. Her aunt Sheila was a big loud-mouthed, jolly woman. Her surname, before she'd married Uncle Jeff, had been Nightingale. Anything less like a nightingale would be hard to imagine, as Peggy Woodstock – one of Sheila's neighbours – had found out the day Sheila had caught her thumping her three year old little girl. They certainly were a tight knit family, the Simmonds.

Both brothers worked in Billingsgate, the big London fish market, which was near London Bridge and all members of the family lived in Fountain Road, Tooting. Their father, and his father before him, had all worked at Billingsgate.

Ruby looked at her empty glass and sighed heavily. What chance had she stood between the lot of them? There weren't going to be any illegitimate babies in their family. Her uncles had said that Brian Brookshaw had to marry her. And they'd seen to it that he did.

'More's the pity,' she muttered.

All responsibility had been taken away from her mother, who had been only to glad to be shot of it, and everything arranged by her uncles. No bride could have asked for more. A great big white wedding, three bridesmaids, a page boy, a bouquet and posies of flowers that were gaudy and far too big, and a reception afterwards at the Fountain public house. All of Fountain Road and more than half of Blackshaw Road had had free booze that day. Come to think of it, it would have been far better if her uncles had seen to it that she and Brian had somewhere half-way decent to live.

Left to Brian and his dad – his mother had died years ago – they'd ended up in these two grotty rooms in Love Lane, Mitcham. Love Lane! That was a laugh, wasn't it? Not much love had been shown to her since she'd moved in. Her father-in-law lived downstairs. He was a bigot and a bully. Like father like son, Brian took pleasure in tormenting her.

Paint factory, the Lavender Works where they made soap and Mitcham Lavender Water, half a dozen pubs, and the Fairgreen with its street traders. Only good thing about this area was Hutton's the fish shop. The mouthwatering smell could send you crazy if you didn't have the money to buy your supper.

Ruby had thought she didn't much like living in Fountain Road when she was a child. Never a day passed now that she didn't wish she was back there with her mother. A long road of small working class houses, it was a proper community of Londoners, most of whom worked hard for a living and were friendly and helpful, good-hearted people. With the ending of the Second World War the old houses had been repaired, sculleries were turned into bathrooms and extensions were built on to the backs. Some houses had telephones installed and, wonder of wonders, television sets began to appear. Fancy sitting in your own front room watching a film.

However respectable they considered themselves, they didn't need much of an excuse to let their hair down. Engagements, weddings, christenings, even funerals were all good excuses for a booze-up and neighbours didn't wait to be asked to join in. An old upright piano, with its top open, would be wheeled out onto the pavement and thumped by anyone that fancied they could knock out a tune. It wasn't like that here in Mitcham. The only friend she had here was Maggie and she was fifty if she were a day.

Ruby spread her arms down onto the table and lowered her head to rest on them. By now she'd had so much to drink that she had dissolved into an orgy of self-pity. Being a mother wasn't so bad if only it wasn't a twenty-four hour a day job. There was no getting away from it, she did love her two little boys. A soppy grin came to her lips. They're little angels when they're asleep. Brian didn't love her and she sure as hell didn't love him. What kindnesses did he ever show her? None.

Tears began to run down her cheeks. She longed to be a little girl again, with no responsibilities. She wanted her mum, her brothers, her uncles, aunts and cousins all to love her, to give her a hug now and again.

Most of all, she longed for her Dad.

Chapter Three

IDA DIDN'T WANT TO go over to Mitcham, but she knew there was no getting out of it. She'd make herself a cup of tea first. Yes, that's what she would do. And perhaps she would have calmed down a bit by then.

She took a match from the box, struck it and held it to the gas jet, put the kettle on and stood staring into space while she waited for it to boil, and when it did she put three spoonfuls of tea into the pot and made a brew.

A burst of wind rattled a picture on the wall as Ida listened to the back door being opened.

'Just in time, am I? That's good 'cos I could murder a cuppa.'

Ida raised her eyes to meet those of her eldest brother and saw that he was studying her. His blue eyes looked troubled and she noticed his sandy hair was streaked with more grey than she had realised.

'Don't look so worried,' he ordered, 'and what are you doing standing out 'ere in the kitchen?'

'I'm trying to get up enough courage to go over and

17

sort our Ruby out, once again. Maggie Marshall's been
on the phone, seems Ruby's lost her job. Maggie said
something about the police so Gawd knows what she's
been up to this time.'

Bert Simmonds put out his hand. The rough skin of his
tobacco-stained fingers brushed against her cheek. 'Don't
let it bother you so much. You should be used to Ruby
and her troubles by now.'

Ida sighed, 'If I live to be a 'undred years old I'll never
get used to that girl and what she gets up to. It's strange,
y'know Bert, Ruby was such a kind, loving, good little girl
till she reached her teens. Now, no matter where she goes
or what she does she always seems to court disaster.'

When her brother made no reply, she sighed again,
pushed a few hair pins tighter into her hair which was
fashioned into a bun at the nape of her neck, and reached
up to the shelf for two cups and saucers.

''Ere, I'll get those for you, short arse. Funny ain't it,
how short you an' Ruby are, the only women left in our
family, while us blokes are so tall,' he laughed. 'Good job
it wasn't the other way round, eh?'

Ida grinned. 'Yer silly sod.'

As she poured the tea out she told herself that she felt
ill, she had stood almost as much as she could take from
Ruby. Still, she'd better get a move on. If she was lucky
she wouldn't have to walk down to the Broadway to get
a bus to the Fairgreen at Mitcham, she could get on the
trolley bus at the top of the road. She put two heaped
spoonfuls of sugar in the largest cup and took it through
to her brother. He was standing in front of the fire staring
into the flames. The tea was scalding but he drank it
almost at once, then set the cup down on a side table.

'D'ye want me to come with you?'

'No, Bert, you've been at work all day. I'll be all right. I 'ope I won't be that long. As long as the twins are all right I'm not staying over there, I don't care what 'appens. I can't be around when that Brian gets 'ome, or else I shall end up saying more that I should, an' even worse, doing something I'd be sorry for.'

Her brother merely nodded at her, then turned and walked across the room. At the door he hesitated and cleared his throat before saying, 'What about Alan an' Norman, shall I get Jozy t'see to their dinner?'

'No, no need, love, they're both gonna be out tonight. I wasn't gonna bother about dinner anyway, there's only me, I'll get meself some fish an' chips or something.'

'Don't be so daft, you come straight into us the minute you get back. I'll be wanting to know 'ow things stand an' you know Jozy, she'll 'ave cooked enough to feed 'alf the street. What's more, y'don't need no telling, she'll be more than pleased to 'ave you eat with us.'

'Yeah, all right then, thanks Bert.'

Her mother had to shout through the letter box at least half a dozen times before she could rouse Ruby enough to come down and open the front door.

'Oh, it's you,' Ruby murmured as she peered round the door, then turned and made for the stairs again, leaving Ida to come in and close the door behind her.

Good God! The living room was a mess and it stank of booze. No wonder! A gin bottle lay on its side and a trickle of gin had run out on to the tablecloth.

'Siddown,' Ruby said, sweeping a pile of kiddies' toys onto the floor.

'Where are the boys?' Ida asked, noting how unnaturally quiet it was.

'Gone out,' said Ruby, 'Maggie's got them. No one 'ere 'cept me.'

Ida settled herself into a chair and slid her shopping bag down between her feet. The vegetables and liver she'd bought could wait.

'Ruby, 'ow long 'ave you been boozing?'

'Oh, don't start as soon as you get 'ere, Mum. What makes you think I've been boozing?'

Before Ida could think of a tactful reply, Ruby added in a quiet tone, ''S only gin with a lot of tonic. Want some?'

'I don't think so,' Ida said, 'I'd rather 'ave a cup of tea. I'll put the kettle on.'

Ruby sat still for a moment or two, looking puzzled, and then pressed her hands down on her knees and got up slowly, like an old woman. She crossed to the dresser and cursed when she couldn't find the bottle. Seeing it lying on the table she made a grab for her glass, upended the bottle only to find there was barely enough gin left to half fill her glass. She cursed again.

Ida touched her hand. 'Why don't you tell me what's wrong?'

'Wrong?' Ruby cried. 'What d'yer mean, wrong? There's nothing wrong. I'm young an' 'ealthy, two great kids who only want me attention twenty-four 'ours of every bloody day. Big bloke for me 'usband who don't know his own strength. A father-in-law that thinks I'm 'ere t'wait on 'im. Lotsa friends who've forgotten where I live. What more could I possibly ask for? Go on, tell me, what more is there?'

Her drink slopped as she tilted her head back, raised the glass and clutched it with both hands. 'Nothing's wrong, Mum. F'get it. 'S just that some days things get on top of me.'

Rather unsteadily she walked towards her mother. 'You and me uncles knew what was best f'me all right. An' I should be very grateful, that's what y'think, ain't it? Get our Ruby married an' she'll live 'appy ever after, that was it, wasn't it? Well let me tell you something, Mum. 'S a dream. Oh yes. 'S nothing but a bloody dream.'

Ida was about to tell her off for swearing so much, but at that moment Ruby looked so sad that she was at a loss as to what to do.

'Things will be better soon,' Ida ventured. 'Oh, Ruby, please don't, don't cry.'

All Ida could do now was stand there and watch, for Ruby had leant her head forward till her forehead was touching the wall and she was sobbing bitterly.

God she needs help, Ida admitted despairingly, she looks more like a wornout middle-aged woman rather than a girl who was only just coming up eighteen. Now was definitely the time to make that tea. Good an' strong, Ida said to herself.

In the kitchen – if you could call it that, for there wasn't even room for a body to turn around – Ida waited until she heard Ruby's sobs grow quieter before she carried the tray in, then she sat down at the table, rolled up the dirty cloth and set out the cups that she had just washed.

'Are you going to 'ave a cup with me?' Ida pleaded.

Ruby answered very quietly now, 'Yes please, Mum.'

'Good, I've made it nice an' strong.'

Ida's thoughts were running wild in her head. She was amazed at this turn of events. Her young Ruby turning to drink had been the last thing on her mind.

It was as they were finishing their second cup of tea that the bell rang and Ida went down to open the door. Maggie came in first, then Joey with Lenny toddling behind him.

21

'There ye are, my luverleys, didn't I tell you I saw yer Nanna arrive?' Maggie was chatting away as she helped the two little boys up the stairs.

Ida closed the door behind them and stared up at her grandsons, a lump had formed in her throat and she had to blink the tears away.

Dear little mites. God bless 'em! Twenty months old now they are, she mused, bonny as any kids she'd ever seen, alike as two peas in a pod, with their fresh creamy complexions and sandy coloured curly hair. Sturdy strong little legs and very forward. They are taking after the Simmonds side of the family all right an' I hope to God they grow up to be as big an' strong as me brothers are.

She gave a weak smile. 'Time will tell,' she murmured as she went along the passage and back up the stairs.

When Ida entered the room, Maggie was busy helping the boys take their coats off and Ruby sat in the one and only armchair completely exhausted. Lenny was the first to twist out of Maggie's grasp and run to Ida.

'Nanna, Nanna,' he smiled, his fat dimpled hands held out in front of him, asking to be picked up.

Joey, named after Brian's father as Lenny had been after Ruby's dad, was not to be outdone and he too ran across demanding to be cuddled and kissed by his Nanna.

'Wait till you see what I've brought for you,' Ida told the boys as she grabbed her shopping bag and delved into it. 'Look. Chocolate buttons for both of you and a colouring book each and some crayons. Let's set you down here on the rug and you can each colour a picture while I pour a cup of tea out for your Auntie Maggie. I'm sure she deserves one, don't you think?'

'Yes,' Lenny piped up, 'we've been on the commom.'

'Auntie Maggie pushed us on the swings.' Joey felt quite important having given that information and now turned over to lay on his tummy, stretched out full length beside his brother. The pair of them now turned their full attention to the serious matter of chosing which picture in their books would they colour first.

Ida's face was solemn now as she stared first at Maggie and then at Ruby.

'Which one of you is going to tell me what's gone on 'ere today?'

Ruby got to her feet, stood still for a moment before turning and saying, 'Come through to the bedroom, Mum.' Ruby sat herself on the edge of the bed and Ida stood looking down on her.

'Well?'

Ruby wetted her lips, blinked and rubbed at her eyes before answering. 'Mrs Morley said she caught me stealing and she was gonna call the police.'

'What?' Even though she knew she had heard right the first time, Ida again said, 'What?'

'You 'eard what I said right enough, Mother, so don't start going on.' And with that Ruby began to cough, a racking cough that wouldn't give over.

'Do you want a glass of water?'

'Yes,' Ruby nodded, 'yes, please.'

Slowly Ida went out to the kitchen, where she was quick to note that Maggie was hard at it clearing up. A good friend indeed was Maggie. Oh yes, without her for a neighbour, things here for Ruby would have come to a head a lot sooner than this.

'How long 'as that been going on?' Ida motioned to the empty Gordon's bottle that Maggie had just tossed into the rubbish bin.

'T'be 'onest, Ida, I couldn't tell yer. First time I've ever seen her this bad, though I've 'ad me suspicions. Can't say that we should blame her, though. You don't know the 'alf of it.'

'So tell me.'

'Not my place, Ida. Just let's say that between that damn 'usband of 'ers and his rotten good-for-nothing father I wouldn't 'ave young Ruby's life, not for all the tea in China.'

Ida let out a deep sigh. 'I wish I knew what to do for the best. About today, 'as she been stealing?'

To Ida's amazement, Maggie threw back her head and laughed out loud. 'She doesn't think so, an' again if yer want be t'be 'onest, I wouldn't exactly call it stealing. More like 'elping the poor. You ought to know by now Ruby stirs up mischief at every turn but there ain't no badness in her.' She roared with laughter again and Ida felt herself in danger of losing her temper.

She shook her head vigorously, 'I'll take a glass of water to 'er an' by God I'll get to the bottom of all of this.'

After Ruby had taken a few sips from the glass, Ida didn't have to asked any questions. Ruby doubled her two hands into fists and thrust them into her lap. Then the words burst from her.

'All I did was give a woman a trench coach. It was only fifty bob, for Christ's sake! Anyone would think I'd given the old bat's jewellery away. Might 'ave been better if I 'ad. Got enough of the stuff. There's days when she wears so many gold chains round 'er neck I find meself wishing they'd choke 'er.' With that she let out a cry and would have fallen forward if her mother hadn't have put out her arms to save her.

Ida now sat beside her on the bed, and with one arm

round Ruby she used her free hand to stroke her hair. 'Aw Ruby,' she whispered, 'I'd like a pound for every time I've brushed and combed this long straight hair. Yeah, and plaited it, tying pretty ribbons on the end of each plait. You know it's still lovely, the colour of corn your grandma used to say. Don't ever think about 'aving it cut an' permed, will you?'

Ruby hadn't answered, but she had stopped shaking and did seem altogether quieter now. Ida pulled Ruby round until she could look into her eyes.

'There! That's better, luv. Everything is going to be all right, things 'ave just got on top of you a bit, but I'm 'ere now an' we'll sort it, you'll see. Aw! Don't make that noise again, 'ere, wipe yer nose and start at the beginning and tell me what 'appened at the shop this morning.'

Ruby did as she was told but it was a good few minutes before she started talking again.

'Well, we'd been quite busy up until about eleven o'clock, with it being 'alf term. Mothers with their kids buying socks an' underwear, all the usual stuff. Then Madam, Mrs Morley, says she going upstairs for her coffee. D'ye know, Mum, I've been there some months now, I know it's only three days a week, nine till 'alf past one, but sometimes we're ever so busy but she still gets 'er break, I don't. She even moans if I ask to go for a pee. Never in all the time I've been there 'as she once offered me a drink.'

Ida could have said get to the point, but she didn't, she remained quiet, only moving to pass the glass of water to Ruby from which she took a long drink.

'Then this woman comes in, I know 'er by sight, lost 'er 'usband soon after I went to work there, always dressed in black she is. Got three boys. The oldest can't be more than about seven. She bought quite a few bits an' pieces ready for the kids to go back to school and then she asked me about winter coats. Well, Mum, you should 'ave seen that woman's face when I showed her some real nice ones, till she looked at the price. She went as white as a ghost, I'm telling yer.'

Ida made sounds of sympathy when Ruby paused to take a deep breath.

'It were me that suggested the raincoats. The boys said that they were nice and that all the kids at school wore them, no one wore overcoats. Their mother wasn't 'alf relieved and we helped all three of 'er boys to try one on.

'Mum, they looked a treat. Navy blue, belted, just the thing with the winter coming on. We worked out that the things she'd already ordered came to just over two pounds five shillings and the two smaller raincoats were two pounds each and the large one two pounds ten. Eight pounds fifteen shillings and three pence in all. Poor woman she almost knelt down to talk to those boys. Said she could buy two of the coats but would one boy mind waiting a month or so until she could save the money for the third one.

'Their poor little faces, Mum. I bet if you'd 'ave been there you'd 'ave felt just as bad as I did. Well, end of the story. I wrapped up all her goods and the three trench coats and only charged 'er for two. She didn't know. Wish I could 'ave been there when she got 'ome an' opened up that parcel! I'd 'ave loved t'ave seen the look on 'er face.'

Well I'm blowed! Ida didn't know whether to laugh or to cry. Say what you like about my Ruby, but mind she's got a good heart. There's not a kinder girl living when you boil it all down. What she said to her daughter was, 'But it wasn't yours to give, was it, Ruby?'

'No, I know it wasn't. But it was so unfair. The Morleys 'ave got so much, especially 'er, and she wasn't gonna lose any sleep over fifty bob that she needn't 'ave known anything about if only she hadn't got such beady eyes when she came down from upstairs an' checked the till and the stock. Mr Morley was nice. I think he was laughing to 'imself till she said she was gonna phone the police. That was when he told me to come 'ome an' not to come back. Still, at least those boys have all got macs to wear to school. They won't get wet when it rains.'

God help us, the girl wasn't the slightest bit repentant. Suddenly the room was illuminated with a flash of lightning which was followed by a deafening clap of thunder, and within seconds the rain was lashing down in torrents.

Ruby flung her arms around her mother's neck and they both began to roar with laughter. When Ida finally got her breath back, her eyes were twinkling as she said, 'You're not 'alf as bad as you're painted, are you?'

Ruby's face became serious now and her voice equally so as she said, 'I don't mean to be a trouble t'you, Mum, but – but I wouldn't blame you if you washed yer 'ands of me.'

'Aw, don't start crying again, please Ruby, don't. Come on, wipe ye face an' let's go an' see what my two grandsons are up too.'

Well, well, Ida tutted to herself, what a turn up for the books. Wait till she got home and told Bert and Jozy, never mind when Jeff and Sheila got to hear about it. The only two that wouldn't be surprised were Alan and Norman. They had long since ceased to be shocked at anything their sister got up to. Half the time the pair of them encouraged Ruby! One thing was for sure they both loved her and there wasn't much that either of them wouldn't do for her.

Things could have been a damn sight worse. Her blood ran cold as she thought about what might have happened had Mrs Morley had her way and the police had been called. But it was true what Jeff was always saying. With Ruby you never knew from one day to the next what she was likely to get up to.

Before opening the kitchen door, Ruby turned her head and said, 'You worry about me, don't you, Mum?' Ida just smiled and gently pushed her ahead. What she said to herself was, I do, Ruby! Believe me I do!

Chapter Four

'GOSH, THAT WAS A darn sight better than fish an' chips, thanks, Jozy.' Ida passed her empty plate to her sister-in-law and leaned back in her chair. 'You make a smashing steak an' kidney pudding. 'Sides which I think 'aving company t'eat with makes all the difference. I 'ate it when the boys are out and there's only me. Can't be bothered to cook 'alf the time.'

'Don't be so daft,' Jozy turned the gas up under the kettle and swung round, leant against the table and folded her arms across her thin chest. 'One more don't make no difference, y'know you're always more than welcome 'ere, but I do think you ought to think about the day Alan an' Norman leave 'ome. 'Cos, like it or not that day will come, Ida.'

'I know. An' I 'ave a funny feeling you're trying t'tell me something.'

Jozy sat down at the table. She looked at Ida, though Ida wouldn't meet her gaze. 'You 'ave plenty of chances to go out with someone if you were so inclined. There's plenty of blokes up the club that would jump at the chance to take you out an' about.'

'Oh yeah.' Ida raised her eyes, 'Like who?'

'Oh, come off it, you don't need me t'tell you.'

Ida tossed her head.

'There's that Ernie, he fancies you. He's always offering t'buy you a drink.'

Ida was straight away up on her high horse. 'Ernie Paige? You must be outta ye mind, he works down the sewerage farm.'

This time they did meet each other's eye and they burst out laughing.

It was minutes before Ida could speak. Still grinning from ear to ear she said, 'You trying to get rid of me? 'Cos if you are, please Jozy, find me someone a bit better than Ernie Paige, 'cos I've no intention of ending me days with a man who stinks to 'igh 'eaven.'

'But Ida, they grow lovely tomatoes down there at that farm near the Wandle. Look what you're missing.'

This set them off again and they were laughing like idiots. Their peals of laughter brought Bert back into the kitchen.

'You two found something funny? I thought you were both upset about Ruby.'

'Aw Bert,' Ida said, wiping the tears of laughter from her eyes. 'It's Jozy 'ere, she's doing 'er best t'get me married off to Ernie Paige, would you believe it. I think she's trying t'get rid of me or something.'

'And why not? Best thing, if y'found yerself a decent bloke.' Bert broke off to smother a grin. 'Not old Ernie though, eh?'

'Why not? 'Cos I'm 'appy as I am and I'd 'ave you both know I'm grey 'aired and getting on in years.'

'If you're grey 'aired an' getting old then I've got one foot in the grave. You're only just coming up forty an' y'know what they say, life begins at forty. Anyway, ain't it about time you both finished clearing the table and made the tea? Jeff and Sheila will be over soon and while we're playing cards you can tell them about young Ruby's latest escapade.'

'Bert!' Ida yelled his name, 'You think it's one great big joke, don't you? She could 'ave ended up in prison, y'know.'

'But she didn't, did she? And look at it this way, sis, our Ruby must be the only one who ever got one over on that Mrs Morley. Bet she'll 'ave a sleepless night or two thinking about 'er fifty bob. Bloody old skinflint. It's well known she wouldn't give a beggar a sneeze if she 'ad a cold.'

Jozy covered the table with a velvety chenille cloth and set out two packs of cards, a pad and pencil, matchsticks and a cribbage board. It was on evenings such as this that Ida felt the odd one out. Four could play a good game and her brothers and sisters-in-law made sure that she always got a turn, nevertheless it would have been nice if she'd had her own partner. As Jozy set a tray of tea down the phone rang and the front door opened at the same time.

'I'll get the phone,' Bert stood, letting his braces dangle over his trousers and the newspaper he'd been reading fall to the floor.

'It's only us,' Sheila's loud voice echoed down the passage. Having pulled the key through the letter box on its length of string and used it to unlock the front door, she and Jeff were in the kitchen before anyone had a chance to answer them.

'Hi ye, sis, y'alright? Bert told me earlier young Ruby's in a spot of bother again.'

'Leave it out, Jeff, let Ida 'ave a bit of peace for a

change. She'll tell us when she's good an' ready.' Sheila spoke sympathetically, 'Won't ye, luv?'

Ida wasn't given a chance to reply because Bert put his head round the door and called to Jozy, 'It's our Terry on the blower, come an' 'ave a word with him.'

Terry was the only child that Jozy had. Shame really, him being an only child he never did seem to quite fit in. Now Sheila had two boys, William, always known as young Billy, and Albert, nicknamed Albie.

Ida grinned to herself. Those two lads and her own two were forever in each other's pockets, she didn't ask and she didn't want to be told what that four got up to half the time.

Jozy came back into the kitchen, her face wreathed in smiles. 'Terry sends love to everyone, I'm glad he phoned,' she said, turning to face Bert, 'about time, wasn't it, though he didn't 'ave that much t'say, did he?'

'Where is he now?' Sheila asked in her forthright manner.

'Said he's in Blackpool, but as to what he's up too, well luv, your guess is as good as mine. He did ask about the boys but never mentioned Ruby, so I thought it best to keep quiet on that score.'

Ida sniffed to herself. Terry wouldn't make Ruby's troubles his problem, he wasn't even close to his own parents. Never had been. Strange that. At least it is to me, she was thinking as she watched Jozy pour out the tea. What with Terry being an only child and knowing how upset Ruby had been when her dad had died, you'd think that would have drawn them together all the more. But it hadn't.

Terry would come home if the trouble was ever bad enough, and if his dad were to ask him he'd go and visit Ruby, after all family was family. He didn't visit his own mum that often. Can't remember exactly when was the last time I saw him. I do remember how smart he looked. Back in the summer it was and he was wearing a double-breasted blue blazer with well-pressed grey trousers. He looked well-off. I'm never sure what it is that Terry does for a living, but one thing I do know he's never short of a bob or two.

Give the lad his due, Ida chided herself. He's generous to a fault when he is at home. Now her own two boys had hardly known their father but they would cross fire and water to get to each other if one was in trouble. And there wasn't much they wouldn't do for their sister. As for me, she mused, I'll never want, not while Alan and Norman are around. Alan had even made her an allowance when he'd been called up to do his national service.

'Come on then,' Jeff called, 'Let's get this game underway.'

The two brothers and their wives settled themselves around the table, Jeff shuffled the cards and they cut for partners.

Ida carried the tray of dirty teacups out into the scullery and set about washing them up. Her children still filled her mind. Like an old hen with a brood of chicks you are, she laughed to herself.

Her boys' characters were different, yet both were good sons. Norman worked for the Post Office. Communications was what he called it. He hadn't passed the medical and so he had been spared his stint of national service. As a youngster he'd had rheumatic fever. He was the serious one yet underneath he was warm and loving. Sometimes, when she thought of Norman, she felt such deep regret that his father hadn't lived to see him grow into such a good young man. Even as a baby he'd been good. It was funny, Norman had never given her a moment's worry.

Alan was a different kettle of fish altogether. His clothes often shocked her and he knew they did! Pink shirt, bright red tie, silk handkerchief in his jacket top pocket. And he was never seen without at least two gold chains around his neck. Entertainment, that's what Alan always insisted he was involved in. God knows how true it was. Oh, he was quick-witted right enough. He'd breeze in bearing flowers and chocolates only for her complaints of extravagance to be answered with a clever remark, 'Mother, I had a hot tip. Cleaned up. So why shouldn't I buy flowers and chocolates for the best Mum in all the world?'

National servive had done that lad a power of good. Not that she had wanted him to go, but say what you like, it made a man out of many a wimp. Even now though, with all that training behind him, he teased her, mimicked her, found fault with her but he still laughed with her, never at her. Yes, my first born may be as deep as the ocean but he's a good son to me.

She emptied the soapy water down the sink, shook the tea towel and hung it up to dry, sighing as she did so. She was a middle-aged lady with three grown-up children who should be off her hands by now. Instead of which, in one way or another, they were still causing her problems. Especially Ruby. Aw! Ruby!

With an infuriated movement she turned from the sink. Was ever a mother on God's earth plagued with such a daughter? Years ago, parents would have given their kids a darn good walloping, though come to think of it, all the bashings in the world probably wouldn't have done a bit of good for Ruby, she'd still have carried on in her own sweet way.

Look at when she was at school. Teachers complaining

she bullied other children. Shopkeepers saying she took sweets not only for herself but for other kids as well when she had no money to pay. The headmistress stating that she was far too cheeky and that she brought home skipping ropes and netballs that didn't belong to her. Ruby always had a ready-made excuse. 'I only wanted a lend of them,' she'd cry.

They say every mother has a cross to bear. God in heaven, Ruby was a heavy one. Yet I suppose I should be thankful that in so many other ways she can be so thoughtful and loving.

Why oh why had she had to get herself pregnant when she was so young? She really could have been such a bright girl. Hadn't she got herself a job down at the Town Hall? And hadn't she always had her nose stuck in a book? That girl used to love the library.

Ida had really worked herself up now. She was vexed with Ruby and vexed with herself for allowing things to get on top of her, yet again.

Not much sound was coming from the kitchen, they all took their game of cards real serious. Soon be time for a beer and a sandwich.

I know, I'll occupy meself setting the bread and things out for Jozy, that's what I'll do.

It was no good. Try as she would, humdrum jobs such as getting the supper ready don't take your mind off your troubles. Clear as a bell she could remember the day she'd collared Ruby about missing a period. Talk about finding trouble! My Ruby runs up the street looking for it!

As for Brian Brookshaw, until the truth came to light and Bert and Jeff went looking for him ready to beat the daylights out of him, Ruby had never once brought him home. She couldn't to this day fathom it out.

Imagine! No one would believe it, she fumed, but that fellow had never even crossed my doorstep, not once before the wedding. Ruby deserved better than him! Even Mrs Walker, a lady if there ever was one, whom Ida had worked for since Len had died, had thought it wrong that Ruby had been forced into such a marriage. Look at the times, in the school holidays, when I've taken Ruby to work with me and Mrs Walker has openly admitted to me that she was amazed at the brightness of the child. 'Self-assured and no mistake,' is what Mrs Walker had said.

Ida's temper changed to a feeling of guilt. Was a lot of it her fault? Should she have let Ruby go to Australia with the Morris family? After all, Andy had been her first love. His family had been sincere in their offer to take Ruby with them, but what mother would have agreed to her only daughter going half way round the world to live, an' her so young an' all?

Did she make the wrong decision? Was the state that Ruby was in really all her fault? No it's not, she told herself with emphasis. I've done me best. Honest to God I have.

'Ida?'

Bert's voice made her jump and she realised that she was trembling.

'Ida, come on. Come and rescue me. Jeff and my old woman between them have taken me and Sheila to the cleaners.'

Ida made a ball of her fist and brushed angrily at her eyes. Thank God for her brothers, and for her sisters-in-law. At least they all got on well together. That was something to be thankful for. As for Ruby, well tomorrow was another day and what can't be altered has to be endured.

And with that profound thought she pushed open the kitchen door and went to try her luck with the cards.

Chapter Five

'I'M GONNA LEAVE THE Post Office, Mum,' said Norman, avoiding his mother's eyes by staring hard at the slice of toast that he was buttering.

'Giving up ye job at the Post Office?' Ida said, a puzzled look spreading over her face. 'You're joking, ain't ye?'

'No, I'm not,' he said, raising his eyes sheepishly to meet hers. 'Now I don't want you to get upset.'

'Upset?' she echoed crossly. 'What the 'ell do you expect me t'do? You're about the only one in the family that 'as 'ad the sense to study an' get yeself a safe steady job an' now you calmly sit there an' tell me you're gonna throw it all away.'

'I'm sorry, Mum.'

'Sorry! What's the bloody good of being sorry if you're gonna do it anyway? What the 'ell 'as got into you?' she screamed angrily. ''Ave y'taken leave of ye senses or something?'

'I'm going into business with Alan.'

'Aw my God! I might 'ave known Alan was behind all

this,' she stuttered, her anger turning to stunned resignation with the realisation that he was serious.

Norman took a long drink from his cup of tea and licked his lips guiltily. He knew how much his job with the Post Office meant to his mother and hated to disappoint her, especially as it was Alan that he was going into business with. She had been a good and loving mother to all of them, but if the truth be known Alan was her favourite, yet she never trusted him. Ruby, bless her, had brought their mum nothing but heartaches. It wasn't the poor kid's fault, she'd been made to grow up far too quickly.

Suppose she looks on me as the sensible steady one, he thought as he braced himself to tell her his intentions.

'The decision to leave the Post Office isn't sudden,' he said woefully. 'I've been thinking about it for some time.'

'Oh really?' Her voice held a note of bitterness.

'I've been faced with a lot of exams to take, and if I want to keep on with what I've been doing I'd have to pass all of them, and honestly Mum, I'm not up to it. Only other alternative is to be down-graded to being a postman, out in all weathers. I don't want that.'

She shook her head from side to side, her face showed despair.

'But with Alan? He never sticks to anything for more than five minutes.'

'Come on, Mum, I'm not that daft. I've been into it thoroughly and I've made the right decision. I know I have. It will be all right, trust me.'

Trust him? She might, but not Alan. Oh no, never Alan. She couldn't bring herself to trust that young man as far as she could throw him.

She didn't reply.

Norman studied her face and was relieved to see her

smile, yet he wasn't happy with what he saw. She looked years older than she was. True it wasn't yet eight o'clock on a Monday morning, still she could have made a bit more effort. Here she was getting breakfast, dressed in her old tatty looking dressing gown, her hair unbrushed and straggly, and the slippers she had on her feet looked as if they were only fit for the dustbin.

Ida felt Norman's eyes on her and she brought her hand to her forehead and ran her palm over her hair, doing her best to tuck the loose strands behind her ears as she shook her head. 'Whatever it is the pair of you are up to I don't wanna know. I just 'ope it works out. I know you're no fool, but just remember this, Norman, brother or not, our Alan is a fly one.'

Norman got to his feet, came to where she stood and held out his arms, 'Oh Mum.'

She hugged him tight and said nothing about how in her heart she was worried sick that he might be biting off far more than he'd be able to chew.

Norman sighed and went to stand in front of the fireplace; looking into the mirror which hung high over the mantel shelf, he made a great show of tying his tie. Then he pulled open the dresser draw and took out his cigarettes and matches, several pencils, a clean handkerchief and a box of throat pastilles, all of which he shovelled into his pocket. Finally he put on his overcoat and wound his scarf round his neck. Although the snow and ice had gone, March had come in bringing bitter cold winds. Norman picked up his gloves, turned and planted a kiss on his mother's cheek, said, 'See ye tonight then,' and went out of the room, closing the door quietly behind him.

Ida was hurt, bitterly hurt. More than she had let on.

Throwing in a good job with the Post Office! Norman

work with Alan? Never! I knew life had been too good to be true. The last six months had at least been peaceful. Ruby seemed to have turned over a new leaf. No trouble. Ida crossed her fingers behind her back as she said that to herself.

The twins were little angels. She had them every Saturday so as to give Ruby a break, and all over Christmas Ruby and the boys had stayed here. Even Brian and his father had come for their Christmas dinner; the whole family had gathered together in Bert's.

God help us, it had been touch and go during the evening when the men had had too much to drink. She laughed out loud at the memory. Old Bill Brookshaw had thought twice about starting anything when Bert and Jeff had got to their feet.

Now what was Norman about to let himself in for? She wished she knew. Why couldn't her two boys have been like the rest of the family and gone to work in Billingsgate? ''Cos I don't want to be forever scrubbing fish scales off me arms and out of me hair, nor clearing away the offal from gutted fish,' was Alan's objection, and Norman had been of the same mind. She couldn't honestly say that she blamed them.

Ah well, she'd been sitting here in her nightclothes long enough, about time she made a move.

The more you did for your children the worse they turned out, or so it seemed. She bent down and jerked the corner of the hearth rug straight. Better think about lighting the fire; the room was quite chilly. I must remember to bank it down though, when I go out. First off, I'm gonna make meself a fresh pot of tea, it would help to soften the shock of Norman's news. I'll make it good and strong, she promised herself as she set about filling the kettle.

* * *

If Norman had been around to see his mother leave the house at ten o'clock that morning he would have had to agree that she had made an effort with her appearance. But then she always did on Mondays, Wednesdays and Fridays, because those were the mornings that she went to 'do' for Mrs Walker.

From Ida's appearance no one would have guessed that she was going to do housework. She was dressed all in navy blue, with a flimsy white scarf tucked into the neck of her coat, and you could see your face in her well-polished shoes. Neat and tidy she was, and that was just how she liked Mrs Walker to see her. She regarded it more as a treat to go to the big house at the top of Wimbledon Hill, rather than going to do a job of work.

Mrs Walker was a large lady with fine white hair set into neat waves, a lovely caring face with bright twinkly blue eyes, and clothes which were obviously expensive. Classic skirts and twin-sets mostly, which never seemed to date. And there was no side to her. She treated Ida as an equal. Come coffee time they always sat together at the kitchen table, and there was no question of Ida being asked to do any of the rough tasks about the house. Oh no. The Walkers kept a handyman to chop logs, fill the coal scuttles from the outside coal bins and to keep the very large garden looking nice. For Ida's jobs, every labour-saving device was provided, including an electric polisher which she used on the parquet flooring that was laid in a lovely pattern throughout the hall and dining room. And Mrs Walker provided a real nice, full-length, pale blue cotton coat for Ida to wear while she was working. Kind of a uniform it was, and that made Ida feel good.

*   *   *

At half-past two, Ida had just turned into Fountain Road and as she came to number five, Mr and Mrs Morgan came out onto their front doorstep. Mrs Morgan was a large untidy lady and her husband was equally as scruffy. They were friendly enough, as was their brood of four children. The two boys made a habit of knocking on doors selling fire wood and offering to run errands for a copper or two. Ida gave them both a curt but friendly nod and would have passed on.

'Coppers 'ave been knocking at your 'ouse,' Mrs Morgan blurted out.

'Don't know what they wanted.' Mr Morgan threw his comment in.

'Guess I'll soon find out,' Ida answered with a wave of her hand while trying to give them a blank look.

'Now what?' she muttered, as she quickened her steps. I knew it, I said so this morning when Norman dropped his bombshell, things have been too quiet for too long. Here I am, having had a lovely morning, got a real nice jumper in me bag what Mrs Walker gave me, ain't hardly ever been worn, feeling at peace with the world and I have to come home to this. I'll bet me last penny it's my Ruby been up to her tricks again.

Jozy opened her front gate and came to meet her.

'''Allo, luv. I've been watching out f'you. I saw the Morgans waylay you. That pair don't miss a trick. Must sit at that front window all ruddy day. Bet they take it in turns to go an' 'ave a pee.' She tried hard to smile but there was a sad note in her voice as she said, 'Come on in, I've got the kettle on.'

'Police come, so they said,' Ida murmured.

Jozy turned away from her sister-in-law, she could hardly bear to tell her. She has more than her share of troubles one way and another, she was thinking. Still it had to be done.

'Yeah, bad news, sorry luv, Ruby's in 'ospital. 'Fraid I don't know all the details. The constable said they were leaving someone on the premises till you got there an' checked the place over.'

''Ow about the twins? Are they all right? Didn't they say anything about what has happened to Ruby? Don't ye know what she's been taken to 'ospital for?'

Jozy turned quickly to face her. 'Ida, don't get yeself all worked up. It's only about 'alf an hour since the copper was 'ere. I said it wouldn't be long before you were 'ome an' that we'd be over straightaway. There's nothing more I can tell you, so don't go torturing yeself by imagining all sorts of 'orrible things. I'll come to Mitcham with you when we've 'ad our cup of tea.' Jozy spoke firmly.

'Thanks,' Ida said, taking off her coat, 'I'll just 'ave to run upstairs an' spend a penny.'

Jozy looked at her back and flapped her hand as if she were trying to wave the trouble away, then she raised her eyes to the ceiling and quietly whispered, 'Dear God, don't let anything awful be wrong with Ruby.'

A policeman was standing in the front garden when Ida and Jozy arrived at Ruby's place.

'Are you relatives of Mrs Brookshaw?' he asked quickly. 'Yes, she's my daughter an' this is Ruby's aunt. Will you please tell us what 'as 'appened?'

'Yes, yes, all in good time.' The constable beamed at them. 'Perhaps we'd better go upstairs, don't want t'stand about out here. Ain't exactly a summer's day, is it?'

Ida felt that at any minute now she would scream, and once she started she knew there'd be no stopping her.

Once they were in Ruby's living room the constable nodded at each of them in turn before he spoke.

'Nasty business, seems her husband lost his temper. No excuse though, is it? Not for beating up on a young lady.'

'Oh my God!' The colour drained from Ida's cheeks.

'Do you know for sure it was her 'usband?' queried Jozy.

'Oh yes, quite straightforward. Neighbours only too willing to give a statement.'

'Where are the children?' Ida almost yelled the question at him, 'and for God's sake don't try palming me off. Just tell me the plain facts and leave us t'sort it out.'

'Well, Madam, your daughter's been taken to the Wilson Hospital, which is on the far side of the cricket green—'

'I know full well where the Wilson is,' Ida rudely interrupted.

'And as far as I can tell you the two little boys are being looked after by a council worker; they weren't here when I arrived. They'll tell you more if you call in at the station, it's quite near to the hospital.'

'I know where the police station is an' all,' Ida retorted.

'The children will be fine.' His voice was gentle now, making allowance for the fact that Ida was frantic with worry. 'Try not to worry on that score.'

'Can you tell us, please, just 'ow badly is Mrs Brookshaw hurt?' Jozy asked softly.

'Well,' he began, hesitated, covered his mouth with his hand and cleared his throat before saying in a very low voice, 'her face was a mess, the ambulance men seemed to think that her left arm was broken and from what I've been told, I'm sure the poor lass will have quite a few bruises on her body.'

The policeman cleared his throat again. 'Well, I'll be on my way. I'm sure my Inspector will be able to tell you more at the station.'

'Yes, thank you.' It was Jozy that had gathered her wits first. 'I'll come down, see you out.'

Left alone in the room, Ida groped for a chair and sat down. It was that or fall down. Her legs felt all wobbly and something inside her head was going hammer and tongs.

After a minute or two she raised her head and looked about her. God! Between them, what had they done to Ruby?

She'd have to take a heck of a lot of the blame on her own shoulders, but her brothers hadn't helped! Oh, they'd acted as they thought for the best. Cost them a packet too. Ruddy posh wedding, all the trimmings, anything to get Ruby married off. Save the gossip and the scandal. Had any one of us ever stopped to ask Ruby what she'd wanted? Would an illegitimate baby have been such a terrible thing? This life they'd pushed Ruby into had to be a bloody sight worse!

Just look at how she'd been living. There wasn't a decent stick of furniture in the whole place. Formica-topped table, metal framed chairs with black plastic seats and what was supposed to be a sideboard shaped out of plywood. Burnt dishes and dirty plates covered the draining board. Amongst all the other things, Ruby had two more against her: she couldn't cook and she was certainly no homemaker.

And that bedroom! She didn't need to go and look to know what she would find. The twins were getting far too big to be sleeping in the same room as their parents. Poor little mites. Had they been witness to this carry on?

If they had she'd bet it wasn't the first row they'd been caught up in.

Something would have to be done. Surely the council could find them somewhere better to rent than these pokey rooms. She had broached the subject more than once; Brian seemed to think that his father had done them a favour by speaking to the landlord and getting them the tenancy. No way could this place be classed as a flat, might be fine for one person on their own, but a married couple with two young babies? It was a wonder things hadn't come to a head before now.

Raised voices brought Ida to her feet. Maggie Marshall came through the door first, followed by Jozy.

''Allo, Ida. Bad business, eh?' Maggie muttered. 'I've said it before an' I'll say it again, that poor girl don't deserve 'alf of what she 'as t'put up with. There's no getting away from it this time. That Brian is a right sod, an' all I 'ope is that he gets put away this time. That'll be the pair of them out of the way. Him and his father. And bloody good riddance if y'ask me.'

Ida didn't know what she was on about.

Jozy, having heard most of the story down in the street, decided to make herself scarce. 'I'll 'ave a look round in the bedroom. Gather up a few of Ruby's things for us t'take up the 'ospital with us. She'll need a couple of clean nighties.'

It was as if Ida hadn't heard a word. She turned abruptly and staring straight at Maggie she demanded, 'How did it start?'

'What?' Maggie looked startled.

'You 'eard me. first tell me what's been going on 'ere an' then we'll get to what you meant by the old man being out of the way later.'

'Well –' Maggie hemmed and hawed. 'Really Ida, it ain't f'me t'say.'

Ida took a step forward, 'Are you gonna tell me?' Her voice was menacing.

'All right. But I don't know all the facts, only what I was told.'

'Just get on with it.'

'Well, y'know your Ruby got that job at the Majestic up at the Fairgreen? Nice easy job, Ruby said it was, sitting on the front desk taking the money an' dishing out the tickets. Real easy—'

'So?' Ida thumped the table in frustration.

'Yeah, well now, mind Ida, luv,' said Maggie very slowly, 'I don't know 'ow much of it is true. It's only what I 'eard Ivy Greenway telling Mrs Mayhew when I was waiting in the queue at Hutton's. I wouldn't like t'bet that it's gospel.'

Ida closed her eyes and muttered, 'God give me strength!'

Maggie took the hint. 'Oh all right, luv. Well, Ivy was saying that Ruby didn't dare go back t'work because if she did, the manager's wife was gonna knock her block off. It seems she came in one evening – his wife, that is – and caught Ruby an' her old man being a bit amorous, like. Ivy said there wasn't 'alf a to-do. Heard the row all through the cinema so they say.'

'So? That doesn't explain why Brian laid into her.'

'Come off it, Ida. Gossip travels fast an' the men are as bad as the women when it comes down to it. Same night it was. In the Bull. Brian got a right old ribbing off his mates, didn't he? You can guess 'ow much he liked that!'

'D'you think it's true?'

'Now Ida!' Maggie blinked and swallowed hard. 'I don't

know, I'm sure. Only one thing I will say – though more than likely I shouldn't – Ruby seemed to 'ave a lot more money to throw around lately. Very generous t'me she's been, for 'aving the twins an' such like. Then again . . .' she broke off and laughed, albeit a laugh that came from embarrassment.

Ida remained silent, and Maggie continued. 'Y'know Ruby would talk to me, when she felt so inclined. Two or three times she's hinted that she and someone – never said who – was working a racket with the admission tickets up at the Majestic.

'There now, I've told you and I probably shouldn't 'ave, 'cos even if it's true that ain't no reason for Brian to 'ave gone bloody berserk. Y'can bet if there was extra money around he saw to it that some of it found its way into 'is pockets.'

'All right. All right.' Ida stretched out her arm. 'Let's leave it there for now, Maggie. Just tell me what you were on about when you said Brian's father was out of the way, and then Jozy an' me can get off up to the 'ospital.'

'I wonder you ain't 'eard about it. Don't ye read the local paper? Bill Brookshaw is in jail. Got six months.'

Ida looked at her in amazement. 'Ruby never said anything.'

'He only came up in court last week.'

'What the 'ell did he do?'

'Drunk an' disorderly and assault, in the Cricketers of all places. Wouldn't 'ave been 'alf so bad if it 'ad been in the Bull. They're used to it in there. But the Cricketers! And what made things worse, he resisted arrest is what the paper said. What the men around 'ere are saying is he put one on the copper an' that didn't go down at all well.'

Ida found herself laughing in spite of everything. 'I bet it didn't,' she grinned.

Jozy put her head around the door. She too was smiling, she hadn't missed much of Maggie's tale. 'I've found a sponge bag an' I've got some washing things and nightclothes in this carrier. We'd better get going, 'adn't we?'

'Yes, you do that,' Maggie urged Ida. 'See if ye can find out where the twins are. Wasn't no need for them to cart the little ones off. I'd 'ave looked after them.'

'I know you would 'ave, Maggie, an' thanks for all you do do for Ruby. We'll see ye later.'

'Are ye coming back 'ere? 'Cos if ye are I'll 'ave a bit of dinner ready for you.'

'No,' Jozy cut in, 'half our street knows the police was at Ida's house this afternoon and when Bert an' Jeff get 'ome they'll want t'know what's been going on. We'd best make straight for 'ome.'

'You could come over to Tooting for ye tea,' Ida quickly invited Maggie. 'In fact you could go now. Go in to Sheila – she'll be worrying, you bet – tell 'er all what you've told me. It's bound to all come out sooner or later.'

'Good idea,' Jozy agreed.

'All right then, ta. I'm glad ye ain't mad at me, Ida. Go on, you two get yeselves off, I'll give this place a bit of a tidy up and then I will get the bus and go to your Sheila's. Don't feel like being on me own. Not tonight.'

'Thanks Maggie,' both Ida and Jozy called as they buttoned up their coats and went down the stairs.

Maggie stood on the landing, watching them go. Ida was such a nice hard-working little woman and she certainly tried to do her best for all three of her children. Shame was that at last Ida was being made to face the truth about the rotten life young Ruby was being forced to lead.

She don't know the 'alf of it yet, an' I certainly wasn't gonna be the one to tell her. Good job the old man is in prison or else there'd be murder done, that's for sure. Wait till she gets to the Wilson Hospital and sees for herself what a state Ruby's in.

A sudden thought came into her head and she gasped. She wouldn't want to be on the receiving end when Ida's brothers were told the whole story. There would be hell to pay.

Chapter Six

THE NURSE WAS SHORT and dark-skinned with fine features that looked even more bronzed framed by her white uniform. She held the door to the waiting room wide open, smiling both at Ida and Jozy as she did so.

'I'll let Sister know you're here. I'll be back in a minute.'

Jozy walked to the window which overlooked the drive. Ida sat down on a long soft couch. The first impression of the Wilson was that it wasn't like other hospitals. For one thing it was very much smaller; take this room, it was full of colour, pictures on the walls and flowers on the windowsill.

The nurse was back. She lifted one hand and beckoned them. 'Sister said to take you straight through to the ward.'

Curtains were drawn around the bed and as the nurse parted them, Ida went one side of the bed and Jozy the other.

Jozy gasped and muttered, 'Jesus Christ!'

Ida found she couldn't speak for a moment, she bit hard down on her bottom lip and tasted blood.

'Mrs Brookshaw, your mother and your aunt are here to see you.' The voice of the nurse was soft and gentle as she bent over her patient.

Ruby stirred, opened her eyes as much as she was able and immediately tears began to roll down her cheeks.

Ida moved quickly and now she was looking full into the face of her daughter. This badly beaten young girl should be out in the world living her life, laughing not crying, and certainly not lying battered and bruised in this hospital bed.

Her eyes were barely open, the right side of her face had been stitched, the blood now dark and dry. Her lips were so swollen it would be a job for her to talk. Her usually lovely silky blonde hair was still fine on the left side of her head; the rest was a mess, matted with dried blood. One arm was cased in a heavy sling.

Oh Ruby! My poor little Ruby. Oh dear God! Oh Heavenly Father! Ida was backing away from the bed. Whatever had her Ruby done to deserve this? Where was that God of love to let it happen? Well this time that sod has gone too far! She wouldn't stop her brothers from sorting Brian out, not now she wouldn't.

I don't care what they do to him after this, she told herself with conviction. He deserved it. Yes. Yes. He deserved all he got.

The nurse pushed past her and grabbed a chair and helped Ida to sit down. A few seconds later, Ida let out her breath angrily, then composing herself, she leant forward and calmly took hold of Ruby's free hand.

'I'm 'ere now, Ruby. Mum's 'ere.'

The flow of tears continued unchecked from Ruby's swollen eyes.

'Please, Ruby, please dear, don't cry, don't cry. Just listen. Auntie Jozy's 'ere with me. The boys will be all right. Maggie's gone on over to y'aunt Sheila's. She an' y'uncles will 'ave it all sorted time we get back. Between us we'll see t' them.'

Ida got no response at all and she raised her own tear-filled eyes to meet those of her sister-in-law's. 'What are we gonna do, Jozy?'

Jozy put her finger to her lips. 'Ssh', she whispered. 'The nurse has just told me that Ruby has been given an injection. She'll sleep now for hours. Best thing for her. They 'aven't set that arm in plaster yet but they will later.'

'I just can't go an' leave her 'ere, not like this.'

'Nobody's asking you to.'

Then as if some bell had been rung, the curtains parted and a tea trolley appeared at the end of the bed.

'D'you both take sugar? And we've got some cream biscuits t'day.' A smiling rosy face topped by a frilly mop cap peered round the screen.

Even Ida managed a weak smile as she heard Jozy saying, 'Ah, bless you. Just what the doctor orderd, eh? I 'ave two sugars an' Ida 'ere, she only 'as one.'

They drank their tea, nibbled their biscuits and talked in whispers for a while. They'd all cope with the twins. Between them it would be a piece of cake. The men would come up and see Ruby tomorrow. What they would do about Brian wasn't mentioned. And by that time Ruby was snoring gently.

They were both standing now, gazing down at the pitiful little figure in the bed.

'Bye Ruby,' Ida murmured. 'I'll be back tomorrow.'

Was that her voice? It didn't sound like it even to herself. Her shoulders heaved and she let out a sob.

'Come on, Ida. We're not doing any good by staying 'ere. Let's get off 'ome. And stop your crying, it don't 'elp any.'

'Shut up, Jozy,' Ida turned on her sister-in-law, 'I'm not crying, I'm bloody well not.'

Jozy turned her head away from Ruby, and she muttered something that could have been taken for 'sorry'. And at the same time she held out her hand.

As they left the hospital and walked towards the bus stop, the silence between them was heavy. Each knew that never before had they felt so sad or so at a loss as to what to do for the best.

'I can't believe it.' Ida was actually smiling as she looked around her brother's kitchen. The twins were there. Playing happily with coloured wooden bricks which were spread out on the big table. Their fair heads, so like Ruby's hair, shone like silk.

Didn't seem possible that they were more than two years old. They got their features from the Simmonds side of the family. Oh yes, thank God, neither of them resembled the Brookshaws. You only had to look at those two little boys to know that they were every inch a Simmonds.

The question was, how would they grow up? Would they take after their father and have his bad temper, and would the way he treated their mother have a lasting effect on them? Not if I have anything to do with it, Ida vowed to herself.

In fact, the whole family was in this warm cosy kitchen, including Sheila and Jeff, their two sons Billy and Albie and her own two, Alan and Norman. The only one missing was, Terry, the only son of Jozy and Bert. Also there was good old Maggie Marshall.

The back door to the garden was thrown open because it was still a lovely evening; summer was well and truly on its way and soon they'd be able to get out and about in their short-sleeved summer dresses. Oh, it would be so nice to see Joey and Lenny dressed only in little cotton shorts with their sturdy little legs getting nice and tanned.

Coming back from Mitcham she had been filled with a cold hate for both Brian and his father, and if the twins hadn't been there when she got back she felt she would have gone completely mad.

'Did you 'ave much trouble in satisfying the council that we could look after them?' Ida asked in a trembling voice.

'No we didn't.' Sheila laughed. 'The minute Jeff came 'ome an' I told 'im what Maggie had already told me, we were off like a shot. Think them posh ladies was relieved to see us. They don't like custody cases at the best of times.'

'We explained where Ruby was, that got their sympathy. Then they asked about the father.' Jeff paused. ''Ad t'bite me tongue a bit there.' This last statement was added with a funny look at Maggie and a quick shake of Jeff's head.

Ida got the impression that Maggie had told Jeff more than she had told her. She glanced from one of her brothers to the other, then she swung round to face her own two sons. Her instinct was right. Not one of them, not even her nephews, Billy and Albie, would look her in the eye.

'Maggie?' Ida was on her feet. 'Suppose you tell me what it is you've obviously told the rest of the family.'

Maggie was trembling. 'I'm sorry, Ida, really I am. Best you don't know. Leave it to y'menfolk.'

Before Ida could go for her, Bert intervened.

'All right, sis. All right, calm yeself down.'

Ida looked first at Alan, then at Norman. They each lowered their eyes, but she noticed that the pair of them had clenched their fists.

Bert took a step nearer to his sister. 'I'm sorry Ida,' he said, 'we're all of us bloody sorry. It's knocked the stuffing out of me, I can tell ye that, and if it 'adn't been for me, your two lads and Jeff's two would be out there looking for Brian right now. But by God I swear both him an' his ole man are gonna pay for it. Just f'tonight we've agreed we'll bide our time.'

All eyes were on Ida now. There was no colour left in her cheeks as she waited for her brother to go on.

Bert heaved a great sigh. 'Suppose if you've got to know, better from inside this 'ouse than from outside.' He took a deep breath and let it out before saying, 'Bill Brookshaw 'as been trying to split Brian and Ruby. And there you 'ave it.'

The noise was deafening. Everyone was talking at once.

Ida laid the bag of fruit and the bunch of flowers on the locker which had been placed at the side of Ruby's bed. She turned, leaned over and quietly kissed her daughter's cheek, saying, 'Feel any better today, d'ye, luv?'

Ruby half smiled, caught hold of her mother's hand and squeezed it, but never made a sound. It had been the same for the past week. She had barely uttered a word to anyone.

Ida loosened her coat and sat there trying to think of something to say. The prospect of an hour's awkward silences had the effect of striking her dumb. She wasn't able to think of a thing to talk about.

When the efficient sister of the ward arrived and briskly said, 'There is a welfare officer here that would like to have a word with you, Mrs Wilcox,' Ida breathed 'Thank God for that.'

56

Sister, all trim and spruce in her navy blue uniform, allowed herself to smile. 'Come along then, she's in my office. You won't be disturbed in there.'

'Sit yeself down, Mrs Wilcox, this is purely an informal meeting so that both you and I can make up our minds as to what is best for Ruby. I go by the name of Mrs Johnson.'

Again, Ida breathed, 'Thank God.' This was no stuffy individual that she would have to cross swords with. This was a nice middle-aged woman that she'd be able to talk to. Ida gave her a broad smile as she let her glance wander over the woman that was seated behind the small desk.

Mrs Johnson was a thin lady with shoulder-length brown hair, dressed in a tweed skirt and a fawn twin-set. Around her neck she wore a gold chain from which dangled a tiny gold cross. She returned Ida's frank gaze, her hands all the while on the desk twisting an expensive fountain pen. In spite of her first-off friendliness, her expression was sort of wary – at least that was how it seemed to Ida – and it was Ida that kicked off by stating: 'So you're saying something has to be done for Ruby?'

Mrs Johnson was taken aback by Ida's blunt question. 'Well, yes. You surely don't believe that your daughter can be allowed to go straight home from hospital?'

'So you're telling me that Ruby should be put away?'

'Oh no.' Mrs Johnson was offended. 'I said nothing of the sort. She's an unhappy young woman who has been badly ill-treated, she needs help.'

'I don't need you t'tell me that,' Ida snapped. 'What I do need t'know is what you're gonna do t'help her.'

Fingering her gold cross, Mrs Johnson returned Ida's glare with an expression that showed no emotion. 'We're both of the same mind then, Ruby needs a break before she faces up to whatever problems led to her being treated in such a cruel way. Agreed?'

'Yes,' Ida spoke softly, making it sound as if she were apologizing.

'Doctor Richards – he's the doctor in charge of Ruby's case, and incidentally the only person who has managed to get her to talk – is of the opinion that Ruby is a very sincere and capable young lady. Nothing wrong with her mentally at all.'

'I should bloody well 'ope not. Oh – sorry, Miss.' Ida covered her mouth with her hand, taking a minute before she added, 'The very thought don't bear thinking about, not of ye own girl it don't.'

'It's all right, really it is, Mrs Wilcox. I do understand, believe me, I have two daughters at home to contend with.'

They smiled knowingly at each other.

'My suggestion, and it has the support of the medical staff, is that we find a place for Ruby in a convalescent home. Somewhere not too far out, where you and your family can visit her. You're lucky there, you have the support of a family. They will all do their bit to help Ruby, I'm sure.' There was by now desperation in the tone of Mrs Johnson's voice, as if she was at times crushed by the sadness of her work.

Ida sighed, 'If you think that's best. Can I ask you one more thing?'

'Of course, anything.'

'Has she said anything about her father-in-law?'

Mrs Johnson took her time in answering that one. Her mind was racing ahead, but it wasn't for her to jump to conclusions.

'All patients differ. Some open up and talk, some just won't be drawn. In Ruby's case I don't know.'

'There's a lot you don't know. A helluva lot. My Ruby gets 'erself into more 'ot water than I'd care to mention. Not that she means any 'arm. Please, don't get me wrong, it's mainly just mischief, but it always seems to 'ave a way of bouncing back on her.'

'Have you tried talking to her yourself?'

'Talk to her? I've done a darn sight more than that. You think I wouldn't stop her if I could? There's been a whole lot of things I'd 'ave liked to stop her doing – getting 'erself pregnant in the first place, marrying that dozy Brian. T'were never my idea for her to get wed. I'd 'ave seen to the baby. Yes I would 'ave. 'T ain't as if I didn't practically bring me own three up without a father.'

'Yes, I appreciate that and I'm sure you would have coped admirably,' Mrs Johnson answered with feeling.

'Yeah, well, it's too late now. Too late for too many things.'

Mrs Johnson rose to her feet. 'I'll do my best for Ruby. That's a promise.'

Ida gathered her coat around herself. 'Thank you,' she murmured, relieved that this meeting was over.

Making her way back to the ward, Ida's thoughts were in a whirl. A convalescent home might be a very good thing for Ruby. Perhaps it would be kind of a nice holiday, but there was one thing she was very sure of. That talk she'd had with Mrs Johnson wasn't the last she'd hear on the matter.

Chapter Seven

THE WEATHER WAS THE best most people could remember. Everything seemed set for a wonderful summer. This, coupled with the fact that Norman now had four days off, had him whistling with delight as he came out of the sorting office on this sunny Friday afternoon in June.

Alan threw the stub of his cigarette onto the ground and stubbed it out with the sole of his shoe. Seeing his brother he grinned, calling, 'Come on, Norm, we've places t'go an' things t'do. Move yeself, get in the car.'

Norman didn't need a second bidding. Alan steered the car into the flow of traffic, crossing the Broadway he drove along Tooting High Street past the Totterdown estate, leaving the markets and the costermongers behind, making for Upper Tooting. At Tooting Bec Underground Station he turned right into Tooting Bec Road.

Here the houses were more imposing, the trees and gardens very impressive. Soon they were driving along the side of the common, nearby lay the avenue of tall oak trees, a sight that most people never failed to admire.

Alan slowed the car down as they neared a spot known locally as York Ditch, a very ancient site that marked the parish boundary between Streatham and Tooting, turned right again and within minutes drove the car between two massive gate posts. There, at the end of the short drive, stood their house.

Or should I say club? queried Norman to himself, for if all Alan's plans became reality they were about to become joint owners of the Cavalier Club.

'It's coming on but there's still a long way t'go before opening night.' Alan broke into his brother's thoughts.

This was Norman's fourth visit to the property and still he was amazed at the sight of it.

This was no ordinary house. It was almost a mansion. Sturdy and strong, this house had stood the test of time. It had twelve rooms if you included the attics, and the ground floor rooms were of a size that Norman had never seen before. The grounds surrounding the property would have you believing you were in the heart of the country instead of Upper Tooting. The main lawn even had a fountain.

Oh yes, to Norman this place was a world apart. The huge front door was solid dark oak, flanked on each side by beautiful bay windows, with tall straight windows above them. And above these were more windows but on a smaller scale.

Alan was first out of the car. He bounded up the wide stone steps, unlocked the door, turned and called to his brother, 'Come on, judge for yourself if the builders have done a good job.'

As Norman stepped into the hall it was as if a signal had been given. Two men appeared, both were smiling. 'Bar's not open yet, but ye can make us all a brew if ye like,' Mr Josling, the eldest man joked, then turning his head and glancing in Norman's direction he stated, 'This is my other son, Fred. He does all the donkey work, mainly crawling about under the floorboards else you'd 'ave met him before. Y'did meet John last time you were here.'

The young man was not unlike his father but not as tall, and where as Mr Josling was constantly smiling, Fred's face had a serious, drawn look. He inclined his head towards Norman, saying, 'Pleased t'meet you.'

He answered, 'Likewise, me too.'

'How's it going, Reg?' Alan addressed the father.

'We're getting there. Yes, now that most of the material 'as arrived we're making progress. Tell ye what though, 'Arry Smith's right annoyed, he's all but finished papering over there,' he nodded his head to the left-hand side of the hall, 'and what d'ye think? The last roll of wallpaper ain't a match. Blew his ruddy top he did. He 'ad to let the electricians go ahead, and the curtain people were breathing down his neck.'

'So what's he done about it?'

'Been on the blower 'alf the morning to the manufacturers. Couldn't get 'a'p'orth of sense out of the local merchants. 'S alright now though. They're putting him two rolls, just t' be sure, on the train tonight. He's going up t'London Bridge to collect them in the morning.'

'Fair enough,' Alan said, and Norman added, 'Can't beat going t' the top when ye want something sorted in a hurry.'

'What we standing about out 'ere for?' Mr Josling asked, moving back a pace or two.

'For the simple reason that you were blocking our way,' Alan smiled.

Norman stood inside the door and marvelled. Since his

last visit the dividing wall had been taken down and now two rooms were one, stretching from the front to the back of the house, with windows at each end and a glorious view of the garden. There were other changes too. For instance a raised circular bar now dominated the centre of the floor space.

Noting Norman's interest, Mr Josling said, 'Carpenters 'ave excelled themselves, wouldn't you say?'

'I would indeed.' The answer was brief but whole-hearted.

'Wait till the french polishers 'ave done their bit.'

Norman smiled and walked the length of the room. Four steps now led up to what would be a secluded area. Anyone sitting up there when the club is open will be able to look down and see all that's going on, he mused to himself.

Now that the authorities had granted a licence to run these premises as a club with membership and to operate an independent restaurant with a drinks licence and the alterations were actually underway, he didn't feel nervous any more.

The licence application had been in the name of their two uncles, Albert and Jeffrey Simmonds, because their solicitor had been of the opinion that any application made by them might be turned down because of their age.

Norman hadn't been at all sure that his mother's brothers would go along with Alan's plans, especially as they were virtually keeping their mother in the dark over it all. He need not have worried. Alan was in fine fettle the night he had approached his uncles. Over a few pints of beer in the Cricketers, plans and dreams had been thoroughly thrashed out and to Norman's amazement both men had gone for it hook, line and sinker.

'We've seen it all on paper; well now, let's see ye get on with it,' had been Jeff's reaction.

'More power t' ye elbow, lads,' Bert had cried, his grin stretching wide. 'You're young and you'll both go places, no doubt about that. The opportunities weren't about when we were your age. Go for it, I say, an' I'm more than pleased that you've chose us to be involved. Just make sure we get an invite to the opening do.'

Absolute trumps the pair of them had turned out to be. Dressed in their best suits they'd attended the hearing in court, waving aside Alan's offer to pay them the day's wages they had lost. And that hadn't been the end of it at all. Advice and experience was on hand now when either of them felt the need to ask. Even a stake in the business had been offered.

'At the moment we're rubbing along fine,' Alan had assured them, 'but thanks all the same.'

'Well, the offer is there should you need it. You'll only 'ave t'ask the once.' Bert had said, his voice firm with sincerity.

To say that after the licence was secure Norman had felt relieved would have been putting it mildly. Now he could begin to sleep nights again! When he left the Post Office in a week's time he wouldn't be walking into the unknown. Like Alan had urged, nothing ventured, nothing gained.

'And this won't be the only one,' Alan's voice made him jump. 'There'll be others, too. Next one up West. Real posh!'

Norman rummaged in his coat pocket, brought out a packet of cigarettes and lit one with the lighter his brother had bought him for Christmas.

'Let's walk before we think about running, eh bruv?'

Alan grinned broadly. 'Oh cripes, you ain't gonna start in on me again about being extravagant, are you?'

'No, course not.' All the same Norman felt his heart begin to thump. Alan always did have such big ideas.

'Come across the hall and see what will be the restaurant when we're up an' running,' Alan said briskly, already walking away. 'That room is practically finished.'

'Good God!' Norman sounded impressed and he was. Again it was a very large room with a high ceiling. And in less than a month it had been transformed. The walls now had light oak panelling. There were long pale green curtains that fell to the floor. The light fittings were real high-class. Only the one strip of bare wall in the far corner of the room indicated the source of decorators' frustration. The whole room had been renovated which was why everything was so new and fresh looking.

'Wait till the furniture arrives,' Alan said, pleased at the look of surprise on his brother's face. 'There's gonna be lots of small separate tables and green leather chairs, same colour as the curtains.'

Norman thought rapidly, going over all the money matters in his mind. He needed to sit down with Alan and thrash the entire business through. It was no good simply letting things drift. Alan had to tell him where all the cash was coming from. There was an awful lot he couldn't figure out. Standing here admiring everything wasn't going to get him anywhere.

'Alan, we don't need to go upstairs today, do we?'

Alan gave him a cautious look. 'Not if you don't want to. You've seen the plans for the conversion. There'll be two great flats eventually.'

'Just thought it was about time we had another discussion. How about we leave here now, go somewhere for a drink? There's quite a few matters we have to mull over. For one thing what about Mum an' our Ruby? We haven't settled that yet.'

Alan scowled. Norman quickly said, 'Of course if you don't want to . . .'

'I'll risk it. Only don't start haggling over pennies. I'll just say cheerio t'the men. Let them know what I'd like them to do t'morrow.'

'Tomorrow's Saturday.'

'Yeah, but they still work half a day.'

Ah well, Norman sighed. In for a penny in for a good many pounds, he told himself as he made his way out to Alan's car.

As Alan drove, Norman was deep in thought. Over the past year he had contemplated marriage. He loved Rose Marlow, he had no doubts on that score at all. He thought of all the times he had held her close, had wanted her, almost desperately sometimes. Why hadn't they tied the knot?

They both had widowed mothers. Mothers that had needed them at home. Hers more than his.

Mrs Marlow was a cripple. Unable to get about much. A nice lady he had a lot of time for. She wasn't a moaner. A good few years older than his own mum, she still coped very well, doing all of the cooking although she wasn't able to cope with the housework. Rose had to pay a woman to do that and being the only breadwinner, that meant Rose had to take a part-time job as a barmaid two evenings a week as well as working full-time in the office of the Co-op.

It irked him that soon now there would be a self-contained flat ready and waiting for him to walk into. What would he do about that?

Alan tapped Norman on the arm to get his attention. 'D'ye want t'go to the Goringe Park Hotel on the junction or will the Castle at the Broadway do?'

'I'm not fussy, the Castle will do.'

Minutes later Alan parked the car on the forecourt and they pushed open the pub door to the saloon bar. They sat down, taking two chairs which were in a secluded corner.

'What'll it be?' Norman asked.

'Don't think I could manage a pint, not with Mum's heavy dinner awaiting us. Make it a whisky and dry.'

The barmaid was a brassy blonde with a friendly smile.

'Any ice?' Norman asked, as she set the drinks down in front of him.

'You've got eyes, 'elp yeself,' she replied pointing to an ice bucket.

'Oh, cheeky with it,' he shot back.

She laughed. 'All you men think us women were put on this earth just to wait on you.'

He shook his head. Maybe she was right. At least as far as he and Alan were concerned. Perhaps we are loath to leave home because of the way our mum waits on us, hand, foot and finger.

Using the tongs he put several cubes of ice into each double whisky and then topped both drinks up to the brim of the glass with dry ginger.

Back at the table, Alan started the ball rolling. 'So, you want serious talk, yes?'

Norman frowned as he stared at his brother. 'I'd say it was about time. How are we doing for money?'

'Well, another five grand wouldn't come amiss.'

'That's what we paid for the property, wasn't it?'

'Yes, you know it was. Six 'undred each we put in and

the bank came across with with just over four thousand and that covered legal fees as well.'

'We couldn't have come up with that kind of money if we hadn't both sold our endowment policies, and the bank manager gave us another five hundred to do the place up.'

Alan threw back his head and laughed. 'That was spent ages ago.'

'I ain't that green. I guessed that much. What I want you t'tell me now, Alan, is what you've been using lately an' where it's all coming from?'

'Oh, Norm, don't act so daft. Didn't we have lunch with Mr Grimes?'

'Yes, he's still the manager of the branch where we bank, isn't he?'

'Gawd, I hope so. An' for a very long time t'come. We'd be in dead trouble without him to back us. He's been all for us from the word go. Remember how he worked out a very thorough detailed account of expenditure for the club and a separate costing for turning the upper part of the house into two flats?'

'Course I remember it. Didn't I spend three nights going over those figures?'

'Well, Grimes sent them off to his head office and apparently the powers that be considered it all to be a worthwhile proposition and they allowed us to 'ave a cash flow of three thousand pounds. That's how come you and me 'ave been signing so many cheques.'

'What exactly do you mean by cash flow? Wouldn't overdraft be a better word?'

'Something like that. For Christ's sake stop worrying. We got that place dirt cheap only because it 'ad been standing empty for so long. We'll make loads of money out of all this. You'll see. Apart from the club there's the land and the bricks an' mortar.' He paused, thumped Norman's shoulder with his fist and grinning said, 'If the worse came to the worse, we could always turn the club into a knocking-shop.'

Norman stared at him. A few seconds later and they were both roaring with laughter.

Now it was Norman's turn to do the punching. 'You'd better be joking, bruv! Mum's mad enough now, can you imagine what she'd be like if we pulled a stroke like that on her?'

Alan's grin was full of devilment. 'I'd leave you t'do the telling, you're her blue-eyed boy.'

'Never in a month of Sundays could I compete with you,' Norman muttered, holding on to his side. The very thought of their mother even getting wind that they might be making a living off the backs of loose women was enough to have him in stitches.

Once they had both stopped chuckling, Alan took a swig of his drink before saying, 'If you're satisfied that I'm not driving us both into bankruptcy I think it's about time we got on to the subject of our sister. Suppose you ain't made any 'eadway in finding Brian?'

'No.' Norman shook his head slowly. 'Apart from those two days we spent touring every known haunt of his, nothing. You?'

'Me neither. Though that's not exactly true. Yesterday I 'ad a drink with Gerry Hicks, seems he's been working on the same job as Brian for some time. He tells me Brian legged it but he's got money owing him, so Gerry reckons he'll turn up come payday an' he's promised to let me know. Says 'im an' some mates will keep a tag on Brian when he leaves the site. With cash in his pocket he's sure t'head for the nearest boozer.'

'God 'elp him!' was Norman's response. 'By the way, who's Gerry Hicks? Name seems t'ring a bell but I can't place him.'

'I did me national service with him, well mostly. You 'ave met him once. He lives in Southfields. Y'know what, Norm, I owe a lot to Gerry. We 'ad one NCO that was a right pig of a bully, I can take a lot but the belittling things that sod 'ad us doing was something else. What with him and the tedium and futility of endless drill and bull it was only ye mates that kept you from going round the bend.'

'And you 'ad a good 'un in Gerry?'

'Yeah, I did an' all. And when I told him about our Ruby, you should 'ave seen 'is face. I don't give much for Brian's chances if Gerry finds him first.'

Norman drew a deep breath, went to speak and then thought better of it.

'Better drink up,' Alan said raising his glass to his lips, 'I swore to Mum we'd both be 'ome for dinner tonight.'

'Yeah all right,' Norman agreed, lifting his own glass. Then shaking his head, amusement showing on his face, he added, 'I haven't told her it's me last week at the Post Office an' come t'think of it neither of us has been brave enough to tell her about the club.'

Alan grinned, 'D'you think she has any idea what kind of business we've set up partnership in?'

'Don't know. An' I sure as hell ain't gonna be the one to tell her.'

'Coward!' Alan was laughing fit to bust now.

Norman made no reply. He too had a grin that spread from ear to ear.

'Quite right,' Alan spluttered, 'we won't meet trouble halfway. We'll get the thing off the ground first an' 'ope she don't get t'find out in the meantime. Tell ye what though, we'll buy her a new dress for opening night.'

'Marvellous! That would be most proper,' Norman was taking the mick. 'We'll also see to it that she has her hair done. How about that?'

'Come on you, let's move, or else it will be our mother what sees to us if we ain't there when she puts the grub on the table.'

There was a pause before Norman got to his feet. He was thinking if the only problem their mother had was finding out that her sons were opening a club, life for her wouldn't be at all bad.

Their Ruby was the problem, and finding Brian and giving him a good hiding might make everyone feel a bit better but it wouldn't solve anything for Ruby. Poor Ruby. Was there ever going to be a time when life would run easy for her? He doubted it.

Chapter Eight

FOR THE WHOLE AFTERNOON Ida had sat by herself and, between bouts of crying, had done her best to think things through.

What she would really like to do was confront Brian, face to face. All she had been told was a load of half-truths.

That social worker, Mrs Johnson, she knew a damn sight more about what had been going on between Ruby and Brian than she was letting on. And as for that Doctor Richards, who was supposed to be in charge of Ruby's case, well, she'd been allowed to see him for about five minutes.

Ida got to her feet, paced back and forth across the room, folding Ruby's clothes up that she had brought from the flat to wash and iron. Next she wrapped up the twins' small garments. It was typical of Ruby that she had put them into soak and never got around to hanging them out on the line.

Five minutes! I ask you. It was only because she had

raised her voice in protest that she'd been allowed into his office at all.

She was quite aware that all patients' notes were confidential, there was no need for him to go on and on about it, treating her as if she were dim and he had to repeat everything twice to make sure that it had sunk in. She was Ruby's mother, for Christ's sake. Surely she had some claim. What gave him the right to be so bloody superior?

Ida supposed that she should have been impressed when Doctor Richards had asked her if she had made any plans for when Ruby was discharged from hospital. She was at her wits' end, if she'd told him the truth. But she had been half expecting this question and had her answer ready.

'My family will see to her. She won't be left to manage on her own.'

The relief had shown on the doctor's face.

Ida knew full well he hadn't wanted to see her. Surely part of his job was helping relatives to cope with what had happened to their loved ones. If it was, as far as she was concerned, he was doing it very grudgingly. He had ended that short interview by getting to his feet, a signal for her dismissal.

As Ida made for her chair to sit down the shrill ringing of the telephone made her jump. At the same moment that she lifted the receiver, Brian's voice bellowed in her ear.

'It's me, Brian. What's all this I 'ear about Ruby being put away in a nut'ouse?'

Talk of the devil! Ida couldn't believe the cheek of him. For a moment she was utterly tongue-tied.

'You . . .' Ida cleared her throat and tried again.

'You've 'eard wrong, my lad. And if you were 'alf a man you be 'ere at my 'ouse wanting to know when an' where you could visit 'er. Not shouting an' 'ollering down the end of a phone line.'

There was a pause. Then Brian said cagily, 'It was all Ruby's own fault, she could 'ave been a bit nicer t'me. Like a bloody iceberg 'alf the time. But try telling that to 'er brothers an' the rest of your damn relations. The word in the pub is that they're out for my blood.'

'Serve ye right if they do catch up with you.' Ida hadn't stopped to think, the words had just tumbled out.

Now she had to hold the earpiece away from her ear. Brian's language was absolutely foul and the things he was spouting on about! God, she wished she had him here right now.

I might be a lot smaller than he is but by God I'd go for him hammer and tongs. She wasn't going to stand here and listen to her Ruby being torn to shreds. True, Ruby wasn't all that she might be when it came to keeping house. But no one could say she was a bad mother. That's one thing you couldn't hold against her. Ruby loved her boys. Found them a handful, but what mother didn't find her kids trying at times? The twins were well fed, always clean and well turned out.

Whatever was wrong between Brian and her was a matter that they ought to sort out in private, and nothing gave Brian the right to set about Ruby so badly that she'd ended up in the state she was in.

Brian hadn't gone quiet. He wasn't going to let her off as easily as all that. 'An' another thing,' his voice was still loud, his temper flaming more with each word he shouted.

Ida told herself to keep calm, she shivered and with

her free hand tugged her cardigan closely about her. She didn't want to come down to his level.

'It's about time someone told you a few 'ome truths. If you weren't such a bloody interfering mother-in-law, Ruby might not 'ave been so uppity. She knew she only 'ad t'come running to you and you'd be down on me like a ton of blooming bricks.'

He's got a lot to say for himself today, must be well tanked up with beer, was the thought that came into Ida's head and she wrinkled her nose in disgust as she imagined the smell of his beery breath.

'I've just about 'ad my fill of you and the rest of ye family,' Brian was still yelling. 'As far as I'm concerned I don't give a monkey's if I never set eyes on Ruby ever again. And while I'm on about it, you can take on the twins, all of you, between you, 'cos you wanna know something, I ain't even sure that they're my kids.'

Ida had listened to enough. She slammed the phone down.

What did he call me? A bloody interfering mother-in-law!

Well, it seems to me I should have interfered long before now. Things have got well and truly out of hand when a git like him can say the things that he'd been saying. But I'll have him. Oh yes I will, she promised herself. I'll live to see the day he gets his comeuppance.

I thought she was only coming here for a fortnight, Ida mused as she walked out of Coulsdon railway Station on her way to make her third visit to the convalescence home to see Ruby. It was beginning to rain.

I just can't face the bus, she admitted as she went towards the taxi rank. As the cab moved off she was hoping against hope that she would find Ruby in a good mood.

Suddenly she shivered. Oh, she felt cold, in spite of the warmth of the taxi. The first report she'd had from the resident doctor of Ambleside House, where Ruby was now, hadn't said a lot. Just that Ruby was concealing her feelings and had slid into depression.

Well, who could blame her? The beating, coming on top of other emotional problems, must have been the last straw.

'Blasted maniac!' the cab driver shouted, braking hard as another car careered down the drive towards them. 'Seven miles an hour it says in hospital grounds. Some don't give a damn.'

Ida didn't want to listen to his moans. She paid him and climbed the front steps.

People were hurrying through the corridors, their hands full with bags and bunches of flowers. Did these gifts help to lift the spirits of the patients? Ida wondered, thinking of all the nice things she was bringing from the family to Ruby. She certainly hoped so.

As Ida came through the door of the main lounge, Ruby saw her and came towards her. Ida stood still, waiting for her. When Ruby got to where Ida was she burst into tears. 'Oh Mum! Am I glad to see you.' her voice sounded urgent.

Ida put her arms around her and hugged her close without speaking, letting Ruby know she realised what she had been through and that she would always be there for her.

Later, over yet another cup of tea that she didn't really want, Ida listened and let Ruby talk her heart out.

'I miss the boys, Mum. Though t'be 'onest, I bet

they're doing a darn sight better with you, Aunt Jozy and Aunt Sheila. Spoilt rotten are they? I've been doing some knitting; the home provides the wool, we get to choose the colours. Thought I'd make zip up cardigans for Lenny and Joey, both blue. They always look nice in blue, don't they? What d'yer think Mum?'

'That's nice. I'll tell the boys the minute I get 'ome.'

'We go dancing twice a week.'

'Pardon?' Ida had to break in. She didn't believe what she'd heard.

'We do, don't we, Peg?' Ruby called across to a girl sitting with her family at a nearby table.

'Don't we what?'

'Go dancing over in the main building.'

'Yeah, we do an' all. It's good, too. Nice music. Men aren't much to write home about, though. Still, gives us a chance to have our hair done.'

Ida couldn't take in what she was hearing. 'Where do these men come from?' she felt she had to ask.

'From the other wing, over the other side,' Ruby told her.

Doing her best to hide her disbelief, Ida asked another question. 'And where d'you get your hair done, you aren't allowed to go out are you?'

Ruby looked across at her friend Peggy and they both burst out laughing.

'Mum! This isn't a prison, we've two or three shops here that open for a couple of hours every morning. We can buy writing paper, stamps, all that sort of thing. We can also buy biscuits, sweets, everything in the toilet line and magazines and papers. The hairdresser's opens two afternoons each week; it's free. Well, it is for a shampoo and set if you get in the queue early enough. Anything more like a perm or a tint and you have to book up and pay for that.'

'You could always buy a home perm from the chemist down the village,' Peggy chipped in. 'I permed that older lady's hair for her last week, you know, the one that always helps give out the dinners.'

'So you do go out,' Ida said, still unconvinced that these young women were being given so much freedom.

'Mum, I've told you. We can go for a walk anytime the fancy takes us. Next time you come we'll walk down to the village. Nice teashop down there.'

'But I thought . . .' Ida stopped, because the image she had had of this place had been sheer guesswork. It was obvious now she had been barking up the wrong tree. 'I'm sorry, I seem to have got the wrong impression.'

'Wednesday morning they have a great market,' Peggy called across to Ida. 'Not many stalls, but not bad for such an out-of-the-way place.'

Minutes ticked by as Ida ran all this information through her mind. She was glad that Ruby had found someone of her own age to be friendly with and she was pleased that they could go out for a walk now and then. Might help to build up Ruby's confidence in herself. God knows it was about time that she had a few pleasures in her life. I must remember to give her some money before I leave and I'll get her brothers to send her a postal order. She'll like that.

'Mum,' Ruby broke into her mother's thoughts.

'Yes, luv?'

'I'm glad you've come today 'cos you can't see the doctor on Sundays.'

'What d'yer mean? Does your doctor want to see me?'

'Sort of.'

'Ruby, don't play games. Either he does or he doesn't.'

'Well, he wants to see both of us – together – at half-past three.'

Ida looked at her watch. 'It's almost that now. We'd better go. Come on, show me the way.'

The doctor that shook hands with Ida was a short wiry man with close-cropped fair hair. He was wearing a white coat which reached well below his knees.

When they were all seated, Doctor Evans broke the ice by asking Ruby, 'Are you happy to be staying here, Mrs Brookshaw?'

Ruby made no answer.

The doctor persevered. 'Being here is giving you a rest and that can only be for your own good.' Ruby stared at the ceiling. 'Mrs Brookshaw, will you answer me, please?'

She sighed. She was getting tired of people telling her that everything they did or said was only for her own good. 'I didn't hear what you said.'

Doctor Evans took a deep breath then let the air pass out between his lips. Ida knew exactly how he felt. Ruby had this knack of irritating people.

The doctor continued. 'The whole purpose of this meeting is to determine whether or not you wish to press charges against your husband.'

'What difference will it make to you?' Ruby was being downright rude. 'Or me either come to that?'

Dr Evans looked away and there were a few moments of heavy silence. He had had one session with Ruby during which she had opened up her heart to him. Since then he had been very aware of this young woman's suffering and he felt he would go a long way towards making allowances for her surly attitude. He sighed to himself. 'All right, Mrs

Brookshaw, I see you are not feeling very co-operative. Off you go. I would like to have a few words with your mother.'

'I guessed you would.' Ruby laughed bitterly as she got to her feet and walked out of his office.

When the door closed behind Ruby, Doctor Evans leaned forward. 'May I speak frankly to you?'

Ida gave a start of surprise. 'Best if you did, I suppose.'

'Well let me start by asking you how much Mrs Johnson told you when Ruby was in Wilson Hospital.'

'Nothing really. Hints mainly. I kind of knew what she was getting at, though. Has Ruby told you more?'

'Well, Mrs Wilcox, we have to be so careful. Push too hard for the truth and Ruby shies away. She is only a very young woman, hardly more than a child, and she feels ashamed.'

'Why should my Ruby feel ashamed? Whatever she's done it was probably little more than mischief, I don't think she ever means to cause trouble, and after all, it's her what's ended up in 'ospital. You're surely not going to tell me you lay the blame on her.'

'No, no,' he hastened to assure her. 'We now know that Ruby has been pestered and persecuted, if not actually abused, over a long period of time, and not only by her husband but by his father as well.'

'Aw my Gawd!' Ida hands flew to cover her mouth and when she did manage to speak her voice was little more than a whisper. 'It's been going on a long time?'

'I'm sorry to have to say yes to that. Ruby has truly been a victim.'

'Here, wait a minute,' Ida's voice was loud and her eyes wide with shock, 'are you telling me that Brian's father's—' she choked on the word, 'raped my Ruby?'

'Mrs Wilcox, please try to stay calm. No, I don't things actually got as as far as what one could term rape,' he told her, at the same time thinking to himself that it hadn't been for the want of trying on the man's part from what he had gathered.

Ida's breath came out in one long gasp of relief. 'Thank Gawd! I don't know what we would've done if it 'ad come to that. Been a different story then, I can tell you that much. When you said Ruby had been a victim – well, I feared the worst.'

Now Doctor Evans sighed, 'Ruby hasn't been treated too kindly by her husband or by his father.'

'Don't I know it.' There was despair in Ida's voice. 'Should I 'ave been aware of what was going on? I didn't even give it a thought. I should 'ave known, shouldn't I? Maggie only gave out hints when Brian laid into Ruby this time. Why the 'ell didn't she come straight out and tell me ages ago?'

Really there was no reply Doctor Evans could make. Mrs Wilcox wasn't talking to him. She was thinking aloud and the poor woman was blaming herself. He played with some papers on his desk, shuffling them into some sort of order. Hadn't any of the family known what sort of man the father-in-law was? Before he could think of something to say, words burst forth from Ida.

'Of all the nice lads in this world, my Ruby 'ad t'go and pick Brian Brookshaw. God knows Brian was bad enough but to be saddled with a father-in-law like that!

'Good heavens, the times she's come 'ome to me moaning about Brian, and you know what I told her? You made ye bed, Ruby, an' now it's you that's got to lie on it. God forgive me.

'You know, when my Ruby was a little girl she was

so timid, wouldn't go anywhere without me. Her father came 'ome from the war and you never saw a little girl more 'appy than she was to 'ave a daddy. Then he died. Then there was Andy Morris, her first boyfriend, he and his family emigrated. Something 'appened to Ruby after that, I don't know what, just something, maybe it was all my fault. I don't know. I really don't know.'

Ida shuddered. 'I wish I could turn the clock back.'

Doctor Evans reached across the desk and patted Ida's arm. 'You know something, Mrs Wilcox, I very often wish the same thing. I'm afraid we can all be wise after the event.'

He closed the folder of papers on his desk and patted it before saying, 'It's a funny thing but I believe Ruby will come through this ordeal a very much stronger person. Can you bring yourself to believe that?'

Ida lifted her head and their eyes met. 'I dunno. I'd truly like to think so.'

He heaved himself up out of his swivel chair and came round to stand in front of her, then said briskly, 'We'll talk again. I have to go. You take your time. I'm just glad that Ruby does have you and the rest of your family. Remember now, we all want what is best for her, and I promise you she'll be home in no time and she will be fine.'

'Thank you, doctor.'

'So you'll stop worrying?'

'I'll do me best.'

She remained seated for a few minutes after the doctor had left the room. Looking round she decided it was a tidy room but so bare and impersonal. Did the words Doctor Evans had told her ring true? In any case this was no place for Ruby to be. She should be home with her family. She got to her feet and decided the quicker she got Ruby out of here, the better.

Ida made a real effort when she got home not to rush over to Jeff's or Bert's. Ruby had been in good spirits when she'd left her, better than she'd seen her for ages, but how long would it last?

What was it Ruby wanted out of life? A nice house? A good husband with a regular job who brought regular wages home? Good food and clothes for her boys? More to the point, what had she got? Not much. Hardly anything at all, as things stood at the moment.

Thinking about Ruby only irritated her; this latest turn-up had to be dealt with and she didn't feel up to it. Not on her own.

She had to keep busy, if only to stop what the doctor had told her going round and round in her head. She tidied the front room, and peeled the vegetables ready for dinner. She even forced herself to think about how she was going to discuss all this with Alan and Norman.

''Cos you'll 'ave to,' she said aloud.

She dreaded it!

I can't help wishing I was miles away. Anywhere other than Tooting and Mitcham and the worries that seem to pile up on my shoulders all the time.

That man! That bloody man! Why the hell hadn't Ruby told her uncles if she couldn't bring herself to tell me or her brothers? Well, something would have to be done. He couldn't be allowed to get away with it.

The chops were under the grill and the vegetables strained and in dishes by the time her two boys walked through the door.

''Allo, Mum,' they greeted her. 'How did you find Ruby?'

'Very much brighter, thank God. Now move yeselves, 'ave a quick wash and sit up to the table, dinner's almost ready.'

She wasn't ready to bring the matter of Bill Brookshaw out into the open. Not yet. The man was banged up in prison anyway, so the telling would only leave her boys feeling frustrated. No, much better that she told her brothers, seek their advice, they'd know what to do and they would deal with it. She had no doubts on that score!

It was almost seven o'clock by the time dinner was over. Both Alan and Norman had changed their clothes and gone out, and it was a very anxious Ida that crossed the street and opened the door to her brother Bert's house.

First words she said as she entered the kitchen were, 'Are the twins settled? 'Ave they been good?'

'No trouble at all,' Jozy looked up from where she was kneeling on the hearth rug, 'I'm just picking up these bricks they were playing with. I swear they get more enjoyment out of knocking them down than they ever do from building them up.'

'Ain't been no bother, ave they?'

'For Christ's sake, Ida! No. They've been as good as gold. They've had their dinner, were whacked out and I've put them t'bed in Terry's room. They were asleep before their heads touched the pillow. Bless 'em. I love 'aving them. You know I do.'

'Don't stand in the doorway,' Bert smiled at her as he came in from the garden. 'Rain wasn't much, was it? And the forecast for tomorrow is a heatwave on the way.'

Jozy laughed, 'Never mind about the weather forecast, give Ida a chance to tell us 'ow Ruby was today.'

Slowly, picking her words carefully, Ida told them what Doctor Evans had told her.

'So Maggie was right.' Jozy's voice was very quiet.

Ida swayed slightly and Jozy guided her into a chair.

Bert splashed whisky into a glass and held it to Ida's lips. The colour had drained from Ida's cheeks and she looked quite ill. After just one sip Ida made to push the glass away.

'No, drink some more,' Bert ordered. 'Come on, get most of it down ye.'

After a while Ida sat up and placed the half-empty glass on to the table. 'Thanks, Bert,' she said sighing.

The kitchen door opened and Sheila came into the room and behind her was Jeff. Jeff with his cautious attitude to life, always taking his time before making a decision, yet such a warm kind-hearted man. It was odd how Ida always thought of him as being the eldest of her brothers, when of course he was the youngest of the two.

Jozy barred their way, guided them into a corner where a hurried whispered conversation was carried on.

What now? Ida asked herself, fully aware that both Sheila and Jeff had been told the facts.

Jeff's cheeks were flooded with colour and his eyes flashed with anger. 'Takes some believing, don't it? A man of his age taking delight in tormenting a young lass! His own son's wife! Gawd 'elp us, what sort of a man is he?'

Ida began to cry. Bert jumped to his feet. 'I think we could all use a drink.' He poured whisky for each of them.

Ida was sadly murmuring to herself. 'People round here don't know the 'alf of it yet. Can you imagine what it's going t'be like when they find out?'

'Oh, sod the gossipmongers.' Jozy bent and patted her shoulder.

'They'll 'ave a field day,' Sheila added, 'but they won't say it to our faces.'

'You women! You wanna try looking at it another way,' Bert told them dryly. 'If the truth does comes out at least folk will realise Ruby 'as been more sinned against than sinner. Heaven knows it's a serious problem. Better for all of us that bastard is banged up where we can't get at him, 'cos if he were about I'd never be able t'keep me 'ands off 'im.'

'Me neither,' Jeff readily agreed. 'I tell you, 'ere an' now, I'd leave the sod for dead.'

Now it was Jozy that began to cry.

'Let's knock it off.' Sheila spoke up firmly, doing her best to cool things down. 'We can't do any more tonight. The twins are staying 'ere with you, didn't you say earlier, Jozy?'

Jozy nodded. 'They're well away, up in Terry's room.'

'Well that's all right then. Ida can come along with us; she don't wanna be on her own.'

Turning now to her sister-in-law she let her know she wasn't going to brook any argument. 'I'll come over 'ome with you, get ye night things an' you can leave a note on the table to tell Alan an' Norm where you are.'

'You'll 'ave t'do as she says, sis. Perhaps now you'll believe me when I tell ye who's boss in our 'ouse.'

'Less of ye cheek, you go on ahead. Me an' Ida won't be long,' Sheila ordered Jeff.

He made for the door, only pausing to look back

and grin at his brother, saying, 'Right pair of ogres we married.'

Even Ida managed a smile as she wiped her eyes and stood up.

Jozy kissed her and said, 'See, you ain't on ye own, you've got all of us,' then nodding in Sheila's direction, she added, 'but ye got t'do as you're told.'

Bert went to the front gate with them, calling out goodnight to them all.

Back in the house he said to Jozy, 'One thing's for certain, there's no way Ruby and the twins are gonna go back and live in that 'ouse. I don't care what 'appens, we've got to sort something out.'

Jozy hesitated for some seconds before saying, 'I'll put the kettle on, make us a cup of tea.' As she went into the scullery she called back, 'As Sheila said, let's leave it for tonight. Tomorrow's another day, let's wait an' see what that brings.'

Setting out the cups, she couldn't help saying to herself, there's an awful lot that needs sorting yet.

Chapter Nine

THE OPPORTUNITY AROSE OVER the weekend for Ida to ask the family if they had given any more thought as to where Ruby might live when she came home.

'She's more than welcome to come 'ere with us,' Jozy stated calmly. 'Don't seem as if our Terry is ever going to come back 'ome to live and it would be great to 'ave the twins near us all the time, wouldn't it?'

It was a lovely summer Sunday afternoon. The back door was wide open, Joey and Lenny were having the time of their lives out there in the garden, splashing and squealing with delight as they romped in the big inflatable paddling pool that Alan had bought for them.

For once the weatherman had got it right and the heat wave had arrived. Sitting around Jozy's tea table were the two brothers and their wives, their sister Ida and Maggie Marshall made up the numbers.

Ida was smiling broadly as she said, 'You know, Jozy, I've enjoyed 'aving the twins an' I know you an' Sheila 'ave as well, but can you seriously say you could put up with 'aving my Ruby 'anging about 'ere, day in day out?'

Jozy turned towards her, she too was smiling, but before she could say a word, Sheila butted in, 'You'd 'ave t'ave eyes out the back of y'ead an' them some to keep up with Ruby.'

Ida laughed, 'I don't think she'd want to come back t'me. Different if she were on her own. With two boys she needs a place of her own. D'you know what, I bet she's worried sick as t'where they're gonna live. Scatterbrain she might be but when it comes to them boys, well, that's a different story.'

'D'ye think she will be 'ome soon then, sis?' Jeff asked.

'Yeah, almost for sure, end of this coming week or beginning of the next, so the Matron told me on Wednesday.'

'Weren't you pleased?'

'Yes, of course I was, but for a moment I was panic-stricken, thinking of her pushing the pram with those two boys in it all over the place looking for somewhere to live. You know we don't know the 'alf of what Ruby 'ad to put up with from Brian and his father. I've found out since, they made her leave the pram at the bottom of the garden, wouldn't let her bring it in the house, and it was always damp and she was afraid the chrome work would go rusty. It couldn't 'ave been easy for her.'

'Bloody nightmare if you ask me,' said Jeff.

Ida bit her lip, 'With the old man being in prison and nobody 'aving seen hide nor hair of Brian I dare say the place is closed up. God knows if the rent 'as been paid or not.'

'I think my landlord's gonna 'ave a flat coming up empty, if it ain't empty already.' All eyes turned now

90

onto Maggie, as she made this statement. 'It's true. I was talking t'the collector last Monday. Didn't give a thought to Ruby. Be a godsend if we could swing it though. Only just round the corner from me.'

'Maggie, you got any idea what's 'appening to Brookshaw's place?' Bert asked, his face now looking very serious. ''Cos we're all of one mind, there's no way our Ruby can go back an' live there.'

'Folk say they ain't seen anything of Brian since the ambulance came for Ruby, but I 'ave.' Maggie was grinning as she gave them this information.

'When?' All voices chorused the one word.

'Twice. Soon after the row he came back. Came over t'me and 'ad the cheek t'ask if I knew where Ruby was. Never mentioned the kids. The next time was late at night. I saw the light go on in the upstairs front room, so I kept watch. Never moved from my front door step till I saw Brian come out with two suitcases. I wasn't 'aving that. Creeping off without saying a word.'

'You never said any of this before,' Ida queried in surprise.

'Let 'er finish,' Bert ordered. 'Go on, Maggie, what did y'do?'

'I was across that road quicker than that, caught him right underneath the lamppost. Did I laugh t'meself! He'd got a great shiner of a black eye. He told me he'd been to his works t'get the pay what was owing to him and now he was off, going on a new job. Wouldn't say where. I did ask him what about the 'ouse, he said he didn't give a monkey's, let his father sort it when he got out. I kept me mouth shut but what I would like to 'ave said to him was good riddance.'

Everyone laughed.

Maggie looked now at Ida. 'Ye never know, he might turn up at your door looking for shelter.'

'He'd get more than he'd bargained for, I'll tell you.'

Jeff spoke up, 'Best thing you can do, Ida, is get yeself over to the estate office early in the morning – perhaps Maggie will go with you – put in a word, like.'

'Course I will. Say what time and I'll meet you as you get off the bus. The office is right by the Fairgreen.'

Bert's voice was a mere whisper as he bent towards Ida and said, 'If you are lucky and they offer you a self-contained flat, grab it. I'll give you a fiver tonight, that should cover three or four weeks' rent which I daresay they'll want you to pay in advance.'

There seemed to be a long pause before she grabbed his hand and said, 'Thanks, Bert.'

Maggie was as good as her word and Ida had to smother a grin as she listened to her explaining why they were there. The agent treated Maggie like a long-lost friend, turning everything she said into a joke.

'Does your daughter have references?' the agent asked, turning to Ida.

She made a helpless gesture. 'She's in hospital, her 'usband's left her, she needs a place to come 'ome to. I didn't think about a reference. I'm sorry.'

He moved towards her, around the edge of his desk. Ida had turned away from him and gone towards the door.

'Hang on a minute.' The young man – who until now Ida had thought was a bit vulgar – was smiling at her and holding out a key. 'Go along an' have a look at the flat, Maggie knows where it is, then come back an' if you think it's suitable we'll talk further. All right?'

'I – I don't know what t'say. Thank you.'

'You're going to look the place over then.' It was a statement, not a question.

Before anything else could be said, Maggie and Ida were out on the pavement. Tucking her arm through the crook of Ida's elbow, Maggie said, 'It's only about ten minutes walk an' it is a gorgeous morning.'

'Isn't it? Too nice t'be indoors. Number twelve Frimley House, the label on this key says. 'Ave you ever been inside these flats, Maggie?'

'No, passed them often enough though. You know where Frimley Gardens is, top end of Love Lane, backs on to Church Road, nice little cul-de-sac.'

And she was right. For one thing, the area was well kept and the pavement was shaded by three trees. It was a small block of just twelve flats, four on each floor. Number twelve was on the top. There was no lift. They climbed the flight of stone steps and put the key into the lock of the front door.

Before either of them had set foot in the hallway they'd each gasped with surprise. The floor was wooden parquet blocks fitted in a pattern. It was the same throughout. Two bedrooms, a half-tiled bathroom, a big front room and a kitchenette at the back. Looking down from the kitchen window, they could see that the land at the back of Frimley House had been divided by a wire mesh fence into twelve gardens. Each plot had a small gate, a coal bunker and a clothes line that stretched from one end to the other.

'Oh Maggie,' breathed Ida, 'You'd 'ave t'be outta ye mind t'turn down the chance t'live in a place like this!'

''Tis nice, ain't it? Pity it's on the top floor. Ruby would 'ave to leave the twins' pushchair downstairs somewhere and she'd 'ave to carry her coal up all those stairs.'

'Don't start creating problems, Maggie, whatever you

do. Ruby's young an' fit enough to sort those kind of things out for herself. How we're gonna furnish it and 'ave it ready for her time she comes 'ome is what I'm thinking about.'

'That's no problem,' Maggie said. 'That Ronnie Carter, the fellow in the office, already let on t'me that all the while old man Brookshaw has been away the rent has been paid on time, so he can't do anything about it. But, and there is a big but, he says providing we only take things that we can prove belong to young Ruby, such as the twins' beds and her personal belongings, he'll allow us entry. If you are gonna take this place for her I suggest that we ask him to let your Alan and Norman come over tonight with a van and fetch what they can. Then tomorrow you an' me can come in, get cracking, give the place a good clean through, make up the beds an' what 'ave you and you'll be able to be 'ere t'welcome her 'ome. Boy, I can't wait t'see the look on Ruby's face.'

'I'll go on the scrounge t'day,' said Ida, 'Sheila will be only too glad to sort some bits an' bobs out and Jozy will too. I wouldn't mind betting Jozy will be 'ere all day tomorrow with us. First thing on the way 'ome I'm gonna buy two tins of dark oak Mansion polish. With plenty of elbow grease these floors will come up lovely.'

Maggie was roaring with laughter. 'Ida! You should 'ear yourself. You're going on nineteen t'the dozen. Don't ye think we'd best get back to that office and sort things out proper like? Good God! You know what's suddenly struck me?'

'No. What?'

'Neither of us know 'ow much the rent is yet!'

'Gawd above, you're right! I never gave it a thought. Bert gave me a fiver and told me to pay about a month's rent in advance. He said they wouldn't rent it to anyone who couldn't pay that much up front.'

'He's about right an' all. Come on, tear yeself away an' let's go an' 'ear the worst.'

They needn't have worried. Mr Carter looked hastily about for somewhere to stub out his cigarette as they came into his office. He found his ashtray and he ground out the stub, turned round and placed the ashtray on a table behind him, before saying 'Well?'

Ida tried to smile but the smile collapsed. She swallowed hard before she managed to get the words out. 'It's a lovely flat. Please – would you tell me what the rent of it is?'

He smiled and again Ida couldn't pinpoint what it was that made her think that he could be a kind young man. Maybe it was the fine lines round his mouth and at the corners of his eyes. It certainly wasn't the way he was dressed, too flashy for Ida's taste.

'Four guineas—' he began, and Ida's heart dropped to the bottom of her shoes, 'would be needed before we could give your daughter the tenancy, I'm afraid. That is the usual procedure, one month's rent in advance. Would you be able to manage that?'

Ida felt she might throw her arms around the neck of this young man and hug him to death. It was an answer to her prayers. Ruby set up in a little palace. Her brothers and her uncles would see that the rent was taken care of. Though to be honest, a guinea a week was a hell of a lot of money. Almost half as much again as the rent on her own house and she had three bedrooms. There again, in this life you only get what you pay for.

Frimley Gardens was a touch of class. That flooring! Ruby wouldn't need any lino. In time she might get some nice rugs to scatter about. And there was a bathroom!

Lenny and Joey wouldn't know they were born. Bath was big enough for them both to get in together.

Now Ida was fumbling at the clasp of her handbag. Oh come on, open, quick, before he changes his mind. She raised one leg up, bent her knee and balanced the bag on it. She still had to wrestle with it but finally found her well-worn leather purse. The black and white five pound note that she had folded so carefully into four was tucked into the back.

The note felt like tissue paper but that five pounds was going to work wonders for her Ruby. It had too. This really was a chance for a new beginning and a happier life, not only for her daughter but her two dear little grandsons as well.

As Mr Carter handed Ida the receipt she glanced across at Maggie. They smiled at each other and for a moment Ida felt choked. Maggie was one on her own. Her husband had died soon after they'd been married. It had happened years ago and Ida didn't to this day know the details.

Still Maggie kept cheerful. She wasn't a moaner. She hadn't got much in the way of material things and many's the time Ida had wished that she would smarten herself up a bit. Having said all that, there wasn't a member of the Wilcox or Simmonds family who wouldn't do a lot for Maggie, and on one thing they would all be in agreement: when it came to helping others, Maggie had a heart of gold.

The following Monday dawned bright and sunny. Was it a good omen? Ida hoped it so. By half past two that afternoon, the three sisters-in-law and Maggie had glanced around the new flat and were each nodding in approval. No effort had been spared.

There wasn't much furniture, but enough to see Ruby all right for the time being. Hand-crocheted doyleys, donated by Sheila, looked pretty laid in the centre of the table and on top of the old chest of drawers. They certainly helped to cover up the scratch marks.

Ida had had her copper going and the chair covers and curtains, old ones of her own, were fresh and clean, as were the covers on the beds. The gas stove, being on rental from the gas company, had been left behind and Jozy had put it to good use. On the ledge in the kitchen were plates of rock cakes, a victoria sponge filled with cream and raspberry jam and a deep apple pie which smelt strongly of cinnamon.

All they had to do now was wait for Alan to come back from Coulsdon, hopefully bringing Ruby with him.

'Nanna! Nanna!'

Ida leant out of the window, smiling and waving at her two grandsons down below in the strip of garden. Seated on a chair by the coal bunker, Maggie sat busily knitting.

'About time they came up an' 'ad a wash,' Ida yelled down.

Maggie waved her agreement and gathered her wool and needles into her patchwork bag. Ida was waiting at the front door for them. They climbed the stairs slowly, even so the children were tired and a little out of breath. They were all dusty, their fine fair hair tousled and their faces streaked with dirt.

Lenny reached Ida first, 'Is Mummy home yet?' he asked.

'No darling, but she won't be long now.'

'Can't we have our tea till she gets here?' Joey wanted to know.

'Don't tell me you've got room for more food,' his nan

laughed. 'You ate three sausages at lunchtime and I know Auntie Maggie gave you a bar of chocolate while you've been down in the garden.'

Joey yawned. 'But we haven't had any tea.'

'Well come into the bathroom, we'll make you nice clean little boys and more than likely by the time you're ready Uncle Alan will be back with ye mum.'

Lenny chimed in. 'Yes, and then we can sit up to the table and have our tea.'

'Will we sleep here tonight?' he asked, almost as if the thought had caught him unawares.

'Of course you will. You've seen your bedroom and Mummy will only be in the room across from you.'

They giggled in a high squeaky fashion as though they thought this moving to a new place was very funny.

Sheila had heard their laughter and came along the passage. Ida had gone into the bedroom to fetch them clean shorts. She stood in the doorway and they did not notice her. The bathroom now looked lived in. Damp towels thrown down on the floor, dusty sandals placed under the washbasin.

Joey asked his brother, 'Is Daddy coming here to live?'

'Nanna never said so.' This was from Lenny who was usually so chatty, but today he didn't seem completely at ease.

'Perhaps we ain't going to have a dad no more.'

Oh! Sheila made a helpless gesture and covered her mouth with her hand. Poor little mites. What Ruby had got to do was buckle down and try to make a good life for these little boys. We all know poor Ruby hasn't had it easy, but with this place and all of her family behind her she at least was being given a chance. A chance a good many girls of her age would give their eyeteeth for.

The boys were changed, their cheeks now glowing, partly from the sun and partly from rubbing with the face flannel. As if on cue the door bell rang.

'Come on, come on, 'ere's ye mum.' Ida ushered the twins down the hallway.

The door was flung wide open, Ruby was down on her knees, her two small sons gathered tightly in her arms.

Over the heads of this group, the like of which had brought tears stinging to the eyes of all four women, Alan shrugged his shoulders and raised his eyebrows. The reason for this action wasn't clear until Ruby stood up straight.

Ida gasped in dismay. Ruby's hair had been cut! And permed!

It was a frizzy mess. Swallowing hard, determined not to say a word, Ida held her arms out wide and Ruby went into them gladly.

'Mum! What can I say? Alan told me everything, even about Uncle Bert paying a month's rent for me. Oh it's smashing. I was dreading coming home. Now I've got me own place. It's wonderful, honestly, it's wonderful.'

'Let's get away from 'ere so's we can shut the door,' Ida pleaded, pushing Ruby along the hallway. 'Go see your aunts, you owe them as much thanks as me. Go on, see the tea we've got ready for you.'

Ida picked Lenny up in her arms and Alan swung Joey up to give him a piggy-back.

'See, I told you Mummy would be 'ome today, didn't I?' Ida said. Over her shoulder she glanced at Alan and mouthed the words, 'Whatever's 'appened to her?'

He came close to her and keeping his voice low he said, 'Wait till you get a good look. Better prepare yeself for a shock, Mum. She shocked me, I can tell you.'

Coming into the front room, after the darkness of the hall, Ida was able to take her time to get over the surprise of the way her daughter looked.

Ruby had kissed her aunts in turn and was now hugging Maggie Marshall. She was wearing far too much make-up, heavy eyeshadow, horrible bright red lipstick and rouge on her cheeks. Earrings dangled as she turned her head. She looked so much older than she was.

Ruby saw her mother's look of disapproval and she plopped down on to the settee, lifting the twins up to sit one on each side of her, giggling at the stir she was causing.

But that wasn't all that shocked Ida – or her aunts, come to that – it was what she was wearing: a tight black skirt that was a decent enough length but which had a slit up the side revealing a lot of leg, and a flimsy red blouse that her underwear showed through.

Jozy broke the tension. 'Lenny, an' you Joey, take ye mum an' show her ye bedroom and where she's going to sleep. Let her see round your new 'ome, come on now,' she ordered, helping Joey to stand down on his feet. 'Off you go while we make the tea, then we can all sit up and eat.'

Once they were out of the room, Alan leaned towards his mother and said, 'It's just her way of showing off. A rebellious act, if you like.'

Ida half nodded.

Then Alan patted her shoulder and with a grin he added, 'Knowing my sister, you can bet it won't be her last.'

'Right. Tea's ready. Come and get it,' Sheila yelled and was almost knocked sideways as the twins scrambled for a chair.

'Sit next t'me, Mummy,' Joey demanded.

Seeing the look that came over Lenny's face, Ruby

quickly replied, 'I'm sitting between you, that way I shall 'ave one of you on each side. Isn't that nice?' Then, almost under her breath, she added. 'Aren't we lucky to 'ave such a lovely new home, an' we're going to be ever so happy here, you'll see.'

The four women, who had worked so hard to make this homecoming such a special occasion, looked at each other and the same thought flashed through each of their minds.

I hope to God that you're right this time, Ruby!

Chapter Ten

IDA ROLLED OVER ON to her side and lay staring out of her bedroom window. The sun was still bright but there wasn't the heat in it any more. Well, she sighed, only a few days to go and September would be gone and by the end of October the clocks would have to be put back and it would start getting dark by about half-past four. The trees on the common were already beginning to show the copper and gold colours of autumn.

Would she be sorry to see the end of 1951? No, she was in no two minds about that.

Years ago, when she was first married and her children had been small, she had loved the winter. Cosy evenings with the fire burning bright and them all seated round the table with board games or picture books to colour. Even when Len had joined the army she had never felt lonely, there was always his leave to look forward to and hadn't Ruby been born in 1933 because of one very special loving homecoming she and Len had shared?

The joy that first Alan and then Norman had brought

to her and Len had been beyond telling. Even though to this day they were different as chalk was from cheese both were damn good sons in their own way.

It was funny, but right from the start she hadn't known how to handle Ruby, and up to this very day she was no wiser where she was concerned. And yet Ruby could be so loving and kind when she wanted to be.

It would bring tears to the eyes of a stone statue to hear her laughing as she romped on the floor with her twin boys. Most times, Ruby looked little more than a kid herself – well, she wouldn't be nineteen until the first of January and eight weeks after that the twins would have their third birthday. It didn't bear thinking about.

Ruby was doing her best to be both mother and father to those boys and for the past few weeks Ida had thought that Ruby had, by some miracle, turned over a new leaf and settled down.

Ida swung her feet over the side of the bed, and the padded quilt slid down onto the floor.

Oh! She'd known that things were going far too smoothly to be true!

She bent and picked up the quilt, folding it neatly and placing it on the end of the bed. She had been feeling so well lately; with Mr and Mrs Walker away up in Scotland she only had to go over to their house twice a week, whenever it suited her. Mainly to pick up the post, seal it into one of the big addressed envelopes Mr Walker had left for her, and pop it back into a pillar box. While there she watered the house plants and put a duster over the lovely old furniture.

The Walkers were so good to her. No matter how long they were away, they paid her wages just the same. There's not many would do that, she often told herself. Her being able to go to Wimbledon when it suited had been great. Several times now Ruby had met her there. The boys were in their element, racing round that huge garden and even Ruby seemed to relax as she sat on the lawn and ate the sandwiches that Ida had taken with her.

Not one Saturday had Ruby missed coming home to Tooting. Ida still took charge of Joey and Lenny, letting Ruby go off for the whole day and do whatever took her fancy.

Had Ruby been taking her on? Laughing up her sleeve whenever she praised her for settling down so well? Why was it that since Ruby had come home from convalescence, Ida hadn't been over to Frimley Gardens once?

She had suggested it but Ruby had said it made such a nice outing for her and the twins to come to Tooting, and Ida had left it at that. Always having a nice meal ready when they arrived and little surprises for the boys.

Since last night things had been going round and round in her head, for now, since having listened to what Maggie had had to say, she had things to think about.

The alarm clock on the mantelpiece went off with such a clamour it made her jump. The time was just seven o'clock. She switched it off and made for the stairs, pulling her dressing gown on as she went.

She glanced at the closed doors of her sons' bedrooms and it occurred to her that she hadn't yet had that straight talk she'd promised herself with those two lads.

All wasn't right there either. And nobody was going to fob her off with a different story. Not this time! They weren't working regular hours, and this club business that she'd only been told the bare bones of, wasn't going at all well. She didn't need to be a clairvoyant to have worked that much out. The thought that Norman had given up a good job and that Alan's ambitious dreams might come to nothing filled her heart with misgivings.

Having filled the kettle and put it on the gas stove, she came back into the living room and set out the cups, saucers and plates in readiness for breakfast. This done, she went back into the scullery, had a good wash and dressed herself.

Finally when the kettle boiled she made a pot of tea, drank two cups from it and was about to fill two large cups which she'd put on a tray when the door opened and Alan's clear voice said, 'I'm up, and so is Norman, he'll be down in a minute.'

'So you should be,' his mother told him, 'it's time you were both up an' about. Never gonna make a living lying about the 'ouse all day.'

Then Norman came into the kitchen, 'Oh good, you've made the tea. Come on then, Mum, pour it out.' He walked towards the window and remarked over his shoulder, 'It's a nice morning.'

The pair of them were irritating Ida. They both were immaculately dressed as if they were off to some special meeting instead of setting off to do a good day's work. Yet for all she knew, that was exactly what they were about to do. She'd given up asking questions. The pair of them only grinned and told her just what they thought she ought to know. Which was never a lot.

There were times when she wished them anywhere but in this house. They got on her nerves and no mistake. More so this morning. This news from Maggie that Ruby had a bloke living in the flat with her was stopping her from thinking straight.

As Ida lit a gas ring and put the frying pan on she was thinking to herself that the sooner she saw these two sons of hers off, the quicker she could get herself over to Mitcham and find out what Ruby was up to this time.

Alan and Norman were now sitting at the table and she had a feeling of pride as she glanced at them each in turn. Alan was still the flash one. He wasn't fitted to settling down. He liked the ladies too much. He was a merry person, with a fancy for the social life. He took chances. There weren't many times when he took life seriously. If he wasn't what you would call reliable, he had lots of charm which made up for his shortcomings.

Norman was the quieter of the two. Now, you could depend on him.

Both were tall, well-built lads but with that well-bred, polished look that came from their father's family. The Wilcoxes were not the big, bruiser-type of men that her brothers Bert and Jeff were. To be honest, she supposed you could have said that Len's family were more well mannered. Certainly not so quick tempered.

Ida smiled to herself. She loved her brothers dearly but no one could call them good-looking. Her boys were, both of them, with their blue eyes, fair hair and that lovely fresh complexion.

She hoped they hadn't got into deep water. Got mixed up with something that was illegal. God forbid she should have the police coming round here. She shook her head quickly. What the hell was she thinking of?

She should be grateful that those two boys had turned out as well as they had. They were both good lads – Alan a bit too big for his boots at times, but then again, wasn't he generous to a fault? What other son bought his mother chocolates and flowers every time he backed a winner?

And Norman, well, he'd suffered. Still did at times but he didn't make a big thing of it. Norman was steady. If anyone could guide Alan it would be his younger brother. She wished with all her heart that he hadn't left the Post Office, but there again, it was his own life to lead as he thought fit. He was a man now and it wasn't for her to interfere with whatever the pair of them were up to.

Ida slid two eggs onto each plate to go with the bacon and tomatoes, and as she placed the breakfasts in front of her sons another thought came into her head. What if this fellow that Maggie insists is living with Ruby turns out to be as bad as Brian was? Aw dear. God no!

She went back to the stove and lit the grill. Pay attention to the toast, she chided herself, and stop trying to meet trouble halfway.

She didn't let her thoughts run riot again until her lads had cleared their plates and she was able to clear the table. She also did her best to keep a smile on her face as they each in turn bent their heads and kissed her goodbye. 'See you tonight,' Alan called from the doorway.

'Yeah, we won't be late, Mum.' Norman echoed.

She didn't breathe out until she heard the front door close, then almost groping her way, she moved to an armchair and sat down.

If they had hung around any longer she would have blurted out that Maggie had told her Ruby had a man living in the flat with her now. And that wouldn't do at all. She had to get going on her own and find out for herself the truth of the matter.

Surely to God it wasn't some bloke that Ruby had picked up, someone she knew nothing whatsoever about, that she'd taken into her home. There must be more to it than that. There had to be.

It had turned eleven by the time Ida reached Frimley

Gardens. She had thought about not making the beds or doing the washing up this morning, but it wasn't in her nature to come out and leave an untidy house. What if anything should happened to her and strangers had to go into her home? Right old slut, they would think. And they'd be right an' all.

As she turned into the cul-de-sac the sound of raised voices hit her and at the doorway to the flats quite a few people had gathered.

'What's up?' she asked a woman who stood on the outskirts of the spectators, her tone of voice expressing both curiosity and concern.

The woman didn't even turn her head, let alone answer.

Ida saw the man who lived in the flat below Ruby. On her last visit he had come up the stairs and made himself known to her. His name was Sam Levy and his wife was Audrey. On being told that her daughter would be moving in with her two little boys, they had said they would be only too willing to keep an eye on her. The fact that Sam Levy had also offered to look out for Ruby and to give her a hand up the stairs with the toddlers or any heavy shopping had made Ida think that they were very nice people to have as neighbours.

She now saw that Sam Levy was standing just inside the entrance with his back to her. She moved quickly, and taking a stand up behind him tugged at his arm, asking, 'What is it? What's up?'

He turned his head, gasped when he saw who it was, then said softly so that his voice didn't carry to the other women, 'There's a woman arrived at Ruby's, been there about half an hour now. There's a boy with her, about twelve years old I'd say, been a right old rumpus going on up there ever since she arrived.'

'How come this lot 'ave gathered 'ere?' Ida asked.

Sam Levy grinned broadly, 'A load of men's clothing came flying out of that top window. That was enough t'draw this lot. Came running, didn't they? Like bees round a honey pot.'

Seeing the look on Ida's face, the colour mounted in his cheeks and for a minute Sam looked very uncomfortable. Turning round quickly he almost knocked Ida off balance. He put out an arm to steady her, but she warded him off, 'I'll go on up if you'll let me pass.'

'Oh, I'm sorry. Really I am. Didn't mean to laugh, can't be very nice for you arriving to find all this. Tell you what, I'll come up with you, make sure everything's all right an' if you like I'll fetch the twins down to our place for a bit. Audrey will love to 'ave them, she'll keep them amused. Best if they're outta the way for a bit, don't you think?'

Ida felt she could have hugged the man. Her grandsons had seen enough quarrels when their father had been around; they were probably frightened to death if the noise that was still coming from upstairs was anything to go by.

She moved in front of Sam Levy now and took the stairs as quickly as she was able.

Ruby's front door was wide open, Lenny and Joey were sitting on the door mat, their heads hung downwards so you couldn't see their faces, only the shining top of their fair hair.

As she bent to kneel in front of them and gather them into her arms, a woman's high-pitched voice came clearly from the living room, screeching, 'I've told you. I am not leaving here without him.'

'Come on, my darlings,' Ida crooned to the boys. 'Come on, don't cry. Mr Levy is going to take you down to his flat and give you both a nice drink. You'll like that, won't you?'

But neither of the boys would be coaxed into standing up. Sam Levy bent low and swooped Lenny up into his arms, while Ida felt Joey's little arms go tight around her neck. 'I'll come back down with you,' she said, hoisting Joey on to her hip.

Audrey Levy was standing at her front door and she held her arms wide to take Joey from Ida. 'They'll be all right. You go back upstairs, see if Ruby is managing. Don't worry about the boys.'

'Thanks,' Ida murmured.

'Come back in before you go. Bring Ruby when things settle down. I'll put the kettle on ready.'

'Thanks again,' was all Ida could think of to say as she climbed the stairs again, wondering what on earth was waiting for her when she got to the top.

Ruby was out on the top landing, all on her own. It was funny but the first thing that came into Ida's head on seeing her was, she's ruined her hair. I bet she has a daily fight to get a brush and comb through that lot.

If Ida had only known the truth, Ruby regretted having had a perm. The more she brushed this frizzy mop, the more it sprang up as if it had a life of its own, though Ruby would no more admit regret than Ida would tell her how awful it looked.

Right now the last thing that was worrying Ruby was her hair.

'Oh Mum, am I glad to see you.' Her voice was trembling, her eyes were red and she was waving her hands about in a distraught fashion.

'Look, Ruby – whatever it is we'll get it sorted. Aw,

come on, what is it? Don't cry. Now – now, nothing can be that bad.'

Ruby had covered her face with her hands and her whole body was shaking. Her mother sighed, putting her arms around her, she pulled her to her chest, saying softly, 'Come on, luv, come on – we'll sort it out.'

For a moment Ruby leant against Ida, taking comfort from her mother's soothing presence. Then pulling a handkerchief down from the sleeve of her blouse, she rubbed at her eyes and blew her nose before managing to say in a low voice, 'Let's go inside, Mum, I've had a friend staying with me and – well – now I'm in a bit of bother.'

Ida swallowed deeply. I bet that's putting the matter mildly, she told herself, as she braced up to whatever it was that was waiting for her inside the flat.

Quite a peaceful scene greeted them both. And that took the wind out of Ida's sails. A man sat on one side of the room, while a woman sat as far away from him as it was possible to get. A young lad was sitting on the floor at her feet.

Ignoring the woman, Ruby made straight for the man. Standing directly in front of him, she turned her head towards her mother, saying, 'Mum, this is a friend of mine, Paddy, Paddy Brent . . .' She floundered, hard put to find the right words. 'He worked at the convalescent home and he's been staying with me – for a break, like.'

This so-called friend got to his feet. He was tall and thin with greying hair. He had a round, red face, a long nose, with a mouth that was set in a firm line. Dressed in grey trousers and a checked jacket, he looked liked a travelling salesman.

'Good morning,' Ida managed to say.

He nodded, moving his eyes over Ida in a way that had her feeling angry. She didn't like the way he licked his lips either. She had a sudden feeling of revulsion, which she couldn't understand.

'Pleased to meet you, Mrs Wilcox,' he said, taking her hand with his own slim, bony one. She couldn't wait to draw her fingers away.

Ruby moved closer to him and he whispered something in her ear. She jumped. She was on edge. She seemed fearful. But then you never knew with Ruby.

Ida was telling herself that Ruby hadn't done herself any good by taking up with this man. To her mind, she'd jumped out of the frying pan into the fire. She steadied herself and turned to face the woman.

'I was wondering when you'd get round to me,' The woman was well spoken. She got to her feet and came towards Ida. She, too, was tall and rather scrawny. Her hair was dragged back tightly from her face, which ought to have made her look severe, but it didn't. She looked anxious even vulnerable and Ida felt sorry for her.

'I'm Mrs Brent, in case you haven't gathered that already, and this is our son, Shaune. We've two more children at home.'

Suddenly the woman smiled at Ida and her smile transformed her face. Ida liked her from that moment.

'It's not the first time that Paddy has taken himself off. He finds it hard to settle. Though he hasn't ever picked on such a young girl as your daughter before.'

This remark caused Ruby to gasp and she started to mutter, 'I – I can't stand this, I can't take much more.'

As much as Ida wanted to rush to Ruby, to put her arms around her, something cautioned her to stay still. Her heart ached for her daughter as she watched her shake her head from side to side, saying, 'I didn't know he was married – I swear I didn't.'

There was no answer.

Ruby now covered her face with her hands and began to cry again. I don't deserve this, she was telling herself, but who was going to believe her?

Paddy had told her he was a widower. It had been a great shock this morning when she'd opened her front door and a strange woman had stated that she was Mrs Brent. She'd topped that by telling her that the boy with her was Paddy's son and that they had another boy and a girl besides.

Why me? Why do all the rotten things happen to me?

All right, she wasn't madly in love with Paddy. She would probably never be lucky enough to find a man she could truly say that about. Paddy Brent had been there when she was feeling low and sorry for herself; he'd made her feel that she mattered to him. You could say that he had come along at the right time, just when she so badly needed someone, if only to save face with her family and friends. Why oh why did she care about what they, or anyone else for that matter, said about her?

The doctor had told her it was because she felt insecure. Too bloody right she did. She'd been knocked about, pushed from pillar to post, left with two children to look after, with no man and no money.

On her own in that convalescent home she'd left herself wide open to Paddy and his lies. Why had she believed him? What on earth had led her to believe that he was any different from all the other rotten men it had been her misfortune to get mixed up with.

Ida knew it was going to be left to her to make a decisive move. Turning quickly towards Mrs Brent, and with her back now to Ruby, Ida said, 'I think it's best if you start making tracks now. Come on son, get up off the floor and get yourself ready.'

Mrs Brent sighed impatiently. 'We're going nowhere till my husband decides he's coming with us.'

'Aren't you?' Ida gave a small chuckle. 'Well, that's no problem, because I'm gonna make damn sure that as you walk out of that door he's gonna be right behind you.'

Now Ida turned to Paddy. She stared up at him, her eyes steady, and she asked, 'You got any other ideas?'

The colour rose in Paddy's cheeks, they were by now a real bright red, and his eyes moved away from Ida and settled on Ruby. 'What have you got to say about all this, Ruby?'

'It's finished.'

'Why, because your mother says so?'

Ruby blinked in surprise. Then her look changed to one of anger. Her heart was banging and thumping. The cheek of the man!

'Get going, Paddy.' Ruby hissed the words at him from between clenched teeth.

'Oh, Ruby.' He made to put his hand on her arm. She struck it away with such force that he staggered sideways. 'Don't touch me!' Her eyes flickered around till they met those of Paddy's wife. 'He's got a nerve, this 'usband of yours, ain't he? I don't suppose for one moment that you've believed what I've told you, can't blame you f'that. I wonder meself now 'ow I swallowed all the yarns he spun me. Still, I'm gonna ask you t'do me one favour. Get 'im out of 'ere before I do him an injury, and just make sure that I've seen the last of him.'

Five minutes later and the three of them were ready. Mrs Brent held out her hand to Ida and Ida shook it. No word was spoken, just a smile one to the other as Mrs Brent went towards the door. Shaune followed his mother with Paddy bringing up the rear, but before going Paddy turned and looked at Ruby, saying, 'I would have been good to you.'

Before Ruby could think of a suitable answer the front door had banged closed, and she and her mother were left standing in the middle of the room in a strange, uneasy quietness, looking at each other.

Ruby was the first to move, she took a deep breath, then slowly she said, 'Thanks, Mum. What would I do without you?'

Ida turned towards the kitchen. 'I'm gonna put the kettle on. God, I need a cup of tea.'

'I'll get the cups out.'

'Did you know he 'ad a wife and three kiddies?' Ida knew she shouldn't have asked that question but it was beyond her to stay silent.

'No. No, I 'onestly believed he was a widower. I've told you that already.' Her voice was loud. 'He was always so damn sincere, at least that's 'ow he seemed to me.'

'But Ruby, you knew nothing at all about him.'

Ida was taken by surprise when Ruby jumped to her feet, saying, 'You can say what you like, yeah and think it. I don't care. I thought he was different. Better than the others.'

'Well, he would have to be, wouldn't he? Couldn't be worse than Brian and his father, that's for sure. You didn't tell me that the old man was sent to prison for bashing a copper.'

'Nothing t'do with you,' yelled Ruby. 'Paddy wasn't like either of them, I tell you. He was kind and gentle. If he'd been given 'alf a chance I bet he would have taken good care of me and the boys.'

Ida had to bite her lip to stop herself from retorting,

well, he isn't doing a very good job of looking after his own family, but she felt she had said more than enough already. She was trying to put herself in her daughter's shoes. Ruby must have been flattered when Paddy started paying her attention. What had the man meant to her, she wondered, was it love? No, surely not that. Just someone to be with. A man of her own which was what she needed most. Now she'd been deserted again. Poor sad Ruby.

She wished that Ruby could cut clean away from here and leave all memories of Brian behind. Take the boys off somewhere and make a fresh start. But who in God's name was going to take on a girl like Ruby, let alone two young boys? He'd have to be a saint. And a wealthy one at that. It was for sure that someone the likes of Paddy Brent was never going to meet the bill.

Ida paused in the act of pouring out the tea. 'I'm sorry I was a bit sharp with you, luv. Come an' 'ave this cup of tea and then we'll go down and fetch the boys.'

She was hoping that this latest development with Paddy Brent would put Ruby on her guard a bit more. Perhaps help her to grow up a bit and to think things through more clearly before jumping in at the deep end everytime.

She half smiled to herself, yeah and pigs might sprout wings and fly. Knowing her daughter as she did, she knew all she could do was just wait and hope.

Chapter Eleven

THE WHOLE STREET WAS up in arms. Everyone was talking about poor old Tom Carter who lived in the big corner house in Blackshaw Road. What a shame no one in the community had bothered to find out how he was managing since his wife had died.

Poor Tom, he'd nursed Nellie, his wife, for nearly two years before she'd slipped away. Nurses, people from the church, neighbours had all been regular visitors when Nellie lay so ill in the front bedroom. Even Ida had popped in of a Friday morning, collecting their weekend list and doing their shopping for them.

With Nellie gone, it seemed as if Tom hadn't wanted folk coming in and out. Very independent he'd become. Ida felt guilty. She should have persevered more. It was the kind of thing you read about in *The News Of The World*, but to happen here, just down the street, was difficult to believe.

She'd heard the news first from Bob Wilson, the milkman, when he delivered her two morning pints. She'd said,

'Morning, Bob,' and his answer had been very solemn. 'A terrible thing has happened. Old Mr Carter has tried to kill himself.'

Ida felt the colour drain from her cheeks and she had to grasp hold of the front gate to steady herself, 'Is he – dead?' she stammered.

'No, not according to the police. I looked through the window, saw him on the floor and phoned straight away. Whether they can save him or not we'll have to wait an' see.'

Tom Carter was a tall reed of a man with hollow cheeks and nice blue eyes that twinkled behind his steel-rimmed glasses. He was a smart dresser and also very clean. He wore old-fashioned shirts with separate collars that were stiff as boards and his trousers were so sharply pressed you could cut your throat on their edge. The raincoat he wore had seen better days but it was always carefully sponged and pressed.

Since he'd been on his own Ida had noticed that he'd taken to carrying a heavy walking stick. He had been a groundsman up at the Oval until rheumatics got to his legs, as he put it. Now he spent some of his days on the seat looking over the duckpond on the common.

His pride and joy was his house, which, he would tell anyone sitting beside him, was the best investment he'd made in his life. 'Struggle it was to make the payments at times but the end has justified the means,' he would declare. He made it sound more like a palace than a house of which he was so proud.

He was also very proud of the job he had held so long and never tired of boasting of the great cricketers it had been his privilege to watch.

Ida wondered what had made the man so desparate that

he had been driven to try taking his own life. Loneliness, was her guess. And she didn't need any telling about that. Oh, she was lucky. More than most. She had her children, her brothers and their wives all around her. But it wasn't the same as having one's own partner. There were still the long nights to be got through.

Since Nellie had died, Tom had kept himself amused by taking in stray animals. Mostly cats. It was common knowledge down the street that Tom fed and loved them so well that even if he were lucky enough to find them new owners, half of them didn't stay long. They constantly turned up again on his doorstep and he never had the heart to turn them away.

Ida went slowly into her front room, her eyes fixed on the window. She didn't open it, instead she stood staring down the street. It was busy, even at this time in the morning, with people going to and fro about their business. There was a motor van drawing up on the opposite side of the road, women were coming out, giving the van driver their bag-wash. A lanky youth was delivering the morning papers, the postman was on his rounds, a middle-aged man in a fawn-coloured overall had a loaded bread basket on his arm. The baker noticed Ida, he smiled broadly and waved, opened her gate and came up the path. She went to open the front door.

'Morning, Mrs Wilcox, luverly day, large tin an' a small hovis, is it?'

'Yes please,' said Ida quietly.

'Well, here you are then, shall I take it through for you?'

'No, thanks, I'll take them.'

Ida watched the man going back down her path. She knew what he'd been after when he offered to take her loaves through to the kitchen for her, and normally she would have been only to pleased to make him a cup of tea, but not today.

She was asking herself, how, with all this hustle and bustle in the street and the comings and goings of tradesmen, could Tom have got so down that he'd wanted to end his life? And how come no one had noticed that he was feeling so low?

He'd got a son, Joe, a real nice lad as she remembered. But as things stood at the moment he hardly ever came to visit his father. He had come to his mother's funeral but his wife hadn't been with him. Fell out with Nellie when they were first married and then they'd moved away. Ida didn't even know where it was the lad lived now.

She felt the pain of guilt again, and began to reproach herself. Later on t'day I'll go up the hospital, see if they'll let me in for a few minutes. Let him know that most of us do care. And when he comes home, if he comes home – Christ! Please don't let him die – I'll make sure that he lets me in that house of his. I'll have him up here to dinner, keep an eye on him. I will. I vow I will. Just let him be all right. Please.

It was almost midday when Alan and Norman walked into the house.

There was something funny going on with those two and Ida could not put her finger on it. They'd left the house before she was up this morning, so what were they doing back here in the middle of the day?

She waited until the pair of them were sitting at the table eating an enormous ham sandwich each, washing it down with great mugs of tea. Alan was the first to finish. He sat back in his chair, satisfied.

'That was real good, Mum.'

Ida smiled. They were both so – so energetic, her two boys, so different and yet so alike in some ways. Bright, happy and lovable. The pair of them were always in a hurry, dashing off here, there and everywhere. It made her tired just to think of it and often she wished she had half of their energy.

She picked up their empty plates and took then through to the sink.

'Right.' Ida's voice was tight as she made up her mind to get some answers from them today. 'It's about time one of you told me what's going on.'

Alan sighed, 'There's nothing for you to worry yourself about, Mother.' He couldn't keep his voice from sounding bothered, whether he would admit it or not.

Norman, who always was the silent one, lit a cigarette and drained his mug of tea. He glanced at the clock up on the mantelshelf. It was one-thirty.

'We'd better be making tracks, Alan. It'll take us about three quarters of an hour to get to Epsom.'

'Oh no you don't!' Ida was annoyed. 'First you tell me nothing of your plans, then in a roundabout way I 'ear that you've got a mansion that you're gonna turn into some posh club. Money was no object, according to what I was 'earing. Now suddenly things 'ave started to go wrong and don't tell me that's rubbish or ask me 'ow I know 'cos I just do.

'I ain't brought you up for all these years without being able to read each of you like a book. Alan's been wandering around looking as if he had won the pools an' then found out that he'd forgot to post the coupon. And as f'you, Norman. Never much t'say for yourself, now I'm beginning to think you're suffering from laryngitis.' Ida had to stop, she'd run out of breath.

Both her boys groaned.

'Come on Alan, tell me what's gone wrong.' Ida's voice was desperate.

'All right, Mother. We were only trying to keep it to ourselves to save you from getting upset. We have run into a few snags.'

'I knew it! Bit off more than you can chew.'

'Mother,' Norman's tone was firm, 'Either keep quiet and let Alan explain or we'll be off.'

Ida looked at her youngest son in amazement. To cover her confusion at being spoken to like that she went to the fireplace and rattled the lever to let the ashes fall through. It was a bitter cold morning, but inside the kitchen it was cosy and the fire didn't need making up.

'Mother, will you sit yourself down.'

Ida did as Alan had ordered.

'Right. I'll tell you in plain language what has happened. We were doing all right, too well, I suppose. The bar of the club, the restaurant, the office were all coming on fine, it's true, but—'

'You ran out of money?'

Alan and Norman looked hesitantly at one another. After a moment, Norman spoke.

'Well, yes,' he acknowledged. 'Through no fault of our own. Honest, Mum, a lot of the trouble we are in is down to the surveyor. The trouble is mainly in the cellars, going to cost a fortune to put right.'

Alan took up the telling. 'Also I was very negligent about the costing for the fire work that has to be carried out before we could hope to get the all clear to open for business.'

Ida closed her eyes and said through gritted teeth, 'God 'elp us.' Then taking a deep breath, she went on, 'It's bad enough to 'ear all this but at least you seem to be acting a bit responsible for once. What I want to know is what are you going to do now? The last thing we need is for you both to lose all your savings.'

'Mum, it's in hand.' The urgency in Alan's voice communicated itself to Ida and she told herself to think before she opened her mouth again.

'We had a meeting with Mr Grimes, our bank manager. Jeff and Bert were there.'

Ida almost slammed her hand down onto the table; she stopped herself in time. So, her brothers had known what was going on, but hadn't thought to tell her. She'd have a word with them later.

Alan knew by his mother's face what was going through her mind but he chose to ignore it. He persisted, speaking slowly. 'It was suggested that if we were to get a few men, each with a bit of money, to invest in the club we could turn the venture into a small company.'

'Alan's not talking about letting strangers in and having a say in the running of our affairs,' Norman patiently explained. 'It would be just our two uncles and maybe two or three friends. It seems the only way. We don't stand a chance of getting another loan from the bank.'

'Find finance for this club, or it sinks. That's what you're saying, isn't it? But for God's sake tell me this, what friends do you know that have that kind of money to invest?'

Alan looked at his mother and then raised his eyes to the ceiling. 'You've got it in one, Mother.'

'Yeah, well, don't sound so surprised. I'm not just a pretty face.'

It was just the kind of remark that was needed to break the tension. They both grinned.

'Well, now you know how the land lies, Mother, we

really do have to be off. We won't be late back. About sixish.' Alan got up from the table and went to kiss his mother.

'You 'ang on a minute. You 'aven't told me who these rich friends are gonna be. By the way, why Epsom? Someone rich live out that way?'

'We're going to see Snowy Freeman,' Alan volunteered. 'Uncle Bert suggested it and he's set up this meeting.'

Ida's eyes shot wide. 'Snowy Freeman! He's your god-father, Alan.'

'Yeah, so Jeff was telling me. Can't say that I can remember him. Tell you all about it when we get back. That's a promise.'

Ida smiled at them both and said what she said to them every time they left the house.

'You drive carefully now, Alan. And mind what you're getting up to.'

'We will. See you later.'

They went out slamming the front door closed behind them.

Ida carried on clearing the table. She'd had a funny feeling ever since she got out of her bed this morning. First Tom Carter, poor old soul. Now her sons were in danger of losing everything.

She sighed. Ruby had been behaving herself. Seemed to knuckle down since that affair with Paddy Brent. She had gone to the social to see about allowances for herself and the twins. Been advised that she had to take a court order out against Brian, which she had, at Wallington Police Court. Much good that it had done. Brian had paid the money in to the court for the first three weeks then nothing. Social had taken over from there, and Ruby had a part-time job.

She sighed heavily. Ruby was behaving herself so now it was the boys turn to give her sleepless nights. Children really were a bind! You did your best for them but it never seemed to be enough.

She began to wipe the kitchen table with a soapy cloth. Snowy Freeman! That name brought back memories. Betty Bailey, herself, Lenny Wilcox and Snowy Freeman had all been in the same class at junior school. A lot of water had flowed under the bridge since then.

Snowy, nicknamed because his hair was so blond it was almost white, had married Betty Bailey. Lenny had married her – Ida Simmonds as was then – and the four of them had started married life as poor as church mice.

Both she and Betty had been pregnant before they'd been married a month. Snowy had stood as godfather to her first and Lenny had done likewise to Betty's first son. The war had split them all up.

So it was true. Snowy had made it and was living out at Epsom. She'd heard as much. Funnily enough Len had always said that Snowy was the boy wonder. Could turn a tanner into a shilling just by looking at it.

She carried on with her housework, she'd better get a move on. She wanted to get the vegetables done and a casserole in the oven before she popped up to the hospital to see how Tom was doing. Perhaps it would be better if she gave the hospital a ring first. Better to know what she was walking in too. She'd had enough nasty surprises for one day.

As she lit the gas oven Ida found she was still thinking about Snowy Freeman. Were Betty and him still together? You never knew these days. So many wartime marriages went sour when the men had come home and divorce had become so much easier than in the old days.

The jangling of the telephone broke into her thoughts.
'Hello.'

'Hello, Mum. It is you, Mum?'

Even from those few words Ida could tell that Ruby was distraught.

'Yes, of course it's me. What's wrong, luv?'

'The police have been to me – you're never gonna believe it. I don't know what I'm supposed to do.' Ruby sounded desperate. She was crying.

'What?' Ida made herself take a deep breath. I knew it, I knew it, she was muttering to herself. This day was turning out to be an absolute disaster. They say trouble always comes in threes. Well, she'd had two bellyfuls already today so she'd better brace herself for the third now.

'Ruby, calm down. I'll be over as quick as I can. I'll phone for a taxi right away.'

'No. No, Mum, don't come 'ere.' Ruby sounded positively terror-stricken. 'I'm in a phone box at the Fairgreen. The twins are outside with Maggie. We'll get on the bus.'

'Don't be so daft, girl. You'll do no such thing. You get in a taxi. All of you. D'you 'ear me? I'll be waiting at the door. I'll pay for the cab. Now, do as I tell you.'

'All right.' Ruby's voice was very faint and the next thing Ida heard was the click of the telephone receiver being replaced.

Ida heaved a sigh. What now? Was ever a mother so plagued with her children as she was? What the hell had Ruby got mixed up in that the police had been round again? Whatever, you could bet your life that Ruby was gonna be made the scapegoat.

She was too jumpy to do anything else other than open the front door wide and stand looking out. As the taxi turned into the road she was out on the pavement, her purse in her hand. She paid the driver and the boys jumped out of the cab with wide smiles on their faces.

'Nan, Nanna, we didn't come on the bus.' Lenny and Joey ran towards her, their chubby arms outstretched.

Ida picked Lenny up and hugged him tight, then quickly set him down and gave Joey a big hug as well.

'I've got the kettle on,' she said turning to Ruby and trying to make light of this visit, 'You couldn't 'ave timed it better.'

She could have kissed Maggie for saying, 'Come on, boys, let's go through to the kitchen, see if ye Nanna's got any chocolate biscuits, shall we?'

Ruby hung back and as the taxi moved off, Ida gently pushed her indoors and straight into the front room.

Ruby was as white as a sheet. Too quiet. Her face screwed up close in a way that Ida knew only too well. Something awful had happened. She didn't need telling to reason that much out.

'What's 'appened, luv? You're feel a whole lot better once you spit it out.' Ruby ran her hands through her hair and immediately Ida felt thankful that at least that terrible perm was growing out. Her hair was no way back to having the long, silky sheen that it used to have but it wasn't half so frizzy now.

This was Ruby all over. She wouldn't say what was wrong until she was good and ready. She came towards her mother, took hold of one of her hands and held on to it tightly, 'Mum, Brian's dead,' she blurted out.

'Aw no!' Panic flooded through Ida. Please, dear God no. He hadn't come back and Ruby killed him? That was more than a body could stand. What about the boys?

They'd send Ruby to prison. Dear Jesus, she's only a lass herself. Aw no. Not prison. Not her Ruby.

Pull yourself together. She could hear the words screaming to her inside her head. Stop overreacting and wait until Ruby tells you what has happened before you start dramatising.

'All right, baby.' Ida was calmer now and this was her own little girl who often got up to mischief but hadn't got a cruel bone in her body.

'What happened? Come on, stop crying and just tell me. Come on, there's a good girl. Please, Ruby.' Her voice was wretched now.

'All right, Mum,' Ruby said flatly. 'The police come, there were two of them, they said Brian dropped down dead. It was down in Wales. I don't know what I'm suppose to do.' Ruby voice had risen and it ended on a sob.

'Of course you don't, darling. I'm so sorry. It must 'ave been such a shock. Now try to stop worrying. Your brothers will see to it. What else did they tell you?'

Ruby rubbed at her eyes. 'The policeman was nice, kind of understanding. He said Brian was playing football, he'd had a load of beer to drink at dinner time. The ambulance men couldn't do nothing. Brian was certified dead when they got to the hospital.'

Ida couldn't help herself. She was consumed with a feeling of hatred for Brian. He could beat up on Ruby, go off and leave her and the two boys without so much as a penny piece, yet he always had the money for a skinful of beer.

It was too bad to place all the burden on Ruby's shoulders. Let the police notify his father, let him pay for the funeral arrangements. Though she supposed that Ruby would want to be there. Time enough to sort all that out later. Get Ruby calmed down was the important thing at the moment.

Ida put her hand gently on Ruby's shoulder. 'You and the boys can stay here with me till your brothers get this sorted out.'

Ruby looked at her mother and gave an embarrassed grin. 'Talk about a bad penny. I'm one if ever there was, aren't I? Always turning up when you least expect me.'

'Don't be so silly,' Ida tried to sound sharp. 'I'll tell you something, shall I? I know you loved Brian in the beginning, but God knows he must have killed any feelings you had for him a long time ago. Now, in my opinion, this could be a blessing in disguise. When it's all over and the dust settles you must pick yourself up, look after the twins and face the world bravely. You've nothing to reproach yourself for.'

Ruby didn't answer, she merely nodded her head towards the door, the handle of which was turning slowly.

Two fair heads peered round. 'Auntie Maggie said to tell you she's made the tea.'

As always when she saw her grandsons Ida was over-whelmed with a feeling of love and affection. They looked like a couple of cherubs.

It might not be nice and it certainly wasn't charitable, but the thought came into Ida's head that these two little mites would be a darn sight better off without their father. And that was her being honest.

Ida stretched, uncramping her legs which had been tucked under her since she'd come to bed hours ago. It was nearly four-thirty in the morning and she was no nearer getting to sleep than she had been at eleven o'clock when she had got into bed. She might just as well get up, go downstairs and make herself a pot of tea.

It had been a wearying day, in fact the past two weeks had worn her out. She supposed some good had come out of it. Her mind was going round in circles, her thoughts drifting to Ruby as she tried to work out what would become of her and her two little boys. She had talked everything over with Jozy and Sheila, but neither of them had come up with an idea.

Thank God Brian's funeral was over and done with. It had been decided that Brian was to be cremated in Wales and his ashes brought back to London. Both her uncles and her brothers had done their best to persuade Ruby not to go, but she'd gone anyway. Alan had gone with her and he said that Brian's father had attended and as he wasn't accompanied by any officials, he had presumed that he had served his prison term and was now free.

'Did you speak to him?' the family had been quick to ask Alan.

'No, he kept well out of Ruby's way and we respected him for that.'

Later, Maggie had found out from the rent collector that Mr Brookshaw had given up the tenancy of the house in Love Lane. That at least was one problem that she didn't have to worry about.

Ida's thoughts turned to her sons. When it came to them she was still in a quandary. Coming back from their meeting in Epsom, they had been full of Snowy Freeman. He was going to be their life-saver. A nicer man you couldn't wish for! Well, she hoped they were right.

Not only was Snowy considering investing in their business, he had offered them each a job to tide them over while all the alterations and repairs were being carried out at the property in Upper Tooting. Snowy, it seemed, owned his own transport company, mainly shifting huge machinery and spare parts for the dry-cleaning business. A lot of the machines that he sent abroad often sent back small parts for repairs and Alan had told her that he and Norman would be driving to Heathrow Airport quite regularly.

Had Snowy merely created a job for her boys because of his friendship with their father? She hoped there was more to it than that.

As much as Norman had hurt her by giving up his steady job with the Post Office to go into partnership with Alan, she didn't wish them anything but well. She really did pray that before long all the difficulties that they had run into would be sorted out and that she would live to see the day that this club was opened for business.

Oh, why was she plagued like this? It was bad enough being one parent on her own without all this added worry.

The kettle had come to the boil and she quickly brewed a pot of tea. By the time she was on her second cup she had let her thoughts drift to Tom Carter.

Maggie had gone with her to the hospital on that first visit. They had both been silent throughout the bus ride up to Balham. When they had finally been allowed to sit at Tom's bedside, they had been shocked at how thin and frail he looked, but he was wide awake and pleased to see them.

He had looked at Ida and frowned, 'I'm so sorry for what I've done.'

'Shhh,' Ida bent over the bed, raising her finger to her lips. 'Now you look here, Tom Carter, we all do things we're sorry for, especially when we're down and things get on top of us. Just you remember, you've got plenty of friends that respect you.'

'Thanks, Ida. You've always been a friend to me and to Nellie. A good one at that. Since Nellie's been gone, the days seem so long. I get a bit depressed and my mind wanders. I find myself doing weird things, putting things away in all the wrong places. Forgetting what I've gone upstairs for.'

'Tom, love, if that's all that's been bothering you, forget it and join the gang. I spend 'alf my time wandering round the 'ouse looking for something I'm 'olding in my 'and.'

'Go on, Ida, you're having me on.'

'Straight up I'm not. Another thing, when you come 'ome, there's going be no more passing my front door. You come in or I'm gonna want to know the reason why. By the way, I'm not sure if you and Maggie know each other but if you don't you soon will. She's an angel. Everyone's friend.'

Maggie came close and shook Tom's hand. 'She's halfway round the bend,' she grinned, 'I'm no angel, I'm flesh an' blood.'

They had left Tom Carter feeling much brighter and the good news she'd heard today was that he was coming home in a couple of days time. She felt silly tears sting the back of her eyes and she blinked hard.

Thinking about Tom made her realise that the week hadn't been all bad. If he had died she would have been feeling a damn sight worse than she did now.

She poured out a third cup of tea. There wouldn't be any use her going back up to bed now. She finished her tea and settled herself into an armchair. Closing her eyes, she said a prayer, asking the Lord God to see that Ruby had an easier time of it from now on and that her sons would be given the strength and the wisdom to surmount their difficulties.

Chapter Twelve

ON THE LAST DAY of the old year the Simmonds brothers
gave a party. They had hired the hall at the back of the
Mitre public house in Mitcham Road, Tooting. Friends,
neighbours and business acquaintances were all invited.

Jeff's two boys, Billy and Albie, came bringing their
girlfriends. Ida was pleased to see that Norman had
brought along Rose Marlow. She had a great affection for
Rose and hoped that before long those two would name
the day.

Alan had invited a young lady that no one had ever set
eyes on before. Ida had greeted her pleasantly enough
when Alan introduced her as Amy Baldwin, but inside
she was seething. Her eldest son could do so much better
for himself. The girl looked tarty! I suppose the men would
say that she was sexy, Ida admitted to herself. More than
likely she had tried to model herself on Diana Dors – now
there was what you would call a sex-symbol – but it hadn't
worked for this Amy Baldwin.

'Don't you like the look of her?'

Sheila had been watching Ida staring at the girl and coming up behind Ida she hadn't been able to resist the comment.

'Dressed to kill, if you want my opinion,' Ida retorted. 'Just look at her, dumplings boiling over. Girls like her ask for trouble.'

Sheila laughed loudly. 'There'll never be a girl good enough for your Alan – every mother feels the same with their first born. Still, I'd like to bet your Alan's not serious over that one. Play the field has always been Alan's motto an' will be for a long time to come, you'll see.'

'Yeah, I suppose so.'

'Anyway, it's New Year's Eve, we're here to enjoy ourselves. Come on, let's get ourselves a drink.'

There was preparation and bustle for the evening going on all around them, and Ida watched as folk arrived, mostly in couples. Snowy Freeman came with his wife Betty and from across the hall she avoided meeting them. Time enough for that later in the evening.

At her uncle's suggestion Ruby had invited a man, and, to everyone's surprise, the man had arrived bringing his small son with him.

Ida sighed. Her heart felt dull and heavy. She felt more lonely tonight than she had done for many a long day. She had hoped that, it being New Year's Eve, someone would have come and sat with her.

Then a few minutes later she had no time to think of her loneliness because Ruby was coming towards her. The twins ran across the floor and into their grandmother's arms. Her face wreathed in smiles, her blue eyes warm and brimming with tears, Ida hugged her grandchildren.

Then she linked her arm through her daughter's and smiled a welcome to the man that stood by her side.

Holding on to this stranger's hand was a small boy. Seeing him, Ida caught her breath. He was so beautiful. His skin was tanned, brilliant big brown eyes, dazzling white teeth and a dimple in his chin.

Ida, more to cover her confusion then anything else, bent her knees and pulled Joey and Lenny within the circle of her arms again.

'Nanna, Uncle Alan said we'll be able to have ice-cream after our dinner if we want,' Lenny said very seriously.

'If your uncle told you that then I'm sure it's right, but first I 'ave t'have a kiss from each of you.'

The twins looked at each other, giggled and then threw their arms about her and planted a kiss on each side of her face.

Ida straightened up.

'Mum, this is Jack Dawson and this is his little boy, Danny.'

Ida put off the moment of actually meeting this new fellow of Ruby's by bending down to cuddle the boy. He really was a lovely child. Unlike the twins, he was plump, cuddly-like and his hair was as dark as theirs was fair.

'Hallo Danny, 'ave you got a kiss for me as well?'

Danny shrunk back, pushing himself close up to his father's side. He was shorter than the twins but Ida thought him to be almost the same age. Dressed in short, red trousers and a white jumper that showed his tanned complexion off, he had a foreign look about him.

Ruby smiled at her mother over Danny.

'He's shy. I've told him you're my mum but he isn't used to you yet.' She bent her head to say to the little boy, 'Look, Danny, this is Joey's an' Lenny's Nanna. D'you want to call her Nan?'

The child made no sound but buried his face deep into his father's side.

'Leave him be,' Ida advised, 'all this noise and fuss is probably frightening him.'

Ida could put it off no longer. She turned to face Jack Dawson and held out her hand. What she saw was a wiry young man, not tall but fit and muscular; his skin was also deeply tanned. He was, she reckoned, about twenty-six or seven, and from hearing him utter only a few words she decided he was definitely a Londoner.

'Have you an' Ruby known each other long?' Ida felt she had to ask.

'Well, quite a while now. I worked with Ruby. Filling in for a friend, doing him a favour.'

'Jack is a chef, Mum. Works away most of the time. Like he said, I got the job as a waitress and that week Jack came to the Grange at the same time.'

Ida's glance flicked over his suntanned good-looking face and briefly met a pair of great dark brown mischievous eyes. Then there was a silence so prolonged that Ida, feeling uneasy, broke it by suggesting that they took the boys off and got them a lemonade.

Ida was lost in thought as she watched them lead the children to the bar, so much so that when Sheila's hand came down on her shoulder she jumped.

'Sheila, I didn't see you come up.'

'Sorry luv, I just want to warn you – Terry's arrived.'

'Why that's wonderful. I'm so glad, that will make Jozy's an' Bert's night. So many family dos that Terry never bothers to turn up to. Hey, what d'ye mean, warn me?'

'He's brought a fella with him.'

'So? What's wrong with that?'

'Wait till you see them together. Jeff told me some time

ago that he'd heard that Terry was shacked up with a bloke, but I never believed it.'

The colour was draining from Ida's face. Poor Jozy! And I think I've got problems! 'Daft, ain't it, Sheila? There's our Bert, a great bruiser of a bloke, only has one child, but that's fine 'cos we all think a son will marry an' give us grandchildren. If it's true, I do feel so sorry for Jozy.'

'Hallo, Auntie Ida.' Terry caught her unawares, but nevertheless her smile showed how really pleased she was to see him. He looked immaculate and he smelt of very expensive aftershave as he put his arms around her and lifted her until her feet were off the floor.

'I've missed you,' he whispered in her ear.

'And we've all missed you, Terry, But God I'm glad you're here now.'

'Auntie,' he murmured as he set her free, 'I want you to meet Peter, Peter Gower.'

Ida saw immediately the feeling these two lads had for each other. They were so alike in looks that they could easily have passed for brothers. Tall and broad-shouldered like all the Simmondses, Terry got his colouring and his physique from his father.

'I'm right pleased to meet you, Peter,' Ida said, meaning every word.

Yes, she was upset for her brother, and for Jozy too. Their only son. Still if they didn't want to lose Terry they would have to accept life as it was today.

Norman came to stand between his mother and his Aunt Sheila, staring as his cousin moved away. When Terry had introduced him to Peter, in to his mind had leaped a word which he had rejected immediately.

Oh no, not Terry. He couldn't be a homosexual. He didn't look or act like that. But then how often did they get to see him? This one cousin had been his best mate at school, then again, he hadn't lived at home since he was seventeen. That Peter seemed a real nice guy. Each to their own, he supposed. Perhaps tonight would break the ice and Terry would come home more often now. He hoped for Terry's sake that his parents would accept the situation. It would probably take a bit of time, but the Simmondses were a strong family and he didn't think they would cut the tie with their only son.

At eight o'clock they all sat down to eat. Candles glowed and pretty flower arrangements had pride of place. Three waiters served the food and the guests that had expected the usual cold buffet were pleasantly surprised to be served steaming hot soup, roast ribs of beef followed by apple strudel with cream, an assortment of cheeses and coffee and brandy.

A five-piece band had struck up and the dancing was going well.

'What d'you think, Alan?' Ida asked her eldest son as they watched Jack Dawson take Ruby onto the dance floor.

'Chef, isn't he? Works away most of the time, doesn't he?'

'So our Ruby says.'

'Seems nice enough. Bit too cocksure maybe. Why the little boy in tow?' Alan asked.

'Ruby said his wife died giving birth to him. He pays a woman to have him all the week, weekends he won't go anywhere without him.'

'Can't be bad then. A lotta blokes wouldn't bother.'

'Surprised are you? That maybe for once our Ruby has found herself a decent fella?' Ida said.

'You *hope*, Mother. Bit early to start assuming that everything is going to be roses from here on.'

'Your girlfriend is signalling you,' Ida nodded her head towards where Amy Baldwin stood, a glass in each hand.

Alan grinned broadly, bent his head and whispered, 'Don't look now, Mother, but your disapproval is showing.'

'You cheeky sod,' she muttered but couldn't keep the grin from her lips.

Snowy and Betty Freeman found Ida in a corner on her own.

'Mind if we join you, Ida?' Snowy's expression was one of amusement. 'It's all going on here t'night, ain't it? Takes us back a bit, eh?'

This was the first chance Ida had had to get a good look at her old friend Snowy. He still had a thick head of hair, more grey now than blond. His face was well-lined but surprisingly his eyes still sparkled with youthful merriment and his figure was good, certainly he wasn't overweight.

The same couldn't be said for his wife, Ida decided, as Betty plonked herself down next to her and breathed a sigh of relief.

'Jesus, I've got to kick these shoes off, they're killing me.'

Ida laughed. 'Things don't alter much, do they Betty? Remember when we went to the pictures in Morden once? You took your shoes off and you lost one. We waited till the lights went up but we couldn't find it an' you had to hobble down the tube with only one shoe on.'

'Fancy you remembering that. I've put a bit of weight on since then. But I see you're still all skin an' bone.'

'Get on with ye. I was never skinny; always short an'

dumpy I was. Scraggy now is what I think when I catch sight of meself in a mirror.'

A grin spread across Betty's face and at the same time she sighed. 'It's a pity really, how we've lost touch over the years. Good pals, all of us, weren't we?'

'We were that. Now you live out at Epsom. You and Snowy made it rich.'

'I wouldn't say we're rich. Just that we do all right. Do you live alone, Ida?'

'No, both my boys are still with me. Don't know for how long though.' Ida turned to Snowy. 'By the way, I owe you a vote of thanks. You're a dear. Don't know what my pair would 'ave done if you 'adn't given them a job. I'm truly grateful, Snowy. What else can I say.'

'Say nothing,' Snowy answered, smiling with satisfaction. 'They're good lads, both of them. Both good drivers too. And while we're on the subject, don't you dare go worrying about their club—'

'Bit off a lot more than they could chew there,' Ida interrupted.

'Nothing of the sort, I'm telling ye.' He gave a great belly laugh. 'Went at it like a bull in a china shop – at least Alan did. But his ideas were sound. Oh yes, very sound. Alan's nobody's fool. Got a good head when it comes to business, has Alan.'

Then reading her mind, Snowy became serious, put his glass of beer down on the table and leant across to take Ida's hand. 'Give them a bit more time and they'll have that club up and running and us few investors won't be a bit sorry that we put our faith in them. You'll see. We'll all be drinking champagne on the opening night.'

'How the 'ell can you be so sure?' Ida asked.

''Cos they've now done what they should 'ave done in

the first place – they've called the experts in. The way things are going now, believe me Ida, you'll end up being very proud of them.'

There was a pause, and Ida was thrilled when Snowy added, 'You'll see. Just wait a bit longer and your pride will know no bounds.'

He got to his feet. 'I'm away to join the men. I'm sure you two 'ave plenty t'natter about. I'll send some drinks over for you.'

Talk! Betty Freeman and Ida Wilcox talked the hind leg off a donkey for the next hour. All they'd been through since they were nippers at school. Sorrows and joys, births and deaths, disappointments, secrets, jokes, tears and laughter. They went through all of their relations, their children, their neighbours. Half the time they were laughing uproariously, the next moment they were wiping the tears away.

The dancing was going very well. Ida spluttered into her drink as she watched the couples move to form a circle, leaving the centre of the floor to Ruby and this Jack Dawson.

My god! What an exhibition! The fella was all arms and legs. He moved with the rhythm like no one she had ever seen and Ruby was in tune with him all the way. This was dancing? No wonder folk were already calling it the Rocking Fifties. The crowd must have enjoyed the performance, as the music came to an end they clapped and roared their approval.

It wanted only ten minutes to midnight. The band stuck up with the conga. The MC urged everyone onto the floor and the long line of revellers snaked its way around the hall. Somewhere a wireless boomed out the the strokes of midnight from Big Ben.

'Happy New Year!' was the cry from all corners. It was 1952.

Everyone was kissing and hugging each other and Maggie came to wish Ida all the best.

'Doesn't Ruby look radiant?' Maggie observed as they stood watching her brothers and uncles line up to embrace her, for this New Year's Day was Ruby's nineteenth birthday. 'I hope that Jack is the right one for her and that she'll be happy this time.'

'Oh Maggie, so do I. Usually Ruby gets what Ruby wants, but happy? That I hope to live to see.'

The night was very cold, the paths already covered with a heavy frost as the guests trod warily to their cars and waiting taxis.

The twins, half asleep, were carried out by their uncles. Ruby and Jack Dawson came to say goodnight to Ida. Jack had Danny cradled in his arms.

'Smashing night, Ma. Thanks t'all of ye family for making me so welcome. Be seeing ye.'

Ida managed a smile. Cheeky beggar! I'll give him Ma. Thinks he's got his feet under the table already does he?

Ruby could read her mother's mind. She grinned. 'See you later today, Mum.'

'I 'ope so love. I've made you a birthday cake.'

They kissed and Ida held onto Ruby for a long moment. Then, seeing her link her arm through that of Jack Dawson, she smiled. Maybe this time! Life suddenly seemed to be holding a lot of promises for Ruby and she hoped that at least some of them would come true.

'Come on, Mum. We're all waiting for you.' Norman's quiet voice brought her back to the present.

'I'm ready, son.'

'Miles away you were. Worrying about our Ruby as usual, were you?'

'There's something about that Jack Dawson that bothers me,' she muttered as Norman wound a scarf twice round her neck.

'Put ye gloves on, it's freezing, an' try being optimistic for a change. At least the fella has a good job; seems to think the world of his little lad. Give them a chance, Mum. Who knows? Maybe him an' Ruby will be ideal for each other.'

I wouldn't put my money on it, Ida was thinking to herself as Norman led her out to the car.

Jack was driving Ruby and the twins back to her flat. When they arrived, Jack told a sleepy Danny to stay in the car while he saw them safely indoors.

Ruby protested, 'Oh no. You can't leave him down here on his own, and – it is dreadfully late – you could—'

'Spend the night here with you?'

'Yes.'

It was a bit embarrassing at first because the flat was so small and Ruby wasn't sure that she had done the right thing, but the following morning she had no regrets.

It was still quite early when Ruby woke up. She crept out of bed, wrapped herself in her warm dressing gown and padded down the hall to her kitchen.

Waiting for the kettle to boil she laid a tray, put three spoonfuls of tea in the pot, all the while making sure that she made no noise, the children had been up so very late and were tired out by the time they had got them into bed. Pouring the boiling water into the teapot, she asked herself a question, Where do I go from here?

She knew that Jack Dawson was going to ask her to give

up this flat and go and live with him in a house he was buying out in Wallington. Would that be a good move? Be like burning her boats once again.

Besides living with Brian hadn't been a bed of roses. She was his wife, or trouble and strife as he called her, and he had thought that gave him the right to do exactly as he liked with her.

She set the now full teapot down on the tray with some force. What was the point of harping on the past? All the things that had happened between Brian and herself, not to mention his horrible father, were better left behind. She had no reason to think of them now. Was she being offered another chance? More to the point, if she took it would it work out for the best?

She carried the tray along the hall and was surprised to see her bedroom door open. The curtains were drawn back but still Jack had switched the bedside light on because this January morning was grey and miserable-looking.

Smiling, she put the tray down and said, 'You're awake then, I've brought us both a cup of tea.' Then she climbed back into bed.

Jack raised himself up on his elbows and grinned at her. His hair looked even darker this morning against the white pillow slip and his chin was rough with stubble. Ruby laughed to herself, he wouldn't be able to shave himself here, not unless he was in the habit of carrying a razor about with him.

She leaned across to kiss his cheek, he quickly straightened up, put his hand on the back of her head and drew her face level with his own. This time he kissed her, not just a peck, a long, lingering kiss that told her he wanted her.

'This is how it should be every morning, waking up to find a beautiful woman ready to wait on me.'

Ruby groaned. 'Oh, the ego of the man!'

He pushed the pillows higher, heaved himself up to lean against them and said, 'Pour the tea, we'll discuss later what your other duties will be.'

Ruby slapped him playfully before turning to the business of filling two cups with tea.

Jack drank slowly in silence, as if he were deep in thought. His bare chest was brown as though he had been out in the sun for a long period, and Ruby thought once more how fit and strong he was and how he had a continental look about him.

Spending the night with him had brought her new knowledge. It had shown her that there was a difference between love and lust. It had been a sweet discovery. It had been a shared experience, good for both of them, not one-sided. She hoped that there might be more to come.

Since Brian's death she had made up her mind that she would devote her life to her boys. She would be satisfied with the fact that she had the joy of seeing them grow up. She had got herself into a routine: working, visits to family and friends, only occasional evenings out when her mother would have the boys. She had kidded herself that was enough. Until she had met Jack Dawson. Now she knew that she had only been living half a life.

If she left the past behind her and went to live with Jack she could have a full life. Was that she what she wanted?

Much later that day, when the children were up, washed, dressed and fed, and Jack was preparing to take Danny back to the lady that took care of him while he was at work, Jack suddenly looked across at Ruby and told her, 'It doesn't have to be like this. I never intended to use you. It certainly wasn't a one night stand. At least not on my part. How about you, Ruby? Will you throw your lot in with me? Bring your boys, take care of Danny and let us all be one family?'

He wasn't offering marriage, Ruby was aware of that. She didn't know how she knew but she did. All for the best really. See how things work out.

There was no hesitation on Ruby's part. She smiled at Jack, went into his arms and with her lips brushing his cheek, she whispered, 'Yes.'

'You'll not regret it, Ruby, love. That's a promise. I'll do my best to be good to you and I'll see to it that the twins don't want for anything.'

Ruby felt then that she wasn't a girl any longer, she was a grown up woman and a mother, capable of making her own decisions.

She just hoped she was making the right decision.

Chapter Thirteen

THE EXTREME WEATHER WAS making life difficult for everyone. Pipes were frozen, the washing stuck to the line. People were slipping on the icy pavements and one of the neighbours had fallen and broken their arm.

Snowdrifts were making travelling impossible according to Alan. He and Norman were working out at the factory in Epsom. They hadn't been home for five days but they telephoned each morning and Ida assured them that both Jeff and Bert were looking after her, and yes, she did have plenty of coal, and no, she wasn't lonely because Maggie Marshall was staying with her.

With an enormous effort Ida straightened up. She had been on her knees, black leading the oven door and the fender. She couldn't do the whole of the grate because the fire was banked up high. It was days now since she had let it go out. Even so she had to keep the doors well shut to keep out the cold. And the blessed wind was a trial. It blew down the chimney, rattling the windows and moving the rags she had shoved under the cracks of the doors to serve as draught excluders.

'Morning Ida,' Maggie called as she inched her way into the warm kitchen. 'My, you've got a lovely fire going.'

'Morning Maggie, the kettle's just coming up to the boil, come an' sit yeself down. I've pulled the table up closer to the fire, breakfast won't take me long.' Ida bustled across from the dresser with two clean cups and saucers and set them on the table.

The kettle hissed and spat and Ida held the brown teapot to the spout to make the tea.

Ida looked at Maggie fondly, but she was too busy with her tea to notice.

How old was Maggie? It was difficult to tell. Maggie was the sort of person who had never looked young. Now, as some sort of compensation she never looked old. She was certainly spritely enough.

If I had to guess I'd say that she was a good ten years older than me, Ida mused. That would put her in her early fifties, yet only the other day Jozy had said that Maggie was talking of drawing her pension soon. Aw well. As long as she stayed fit and well what did it matter.

Tom Carter was one of the reasons that Maggie was full of herself at the moment. With Ruby now moved out of Frimley Gardens – or should she say hounded out by gossiping old biddies – Maggie might have been feeling very much at a loss as to how to fill her time. God works in a mysterious way his wonders to perform. With Ruby no longer just around the corner, Maggie came to Tooting more often and from the day that Tom had been discharged from hospital Maggie had fussed over him like an old hen.

Jack Dawson now had Ruby and the twins installed in his very nice house out at Wallington. Everything, on the surface, seemed to be working out very well in that quarter. Time would tell. Maggie wasn't about to agree that Ruby had done well for herself. Well, not yet.

'What's the weather forecast? What sort of a day is it gonna be?' Maggie asked.

'No change, according to the wireless.'

They both turned their heads to peer out of the window. The clouds had never lifted. If it weren't for the snow lying thick on the rooftops, making everything look white and fresh, it would be depressing.

Ida heaved herself to her feet and went out into the scullery. She lit the rings on the top of the gas stove and soon the air was filled with the lovely smell of bacon and eggs.

With breakfast over, there were the usual preparations for Sunday midday dinner to be seen too. Tom Carter was coming up to join them. True to the promise she had made to herself, Ida had Tom up for a meal quite frequently now.

On fine days and holidays Ida showed off and they set the table in the front room. Today it was far too cold. If the boys had been home they would have insisted that their mother had two fires going, but Ida was more careful with the pennies. Besides, who knew when the coalman was going to come down their street again. Even the milkman had missed two days last week. He'd had to find a replacement to do his rounds because he had fallen and broken his ankle and was now hobbling about on crutches.

Usually Tom's visits were on a Sunday, and Ida, seeing how very much taken Maggie was with Tom – and he with her come to that – she had made a point of asking Maggie on the same day.

'Our Mother's a matchmaker,' Norman had said aloud to Alan one Sunday morning as he got himself ready to go out.

'Yes, pity she don't start up a lonely hearts club,' Alan had teased.

She hadn't answered but she had wondered whether they were right where Maggie and Tom were concerned.

Sometimes Tom came unheralded. Seeing him on her doorstep never failed to please her. He would come in, sit with her, drink tea, play a few games of cards. Once he had taken her to a restaurant in Balham, where they had had a lovely meal and drank a bottle of wine between them and talked over old times and agreed how the years were now flying by.

They were good companions. There were times when she was curious about his intentions towards Maggie, but decided it wasn't her place to ask.

The joint of beef was sending out tempting smells from the oven at the side of the grate. No gas oven could roast the meat like the good old hob. Maggie stood on a chair and lifted down from the dresser a large meat dish. It was one of a set of three. Long and deep with raised curled edges, the dish was patterned with colourful wild birds. Maggie set it on the table and stood back.

Ida knelt and with a heavy kitchen towel wrapped around her hands, she opened the oven door, lifted the black enamel baking dish out, rose to her feet and set it down.

'Just how we like it,' she crowed, spearing the joint

with a long-pronged carving fork and transferring it onto the dish.

''Cor, I'll say, look at the blood running. Can't bear beef that's cooked to a frazzle. You are a smashing cook, Ida.'

'I'll second that.' Tom Carter was a sight for sore eyes. He had entered the house so quietly, using the key on the string, they hadn't heard him even though he had stomped on the doorstep to remove the snow from his galoshes.

His face glowed with the cold, but he looked remarkably fit; upright as ever and well turned out.

'Here, my contribution, a hot toddy I thought would be the order of the day,' he said as he drew a bottle of whisky from a bag and set it down on the table.

'Tom, you didn't 'ave t'do that but thanks all the same. Here let me 'ave ye coat an' things. Come near to the fire, Maggie's set three armchairs round so's we'll all be warm.'

'Warm? It's gorgeous in here,' he said, removing his glasses because they had steamed up. 'Thank God none of us have to venture outdoors today.'

Ida grinned. 'Well that's all right then. I'll get the glasses an' some brown sugar.'

With Ida away in the front room, Tom glanced at Maggie.

'How have you been coping with the weather?' he asked.

'As you can see, Tom, I've been lucky. Came here beginning of last week an' Ida wouldn't 'ear of me going back home.'

'That's what friends are for. We're both of us lucky to have such a nice lady as Ida for our friend.' He sighed as he finished speaking, then in a very sad voice he added, 'God gave us our relations, thank Christ we pick our friends.'

Ida came back into the living room in time to hear that last sentence.

'Whatever's the matter, Tom? I can't say that's true for me. I wouldn't be a day without any member of my family.'

'Ida, my dear. I didn't mean to upset you. That was a very selfish remark and I apologise. I know only too well how kind and caring your relatives are.'

'Tom, what prompted you to say that?' Maggie's voice was very low as she asked the question. 'You haven't any relations living, have you?'

'Only my son.'

'Has Joe been in touch?' Ida was quick to ask. It would be the first time since his mother's funeral if he had. The hospital had notified him when his father had attempted to take his own life, but as far as she knew he had not come to see his father.

'Yes, Ida, Joe's been in touch. More's the pity. He and his wife seem to think I am unable to care for myself. Think I would be better off in a home.'

'What?' The one word was uttered simultaneously by both women.

Tom's face had a solemn look and the tears in his eyes were in danger of spilling over.

'Here Maggie, fill a jug with some of that boiling water, I'll open this bottle. Before we do or say another thing, a toddy is in order. And move those saucepans to the back of the hob, there is nothing that will spoil. We'll put the Yorkshire pudding in later when Tom starts to carve the meat.'

Maggie did as she was told. Ida poured the hot water into each glass, added three spoonfuls of dark sugar and then a generous amount of the whisky. 'Here's to good friendships,' she toasted, stirring briskly and handing the first glass to Maggie.

They sat around the fire, hands cupped around their glasses, and sipped their drinks. The silence was fine. A silence that is only good amongst people that care for each other. The flames in the fire were flickering blue.

'There'll be another heavy frost tonight,' Tom murmured.

'Now Tom,' Ida began, 'If you're having difficulties, let's be practical and talk about them.'

'Well,' Tom sighed, 'I kinda brought it on myself, didn't I? Joe wouldn't be raising objections to my living alone if I hadn't been so foolish.' He read the expression on both of their faces and did his best to smile. 'I'll be all right,' he assured them.

'There's more to this than you're telling us, isn't there?' Ida queried. 'What is your son on about? Where would you go? No, we'll not stand for that. Away from everything you're used to, everybody you know! Does your son 'ave an interest in your house?' she asked cautiously.

'Ida, I've thought about that long and hard, and you know, I've come to just that conclusion. Much as I hate to admit it, I think Joe would like to move in. He has suggested that him and his wife Annie, and their two children, should come and look after me or he'll sell the house from under me, and put me in a home.'

'Could he do that?' Maggie cried.

'Who knows.' Tom sighed heavily. 'If he could get a doctor to state that I was no longer safe, a danger to myself . . .' He didn't finish the sentence.

Ida drew herself up straight. 'Now, drink up the pair of you. Children, all children, I've come to the conclusion, are a worry. But they are not going to ruin our Sunday dinner. Move yourselves. You, Maggie, set the table. You, Tom, start carving and I'll pour the batter into the meat tin, that fat must be hot enough by now.'

'Better do as she says,' Maggie laughed.

'You 'ad, an' all. We've got all the afternoon to talk about this. One thing's for sure, Tom Carter. You might be a whole sight more brainy than I am, but if you're laying awake at night worrying yourself sick about what that son an' his wife are going to do, then you ain't the man I thought you was. You'll set them straight. Me and Maggie will see that you do. All right?'

'Yes ma'am.' He gave Ida a mock salute and at least by now he looked a darn sight more cheerful.

One of the reasons that Ida Wilcox got on so well with her neighbours was that when she promised to do something, she always kept her word.

She rang off, putting the telephone back on its stand, and leant back in her chair. Now, she had set the wheels in motion. Joe Carter would have the authorities to deal with if he intended to continue with his threats to his father.

Am I an old busybody? she asked herself. I don't think so, was her answer.

Tom Carter was only in his early sixties. The main reason he had retired from his job hadn't been ill health, at least not his own. He had given up work solely to look after Nellie. True, he had aged since she had died, perhaps one had to agree that he had let himself go a bit. Probably the house as well. Wasn't that understandable?

It didn't mean that he could be shuffled off into some

home to end his days just waiting to die. Nobody in their right mind would wish that on such an honourable man as Tom. It was because his father had made the mistake of trying to end his life that his son had pounced.

Whatever had driven Tom to do such a thing, he had survived. He was doing his best to put it behind him. He didn't want to talk about it and he shouldn't have to.

Get this bad weather over and spring would be on the way. He'd be able to get out, go up the common, meet and talk to people. I'll see that he does too, Ida promised herself. I might even be able to persuade him to look for a part-time job. Something that would occupy his time and keep his mind alert.

The lady from the Citizen's Advice Bureau, having listened to Ida outline Tom's problem, had assured Ida that she had done the right thing by telephoning them, that she was only too willing to help and that she would ring back as soon as possible.

What if the powers that be decided that Tom's son was right? A residential home. That shouldn't happen to Tom of all people, who had never been sick in his life. A touch of the old rheumatics was only to be expected at his age. Tall, strong, vital, interested in so many subjects, but most importantly, a kindly man who thought of others.

Look at how he had nursed his wife. He could so easily have had Nellie admitted into hospital but even though she lingered for a very long time, his determination to let her die in their own home had never wavered.

Now Ida sighed heavily and as she did so the telephone rang. Very slowly she picked up the receiver. 'Hallo.'

A man's voice came down the line. 'Mrs Wilcox?'

'Yes, speaking,'

'You kindly rang us concerning the welfare of a Mr Thomas Carter?'

'That's right, I'm worried about him.'

'Yes. I understand. The best thing would be for us to arrange for a welfare officer to go and see him, talk things over, and, if necessary, see if they could come to some sort of arrangement. I'm sure they'll do everything possible to allow Mr Carter to go on living in his own house. With help, if that is what it takes. I'll set the wheels in motion and then I'll be in touch again.'

'Oh thank you, thank you very much.'

'Not at all. We're pleased that you have put us in the picture. Someone will contact Mr Carter, probably tomorrow. Goodbye, Mrs Wilcox.'

Ida was smiling broadly. She felt very much better already, even optimistic.

She climbed the stairs and went into her bedroom. I know what I'll do, I'll give this room a jolly good clean out. God knows it can do with it. She was about to strip the sheets from the bed when there was a knock on her front door and she muttered 'Who the 'ell can that be?'

'Tom!' Ida spoke his name with surprise because he hardly ever knocked, then she noticed the young couple standing behind him.

Joe, Tom's son, she barely recognised. Right smart he looked, thick heavy navy blue overcoat, bowler hat and real leather gloves on his hands. The girl, presumably his wife, was small and neatly dressed in a red coat which had a fur collar. But she was wearing far too much make-up and Ida could smell heavy sweet perfume from where she was standing.

Tom opened his mouth to speak but he was unable to

get the words out, he was gasping. Ida knew there was something very wrong. She opened the door wider.

'Come on in, all of you.'

Through to the kitchen they trooped and Tom had to sit down straightaway as he could not get his breath. His face went grey and his forehead was covered with perspiration. Ida fetched him a glass of water, holding it for him while he searched in his pocket for a handkerchief with which to wipe his face. She watched as he gulped at the water, then slipped her arms around his shoulders.

Joe Carter watched in silence as Ida cared for his father. Then he spoke. 'I'm sorry we've bothered you, Mrs Wilcox. My Father insisted we came along and told you of our plans. By the way, this is my wife, Doris, I don't think you've met before.'

Ida did her best to smile at them both. 'Well, you're here now so why don't we all sit down and then you can tell me whatever it is your father would like me to know.'

Joe Carter looked guilty. 'You know what happened to my father a while back?'

Ida nodded sadly, looking across to where Tom lay back in the chair. He was such a gentle man, so easy to love. She did love him, like another brother. What he needed was someone to share his life with, to care for him and see that he got enough rest. Wasn't that what we all need in this life? she asked herself.

She leant towards Tom, saying, 'Are you all right?'

'Yes, Ida, I'm all right. Just listen to what they have to say. I can't believe it myself.'

A cynical expression swept over Joe's face as Ida turned to face him. 'Course he's not all right. Any fool can see that. And he won't be, not all the time he's living alone in that great rambling house. We've sold our house. Going to put our furniture into store until we sort out all father's rubbish.'

The cheeky blighter! Ida had to bite her tongue. Tom had some beautiful pieces of old furniture in that house. Rubbish indeed!

'Yes, we'll be moving down here in about a fortnight's time,' Joe's wife added for him, her voice rising to a high pitch as if she felt she had come out on top.

'You 'aven't wasted much time, 'ave you?' Ida spoke without thinking. Turning to Tom she asked, 'Is this what you want?'

'Course it's not. Do you think I'd be better off, sharing my house with them?'

'That's up to you.'

'Don't look that way to me. Don't seem as if I'm going to be given a say in the matter. They've arrived. Stated what they are going to do without so much as by your leave. I don't know Doris from Adam. And Ida, let me tell you another thing, they have two children that I have never even set eyes on. My own grandchildren! Now, doesn't that make you wonder as to why they should suddenly concern themselves as to where I live or whether I live or die?'

'What's it got to do with this woman?' Doris's eyes were blazing as she nodded her head towards Ida before glaring at her father-in-law.

Ida would have liked to ask this Doris where her manners were. The cheek of the girl, shouting and being so rude, especially as she was in someone else's house. Still, she'd let it go for Tom's sake. It would be stupid if she answered her and they got into a slanging match. Now of all times she had to keep cool.

'Now Mrs Carter,' Ida spoke softly, keeping her temper well under control. 'If you'll just sit still, I'll put the kettle on and make us all a cup of tea.'

'We haven't come here for tea.' Doris Carter leaped to her feet. 'Don't really know why we did come. Joe, it's time we were going. You shouldn't have given in to your father's whim. Involving neighbours in our business. I've never heard the like of it. Come on, Father, on your feet.' She was bawling now.

'Doris! Aw, for God's sake, keep your voice down, do you want the whole street to hear you?' Joe spoke harshly but he shut up when his wife turned her gaze on to him.

Her voice lower, she leant towards him, saying, 'You think they don't know already? Daft old man, trying to commit suicide. If we walk away, leave him on his own, God knows what he'll get up to. More than likely burn the house down then the whole town will have something to talk about. You'll have to speak to him, Joe. Make him see sense. He won't listen to me, I'm only his daughter-in-law, but you let him know that if he tries to pull any more daft tricks we'll have him put away. Do you hear? I mean it. I'll go to the authorities myself if you won't do it.'

Ida pushed her way through to the scullery, if she stayed in that room she'd end up saying a whole lot of things that weren't her place to say.

'Don't go, Ida,' Tom began to laugh. It was a deep rollicking kind of laugh that didn't seem to match this refined gentleman. Although Ida couldn't as yet fathom out the reason for it, she wanted to laugh with him. She kept her eyes on him. Never, never had she seen Tom like this. He was sitting up straight, looking at his daughter-in-law as if he were seeing her for the very first time. And Doris was backing away from his look.

A few moments ago Ida had thought that Tom was afraid of this pair of youngsters. That he would give in, let them move into his house and more than likely make his life a misery an' all.

Now she wasn't so sure. Wouldn't it be marvellous, absolutely marvellous, if he stood up to them. Told them where to go.

She moved slowly, trying hard not to smile. She was going to make that tea for her and Tom whether they wanted a cup or not. She closed the door behind her. She wanted to eavesdrop, but thought it better if she didn't. Knowing what she was like she'd have to open her mouth and put her two pennyworth in. It was up to Tom now and to be honest, the least said the better.

The scullery door inched open and Joe joined her. 'I've got to apologise again, Mrs Wilcox. This shouldn't have happened. Me an' Doris are going to get off now. I will say this, Doris was acting with the best intentions. All for my father's own good. Us being on the spot seemed the lesser of two evils. I didn't want me father put into a home. I'll come and visit him again soon. On my own. Have a long chat with him.'

'All right, Joe. That's probably the best thing.' Ida had to force the calm words out. What she really would have liked to have said was, take that stroppy bitch outta my sight and for God's sake learn to be a man and stand up to her.

'I'll phone you from time to time. Will that be all right?'

'Course, course. Any time.' Ida did not protest at their going or ask any questions as to their intentions.

'Oh, one more thing. Do you know if my father sees a doctor on a regular basis?'

'No.'

'Well, he should, you should tell him that.'

Ida bit her lip hard. She wasn't going to tell him what to do. Tom wasn't a child, neither was he going mental. Left alone he would manage fine with a little help from his friends.

As they entered the kitchen she heard the front door open and knew that Doris Carter had made her exit. She smiled at Tom and he smiled back. 'I won't be a minute, I'll just go to the door with your son.'

She was more than pleased when Tom got to his feet and held out his hand to the younger man. Joe went one better. He wrapped his arms around his dad's shoulders and drew him close. 'Take care, Dad. I'll get up t'see you as often as I can.'

'It's all right, son. I know where you are if I need you.'

'Yeah,' was all that his son managed to reply.

Ida accompanied Joe to the front door, and there they looked at each other in awkward silence for a moment before Ida said, 'Well, goodbye, Joe. Don't worry about him too much. He has got good friends that keep an eye on him.'

'Goodbye, Mrs Wilcox. Thank you, thank you very much. I will keep in touch.'

'Make sure you do,' Ida answered from the front gate. Then she watched Tom's son walk the length of the street before she went back indoors.

'He was a sweet boy as a child,' were Tom's first words as she came back into the kitchen. 'He had nothing to speak of in the way of looks but he was intelligent.'

Ida was looking at him now, waiting, and he leant his shoulder against the mantelshelf for a full minute before he spoke again.

'His mother was so cross when he rushed into marriage and so annoyed at the way Doris and her parents brushed us off at the wedding, almost as if we were complete strangers, which I suppose we were, to tell the truth. Joe met her when he was away at college. Never brought her home, only the once.'

'Do you think they have sold their house?' Ida ventured.

'I doubt it. Probably put it on an agent's books. Testing the market, like.'

'Tom, can I ask you something?'

Tom paused as Ida continued, 'I know Joe's your son, but do you think he's got his eye to the main chance?'

'If you mean is he and that wife of his after either having my big house for themselves or alternatively selling it for a very good price, then yes, I have to agree with you.'

'I think your Joe was being egged on. You shouldn't 'ave laughed at him the way you did. It must be hard for him, being torn two ways.'

'Life's hard for all of us, Ida.'

'But they're young, they see things differently to what we do. All the youngsters seem in a hurry to make money. Makes ye wonder where it will all end. Still, you 'andled that very well.'

'Maybe, but it's not over yet. Must admit I'm glad t'see the back of them for now.'

'What's not over – 'ave I missed something?' Maggie came bustling into the kitchen, her cheeks glowing from the cold air. 'I've bought us some Bath buns, didn't know you'd be 'ere, Tom, but I'm glad you are.' She tugged her

woolly gloves off, unwound her scarf and looked at Ida.
'I was about to ask you t'make the tea, but from the look
on your face you'd better tell me what's been going on.'

Tom got to his feet. 'I'll tell you in a couple of
sentences, Maggie. My son and his wife have paid me
a visit. Must have travelled all night seeing as how they
live in Cornwall. They want to sell their house, chuck
all my furniture out and move their own into my house.
They think I'm too old and decrepit to be allowed to live
on my own.'

'Perhaps they're worried because you've been ill.'
Maggie's voice was quiet.

'Look Maggie, let's call a spade a spade. I have not
been ill. I tried to take my own life. Made a bloody mess
of it, but that doesn't give my son and his wife who barely
knows me the right to assume that I'm a doddering old
fool. Having said that, let's all have some tea.' He walked
through to the scullery to make it himself, leaving both
Ida and Maggie staring at his back.

Maggie was lost in thought as she ate her bun and
drank her tea. She could hardly believe it. Tom's own
son. Yet the relationship between them could never have
been close because Ida said she'd hardly set eyes on the
lad since he'd got married.

Thankfully Tom had stood up to him. The very idea
of Tom living in a home for the elderly was terrible. She
was bristling with indignation. 'Tom?'

'Yes, Maggie.'

'I've been thinking. How would it be if I come over
a couple days a week? Did a bit of cleaning in that big
'ouse of yours, a bit of washing an' ironing, might even
try out me cooking skills on ye.'

A big smile spread across Ida's face as she cried,

'Why Maggie, that's a great idea. What d'ye think Tom?'

In spite of himself and the way he was feeling, Tom laughed and said, 'With two determined ladies like you, I won't dare to argue.'

'Then you'll let me? I do miss 'aving Ruby an' the twins near by. Some days seem so long. You'd be doing me a favour.'

'Oh that's different then,' he chuckled, 'if it's me that would be doing you the favour.' He turned to Ida and gave her a saucy wink, seeking her approval, and when she nodded her head he added, 'Maggie I would love to see you anytime. Why don't you come down home with me when I go? I'll show you around. Let you see what you're letting yourself in for.'

'Oh, Tom, that'll be great.'

The expression on Maggie's face was a joy to see and Ida heaved a great sigh of relief. Perhaps some good had come out of today's disturbance.

When they were wrapped up warmly and ready to leave, Tom came to stand in front of Ida and deliberately hugged her close. 'Thanks for everything, Ida. You are one in a million.'

He broke free and as he walked out of the room he put his arm around Maggie's shoulders and led her down the hall to the front door.

Maggie half turned and looked back, calling to Ida, 'Don't come out in the cold. I'll spend an hour or so with Tom, but I'll be back about four.'

Ida closed the front door behind them and returned to the warmth of the kitchen. On her own now, Ida suddenly felt very lonely.

Chapter Fourteen

IDA HADN'T ANY IDEA when she had fallen asleep but she woke at first light. She heard the sparrows start their dawn chorus. She heard the traffic moving along the main road, and she wondered if it was going to be as hot today as it was yesterday.

She was so disturbed. Not knowing what to do or even what to say. Nothing was probably the best policy but she just couldn't stand by and wait any longer for the balloon to go up. Because the way things were going it wouldn't be long now before it did.

It was getting on for two years since Ruby had moved to Wallington to live with Jack Dawson. To start off everything in the garden had been roses. The trouble was that as usual Ruby didn't know when she was well off.

'If I had anywhere to go I'd be off like a shot,' she told herself thinking aloud. 'I'd just like to get away, give meself time to think. Not that if I sat and thought every hour of the day that God sends it would do much good.'

The first Christmas that Ruby and Jack had been together she went to stay with them. She'd only gone the once. It wasn't a happy time. It had been one big row after another. She had relived that couple of days so many times.

Jack Dawson wasn't working over the holiday and his house was warm and cosy; the furniture a bit scruffed and scratched but what did that matter with three little boys in the house? I still think Jack is a bit arrogant, too sure of himself, knows everything there is to know. But then again he is generous to a fault, very kind, at least to me he is. Half her family thought he was marvellous, the other half couldn't stand the sight of him. That's the way it was with Jack. You either loved him or you hated his guts. One thing was sure he was master in his own house. When he spoke the kids jumped.

Why wasn't it like that between him and Ruby? She twisted him round her little finger. Well, she had done so far, but even a worm will turn and Jack was no worm. He had had enough. Or nearly enough. Ida couldn't tell how she knew. She just did.

The main cause of the trouble was jealousy. The boys played Ruby and Jack off one against the other. Depending on who was offering what. That's what it boiled down to. That and greed. Spiteful greed at that. And who could blame the kids, living in an atmosphere such as they did?

They were well fed, the best of everything, Jack saw to that. New clothes were never a problem and more toys than Ida thought was good for them.

The twins were five now and – hard to believe it because he was so much shorter – Danny was six. All three now went to school.

The trouble stemmed from the fact that Jack was quite happy to live with Ruby, but not marry her. Another factor being that Danny was such an incredibly lovely child to look at. Not that the twins weren't. They still had fine sandy hair and creamy complexions, against which Danny's dark thick curly hair, tanned skin, and enormous brown eyes set him apart.

When Danny chose to smile, it was brilliant, his dimple showed and his whole face lit up. But that didn't happen too often. Mostly only at weekends when his father was home.

Very often, when Ida visited, she thought how pitiful little Danny looked. Jack's parents lived in Spain. They ran a bar out there. They had come home for a visit last Christmas, staying a week with Jack and Ruby.

There had been ructions. Ruby's version was that they spoiled Danny rotten, ignoring her two sons. That they were everlastingly telling Danny how beautiful he was and what a pity his mother hadn't lived to see him.

Jack – a man of few words at the best of times – had merely told Ida that Ruby had been set to make mischief.

You couldn't get away from it. When Jack wasn't in the house, any trouble and Danny got the blame. It was always him that was grabbed by the arm and practically thrown up the stairs to stay in his bedroom until he owned up.

Ida hated to admit it, but Ruby was making both Joey and Lenny crafty. They were getting away with all sorts of pranks, knowing full well that Danny would get the blame.

Ah well, I've laid here long enough. She threw back the bedclothes and put her feet to the floor. If it wasn't for the fact that Ruby meant so well, caring for the twins like a mother hen, always wanting nothing but the best where they were concerned, she'd go over there and tell her a few home truths.

Half an hour later she was saying to herself, shame to waste such a lovely day. The kids were probably getting on Ruby's nerves; the summer holidays the schools gave them were far too long.

She stood at the back door, looking down the garden while thinking. It really was a lovely day. She'd get herself over to Wallington, that's what she'd do. Persuade Ruby to pack up a picnic and they could all set off, spend the day on the common. I'll treat the boys to a boat out on the lake.

She felt heaps better now that she had it all planned.

Ida got off the bus. Ruby only lived just off the main road, she'd soon be there. But first she turned into the local grocers and did some shopping. Crusty bread rolls, thick slices of ham carved off the bone, the makings of a salad and lots of fresh fruit, three sherbert dabs and a couple of bottles of lemonade.

Ida arrived to find the front door wide open and coming from upstairs the sound of Ruby screaming at the top of her voice. The twins were playing on the opposite of the road, on a site where the houses had been demolished soon after the war.

'Nan! Hallo Nan!' they called, racing across to meet her. Before she opened the gate, she set her shopping basket down on to the pavement and stood still, arms open wide. They flung themselves at her, and were instantly hugged tight. Ida tickled them, they wriggled, and soon they and their grandmother were shrieking with laughter.

It was Lenny who finally put an end to the frolics. He wriggled himself away from his grandmother's arms, and with great determination said, 'We've got t'go. That's our bat an' ball those boys are playing with, and anyway, I'm the captain in this game.'

Ida sensibly let him go. 'Just a second,' she called, grabbing hold of Joey's sleeve and giving it a tug, 'Where's Danny? And what's up with ye mum?'

Joey looked at her, giggled and then quickly covered his mouth with his hands.

Ida bent low and spoke very quietly. 'I asked you a question. Now, be a good boy an' answer me.'

He took an enormous breath before uttering, 'Mummy made an apple pie. Then she found someone had took a lump out of it.'

Ida shook her head in disbelief. 'And Mummy said it was Danny?'

Slowly, his cheeks flushed up. 'Not really.'

'All right. Off you go an' play.' There was nothing for it but to go into the house and face Ruby.

To her total surprise she received a warm welcome. The living room was tidy. There were flowers, nicely arranged, set in the centre of the table.

'Would you like a cold drink, Mum? We could have it out in the garden.'

Ida forgot her good intentions. That little boy shouldn't be shut away upstairs on a lovely sunny day like this. What if he had taken a piece out of an apple pie? It was nothing to get so upset about.

'Where's Danny?' Ida repeated the question she had asked of Joey.

Ruby's expression changed. 'Up in his room an' that's where he's gonna stay all day.'

Not if I have anything to do with it, Ida decided, pondering as to what was the best way to tackle Ruby. She was so incensed by the whole business that she had to breathe deeply before speaking. 'I hope not. I thought we'd make a picnic up. Take the boys up on the common.'

Ruby walked from the room without bothering to answer her mother. When she returned she was carrying a tray with glasses and a bottle, also a glass jug filled with iced water. 'Mum, don't start on me about Danny. I do me best. It isn't that I'm not fond of him, it's that just when I think we're all getting along fine, he does something bloody awful again. He's a right little monkey, Mum. He really is. I'll end up killing him. He can stare me straight in the face and swear he hasn't done anything wrong when all the time he's lying through his teeth.'

Ruby had worked herself up into a right paddy. She looked just about ready to kill anyone that spoke out against her so Ida kept her mouth shut.

Surely this couldn't be right? And it couldn't go on for much longer. Maybe Danny was a little sod. She wouldn't be a bit surprised, most little boys were. Maybe he was after getting a bit more attention. After all, he couldn't have had much loving in his little life. He'd never known his own mother. His grandparents didn't even live in this country. A woman had been paid to look after him for at least five days out of the week and even now he only got to see his father at weekends. He could be the cause of the trouble, five maybe even seven times out of ten. But not ten times out of ten! Even Ruby couldn't think that Lenny and Joey were that good. She'd have you believing they were angels next.

Having poured lemon barley into two glasses Ida

topped them up with water, letting a couple of ice cubes clink in as well. Then she hitched herself onto the couch where Ruby had plonked herself, turned towards her, took her hand between her own and, looking into Ruby's eyes she said, 'I thought things were better between you all. Why can't you accept Danny? Can't you see what you're doing? You're making a rod for your own back.'

'Danny's all right.' Ruby insisted, 'He's got t'learn that he can't always get away with telling lies.'

Ida really had meant to keep her tongue between her teeth but having started there was no stopping her now. 'Yeah, well, that's as maybe. You know my feelings by now. That child is unhappy. He doesn't feel wanted let alone loved.'

'He's a bloody little terror. You don't 'ave to put up with him day in, day out. He might look like an angel to you but there's a devil in him. He gets up to more tricks than half a dozen other kids put together.'

'That's enough! This business has gone far enough. Jack must dread coming 'ome 'ere of a weekend. I know for a fact he's 'ardly inside the door and you start on at 'im. Danny's done this, Danny's done that. You don't give the bloke a chance, do you?' She pressed on, not giving Ruby time to reply. 'I know you 'ave a lot t'put up with. And I know Jack's no saint. Seems t'me that half the time he's yelling at you, wanting t'know why it is that every time something happens his kid gets the blame.

'Then there's you, screaming that he doesn't treat your kids as well as his own. If you're together and if you want to stay together, don't you think it's about time that you started calling them *our* kids? Combine them. Stop dividing them. Let them realise that you do intend to be one family.'

After a while, Ida said, 'You're not answering my question. Do you really think that little boy is the main cause of the trouble?'

'No.' Ruby's head hung low.

Ida watched her. Her own heart was heavy. She saw this daughter of hers bowed down with problems, mainly of her own making. Her dear little face, so serious now, but which could light up so unexpectedly in a smile. The long fair hair, the lovely blue eyes, she was still so young. There should be more to life for her than all these upsets and quarrels.

Ida made a decision. She got to her feet and said, 'I'm going upstairs to see Danny. On a brilliant summer's day like this is, those kids ought to be up the park or on the common, not one of them shut in his bedroom and the other two mucking about on a bomb site. Can I bring Danny down?'

Ruby lifted her eyes to meet those of her mother and did her best to smile. 'Aw Mum . . .' She couldn't go on, tears overspilt and ran down her cheeks.

Ida could see that she was very hurt. 'Come 'ere.' She said, 'It's all right, dear, don't start getting upset. We'll all go out. It'll be lovely up on the common. Drink some of this,' she commanded, handing a glass to Ruby. 'I noticed you didn't put anything stronger in that jug.'

Ruby ignored her joke and her face was straight as she said, 'Mum, I'm sorry. Truly I am. I do try.'

She held out her hand and Ida took it between hers, squeezing it with a great deal of pressure. All the while Ida was saying to herself, Don't cry! For God's sake don't cry.

174

Quickly she pulled herself together, placed a hand on Ruby's shoulder and said, 'I'm going up to see Danny. You put the kettle on.' Then she went upstairs, thinking as she did so, Thank God for one thing; Jack isn't here.

When she reached the bedroom she found Danny crying bitterly. 'Aw luv, come 'ere an' give ye Nanna a cuddle.'

The little face remained looking at the wall, the tiny shoulders heaving. Ida sat down on the bed, and soon she was crying softly. The sight of that dejected little boy was too much. She crossed her arms over her chest and began to rock to and fro. For the first time for many a long year she felt helpless.

It was a few minutes before she cleared her throat and managed to find her voice. 'Come on, Danny. It's me, ye Nanna. I'm not cross with you. Come an' let me wipe ye face.'

'You're not . . .'

Ida couldn't be sure if it were hiccups or the boy was choking on his sobs.

Danny tried again. 'You're not my Nan – Lenny an' Joey – they said you're their Nan. But they share my dad.'

It was like a knife twisting in her heart. How cruel children could be to each other. How could Lenny and Joey say such a thing to this poor little mite? What her daughter felt was rubbing off on to her own children making matters a whole lot worse.

Ida closed her eyes and leaned her head against the wall. She screwed her eyes up even tighter. It was easier to keep the tears back if you didn't open your eyes. When she opened them it was to see that

Danny had moved and was now standing in front of her.

'Lenny and Joey didn't mean it.' Ida spoke very softly and gently, 'Tell ye what, Danny, I'll take you back downstairs and make you a nice cold drink. How about that?'

'I don't want to go downstairs . . .'. He balked as Ida tried to pick him up and he looked around him in a panic. 'Mummy said I've got to stay up here. I can't come down.'

Ruby, Ruby, Ruby, Ida sighed to herself. Why the hell doesn't she count her blessings?

With that disastrous marriage to Brian behind her, she had met Jack, a hard-working, good-looking, fit and healthy man who was lonely. Jack had taken Ruby and the twins on and all he asked in return was that she included his little son in the arrangements.

Give the fella his due, he'd stuck to Danny from the day his mother had died giving birth to him. It couldn't have been easy. Not with the odd hours he worked. Banquets, dinners, race meetings, he travelled the length and breadth of the country to earn good money. He was certainly a good provider. Nice house, all furnished, bed linen, china, the lot. Why couldn't Ruby appreciate it all and admit that she had fallen on her feet?

Jack made it plain that he loved Ruby and was doing his best to love and care for the twins. Ruby was quick to say how much she loved Jack, couldn't she include little Danny in that love? Was it too much to ask?

Ida raised her head and turned her gaze onto Danny. She thought he looked like an endearing old teddy bear. His hair was tousled, his cheeks streaked with tears and those long dark lashes wet against his chubby red cheeks.

I wonder what he's thinking? She had asked that question of herself many times and still had no answer. Did he hate Ruby? Oh no! Surely not. Ida felt sick at the thought of it.

Then suddenly he held out his hands to her in a hopeless sort of way. Gently she put her arms around him and bent and kissed the top of his head. His lips brushed against her cheeks, 'Oh Danny, oh Danny.' She kissed him again and heaved him up to sit beside her.

Somewhere in the room a fly droned, blundering against the glass of the window. It wasn't a nice sound.

'We'll go down in a minute. I'll wash your face and then we'll have something to eat, but we're going to take a picnic up to the common. You'll like that won't you?'

'Nan, are you gonna come?' Then he added very wistfully, 'I hope you are.'

Ida sat very still beside him. She stared at the fly, still trying to get out into the sunshine. Her hands began to shake. If she didn't do something quickly she was afraid she would start to cry again.

She leaned forward, put her finger beneath Danny's chin and raised his face. 'Of course I'm coming with you. We're all going an' we're gonna have a lovely time. You'll see.'

The smile he gave her lit up his face. She lifted Danny up in her arms, hoisting him up against one shoulder. He might be six years old, but he was still a podgy, cuddly little boy with those huge dark eyes that tore at your heartstrings.

Whispering into his ear she told him, 'You're bloody lovely. You know that, Danny Dawson? You are. You're bloody lovely.'

She set him down on his feet. 'Come on now,' she said, taking hold of his little hand. 'We'll go downstairs.'

He tugged at her arm, she had to lower her head to catch what it was he said. 'Nanna, I think you're bloody lovely too.'

She lifted him up again, holding him close. Too full to form an answer. With him in her arms, his soft cheek resting against her own, she carried him downstairs.

'I've done all the food. The basket is packed,' Ruby told her mother as she handed a glass of orange juice to Danny.

He didn't look up as he took the glass, but very quietly said, 'Thank you.'

'That's a good boy,' Ruby smiled at him and was immediately rewarded by an answering smile.

'Tell you what,' Ida called from the scullery, 'you give Danny a wash while I go and buy some ice-cream. We'll call Joey an' Lenny in, the boys can 'ave the ice-cream while you an' I 'ave a cup of tea and then we'll all set off on our picnic. How does that sound?'

'Fine by me,' Ruby called back and as Ida appeared with a basin she was thrilled to see that Danny was looking up at Ruby, his big brown eyes shining, showing just how delighted he was.

'You'd better let me cover that bowl with a cloth and then wrap it up in some newspaper,' the shopkeeper offered kindly, 'else you're gonna have it all melted time you get back home.'

'Well, thank you. It's good of you t'bother.'

It wasn't a minute before the man came back carrying her bowl, which now contained ice-cream well and truly wrapped up.

'Don't bother to bring the cloth back, missis, any time you're passing will do.'

'Thanks again. I'm obliged to you.'

'That's all right. I hope you an' ye kids enjoy the treat.'

They both laughed, then Ida went out of the shop, walked a few yards along and turned the corner.

Even from this distance she could see the group of boys playing on top of the piled up rubble and as she drew nearer her first thought was, talk about grubby angels. Lenny and Joey both looked as if they could do with a jolly good wash. Still as her own Mum always used to say, that's only a bit of clean dirt. Being out in the open air never hurt anyone.

Around the site there were stacks of new bricks and piles of sand. Word was, according to Jack, six new houses were to be built there. The local children would miss having that site to play on.

Most of the kiddies were stripped to the waist, their bodies already a deep shade of brown. The twins were wearing nice blue shorts and thin cotton short-sleeved shirts. Ruby was sensible. She made sure her boys were covered against the hot sun. With their fair skins they burnt so easily.

Ida drew level and smiled with relief.

Danny was standing on the bottom rung of the gate, his fat little hands grasping the upper ledge. Ruby was singing to him as she swung the gate back and forth giving him a ride.

'I'll take this ice-cream through, put it in the shade.

179

Ruby, you'd better call the boys to come and eat it now or it won't be worth 'aving.'

As Ida went inside the house she laughed out loud at the racket Ruby was making.

'Joey, Lenny, ye Nan's been for ice-cream,' their mother yelled at the top of her voice. 'No, you can't finish that game. Get yeselves in here, now.'

Ida was out in the scullery standing the dish of ice-cream in a bowl of cold water when she heard the screech of brakes and the grinding of metal. Ruby's terrible scream tore through the house.

She couldn't move. She was rooted to the floor. When her legs did carry her out into the street the first thing she saw was the huge lorry and Ruby kneeling in the middle of the cleared bomb site beside one of her boys. She couldn't tell which one.

Her breath rasped and she felt as if someone were strangling her. Aw no! No! Please God. No!

Her eyes wide with horror, her chest still heaving, she made herself step off the pavement and cross the road. She had to walk around the huge open back lorry and push past people that had already gathered.

The very sight of Ruby's stricken, terrified face as she murmured confused words to Joey made Ida feel sick. She knelt beside her daughter in the dust. Ruby straightaway grabbed at her arm.

'Mum, Mum . . .'

Ida couldn't understand a word. Ruby's eyes were half out of her head. Her nose was running and spital was dribbling from her mouth. The front of her blouse was stained with blood. She was trying desperately to get her mother to do something, pleading as if her very life depended on it.

Ida looked up and a man assured her that the ambulance and the police were on their way.

Joey was moving! Oh thank God. He was alive!

Ruby was sobbing loudly now and suddenly her incoherent words got through to Ida. Oh, dear Jesus, she wanted to know where Lenny was!

Ida was terrified. She didn't want to stand up but she knew she had to make herself do so. The same man that had told her the ambulance had been called took hold of her arm.

'It were that lorry. Backed in to make a delivery, came up over the pavement. Suppose he couldn't have seen the kids running.' He inclined his head to the side. 'That little 'un got the worse of it. I saw it. He bounced like a rag doll and finished up trapped beneath the truck's rear wheels.'

In the commotion of the police cars and the ambulance arriving, no one noticed Ida bend over double and vomit all over her shoes. It must have been at that moment that Ruby too became aware of what had happened. A low moan errupted from her mouth before she opened it wide and shrieked, 'My boys, not both of them. No. No. It couldn't be – my boys . . .'

A policewoman ran and caught hold of Ruby as she collapsed. Ida, sobbing uncontrollably, moved near to where the ambulance men were attending to Joey. Once again she knelt and gently held his hand. She was blubbering quietly, 'He's alive. Our Joey is alive.'

The ambulance men lifted him on to a stretcher. Ida got to her feet, leant over and softly stroked his hair. It was matted with blood.

Sirens, men, women, the whole area was like bedlam. Lenny was dead. Ruby wouldn't have it. The ambulance men fought with her, persuading, pleading for her to come away. They needed to shift the lorry.

Ruby lay half under the truck, her bare legs stuck out in what was still hot sunshine. The policewoman had to wipe away her own tears as she listened to Ruby willing Lenny to be alive.

There was just stunned silence as two policewomen finally led Ruby away. Sitting in the ambulance, the door wide open, Ida watched as a constable took charge of Danny. His little face was ashen. In deep shock, his eyes were enormous. Poor little mite. He'd seen it all.

Ida felt she wanted to go and tell the officer to take good care of the lad. But if she were to say anything, her words wouldn't make any sense. What could she do for Danny now? Nothing.

She'd been assured that Jack would be contacted. Well, the sooner he got here the better. Joey died on the operating table, just thirty minutes after they arrived at the hospital.

Ruby had been given sedatives and the doctor's advice was that she be admitted as a patient at least for one night. Ida was grateful for that. Almost out of her own mind with the ghastly knowledge that both of her grandsons were now dead, she didn't think she would have been able to cope with Ruby. Not today! What on earth could she possibly say to her that would do any good?

The police came to tell her that her family had been told of the accident and that her sons were on their way to the hospital. As the police went out, a nurse came into the waiting room and handed Ida a cup of tea. Very kindly and speaking softly, she said, 'Try and drink it. It might help.' Then she opened a window and pulled the curtains back as far as they would go.

The breeze that fluttered in was most welcome, but it was difficult to believe that outside the sun was still shining brilliantly. It was still only early afternoon.

This was the day when everyone was going to be happy. Ruby had made her peace with Danny and they were all going for a picnic on the common. A boat out on the lake. Oh, wouldn't the boys have loved that!

Now there were no boys, only Danny, and he didn't seem to belong to anyone. Perhaps it wasn't true. She knew damn well it was.

Thank God that for a few hours at least, Ruby would be oblivious to what had happened. Ida felt she would never swallow properly again. The lump in her throat was choking her.

Life had hardly begun for her grandchildren and then on a lovely warm sunny day, when they were dashing to come indoors and eat ice-cream, a lorry had reversed on to an empty site and in a split second their lives had been wiped out.

Why the hell had she decided to come to Wallington today? Why the hell had she had to interfere? Why the hell had she bought ice-cream?

Ruby! Her poor Ruby! First her husband and his rotten father lead her a dog's life. Free of Brian, there had seemed to be a chance of happiness for her when she'd met Jack Dawson. Now this utter disaster. It was unbelievable. What more could life possibly throw at her?

Ida sighed heavily. It seemed that the less Ruby expected from life the better off she would be. This blow might prove to be too much for her.

Let's face it, losing both your children could drive any

mother over the edge. Ruby might be a lot of things, but a bad mother she wasn't.

Dear God whatever will she do now? Ida didn't know the answer and she doubted that there was anyone on this earth that did.

Chapter Fifteen

AT TEN O'CLOCK THE crowds began to gather in Fountain Road. The twins were being taken to be buried from their grandmother's house.

Men, women and children, they came from Mitcham, where the boys had been born, they came from Wallington where they had lived for the past two years, they came from the school where Lenny and Joey had attended for just two terms.

Neighbours, friends and relations came to the house. Bert and Jozy first, and with them Terry and Peter Gower, followed by Jeff, Sheila, Billy and Albie. Maggie Marshall came holding onto the arm of Tom Carter. Snowy and Betty Freeman came. It was no surprise when Mr and Mrs Walker arrived. Ida had worked for them for a good number of years and she had talked incessantly of her grandchildren and their doings.

They were like people in a trance, all wore similar expressions on their faces. But once Alan and Norman had made sure that everyone had a drink in their hand, it was as if they began to thaw.

Ruby began to cry slowly and painfully. Alan wrapped his arms about her, letting her bury her head against his chest.

Sheila and Jozy were openly crying. Maggie couldn't control her sobs. All she could think about were the times she had nursed the twins when they were babies.

Norman too began to cry. Doing his best to hide his tears, he slipped out of the room and went upstairs.

Ida felt she hadn't any tears left to cry. Thank God neither she nor Ruby had had to go to the mortuary. Alan and Norman, with help from their uncles, Bert and Jeff, had seen to all that. She had been over to Wallington the very next day, before they'd even fetched Ruby home from the hospital. She had got on a bus and gone to the house.

Why did she want to return there? Why? It should have been the last place on this earth that she would want to go to. Somewhere at the back of her mind she had the faint idea that she would feel better if she went into the twins' bedroom.

Yet there was another reason: Danny! She felt guilty about leaving him. What else could she have done? Had she known that Jack would be there? Probably.

She'd taken a deep breath as she rang the doorbell.

'Come in,' Jack's voice trailed away as Ida stepped over the threshold.

Then they were standing in the hallway gazing at each other, deep sorrow showing in their eyes.

'I'll be gone from here by the weekend. Ruby's welcome to the house if she wants it.'

'No. No, I doubt she'll even come near. And you mustn't do anything in a hurry, you should let the dust settle first.'

186

'Does she want to see me?'

Ida shook her head. 'Give her time.'

'No, Ma. It's over. It's got to be. Danny is the last person Ruby would want around and I'll never leave him.'

Ida nodded her understanding. 'What do you intend to do?'

'I don't know.'

'What about Danny?'

'We'll see. We'll see.'

Then as if deciding that Ida was owed more than that, he said. 'Come through, you'll have a cup of tea.'

He said nothing more until the tea was made and a tray set down between them. 'To tell you the truth, Ma, I'm going down to the West Country. Get a job in a hotel. Live in. No more casual work. I'll sell the house in time. Use the money to send Danny to a private school, probably as a weekly boarder.'

'You'll go mad. Miles away from London. And you won't earn the kind of money you've been used to.'

'I'll be all right. You've enough trouble on ye plate without taking me and Danny on as well.'

Ida opened her mouth to protest but Jack stopped her. 'We'll be all right, I tell you.' He looked around the room. 'I – I just want to get away for a bit. Anywhere away from here.'

Ida hung her head. She couldn't bring herself to ask where young Danny was. Did she want to see him? Half of her longed too, the other half recoiled at the thought of cuddling him when her own two grandsons were laying in their coffins.

She stood up. 'I'd best be going. Don't really know why I came.'

'Ma,' Jack's voice trembled, 'I'm ever so glad that you

/9j/example

did. I'll let you have an address when I get settled. If you want me, anytime – anytime.' He didn't elaborate.

'I know, I know, Jack. Goodbye.' She had to turn away before the tears started to run down her cheeks.

'Goodbye Ma,' she heard him say as he closed the door behind her.

A murmur went through the crowd as the hearse turned into the street.

Jeff turned away from the window. The moment they had all been dreading had arrived. He moved across the room to where his sister sat and with great compassion he leant over her and took her arm. 'They're here, luv. Come on now, on your feet, that's a good girl, put ye hat on. Alan is seeing to Ruby.'

Ruby went out first, supported by her eldest brother, with her mother and other brother only a few steps behind. They walked slowly, heads bent, dressed all in black, their gloved hands clasped tightly as if in prayer.

The two small white coffins were laden with flowers, and both women could be heard to gasp as they entered the funeral cars.

No one who attended the funeral service of the twins would ever forget just how moving it was. The church was overflowing with flowers, and the grave itself was surrounded with pretty posies and little white cards written with such feelings of kindness and love.

A choir of older children from the school led the singing of a hymn, their high, clear voices soaring as the mourners took their places in the pews and knelt in prayer.

As the two coffins were carried up the aisle, the full impact of the tragedy hit Ruby and she wept uncontrollably. For Jozy and Sheila it was all too much and the sight of the coffins made the deaths even harder to bear. Maggie sobbed and Tom did his best to comfort her.

Still Ida remained dry-eyed. She had gone beyond tears as she felt again the pain of losing her two young grandsons.

When they arrived back at the house, it was still not over. There was the agony of having to feed everyone and to thank them all for their kindness.

What seemed liked hours later to both Ruby and her mother, it did come to an end. Everyone had gone. The evening passed in silence. Alan and Norman had gone out, saying they probably wouldn't be back until the morning. Who could blame them?

Neither Ida nor Ruby were hungry and hardly touched the food that Ida had prepared. Ruby's face was tight. Her eyes red-rimmed from crying. But there was something about her that Ida couldn't put her finger on – it was almost an air of expectancy. But what more was there that could take place?

Choosing her words very carefully, Ida asked, 'Do you want to talk, Ruby? Have you thought what you would like to do?'

Ruby turned her dull eyes to look at her mother. She looked empty, drained, unable to think.

Ida burst out, 'Ruby, luv, life has to go on. I mean, you'll make yourself ill at this rate. Say something. Talk to me.'

'What is there to say, Mum? Nothing you, I, or anyone else says will bring back Lenny and Joey.'

She got to her feet, came to where her mother sat, bent low and very tenderly placed her lips against her cheek. 'Try not to worry about me, Mum. Now, if you don't mind, I'm going up to bed.'

Ida blinked rapidly before she pulled Ruby to her and held her tightly. 'Try an' get a good night's sleep,' she whispered, but now she was in no two minds about what Ruby was going to do. She hoped against hope that she had jumped to the wrong conclusion.

The night was a long one. Ida didn't even try to sleep, she knew beyond a doubt that it was impossible. She lay on her back, her ears waiting for the sound she knew would surely come.

Although Ruby had been a trouble to her from the day she was born, she loved her. In a peculiar sort of a way her whole life had revolved around her daughter. More so since the twins had been born. She hadn't realised just how much those two boys had filled her life until they were gone from it. Seeing them at least once during the week and waiting for Saturdays so that she could have them to herself for the whole day. Ruby bringing them to Sunday tea whenever she felt like it. It was as if there was no pattern to her life now.

Daylight was beginning to creep through the crack in the curtains. She closed her eyes, then slowly opened them again as she heard the bedroom door open.

Ida knew now she hadn't been wrong! She waited for her own door to open, but it didn't. She heard Ruby's footsteps going down the stairs. She imagined her filling the kettle, placing it on the gas to boil. She hadn't long to wait.

The sound of the front door being opened and then gently closed had her lifting herself slowly from the bed and dragging herself across the room. From the bedroom window Ida watched Ruby walk away up the street, and she knew she had to let her go.

She smiled a bittersweet smile as the memories of Ruby

as a child came back to her. And as the memories deepened, the smile became sad. 'Oh, Ruby,' she whispered, 'Oh, Ruby.'

Sorrow was one thing but at this moment Ida felt she was being made to suffer more than was humanely possible. In the time between that dreadful accident and the funeral she had drawn on a strength that she hadn't realised she possessed. She had never left Ruby alone for a minute, always making sure that an aunt, uncle or brother was with her. Keeping Ruby's spirits up to the best of her ability, trying to convince her that in time there would be a future for her. Looking back, she didn't know how she herself had kept going, let alone Ruby.

Oh, she'd miss her. How she'd miss her. Where was she going to go? However would she manage on her own?

She wanted to beat her fists on the pane of glass, shout and holler, Come back! Don't go, please don't go! She couldn't allow herself to do that. Whatever lay ahead for Ruby, it was never going to be an easy path for her to tread. But come what may, it had to be of Ruby's own choosing. She wasn't a little girl any more, twenty-one years old and enough bad experiences behind her to fill three lifetimes.

She wouldn't hold it against Ruby, going off like that. For once she would mind her own business and allow Ruby to stand on her own two feet. The tears were running down her cheeks and she said to herself, 'I thought you had no more tears left to cry.'

She put out her tongue to lick the salt drops away and murmured, 'Don't let anything happen to her. Keep her safe. Let her find some happiness.'

Just who she was asking to take care of Ruby she couldn't fathom. Her faith in God had been badly shaken. Why had two little children, whose lives had only just begun, had to die?

Wearily she returned to her bed, crawled thankfully beneath the warm sheets, buried her head deep into the pillow and whimpered like a child.

She hadn't been wrong. Ruby had left. Gone away to be on her own. And she needed no telling that it would be many a long day before she set eyes on her again.

With that knowledge she closed her eyes and finally fell asleep. But it was a shallow sleep, fraught with fear, and an overwhelming feeling of loneliness.

Part Two

1967

Chapter Sixteen

IN THE THIRTEEN YEARS that had elapsed since the twins had died, everything from an outsider's point of view had seemingly gone well for Alan and Norman Wilcox and also for the Simmonds side of the family. Not only had the Cavalier Club been extremely successful, Ida's two sons had extended it by building onto the back of the premises.

Alan and Norman were both well satisfied. Things had gone from good to better. The business was flourishing, the order book for the restaurant and the newly-built function hall at all times bursting, and they now had a healthy sum of hard-earned money sitting in the bank earning interest for them.

With these considerable achievements the Wilcox family itself had expanded in a truly surprising fashion. Norman had been the first to marry. The death of Rose Marlow's crippled mother in 1955 had allowed them to bring the date of their marriage forward. Within a year Rose had given birth to a daughter, whom they named

Anne, after Rose's mother. A talkative little girl, though rather plain to look at, she had already decided that as soon as she was old enough she would be a teacher. The next four years had given Rose and Norman two sons, Roy and then Garry, both healthy normal boys.

Alan, as everyone had expected, had taken his time. And wonder of wonders, he had done remarkably well for himself, choosing for his wife a woman he had met by chance in the bank, of all places. Iris Donnelly, a well-bred, educated young lady that Ida had not only approved of but had come to love just as much as Rose.

Iris had a pigeon pair, first John, and then Joanna, within three years of her and Alan having been married in 1957. Both children were doing well at school and Ida considered them to be a well-adjusted family.

Jeff and Sheila hadn't been left out in the grandparents stakes; their sons, Billy and Albie, had both done well for themselves.

Billy and his wife, Linda, had only the one child, Jodie. A bonny brilliant child was Jodie. Oh, yes, a clever one. Relations and friends alike said this. Probably why Linda and Billy had chosen to only have the one child. Her private education was costing a fortune.

Albie and his wife, Mary, had gone back along the line to produce twins Julie and Karen. And to be honest, Ida had breathed a sigh of relief that they were both girls. Twin boys would have brought back a lot of painful memories. Not that Ida begrudged these youngsters their happiness and was always thrilled to be included in the activities of these young families, but, though time did heal, the hurt never really went away.

The reason for going back and reliving so many memories on this bitterly cold February morning was the fact that had Lenny and Joey lived, they would be eighteen years old today. Her grandsons would be grown up young men. Ida replaced the photograph of the twins, taken when they were three years old, back on the shelf.

They say it is better to have loved and lost, than never to have loved at all. She wasn't so sure.

Ida spared a thought for her eldest brother Bert and for her well-loved sister-in-law, Jozy. They hadn't been blessed with any grandchildren. Their only son Terry still lived with Peter Gower. Again, there wasn't a friend or relative that didn't love both Terry and Peter. They were happy together and they were kind and considerate to all their relatives. Which was more than you could say for some.

She recalled the night before her daughter had walked away from this house.

'Don't worry about me, Mum,' Ruby had said and Ida now found her hand was touching her cheek as she recalled the gentle kiss that Ruby had placed there before going upstairs to bed.

With hindsight, there had been no need to worry over Ruby. She, too, had done very well for herself. Ida was well aware that Ruby had gone through sheer hell in those first lonely years on her own. God, she was only twenty-one.

'She's thirty-four now,' she exclaimed with a little shock, and wondered at how quickly the years had sped away.

If Ida had to describe Ruby now, she would say not only was she her daughter, she was her best friend. Ruby hardly ever came home – only twice in all these years – but they were close. Never a birthday or Mother's Day passed without a bouquet of flowers being delivered. Not a week passed without a phone call or a letter, even if it were only a few short lines written in another country, for Ruby was now an air hostess.

It hadn't been an easy path for Ruby. When Ruby had first left home, Ida had discovered, to her dismay, that her daughter was living in a bedsit in Manchester, working nights in a fish and chip shop and serving behind a bar in a public house at lunch times. Working hard, doing anything that would help her put out of her mind all that had happened during that dreadful day when her two little boys had been killed.

They sometimes met in London. Ida, bursting with pride, would follow Ruby into a restaurant where Ruby had always booked a table in advance. On the last occasion, Ida had been waiting on the Embankment, staring into the dark waters of the old Thames, thinking that was what London was all about, the whole of the city revolving on and around the Thames.

Ida had watched as this different daughter of hers came towards her, the sophisticated hair-do, the make-up, the smart suit, the upright way she held herself. With Ruby being so short, the high-heeled shoes she wore did a lot for her bearing. She had certainly altered. But still those lovely big blue eyes.

A little girl no longer.

It warmed the cockles of her heart to see how well Ruby was doing for herself.

'Oh, well.' Ida stood up and tied on her pinafore. Talking aloud to herself – a thing she did a lot of lately – she murmured, 'It's a rotten morning, not only very cold but damp as well. Gets right down into ye bones does this damp.'

She filled the kettle and placed it over the gas ring. 'I'll push the Hoover around upstairs, clean the bathroom out, do me little bit of ironing, then about twelve I'll take the flowers to the cemetery.'

Her thoughts turned again to Ruby. She was miles away. She wouldn't come. But then she never did. Still far too painful. I'll lay a pound to a penny she's here with me in thought today.

Would Ruby ever meet someone? Get married again? She doubted it. Career, that's what Ruby concentrated on.

Ida climbed the stairs with her dusters and tin of furniture polish. A waste of time this was really. She hated these spare bedrooms, remembering when they'd been occupied by her three children. She whipped in and out of them once a week, flicking the duster around and giving the curtains a good shake.

With all her jobs done, Ida decided to have a bath before getting dressed to go out. 'An' I don't think I'll bother about getting meself anything to eat. I'll treat meself to a bit of lunch while I'm out. Yes, that's what I'll do.'

She shook plenty of coloured bath crystals into the steaming water and then lying back, feeling totally relaxed, she allowed her mind to drift again.

It seemed as if everyone she knew was settled. So often these days she felt tired, not so much from physical fatigue but because of a sense of emptiness. Who did she have that she could call her own?

Oh yes, she had plenty of family and no doubt they all loved her. But who exactly would miss her? She had no partner. No one that on social occasions she could be paired off with.

She was wondering – another thing that she did so often

lately – just where was she going. What purpose did she have in life? Maggie had told her only yesterday that she ought to think about getting a job.

She'd been so shocked by the suggestion that she'd rounded on Maggie, 'What d'yer mean? Me get a job? Who the 'ell d'ye think is gonna want to employ me?'

All Maggie had done was grin. 'Ye don't know till ye try. Sitting in here all day long feeling sorry for yeself ain't ever gonna get ye anywhere.'

Easy enough for Maggie to talk, she was home and dry; where as since both Mr and Mrs Walker had died, Ida hadn't gone out to work. There was no reason why she should. She didn't need the money. Her sons saw that she had a regular income and Ruby was more than generous to her. All the same it might be worth thinking about. Get her out of the house. Enable her to meet people. What kind of a job would suit me? There ain't much that I'm any good at.

She leant forward, turned on the tap and wiggled her toes about as more hot water gushed into the bath. It was hard not to laugh when she thought about Maggie. To be honest, she was probably a little bit envious.

She smiled now at the recollection of Maggie's face on the day she'd asked her advice about getting married to Tom Carter. Maggie's jaw had dropped when she'd laughed out loud at the suggestion. Maggie had never been any good at hiding her feelings, especially if you caught her unawares, and the look of blank disappointment on Maggie's face had been too much for Ida. She hadn't meant to be cruel.

'No need to ask me, Maggie, luv,' had been Ida's quick reply, 'but since you 'ave, I say go for it. Wonderful! For both Tom an' yeself. You're there most days of the week anyway. And God knows that great big 'ouse could do with another body living in it.'

Maggie face was wreathed in smiles now.

'Mind you, you won't get much encouragement from Joe Carter, nor from his snooty wife, Doris. If I were you, I wouldn't bother sending them an invitation to the wedding.'

Maggie and Tom's decision to get married had soon become common knowledge After all they'd been good friends for a long time. Neither of them would be getting a pig in a poke. As it turned out as they were as happy as any two people could be.

Both of them now having turned seventy, it was as if they had taken a new lease on life. They got out and about all over the place. They never failed to ask her if she wanted to go with them, a fact that was greatly appreciated by Ida, but she didn't feel that she could play gooseberry all the time.

Those two were made for each other. Things had a way of working out for the best. Well sometimes, anyway. There was no denying that. But why did it always happen that way for everyone else and not for me?

She finished washing herself, got out of the bath, reached for the big towel that lay folded over the back of the chair and wrapped it tightly around herself. She thought of why she was taking flowers to the grave of her grandsons today. She wished with all her might that instead she could have been icing a cake for them on this special birthday when they would have been eighteen years old. As she went downstairs she was still wishing that she could turn the clock back.

Ruby Wilcox wasn't in a foreign country today. She had

her feet firmly planted on the ground in Lancashire. And she was well aware of what day it was.

When her whole life had collapsed, leaving her nothing worth living for, she had left London, where she had been born, got on the first train going north, took on the surname of her childhood and worked like a dog. Two sometimes three jobs at a time. Anything that would make her so damned tired she would at least have half a chance of blotting out the nightmare of that day when she had lost both her babies.

Hard work she found she could take, but loneliness was something else. Her mother, brothers, cousins, aunts and uncles would never know how much she missed them. Nor how many nights she cried till there wasn't a tear left in her to shed.

She had felt guilty over the way she had walked away from Jack Dawson and his young son Danny. A sharp clean break had been necessary. She had made that decision then and even now she knew it to be the right one.

Their being together hadn't worked that well. A lot of it being my fault, she freely admitted, though thinking back it had been a case of six of one and half a dozen of the other.

Could she have remained with Jack? Perhaps have married him? The answer to both questions was a definite no.

How about Danny? Even if she could have faced the prospect of watching him grow up, she knew it wouldn't have worked. Danny would have continued to make her life a misery and she his.

No, as regards Jack Dawson, what she had done had been for the best. One thing she was pleased about. Jack had kept in touch with her mother and from her letters, she'd learned that from time to time Jack brought Danny to see her.

Jack still lives in the west country, her Mother had written, *He's got a little house, married again, and now that Danny's older he goes to boarding school. Jack's always telling me they've got a nice spare bedroom and if I'd like to go and stay with them he would come up to London to fetch me.*

Ruby bit her lip as she recalled this particular letter. She would have liked to have asked her mother so many questions. Would she go? See if Jack and Danny were happy in their new life?

It was all too difficult for her. She had had her chance and she'd blown it. Perhaps later on, when I go home next time, Christmas maybe. Yes, I'll make an effort this year and then, maybe Mum and me can sit down and talk about them.

She raised her hand at this thought, brushing at her eyes. Thinking of Jack and Danny still made her feel uncomfortable and loaded with reproach. Even after all this time she still felt guilty.

With time to consider her life, Ruby had decided that it was not too late for her to do something decent and useful with it. She wondered if she might be able to go to college. Start to get herself educated. The prospect of making an application had been daunting. To put it mildly she'd been frightened of failing the entrance exam.

She did make it to college and, with a great deal of dedicated swotting and sheer determination, she had after two years secured a place for herself at Manchester University. Once there, she had received so much encouragement from the men and women who were devoted to teaching and studying that she hadn't found it so hard. Obtaining a good job hadn't been so difficult since she was able to show her degree in Business.

Weekends were still the worse. Wherever she went for a walk there were always children squealing with delight as their parents pushed them on swings, swung them round, hugged them tight, bought them sweets and ice-creams. Ruby would watch helplessly, hating herself for what she knew was utter jealousy.

She was so alone. So far from home, from London, everyone she knew and loved.

Work had been her saving grace. And today she was going after yet another new job. Being an air-hostess had been marvellous to begin with. It still meant long lonely nights in far away places. Though to be honest, she had met and made so many friends from all walks of life, and she'd be the first to admit that it was her own fault that she didn't allow anyone to get too close to her.

Ruby sat by the table at the window in this plush waiting room and wondered what this interview would be like. It was because of an advertisement in the *Guardian* that she was here. More than half the business in the city of Manchester seemed to be connected either with the manufacturing or distributing of cotton. The position she was about to apply for had no such connection.

A side door opened; a well groomed blonde appeared. Ruby turned her head slowly and they exchanged glances.

'Don't look so worried,' the receptionist said softly, 'Mr McKenzie will see you now.'

Ruby smiled her thanks and as she drew level, the young lady whispered, 'He doesn't bite – he's nice really.'

'Come in, have a seat.' The man, who obviously lived

a lot of his life outdoors, nodded her to sit across from his desk. He was very good-looking, bushy hair bleached by the sun, his face quite tanned. 'I liked your application letter. Very much to the point. Saves time.'

Ruby's impression was that he was a man of few words, and his accent was pure Scottish.

'What's your professional experience?'

Ruby shrugged. 'Mainly what I put in the letter. Technical college. Then I was lucky enough to get a place at university. After that I joined a firm of solicitors, Oakley and Bennett, I worked there as a clerical assistant for a couple of years.'

He looked serious, 'There's no luck attached to being given a place at university. You must have earned your qualifications.'

A buzzer on the intercom rang, he pressed a button and spoke to who Ruby supposed was his secretary.

'Yes?'

'Mr Henderson on the line for you, sir.'

He looked at his watch and then at Ruby, 'It is important, would you excuse me for a moment?'

Ruby nodded and made to stand.

'No, please, stay where you are. I shall only be a few minutes.'

Ruby tried to keep her eyes lowered. The carpet on the floor was a dove-grey. Thick and expensive, she decided, but then everything about this place and the man himself smelt of money.

A plaque on the front of the large desk stated *Ian McKenzie*.

Ian! The name suited him well. Strong, tough and very businesslike. Dark suit, immaculate white shirt and plain tie. Ruby thought him to be in his late thirties.

'Fine, fine.' He ended the conversation abruptly, leaned across the desk and replaced the telephone receiver.

Again he looked at his watch. It was twelve-thirty.

'Miss Wilcox.'

'Yes?'

'I have a free hour or two. Will you have lunch with me?'

Ruby was flustered. 'What now? Today?'

He smiled at her confusion. 'Yes, right now.'

For an instant she hesitated, and then made up her mind. 'Thank you, Mr McKenzie, that would be nice.'

She gathered up her coat, gloves, and bag and he took hold of her elbow as he steered her towards the lift.

The restaurant he chose was a short walking distance from his office. It was clear from the way the waiters treated him that he regularly came here for business lunches. They climbed the stairs to a dining room on the first floor. The windows were huge and in the distance Ruby had a clear view of the busy Manchester Ship Canal.

The waiter took her camel coat and she was glad that she had worn her grey suit with a heather-coloured jumper beneath. She could see only one other woman in a sea of business men.

'Good afternoon Mr McKenzie.' The wine list was offered. Ian McKenzie ignored it. 'A bottle of the house white,' he ordered. Turning his attention to Ruby he asked, 'Now, what would you like to eat?'

Ruby couldn't decide. Used as she was to eating out, this menu was terrifyingly large and mostly in French.

'I could make a suggestion, poached salmon to start with, followed by the roast lamb.'

Ruby nodded her agreement.

The wine waiter came back. The bottle was expertly opened and the wine poured, Ian waving away his right to taste it first.

Ian was silent, busy with his thoughts. This was not the classic example of an ambitious and clever woman. To him – always quick to judge and very seldom wrong in his snap judgements – Ruby Wilcox seemed a very capable young woman. One that wasn't a chatterbox. He couldn't stand women that talked too much. She was intelligent, that much was sure. Determined. Not much would daunt her. Still, there was an air of sadness about her, almost as if she had had to forfeit a lot to get where she was today.

She wasn't that young. About five years younger than himself, he guessed. She wore no rings on her fingers, had she ever been married? Probably yes, but perhaps like himself, it was a case of once bitten, twice shy.

'The position I'm offering is very different from anything you've tried before. It is in Scotland for one thing.'

Ruby set down her glass, her hands were trembling. 'I'm aware of that. The advertisement made it quite clear.'

'You wouldn't object to that?'

Ruby was in danger of becoming annoyed. 'I considered that well before I applied.'

'I have a housekeeper and also several men who work on the estate. What I need is a secretary come bookkeeper. The books alone can be a very demanding job.'

Ruby couldn't think how to reply to that but was saved by the arrival of their first course. She suddenly realised how hungry she was, took up her fish knife and fork and began to eat.

'It's not just the work – there are other things to be considered. My property is set in acres of moorland, but we're not far from the sea. 'Tis very beautiful in the summer months. The house and gardens are sheltered by the hills, still we get snowed in for many weeks. Would that be a problem?'

Ruby was thinking of a month she had spent with a friend from college. At that time Scotland had seemed to be the answer to all her prayers. Peace and tranquillity, it had been balm to her soul. She'd vowed then that she would come back to live there one day.

Tired of flying around the globe, not getting the chance to see very much of other countries, merely being at the beck and call of the passengers on the aircraft. She had considered giving up. Going back to live in London. It wasn't a pleasant prospect. She had to go on, not back.

At this point waiters interrupted, one removed their empty plates, another served the lamb.

'You're giving a lot of thought to your answer. How about coming up to Scotland for a few days next week? Get the feel of the place.'

Was he serious? Was he trying something on? Would she be alone, out in the wilds with him?

He could guess at the thoughts that were running through her head. 'Eat your lunch. Decide later.' He seemed quite untroubled about it all.

The tender lamb, the roast potatoes, the broccoli and onion sauce had all been eaten, the wine glasses refilled and a sweet served.

'Would you like coffee?' He asked, glancing at his watch.

'Can you spare the time?' Ruby boldly asked.

He grinned and nodded his head, so Ruby said that she

would. The waiter brought their coffee, black, steaming and smelling great, with a pot of thick yellow cream.

'I can find out all I need to know about you.' He suddenly told her.

Ruby found this statement disconcerting and it showed in her face. Quickly he smiled before saying, 'So, it's only fair to tell you a bit about myself. I have only a minor interest in this Manchester business, the chief shareholder is my brother Andrew. Scotland is my first love and I spend as much time there as I am able. For some time I did have a male secretary. It didn't work. Me being away for long periods caused problems. Mrs Patterson objected to being alone in the house with him. Catherine Patterson has taken care of me and mine for years as well as everything else about the house. So, there was no contest.'

Ruby cleared her throat before quietly saying, 'I think I would like to accept your invitation.' Then, with what for her was a very rare smile, she pushed the sugar bowl in his direction. 'That's if you meant what you said.'

'I never make a statement that I don't mean or promise something that I cannot deliver.'

That was the end of their conversation. They drank their coffee in silence. Outside the restaurant, he ordered a taxi for Ruby. They said their goodbyes on the pavement. He promised that he'd have the travel details in the post to her first thing in the morning.

The taxi moved off. 'Bye,' she mouthed, leaning forward and raising her hand, but Ian McKenzie had already gone.

She sat back in her seat and looked at the passing crowds. It was just beginning to rain, umbrellas were being put up, heads down; folk were in a hurry wherever they were going.

What a day this had turned out to be. She could feel her heart thumping with excitement. Had she got the job? Seemed like it. A lot depended on those few days she was going to spend in Scotland.

An entirely different way of life, he had said. Well, he was an entirely different kind of man to anyone she had ever met before. Would it all work out all right? She hoped so. Oh, yes, she hoped so.

Chapter Seventeen

MAGGIE CARTER, AS SHE was now, caught up with Ida as they turned into Broadwater Road.

'I guessed you'd be along here about now,' Maggie said, transferring the pot plant she was carrying into the other hand.

Together they walked towards the cemetery gates. The ground was hard and slippery, and as they were holding arms they slithered along together.

There was silence between them as they looked down on the well-kept grass that was the grave of Ruby's two little boys. Ida bent her knees; she had to tug hard to get the spike at the base of the green enamel vase out of the hard ground, then removing the dead flowers, she said, 'I won't be a minute, I'll just fill this with clean water.'

Left alone, Maggie folded her shopping bag to form a kneeling mat. The ground was very frosty but at least it was fairly dry. She knelt, took the small garden fork which was always kept at the head of the plot, and by scraping hard managed to clear a small surface of the earth. With both hands she wriggled the plant pot this way and that, until it was set secure enough not to blow over. Then she scooped the loose earth back around the base of the pot, patting it firm, thinking that it would help to keep the roots of the plant warm.

Ida returned. 'By, my hands are cold, that water's freezing,' she said, as she pushed hard to get the spike of the vase back deep into the grass. She unwrapped the spring flowers she had bought. 'They won't last long out here in this bitter cold wind,' she whispered.

'Never mind, luv, they look pretty, especially the pink tulips. Must be forced. They've never been grown out-doors, 'ave they?'

'No, don't suppose they 'ave, Maggie. You were the most sensible,' Ida told her as she looked at the pot of bright yellow chrysanthemums that Maggie had brought. 'Look like a ray of sunshine, don't they? An' they'll last a while an' all.'

They picked up the paper wrappings and tidied a few tufts of grass. Then Ida lowered her eyes and dropped her head as if in prayer.

'Eighteen! Not fair, is it?' she muttered, more to herself than to Maggie.

'Come on. Come on now.' Maggie made her voice sound cheerful. 'Let's go an' treat ourself to a nice 'ot drink.'

There was a little embarrassed silence between them as they pulled on their woolly gloves, wound their scarves tighter around their necks and pulled their hats down lower over their ears before linking arms again. Ida broke it by saying, 'You're a good pal, Maggie. And you never forget.'

'Works both ways, luv. I'd still be on me own if it

weren't for you. You and all yours made me part of yer family. And I ended up with Tom. That was down t'you an' all. As for never forgetting, well, I ain't made of stone. Many's the day I 'ad those babies t'meself whilst Ruby was at work. God knows it wasn't fair, what 'appened.'

Ida sighed. 'I think the reason Ruby never visits the grave is because it would bring it all back. Pity.'

Maggie looked into Ida's eyes, her own soft with kindness, her voice expressing it too as she said, 'Don't suppose poor Ruby will ever be able to get that awful day out of her mind, but give her credit, she's upped an' faced life squarely, ain't she? She never forgets to write. Tom looks forward to getting her cards. Keeps everyone of 'em in a scrap book.'

By now they had reached Tooting High Street and the hustle and the bustle served to drive away some of the sadness they were both feeling.

Ida swung round towards Maggie, 'I don't usually have anything to eat while I'm out, always a cup of something but that's all. I usually do me bit of shopping an' go 'ome. Today I'm gonna splash out. Wanna join me? I'll treat you.' Then quickly changing her tone of voice to what was for her a posh accent, she added, 'Where would you like to eat? Do you have a preference?'

They both laughed loudly. It was as if they had thrown off their gloom.

'You don't 'ave to treat me. We'll go 'alves.'

'No we won't,' Ida insisted. 'I said it's my treat. Where shall we go? And don't say up the market, I don't fancy that cafe, not today.'

'All right, since you're in the money, let's try that new place the other side of the Broadway. They do a set lunch, three courses; people 'ave told me it's not bad. What d'ye think?'

'Why not? But for God's sake let's get a move on, me feet 'ave frozen in me boots. Here! What say we 'ave a tot of whisky in the Castle, just to warm us through first? We do 'ave to pass the pub.'

'Be a sin not to,' Maggie grinned broadly. 'As you say, luv, we do pass the pub, 't ain't as if we'd be going out of our way.'

With their clothes loosened and a tot of whisky loaded with hot ginger wine, the two women settled in front of the log fire and counted their blessings as they sipped their drinks.

'Thought any more about getting a job?' Maggie shot the question at Ida, taking her by surprise.

'What's the idea? You wanna get rid of me or something? If I go out t'work I won't be there when you feel like popping in for a cuppa tea, will I?'

'No one's suggesting you go full time, an' the reason I've brought it up again now is 'cos 'Emmings have got a card in their window, asking for a part-time assistant. It says you 'ave to apply within.'

Hemmings the bakers! A bit posh for the likes of me, quickly passed through Ida's mind. It wasn't the normal run of the mill baker's shop. Ever so nice, the bread was smashing, baked on the premises and often a loaf was still hot when you bought it. The cakes melted in your mouth and the jam doughnuts, well, there wasn't any better to be had no matter where you went. Cost a bit more though, but that was only to be expected, since they wrapped the loaves in big sheets of white tissue paper and put the cakes in boxes. It's not the kind of shop that I'd use every day. Besides, I ain't never done any shop work.

'I'll think about it,' Ida promised, taking a long slow drink of her hot toddy.

'God give me patience,' Maggie breathed, 'how much longer are you gonna mooch about in that house all on ye own? I'll tell ye what, I'm taking no more excuses, we'll 'ave another one of these.' She picked up her own glass and took a big swig, 'Then we'll go an' eat, an' after that I'm coming in t'Emmings with ye. At least ye can ask what the hours are. That won't 'urt you.'

Not for the first time, Ida looked in amazement at Maggie. She could be a right old tartar when she liked.

Having had a second hot toddy each, they came out of the Castle in a much jollier mood than when they'd gone in. That was until they found that it was raining heavily.

'More like sleet than rain,' Maggie moaned, 'if this lot turns into snow we'll be in for it all right.'

'Oh, stop complaining,' Ida said as they paused for a moment in the shelter of a shop doorway.

'Just look at those blasted kids.' Maggie pointed a finger looking towards the island in the middle of the busy Broadway. 'I don't care what they do t'themselves but the way they're carrying on out there, they're gonna cause an accident, an' it won't be them that ends up getting 'urt.'

Ida stared in amazement. 'That lot call themselves hippies, don't they?'

'I know what I'd call them.' Maggie was off on her high horse. 'A load of daft lazy buggers. Ought t'be made to get a job.'

There were more girls than boys in the group. One girl in particular was showing off. Doing some kind of a dance. Jumping on and off the island narrowly missing the traffic.

She was wearing a plastic mac over a long dress that almost touched the ground, her long wet hair hung in separated strands on her shoulders.

Several rows of beads were woven around her forehead and several more strings of beads were dangling from her neck.

The group as a whole were irritating the people who were trying to get past and go about their daily business.

'Good, about time too,' Ida said, as they watched two police constables approach the hippies.

'Yeah, well, if that lot's daft enough to 'ang about in this rotten weather, don't mean to say that we 'ave to. Come on Ida, best foot forward, me stomach's telling me it's time we 'ad our dinner.'

'I've got t'admit this place ain't 'alf bad,' Ida remarked as she wiped her lips on the thin paper serviette.

The pair of them had finished their steak and kidney pie with three vegetables, and what with having had a bowl of soup before that, they were feeling pretty full.

'D'ye fancy any pudding?' Ida asked.

'No thanks, luv. That was a lovely dinner but I'm full right up.' Maggie reached for her purse, but Ida stopped her.

'There's no need. I said I'd treat you an' I meant it.'

The cafe was busy, people were waiting for a table, so they scrambled to their feet, collected up all their belongings, dealt with their scarves and tugged on their hats.

'Ready?' Maggie asked.

'Just about. Be glad t'get 'ome. You'll come in an' 'ave a cuppa with me?'

'Not so fast. 'Emmings is only two doors up the road

an' you, my friend, are going to see about that job if I 'ave to drag you in there.'

'All right. I wasn't trying t'chicken out, I just thought we'd leave it to another day.'

'Never put off till t'morrow what ye can do t'day, is what Tom is always telling me. Come on Ida, the man won't bite you, you're only going t'ask the details.'

Minutes later a big fat man dressed all in white was thanking her for coming in his shop. He looked every inch the jolly baker, his round red face smiling at her.

'What did you say your name was?' Mr Hemmings asked, leading the way through the shop and a store room and into a small office.

'Mrs Wilcox, Ida Wilcox.'

'Thanks again for calling in.' He shook Ida's hand.

She, feeling flustered, added, 'Pleased t'meet you.'

'Sit down, my dear.' Mr Hemmings nodded to an upright chair. 'As you probably know, this is a family business, just the wife, my son and myself. Always have had two part-time ladies, now one, Mrs Harris, has upped an' moved away. Pity really. She's been with us eleven years.'

Well, that said something for them, Ida thought quickly, a body wouldn't stay at a place of work for eleven years if they weren't nice people to work for.

She smiled at Mr Hemmings.

'The hours would be eight till twelve, or two till six. You can chop around some weeks, if you like. Vera Brightwell – she's our other part-timer – is always willing to fall in with what suits. Vera and Mrs Harris sorted it out between them fine.'

Sounds a friendly sort of woman. Ida's thoughts raced ahead. Mr Hemmings had called his other employee Vera.

That's nice, much better than working with someone and calling them Mrs Brightwell all the time. Bit of a mouthful a name like that was.

'Oh, I forgot. We do need both women to come in all day on Saturdays. Eight till four, with three quarters of an hour for your dinner. Have you got any young children? Would that be a problem?'

For the first time Ida relaxed. She grinned. He was having her on. Young children! Bit old in the tooth for that. 'No, that would be all right.' Ida spoke quietly, surprising herself that she was accepting the job.

Mr Hemmings talked on for a few minutes, giving her more details and finishing by saying, 'All your white overalls are provided and of course the hat. Must wear a hat in the shop, regulations an' all that.'

Now Ida had to surpress her grin. She could just see the smiles on the faces of her sisters-in-law if they came into the shop and saw her wearing one of those silly hats.

Encouraged by all this friendliness, Ida stood up and said, 'Well I'll see you on Monday morning, then. Thank you very much.'

'Thank you, Mrs Wilcox. I'm sure we'll get along fine. I'll introduce you to my wife and Vera on the way out.'

'How was it? Tell the truth now.' Maggie was impatient to hear all the details.

'Not too bad at all.'

'Good, good. I was dreading ye coming out, thought ye might be in a right ol' temper.'

'No, it weren't no trouble, much better than I thought. I'm gonna start work there next Monday.'

Maggie grinned broadly at her. 'See, you only 'ad t'make the effort.'

'Yeah, well, let's get away from 'ere before we freeze to

the spot. It was ever so warm in there and the smell was gorgeous, but ye don't 'alf feel it when ye come out.'

They linked arms, turned around and set off for home. Maggie was well pleased with herself. She had done her dearest friend a great favour, she was sure of that. Ida badly needed to get out and about more. Meet people instead of being couped up on her own for hours on end.

Ida found that she had surprised herself. She had got a job. She felt happy. It was the sort of happiness that she had not experienced for years. It's because I'm fifty-six coming up fifty-seven years old and I've just discovered that I am not on the scrap heap, I can do something useful. Serving bread and cakes couldn't be that difficult. Anyway, we'll see. At least now life wouldn't be a dull daily routine. She had something to look forward to, something different. I am going to enjoy every minute of it, she promised herself.

Turning her face to Maggie, she said, 'Come on, let's walk a bit quicker, I'm dying for a cup of tea. And thanks, Maggie, for the job I mean. I think it's going to work out all right.'

Maggie smiled to herself. Ida hadn't sounded so optimistic for a long time.

Ruby didn't have such a caring friend as Maggie to urge her to go for it, so she kept repeating to herself that a change was as good as a rest and that going to Scotland for the weekend didn't necessarily mean that she had to accept this job. Treat it as a free holiday, she smiled to herself, give yourself a chance to see how the other half live.

It was amazing how simple, how straightforward, things became as soon as you had reached a decision. Problems ironed themselves out, difficulties faded away. Perhaps a few doubts still lingered but right now she wasn't going to think about them.

Ruby leaned back in her seat, opened her magazine, smiled at the hostess and told her, yes please, she would like some coffee. She was on her way to Edinburgh. Excited at the thought of meeting Ian McKenzie for the second time.

Ruby came out of the airport to be met by a huge man who certainly hadn't bothered to dress for the occasion. His clothes looked as if he had worked out in the fields in them for days on end. He wore corduroy trousers and an old tweed jacket which had leather patches on each elbow. His grey hair blew in the wind, but his smile made her feel truly welcome.

'Mr McKenzie will be back at the house time we get there,' he told her, leading the way to a big black Austin car. 'I'm Alisdair, generally know as Ali, one of Mr McKenzie's keepers.'

Seeing Ruby's puzzled frown he explained: 'The estate has deer, grouse, pheasants and cattle. Then there's the water, has to be kept free of weeds. Most of the men are known as keepers.'

Ruby had to listen hard to catch his every word. His Scottish dialect would take a lot of getting used to. But then who was she to complain? When she'd first left London, the people she'd mixed with in Manchester had taken the mickey out of her cockney accent something rotten. Even more so during her time at college. She smiled to herself, she would never admit it to her family but before she had applied for the job with Oakley and Bennett she had attended elocution lessons. She smiled again, that wasn't to say there weren't times when she lapsed back into pure cockney, especially if anyone took her to be a fool.

Ruby had her first surprise when she came out of Turnhouse Airport; she had imagined it to be very near to Edinburgh.

'Do we not go through the city?' she queried, as the car drove through a small village.

'No, Edinburgh is six miles in the opposite direction, and Queensferry is six miles the other way. Muir House is set apart, outside of Queensferry. Could say Edinburgh City is twelve or thirteen miles from the estate if you wish to visit the castle whilst you're here.'

After only a mile or so the scenery changed abruptly. The road was empty now and the car was winding gently upwards. The day was cold and bleak, the wind strong and bitter. Great bunches of cloud moved slowly across the sky, but every now and then a blue patch appeared, allowing a gleam of wintry sunshine through. Ruby had never been this far north before and she was staggered by the difference in the countryside. As far as her eyes could see there was nothing other than moorland covered with a mishmash of winter grasses and great tracts of colourful heather. Then banks of snow began to appear, the white standing out against the sombre dark moors, laying where it had been trapped in ditches and under hedges.

'You'll be able to get a glimpse of Muir House in a minute, we're almost there.'

'Have you had much snow?' she ventured a question.

Alisdair clicked his tongue. 'Depends what you call much. Afore Christmas we had six inches or more. This road is good today, usually it is ice-rutted.'

When Alisdair turned off the road, Ruby got another

surprise. Muir House was not at all as she had imagined it to be.

She had expected some kind of mansion or even a castle. Her imagination had certainly run riot. This was just a big square house with many windows and lots of chimney pots. Ian McKenzie appeared from round the side of the house just as Alisdair climbed out from behind the driving wheel of the car and held the passenger door open for Ruby.

Ian came towards her, his feet crunching over the gravel, his hand outstretched in welcome. 'Miss Wilcox.'

Ruby smiled. He looked just as she remembered, although he was dressed very differently. He was now wearing thick, dark brown trousers and a heavy Fair Isle patterned sweater. Same bushy sandy hair, same nice grey eyes, same healthy overall look.

She walked towards him and they met in the middle of the gravel.

'Hallo, Mr McKenzie.'

They shook hands.

'The house is not what I expected but the view is wonderful.'

'Most folk are disappointed by the outside. I promise you the inside is worth a look. As to the view, not much of a day to see it on. Come along, let's get you inside.'

He took her one suitcase from Alisdair, had a few words with him that Ruby couldn't catch and then hurried her indoors.

Again it was nothing like she had imagined. Big, was the only word that sprung to her mind. Very much bigger than the outside would lend one to believe.

'Take your coat off, go to the fire. I'll see if Catherine has the tea ready,' Ian said.

The fireplace was enormous and the heat that the fire

was throwing out was wonderful. Banked up piles of logs and peat were smouldering, and there were two baskets of peat and logs sitting near the hearth. Enough there to keep that fire going for days, I shouldn't wonder, Ruby thought to herself, as she settled down in front of it.

Ian reappeared beside a lady bearing a heavy tea tray, whom Ruby supposed was his housekeeper.

'There,' the lady said triumphantly, setting the tray down on to the table that Ian had dragged close to the fireplace.

She was quite red in the face, as if she had been cooking, which judging from the lovely smells coming from the food, she obviously had. She straightened up, tucked in a few stray grey hairs which had escaped from her bun and turned to smile at Ruby.

'This is Mrs Patterson, Miss Wilcox.'

Before Ian could say more, Mrs Patterson interrupted him abruptly.

'It's many a long day since you, Ian McKenzie, referred to me as Mrs Patterson. If this young lady is to be a house guest for a few days I suggest we begin as we mean to go on.'

She elbowed her way past him, her hand outstretched to Ruby, a broad smile on her lips. 'Welcome to Muir House, lassie. I'm going to use your Christian name and you shall do the same for me. We'll no bother to stand on ceremony. I'm Catherine and you are?'

Ruby looked first at Mr Mckenzie and had to hold her laughter in check as she saw a spark of wry amusement glimmering in his eye.

'Aye well, we'd best humour the old Scotswoman. Apparently I shall be Ian and you shall be Ruby. Now, my fine Catherine, will you feed us or no?'

Catherine Patterson wasn't very good at concealing her smiles either as she said, 'So Ruby it is. Thought you'd like a bite of something before lunch; you must have left your home pretty early this morning. Let's see if I can tempt you. There's a batch of Highland scones still warm from the oven, and real heather honey there beside the butter.'

Ruby hesitated. Ian drew three upright chairs around the table and she began to relax as she watched him pour out the tea.

The silence between them as they ate was comfortable and Ruby felt so at ease that she thought how nice it would be to curl up and go to sleep in front of this great fire.

'I'd best be seeing to the lunch.' Catherine Patterson gathered the china onto her tray and departed for her kitchen, saying as she went, 'Your bedroom is nice and warm, Ruby, I hope you'll be comfortable.'

Ian picked up her suitcase and led the way.

'Catherine has put you in a room on the first floor – here we are. There's a bathroom right opposite. I have rooms at the top of the house and Catherine has her own apartment on the ground floor, so no one will disturb you.'

Ruby walked across the bedroom. 'I think this is perfect.' She set her handbag down on a chair and looked about her. There was a window facing out over neat grounds and a wide, deep windowsill. She could see the stable yard.

On the table beside the bed there was a small glass vase of primroses. She thought how kind it was of Catherine Patterson to have put them there.

'I'll leave you to settle in,' he said, and went out closing the door behind him.

Ruby sat on the windowsill and had a good look around the room. Dark coloured paper on the wall, large old-fashioned furniture, and yet the room had a good feel about it; a deep comfortable armchair and everything else that a person could possibly need. There was even a small fireplace in which a stack of peat was smouldering. How many modern bedrooms could boast a fireplace today, she wondered. There was a washstand with a marble top, on which stood an enormous china jug and bowl, and a pretty china soap dish, which held a shell-shaped tablet of pink soap. On a free-standing wooden towel rail folded towels had been hung.

Suddenly she found herself thinking back to her early days when she had lived first in Tooting and then in Mitcham. She was nothing like that young daft girl, she was a different person altogether now. Oh dear God, the mistakes she had made then! And how dearly she had paid for them!

Here she was now in Scotland, in a house she had never set foot in before, staying with a man whom she had met only very briefly and who might very probably turn out to be her employer.

She giggled, and the sound of her own merriment made her jump. Her own mother would more than likely say that she had taken leave of her senses.

Again her eyes swept around the room, and it seemed, all at once, the most natural thing in the world for her to be there.

During the course of the next few days, Ruby realised Catherine Patterson was much older than she looked. She learned that Catherine had been at Muir House since she was a very young girl, as nursemaid to Ian and his younger brother Andrew, before becoming the housekeeper.

Although she had formed the opinion that Catherine

Patterson could be pretty formidable if the mood took her, she also found that she liked her very much and was sure that given time they would become the best of friends.

The weather had closed in, a great deal of snow had fallen during the night, making it almost impossible for Ian McKenzie to do as he had intended and show Ruby around the area.

Ruby wasn't in the least put out. From the comfort of her warm bedroom she stared at the white wilderness. To her it was like a picture from a child's story book, the snow bringing with it that stillness that only comes when every branch and twig are covered with what seems like cotton wool.

And the deer! Ruby thought it amazing that she could stand at the window and pick them out in the snow.

Being restricted to only short walks, Ian had driven her down to see Queensferry beach. Ruby had sat in the car and stared spellbound.

'What a lovely stretch of sand!' she exclaimed.

'In the south you have some beaches with shingle, here in Scotland we only have sandy beaches.'

Ruby smiled at the sound of pride in his voice

For the rest of the day Ian devoted a lot of time to explaining the workings of the office which was situated behind the dining room and had a door that led to the grounds; a door that the men who worked on the estate used when they needed to come into the office, thus saving them coming through the main hall.

Early next morning, two sturdy men were in the office when Ruby came downstairs.

'Don't go, Ruby, stay and help me weigh up the pros and cons of my keepers' plan.' Ian had called to her as she was about to back out of the room. Between the three men it had become something of an heated argument.

Later, while in the kitchen having coffee with Catherine, Ruby had made a confession. 'When Ian is emotional he speaks so quickly, then his Scottish accent becomes more pronounced and, Catherine, if you were to ask me what all that controversy was about earlier, I couldn't for the life of me tell you. I only understood about one word in three.'

Catherine Patterson laughed loud and long. 'Saints above, lassie, that's nothing to be fretting yourself about. If I were to come down to London – and that would be a first, let me tell you – I have me doubts that I would be able to follow a conversation, never mind the sort of clash that you were a witness to this morning.'

Yes, Ruby told herself, in this good woman I will have a confidant and a friend if I decide to come up here to live.

With that thought she leant across the table, picked up the coffeepot and poured herself a second cup. She had stopped feeling intimidated or even shy. In fact she was beginning to feel very much at home.

The weekend began to come to an end. Her last dinner was over.

Ian finished his port and stood up. 'Perhaps,' he said softly, 'I should leave you two ladies alone. I shall drive you to the airport in the morning, Ruby, and you can tell me on the way if you have come to a decision. Good night to you both.'

The door closed behind him. Catherine put more logs on the fire, then she and Ruby drew their chairs up to the blaze.

It was as if they had known each other for much of their lives. Despite the age difference, there was a trust between

227

them. They spoke of many things, each aware that all was being said in confidence.

One thing Ruby did learn was that she wasn't the only one to have suffered in the past. Ian McKenzie, as a young man, had taken a bride.

'A disastrous marriage,' Catherine quietly told Ruby, adding, 'Not that it made him bitter. There's more to tell but that will be up to him. Things in general do go right for him and for his brother Andrew, maybe because they both care for people and people respond accordingly.'

'What time is it?' Ruby suddenly asked.

'Late. And you have to be up early in the morning.'

Slowly Catherine Patterson got to her feet. It was a long time since there had been another female at Muir House. She hoped now that was about to change. This young woman had her head set right on her shoulders. She had seen a lot of life and although she hadn't been too free with her confidence, she could tell that life hadn't always been kind to Ruby. Here in Scotland she might even find happiness.

'Goodnight my dear.' She took Ruby's head between her hands and kissed her forehead. 'Sleep well and I hope you make the right decision.'

Ruby lay awake for an hour or more. The heavy curtains moved as the cold night air flowed in through the slightly opened window. In the hearth the peat fire burned steadily, and its flicker and glow made patterns on the ceiling. She lay there calmly telling herself that she was going to give this new life a go. She was going to come and live in Muir House, Queensferry.

Only the date had to be decided. And that would be up to Ian McKenzie.

Chapter Eighteen

AUGUST BANK HOLIDAY. IDA couldn't believe how quickly the last six months had gone.

She had never been happier. Life – her life – suddenly had a meaning. She got up in the morning and had a reason to get dressed, taking care over what she chose to wear. Even using a little make-up.

She really liked her job at Hemmings the bakers. Every hour that she was there was different.

The young kiddies came with their large shopping bags, before setting off for school. Mr Hemmings sold bread left over from the previous day at greatly reduced prices. Mums sent their kids, knowing that Freda Hemmings was a soft touch and often added a few bread rolls at no extra charge. Make-weights, Freda called them, and if the kiddies were cheeky enough to ask she more often than not gave them a doughnut to eat on the way home.

'You'll be the ruin of me.' Her husband would mutter. Her son, George, would smile at his mother and wink at

Ida. They were all well aware that the old man had a heart of gold.

Then came the housewives, some well-off, choosing with care an assortment of fresh cream fancies. Women with children buying bath buns, Chelseas and plenty of bread, the cottage loaf being the favourite. A small loaf baked on top of a large round one, you got four knobbys instead of the usual two on an ordinary loaf.

Towards dinner time the workmen came in. Road sweepers, postmen, van-drivers and building workers all knew the worth of Mr Hemmings' rolls. He never stinted. Large crusty rolls, brown or white, filled with cheese, ham, salt beef or salami sausage and the customers told to help themselves to mustard or pickles.

There was always something going on. The shop was never empty. Saturdays were the best of all. Rushed off their feet for the first four hours, but then the Hemmings took over serving for a while and let Ida and Vera go out back and have their lunch together. A generous feed, provided free.

This was the forty-five minutes that they both looked forward too. Gave them a chance to have a good natter. Catch up on all the gossip. It had turned out that Vera Brightwell only lived two streets away from Ida. They were practically the same age, give or take a year or two. Vera had only one daughter and she was married with three children but they lived in Australia. Still, Vera was lucky. She still had her husband, Fred, and he was a postman. Good steady job that was.

Today being a public holiday the shops were all closed.

Sheila and Jeff were having a party. Living on the opposite side of the road to Ida, their garden was very much longer and as the weather was good, everyone had turned up.

Sheila liked it that way. She never minded the work. It was her way of making sure that the grandchildren, as much as their parents, knew what families were all about. Being there for each other when needed was what mattered. Or it should be.

Sheila was well contented as she sat at the garden table outside the back door, keeping an eye on the children as they helped to carry plates of food out from the kitchen.

There were three of her own grandchildren. Jodie, who at the age of twelve was too clever by half; then the twins, Julie and Karen, who were almost ten. Funny how life turned out. She had two boys, now her sons and their wives had all girls.

Helping them were John who was nine and his sister Joanna, just seven. They were the children of Ida's eldest son Alan and his lovely wife Iris.

All the family had all been so pleased when Ida's son, Norman, had married his long-term sweetheart, Rose Marlow. If ever a match was made in heaven it was that one, Sheila assured herself, as she watched their two young ones, Roy now ten and Garry just eight, tear off down the garden shouting back that only girls helped in the kitchen. Their sister Anne was Rose's first born; at the tender age of eleven was already showing signs of becoming a great beauty and she had that kindly nature that endeared her to everyone.

There was some sort of ball game going on down at the far end, she couldn't for the life of her make out what it was, still, men never grew out of knocking a ball around. Always were and always would be little boys at heart.

Her husband Jeff and his brother Bert were there – you could hear their voices above everybody eles's. So was Tom Carter. He was a marvel! Best thing that ever happened to him, the day that he married Maggie. That couple were now well and truly part of the family, affectionately referred to by all the kids as Auntie Maggie and Uncle Tom. And her Jeff especially had a lot of time for old Tom, there was nothing that he liked better than to talk cricket with him.

There were at least six young men down there. Suppose they are more like middle-aged men now, Sheila smiled to herself.

Ida's two sons, Alan and Norman, God they'd done well for themselves! Mind you, Jeff, Bert and Snowy Freeman had had to come to their rescue at one time but they had proved themselves worthy of that trust.

Then there was Terry with his long-term companion Peter Gower. Peter was well and truly accepted and loved by every member of the family and no one would have it any different.

There were times, though, when her heart ached for Jozy and Bert. Being deprived of grandchildren must hurt, though they never let it show.

And last but not least there were her own two sons, Billy and Albie. Sheila lifted her eyes to the bright blue sky and thanked God, as she did on many an occasion, for those two lads. They were by far and away the best thing that had ever happened to her. God forbid that anything should happen that would keep them and their families from visiting her and their father at least once every week.

There was only one person missing that would have made this family completely whole. Ruby.

Wasn't it bad enough that Len, Ida's husband, had been taken a prisoner during the war? Then to come home in such a terrible state that he hadn't lived for much more than a year. Such a nice, kind, gentle man was Len. He didn't deserve to die so young. Surely Ida being left on her own with three children to bring up ought to have been a full share of sorrow for anyone. But to have had all the pain and heartache that she and her Ruby had had to bear was asking too much.

Sheila sighed heavily then chided herself. Today was not the day to be sad. The sun was high in the sky and she didn't need anyone to tell her how lucky she was, in fact all of them were, to have each other.

Ruby was still filling Sheila's thoughts. If her letters were anything to go by then she had landed on her feet. Ida certainly thought so. Never tired of showing the photographs around, Ida would explain that this was the great house in which Ruby now lived and worked. This was Ruby, out walking with two dogs and an older lady companion, both of them dressed in heavy tweeds that made them look as if they had been born and bred on those Scottish moors.

Six months Ruby had been living in Queensferry now and one could only pray that she was happy. God knew she deserved to be.

Ida interrupted Sheila's daydreaming. 'Food's all ready, do you want us t'make the tea? Jozy thinks we ought t'use three pots, what d'you think?'

Sheila, having done most of the baking the previous day, had been urged to take it easy. The kitchen was full of women, sisters-in-law, daughters-in-law, grand-daughters and Maggie, who, even at her age, would never sit down when there was work to be done.

Now Sheila got to her feet, saying, 'I set three pots out on the windowsill, I thought we'd need all of them. I'll go down and tell our lot that tea is ready, no good calling them, they'll never hear me, not with the racket they're all making.'

All the women were seated around the big wooden table, the children and the men sitting down on the grass. It was a jolly party, everyone's tongue doing its fair share of wagging, and the garden echoed to children's laughter, giggles and good tempered teasing.

After tea, when the table was being cleared and the youngsters were racing around again, Ida sat with Jozy, each silent, both busy with their own thoughts. Ida thinking how lucky she was to have three young grandsons and one young granddaughter but still missing her only daughter and thinking if only Ruby were here then life would indeed be perfect. But then again, no one had everything. Not in this life they didn't.

Jozy's thoughts weren't that different. She was the only one here who didn't have any grandchildren. And was never likely too.

Count your blessings, she urged herself, two caring sons instead of one. And Peter was surely a son in every sense of the word. She had more than enough nieces and nephews to buy birthday and Christmas presents for and hardly a day went by that one or the other wasn't on her doorstep proving what a favourite aunt and uncle she and Bert were.

'Mad lot, ain't they?' Sheila cut into their thoughts, at the same time covering her ears against the screaming that was going on.

They laughed.

'You're the mad one, 'aving us all every high day an' 'oliday,' Ida retorted.

Sheila smiled and Jozy said, 'Get on with ye, the day they don't all turn up is the day that our Sheila will go mad.'

Sheila knew that to be true.

The local pub, the Fountain, was always full to bursting every weekend but with this being a bank holiday evening it was packed to the doors.

'You women go out in the garden with the kids,' suggested Bert, 'You're sure to find an empty table an' if not, well, it won't 'urt ye t'sit on the grass. We'll be out with the drinks in a minute.'

'Yeah, some minute,' Jozy muttered as she watched their men elbow their way to the bar. 'Ye can bet ye life we won't see them before they've got at least one pint inside them.'

'Not t'worry,' Maggie soothed, 'We won't die of thirst. Come on, let's see what the youngsters are up to.'

The women pushed their way through the throng to the french doors that were propped wide open on this balmy evening by empty beer crates.

The boys had been fortunate to find two wooden tables that had been recently vacated. They dragged them together just as their grandfathers, fathers and uncles appeared with trays of drinks.

'Wonders will never cease,' Jozy was muttering again.

'Don't knock it,' Sheila warned her, 'They're being kind-hearted, got the holiday spirit.'

'Well, if they ain't we soon will 'ave,' Ida laughed. 'Look at the tots of gin an' whisky – they're doubles!'

'Course they are,' Bert spoke up. 'Ye don't think we're gonna keep traipsing back and forth t'the bar do ye?'

There wasn't any time for replies, small hands were coming from all directions.

'Did I get a ginger beer?'

'I want crisps, please.'

'I'd rather have lemonade, Uncle Bert, but I don't mind crisps as well.'

'Quiet! Line up, the lot of you. A drink, a packet of crisps an' a bag of peanuts for each of you. What you don't like or don't want, swop. Now scoot and leave us to 'ave our drink in peace,' said Alan firmly.

The children needed no second bidding. They were off across the grass, giggling and shouting.

'They're all lively tonight,' Maggie said, as Tom bent over her saying, 'Here you are, love, you always have to be different to the others, we got you a port and lemon.'

The holiday atmosphere in the pub had spread to those outside in the garden and it wasn't long before the singing could be heard more than two streets away.

Alan and Norman fought their way through the crowds to fetch a second pint for each of the men.

'Cor, dearie me, Mother,' Alan's smile was broad as he told his mother and aunts what was going on inside the pub. 'That singer! She's wearing high-heeled shoes, loads of make-up, a curly blonde wig and very little else. No wonder it's hot and humid in there.'

Norman looked a trifle dishevelled himself as he took a long drink from his glass. Then setting it down he grinned at his brother. 'What do you expect? You can bet they pay that pianist a mere pittance and although that blonde is almost certainly doubling the pub profits tonight she will probably get paid even less. Just think how much we'll pay out in wages at the club this week. Double time for this weekend.'

'Thank God we can afford it,' Alan said quite seriously before bursting into laughter. 'This isn't exactly on par with the Cavalier is it? Anyway,' he paused, bent down and locked his arms around his mother's shoulders, 'what's money,' he whispered to her, 'when we can be with you and all the family?'

By nine o'clock there were people standing in groups in the garden, swaying to the infectious rhythms and melodies that were coming from the bar, and everyone seemed to be having a great time.

'I'm gonna 'ave to go t'the toilet,' said Ida.

'I'll come with you,' Maggie offered, getting to her feet.

Ida put out a hand to steady Maggie. She wasn't looking much older but her hair showed more grey and her movements were not so quick as they used to be.

'You enjoying yeself, Maggie?' Ida asked as they stood back to let a stream of girls come out from the ladies.

'Course I am.'

Ida held the swing door wide to let Maggie enter first. 'My, it's hot in 'ere. We don't want to 'ang about too long, it don't exactly smell sweet an' fresh either does it?'

There was only one cubicle free and Ida told Maggie to take it.

'Hi ye Ida, what you doing 'ere?'

Ida looked amazed as Vera Brightwell turned around from the mirror. Like herself, Vera was a short woman. Her hair was dark brown and she had nice eyes. Ida thought of how much she had come to like working with her. Her voice was always full of laughter and her accent was pure cockney.

'Well, I could ask you the same question,' Ida smiled. 'You look so different tonight, you've 'ad ye hair done and that frock you've got on ye didn't get up the market.'

Vera grinned. 'No, me and my Fred 'ave been dancing. We've only called in 'ere for a quick one. That reminds me, Ida, there's something I've been meaning to ask you fer ages. What d'you do on a Monday night normally?'

'Me? Nothing much, a bit of ironing maybe, if I've managed t'get the washing dry. Why?'

'Well, me an' Fred thought ye might like to come dancing with us.'

''Ere, 'ang on a minute, you told me before that the dancing you an' your Fred do ain't all ballroom dancing. Sequel dancing I think you said it was, an' I ain't got a clue what that is. 'Sides, I ain't got a partner an' if you think I'm gonna come with you and sit there like a wallflower you got another think coming!'

Vera drew herself up, looked Ida straight in the eye and said, 'If you'd just let me get a word in edgeways I might be able to explain. In the first place we go to Peggy Spencer's Dance Club, which is near Crystal Palace. We do all sorts of dancing, including Latin American.'

'Aw my Gawd!' breathed Ida.

Vera ignored her. 'Secondly, Peggy Spencer is one of the best dancing teachers in the world, I'd say, so even you could learn. Thirdly, sequel dancing is the easiest of the lot because everyone on the floor is doing the same thing, so you just 'ave to follow the one in front.'

'All right, all right. No need t'get out of ye pram. I know you were only being kind, but that still don't answer my query about a partner. And another thing, how do I get there?'

'Ah,' smiled Vera, 'at least you are considering it. Partners? Well, can't promise you'll always get a man to dance with, though there are a few loners floating about. But being short there's no end of women who will be only too glad t'be ye partner.'

'You can't be serious. Women taking the part of men, an' you want me t'join in?'

'Beggars can't be choosers, luv.'

'Yeah, well, I ain't reached the begging stage just yet.'

The doors of all three cubicles opened at once; two young women and Maggie emerged at the same time. All three were grinning broadly and it was obvious that they had heard the whole conversation.

Looking at Ida, the oldest of the women said, 'You wanna go, luv. Ye never know, ye might enjoy it.' With that, she and her mate linked arms and made for the door, but before going out they turned their heads and said, 'Best of luck, luv.'

Maggie couldn't control her laughter and only just managed to say, 'I really don't know why you don't go.'

'There ye are,' said Vera, 'listen t'Maggie. If it weren't for 'er, you never would 'ave come after the job at 'Emmings an' you an' I would never 'ave met.'

It was sickening to Ida, being told by one after the other what she should do. 'All right!' she cried out loud, 'I know I don't lead a very exciting life like the rest of you, so I'll come. Just the once, see what it's like. I must be barmy but if as you say, Vera, there are a few spare blokes then I reckon if I put on all me glad rags, fish out a pair of high-heeled shoes that I can dance in, then I'll stand as much chance as the next one of catching meself a partner.'

'Good on yer,' said Vera, most satisfied with the outcome. 'I'll see you at work during the week but just so's yer don't start 'aving second thoughts, I'm telling ye now, with Maggie as me witness, me and Fred will pick you up at 'alf past six next Monday night. Did I tell ye my Fred 'as bought himself a car? No, well he 'as, a little Ford so there's another worry solved. How ye get there an' back. All right?'

Ida stood nodding her head, wondering what she had let herself in for. But seeing the amusement on Maggie's face and the merriment in Vera's eyes, the light suddenly dawned on her.

She was going dancing.

How long since she had been on a dance floor? God alone knows, she answered her own question.

Well, like it or not, she was committed now. It might turn out to be a whole lot better than she was imagining. What she had said in jest might just turn out to be true.

You never know, she smiled to herself. I might find meself a bloke.

Chapter Nineteen

FOR RUBY, THE PAST three weeks had been one long round of work, walking and sleep, roughly in that order. Now bank holiday Sunday was here, Ian McKenzie was off to India with his brother Andrew and several other executives from the cotton trade.

Ruby surprised herself with the thought, I shall miss him.

The house seemed empty when he was only away from it for a few days at a time. Not that she was complaining, she still found it quite hard to believe that she, born and brought up in London, had taken to living up in Scotland like a duck takes to water.

Catherine Patterson had indeed become a friend and the life they shared was a good one. Ruby found the work that she had to do was demanding at times, but never boring. She had learnt as she went along the intricate ways there were to running a large estate and the Laird, as Catherine so often referred to Ian as, had been a patient and understanding teacher.

The Laird! God, she had been ignorant. When she had first heard Catherine say Laird, she had mistaken her Scottish accent and presumed she had meant that Ian was a lord.

'Good Lord, no,' Catherine had said in answer to her query.

'Then what is the difference?' Ruby quietly asked, hoping that she didn't sound too naïve.

'Well lass, Ian McKenzie is a Laird simply because he is the owner of all the land on a Scottish estate, as his father was before him and his father also. Not a lord as in England, no, not a titled nobleman like the eldest son of an earl.'

Ruby had thanked Catherine but all the same it did make her wonder. It had taken an old lady who had been born and bred in Scotland to explain the perplexing difference between the English and the Scottish aristocracy to her.

This morning Ruby had dressed with care. Alisdair was driving Ian to the airport but they weren't leaving the house until eleven o'clock. First Ian was going to Manchester; it would be Tuesday before he left the country. She, Catherine and Ian would breakfast together this morning as they usually did when he was at Muir House.

She had put on a most beautiful dress, sleeveless and very light, for contrary to what she had thought when she had first come to Queensferry, Scotland was not always cold, indeed since the beginning of May they had had very good weather. She had swept her fair hair up, away from her face and with her suntanned arms and bare feet thrust into sandals she knew that she looked a picture of health.

A strand of hair had worked loose and Ruby tucked it

behind her ear and wiped her hand across her forehead. From across the breakfast table, Ian's voice came quietly, 'Are you hot? Shall I open the french doors?'

Ruby realised that he had been watching her and this made her feel self-conscious. She put her hands back in her lap and shook her head.

'No, I'm fine.'

He picked up his cup, drained the rest of his coffee and got up from the table. He walked to the fireplace and leant his elbow on the mantelshelf.

Ruby lifted her head and returned his look. She decided that her first impression, made six months ago, had been right: Ian McKenzie was a good-looking man. He was also fair-minded. Straight in all his business dealings and tough with anyone that thought differently.

He looked, if anything, even more healthy than when they had first met, with his suntan, his bright eyes and sandy hair. He took Ruby unawares by suddenly saying, 'Are you happy here, Ruby?'

'Yes, thank you. Very happy.'

'Has Scotland lived up to your expectations?'

'Yes, once I became aware that it is not winter all the time.'

Ian laughed. 'This year summer has been great. It isn't always so.'

Ruby thought he looked quite boyish when he laughed.

'The only thing spoiling it now is that I have to go away. Two, maybe even three months. I can't get out of this trip. I am committed.'

He'd taken Ruby by surprise again. He sounded as if he were reluctant to leave Scotland and for more reasons than one.

'Oh,' Ruby smiled, feeling foolish. 'I imagined you

businessmen looked forward to travelling all over the world.'

'Normally I would agree. When I got divorced I couldn't leave the country quick enough. I was twenty-five years old. You'd have thought I'd have been old enough by then to cope with the situation, but it did something to me. Turned my life upside down. Nothing's ever been quite the same. Until you came here.'

Ruby couldn't believe what she was hearing. He had never before mentioned that he had been divorced. From Catherine she had learned that he had been married, she didn't know why but she had presumed that his wife had died. She couldn't have made a reply. Not to save her life.

Firmly but quietly, Ian McKenzie continued. 'I would like you to know that Muir House has a welcome feeling about it now. Even when I've only been down to Manchester I feel it on my return. I suppose it's something to do with the people who live in the house – in fact, I know it is. There has been a great change since you came here, Ruby.'

Silence hung between them. A moment later there came the sound of a car coming down the drive and soon the engine was cut as it stopped in front of the house.

'I must go and fetch my things down, if you'll excuse me.'

Ruby watched Ian gently kiss Catherine Patterson goodbye, telling her he would write and telephone at regular intervals.

'You'll be fine, besides the dogs you have Ruby for company this time,' he said, then quickly he added, 'Jock will see the men carry out their tasks.'

Catherine smiled and Ruby knew why. She had heard the tale of Jock Dunbar a good many times. He had lived on this estate as man and boy and demanded his proper title of head gillie.

Thank God he doesn't resent me, in fact to him I'm quite a bonny lassie, Ruby mused. It was far better to have Jock as a friend rather than as an enemy.

There was nothing for it but to take the hand that Ian McKenzie was holding out to her.

With Ruby's hand held tightly in his they gazed at each other. His silence said a whole lot more than any words. Having held her hand for far too long, Ian slowly let it go. 'Be here when I get back. Promise?'

Ruby nodded her head and within seconds he was in the car and the car was disappearing down the drive.

Ruby let out a deep breath and began to relax a little.

The sun was indeed shining as Catherine led the way up the beach, and Ruby followed, straggling a bit because she was laden with their picnic basket. There seemed to be a strict rule about Catherine Patterson's picnics. Everything but the kitchen sink had to be brought with them.

Ruby watched as Catherine laid out the tartan rugs on the sand, near enough to the old stone wall to enable them to rest their backs against it if they wished to sit up and read their books.

The sound of the sea could almost hypnotise one, Ruby thought as she sat staring out at the sun glistening on the gentle waves that lapped on the shore.

Catherine Patterson, dressed in a cool navy blue dress that had a thin jacket to match, pulled her straw hat well down over her forehead to shield her eyes from the sun and secured it to her bun with a sharp hatpin. Then turning to face Ruby, she smiled knowingly, before saying, 'Ruby, with Ian away and the house to ourselves we can more or less please ourselves what time we get back. I think you're going to miss the Laird. Would you like a cool drink before we set out our lunch?'

Ruby turned her head and looked at her. Her pale blue eyes held a certain gleam in them, but otherwise she was straight-faced. 'I think a drink now would be very nice.'

To the flask of home-made lemonade Catherine had added crushed ice; even glasses had been brought to the beach – there would be no mugs to drink from for Miss Patterson.

'Oh, that really is refreshing,' Ruby smiled her appreciation and then lay back on her rug, resting on her elbows.

The tide was coming in, each wave was crested with white foam, sending spray far and wide as it burst onto the sand. Ruby leaned forward, meaning to ask Catherine whether the boat that was tied up took passengers for trips or if it was used solely for fishing trips, but at that moment two young kiddies ran to the water's edge.

Wheeling seagulls swooped overhead screaming loudly and the two children turned and ran back along the sand. Further back the sand was soft and dry except for the shallow pools that never seemed to disappear. This still water fascinated the toddlers and their attention was caught by shells that lay nearby.

Suddenly one child – it appeared to Ruby to be a boy – lurched forward and on chubby little legs tottered towards the sea's edge again. A wave crashing in must have frightened him for he made to turn, slipped and finished up sitting in four inches of salt water.

He began to cry and his first wail was hardly out when

the other child began to scream in fright. Ruby was on her feet in seconds and running like the wind.

A lady and gentleman beat her to it. Ruby stopped in her tracks and silently watched as the young mother picked the boy up and carried him back along the beach to where the father had set the other child down on a heap of gaily coloured towels.

Ruby couldn't resist the temptation, she walked behind, watching and listening.

'Jamie, you're not hurt,' she heard the mother say as she held the boy close and laughed into his neck. 'I know, the water was cold,' she tickled him and the boy chuckled.

Ruby turned away. Watching them, she had been filled with a longing that had brought tears stinging to her eyes. It was a long time since memories had flooded back like that.

She wondered about the way she often looked back with regret for what might have been – indeed should have been. Was one meant never to forget? Should she have felt that surge of protectiveness when she had thought that child was in danger?

Like it or not, it still hurt when she saw families together. Whole families. She could be home with her own kith and kin on this lovely bank holiday weekend but would that make her feel any better? A whole lot worse, more than likely. She would see her nieces and nephews and be envious of their parents.

She'd be the odd one out. Just as her mother had been over all the years since her father had died. But there again her mother had had three children, she hadn't been entirely on her own.

At this thought a wry smile came to Ruby's lips. I bet there were many times when my poor Mum must have wished that she'd never set eyes on me! At least since I've left home we have become the very best of friends, and that thought reminded her that she had, the last time they had met, made a rash promise to go home for this coming Christmas.

It would be the first Christmas she had spent in London since she had lost the twins. Would she be able to go through with it? She pushed the thought to the back of her mind.

Catherine was sitting up with her arms wrapped around her knees, watching Ruby walk slowly back up the beach. She thought of the warmth that Ruby had brought into her life and was amazed to realise that were the girl to leave Muir House now there would be a great void in her own life.

She wasn't the only one that the coming of Ruby Wilcox had made an impression on.

I might be old, but I'm not yet blind and Ian McKenzie's outlook on life has brightened a whole lot since that lass has taken up residence. Take this morning, does he think I didn't notice? Seems he didn't care if I did, or maybe again he wanted me to observe that he held onto her hand for a lot longer than was necessary.

There was one thing that she was convinced of. Ruby had had her share of troubles. Not that she ever talked of them. It went too deep for that. There was many a time when she would turn her head over her shoulder to glance at Ruby, only to see that her eyes were bleak and sad, and she would be moved to sympathy for her.

Being a wise old bird I keep my own counsel and don't ask questions, she softly told herself. There may come a day when that lass needs to talk and then I'll be there for her. Oh yes, without a doubt I shall be there.

Slowly she got to her feet, brushed the sand from the hem of her dress and called out to Ruby, 'I'm feeling hungry, how about you?'

Ruby called back, 'I'm coming.'

'Well hurry up, and we can savour all the good things I've packed into this picnic basket.'

Perhaps because of the picnic – which had lived up to Catherine's best – or it could have been the wine that she had provided to go with the good food, or maybe it was the fresh sea air, then again it could be the kindly way that Ian had said goodbye to her, whatever, all these things rolled into one made for a very tired but a contented Ruby that bade Catherine goodnight before making her way up the great staircase that night.

Chapter Twenty

'MOST OF THE TEA is ready now,' Ida told her eldest son as she refused his offer of help. 'Besides my kitchen wasn't built for big fellas like you to work in.'

Alan had been feeling a bit guilty. Since him and Norman had opened the extension to the Cavalier Club his visits to his mother had grown less and he had decided to make up for this neglect by bringing his wife Iris and their two kiddies, John and Joanna, to have tea with her on this Saturday afternoon.

It had been a long hot summer and Alan was not sorry to see the autumn fast approaching. During the winter months they could be sure of a full order book. The Cavalier had become very popular with firms holding their staff dos there.

Enlarging the business had brought its problems. For one thing, neither Norman nor himself lived on the premises now. They employed a caretaker and his wife for that sole purpose. They both now owned large houses in Streatham. However it did mean dividing his time between two locations, three if he counted the office which they still kept at the top of the club.

Norman had volunteered to go in there today. Even Saturdays there was the question of the post. Wouldn't do to let a good booking slip through their fingers.

These days they had a restaurant manager, two waiters and two waitresses, two chefs and five kitchen staff, the receptionists and front desk personnel, not to mention the cleaners, but no employee touched the post. Just Norman and Alan discussed the merits of all inquiries and sent out the quotes. It was also down to them as to how much free hospitality was granted to any one firm or customer.

One thing him and Norman would have to give their full attention to was the family get-together that they had agreed to host for this coming Christmas.

'Son, go over to Bert's and fetch your children, will you? I'm just about to make the tea,' Ida said.

Alan was brought up sharp. He'd do well to try and forget the club just for this one afternoon. He owed his mother that much.

'All right, Mum, I'll only be a minute.'

'You really did go dancing, Nan?' Joanna giggled.

'Hang on a tick, you're not supposed to ask your Nanna questions like that,' her mother said, giggling herself.

They were all seated around Ida's table, which was laden with all the good things she had spent the whole previous evening preparing. The children obviously thought the fact that their grandma had gone dancing was a great lark and Ida was quite willing to let them have their fun.

She busied herself cutting the iced sponge cake into portions and let her mind roam back to the previous Monday evening.

She'd had a great time. Nearly never went, she mused, not even ready when Vera and her husband Fred had called for her. Well, that wasn't strictly true. For an hour or more she had deliberated over what she would wear, racking her brains as to how to do her hair.

She had finally decided to sweep the sides up and roll the top high, clipping it all in place. Then, after all that effort, she had decided she didn't like it one bit and had torn out the hair clips and brushed it all out shaping it into the french pleat that she normally wore when she was going out.

After that, she had put on her best dress which was a light navy blue, had a tight-fitting bodice, long sleeves and a flimsy skirt that fell in folds to below her knees. Then she had stood in front of the mirror and in some exasperation had made up her mind not to go.

She didn't have a decent coat, not a coat that she could wear over this dress. She couldn't go without one because the evenings were drawing in and it would probably be quite chilly by the time they were ready to come home.

'Ida, come on! Fred's kept the car running, we don't want to be late.' How well she remembered Vera calling up the stairs. She had swung the coat around her shoulders and clutching the lapels, had run downstairs to find that Vera was already back in the car and that Fred was standing on the pavement holding the door open for her to get into the back.

'What kind of music did they play?' Iris asked as she took away the plate that Joanna had eaten tinned salmon, cucumber and tomatoes from and changed it for a clean one.

'Oh,' Ida sighed and Iris turned to look at Alan. They both grinned as his mother almost sang, 'It was my type of music. Music that you could really dance too. Music from the fifties.'

'A big band, was it then?' Alan couldn't keep the chuckle from his voice.

'You, my son, are asking for a clip round the ear,' Ida told him in no uncertain terms.

John nudged Joanna. 'Nanna's going to give our Dad a whack.'

'What for, Nan?' Joanna quibbled, 'Dad only asked you if you danced while a big band played.'

The three adults had the grace to look sheepish.

'Because, my love, your father knows full well that it was a dance school that I went to, not a dance. It was held in a very large room, there were lots of very nice people there and the music we danced to was from gramophone records, great love songs from the 1950s hit parade.'

Joanna covered her mouth with her hands to smother her giggles. Her parents laughed outright and John merely grimaced, saying, 'Eeh, did you get all romantic, Nan?'

Even Ida had to laugh. 'Fill their cups up, Iris, and cut that fruit cake, I'll go and fetch the trifle.'

As Ida left the room she was saying to herself, 'My grandchildren are too knowing for their own good. Talk about out of the mouths of babes an' sucklings, 'cos that was exactly how I did feel. And who wouldn't feel romantic – listening to the dreamy sounds of Perry Como, Dean Martin, Nat "King" Cole and the happy songs of Connie Francis and Rosemary Clooney?' And there had been that nice chap, Mike Moffett. He'd danced with her several times.

As if Iris had been reading her thoughts, she watched her mother-in-law set the large bowl of trifle down and go back out to the kitchen to fetch the sweet bowls, before asking, 'Did you find yourself a partner, Mum?'

Ida let her eyes roam around the table, settling on her eldest son. 'Yes I did,' she said indignantly, 'And very nice he was too.'

'I'm pleased for you, Mum,' Alan said, doing his best to keep a straight face.

At the age of nine, John was forever asking questions and now he faced his grandmother and quite seriously asked, 'Did he come up to you and say, "Please may I have this dance?"'

'Well, no, John, it didn't 'appen exactly like that.'

'So what did he say? I bet it was something daft.' stated John.

'Or sloppy,' Joanna giggled again.

'Stop pestering your Nanna and eat your tea,' their mother implored.

'Oh crumbs, I can see I've started something,' Ida was grinning broadly.

'Keep quiet then an' I'll tell you 'ow I met me first partner. Peggy Spencer said we were going to do the Paul Jones, 'cos it got everyone going and we all got to dance with each other.'

'Nan,' Joanna's eyes were wide as her little hand plucked at her grandmother's sleeve, 'I don't know what the Paul Jones is.'

Ida patted her head, 'Course you don't, luv, but I'm just about to tell you.'

She took a deep breath and gave her son a look that defied him to make any more sarcastic remarks.

'Everyone gets on the floor, men form one circle, ladies another, you all hold hands and kind of trot around, each circle going in a different direction, men facing the ladies.

255

It's kind of like ring-a-ring of roses. When the music stops, the person opposite to you becomes your partner. The tune changes and this time it was the Gay Gordons. I told this chap I couldn't do that. Know what he said? Neither can I, that makes two of us! Anyway, we managed somehow and after that we were good friends.'

When the laughter had died down, Alan wiped his hand across his eyes and said to his mother, 'So you're going to go again.'

Ida winked at her grandchildren, 'Let's see 'im try an' stop me. I'll be on the telly in *Come Dancing* before you know it.'

Ida stood at her front gate seeing Iris, Alan and the children off.

Joanna hung back. 'Nan, will you tell me what happens at the dance school when I see you next time?'

'Did I promise I would?' asked Ida.

'Well, you didn't exactly promise but you will won't you, please?'

'Yeah, course I will, my luv, an' if me partner wants to put me on his big white 'orse an' carry me off I'll tell 'im I can't go 'cos I wouldn't leave my lovely grandchildren.'

'D'yer mean that, Nan?'

'Cross me 'eart an' 'ope t'die.'

'That's all right then because I would miss you ever so much. So would John. He would, you know.'

'Give us another hug now then.' Ida held her arms wide and Joanna wrapped her own little arms around her grandmother's waist. 'I'll see you soon pet, be a good girl.'

Ida waited until Alan's car had turned the corner before she went back inside the house and closed the door.

The living room seemed depressingly empty. She felt lonely. She even felt like crying. She wouldn't though, she would busy herself clearing up and making the place look tidy again. She laughed as she thought about the way Alan had teased her. All right for him. He led a full and busy life. Iris was a lovely girl, an ideal wife and those two kids of theirs were a joy to behold.

Oh, come on, she chided herself, don't start feeling sorry for yourself. Life is a helluva lot more interesting since you've started working at Hemmings the Bakers.

'Sides, now she had something else to look forward to. Dancing lessons! At my age? Then again, hardly a soul that had been at Peggy Spencer's had been all that young. Most were in their late forties and fifties. Some were even older and so she wasn't complaining. Quite the reverse. It was extraordinary really, just how she and Mike Moffett had hit it off right from the word go.

Over the past week she had thought about him a great deal. Even when they'd been busy at the bakers he'd never been completely out of her mind. After all, he had partnered her for most of the of the evening after the Paul Jones.

She could easily picture him. He had told her he was a widower and that he earned his living as a London docker, and that was exactly what he looked like. Not over-tall compared to her brothers but a good three inches taller than herself, thickset and broad as they come, with a ruddy complexion. His hair was still dark with only a sprinkling of grey; his eyebrows bushy and his deepset brown eyes were merry.

Off the dance floor he seemed rather awkward, never knowing where to put his hands – hands that were very large, the backs covered with dark hairs and which showed every sign of hard work.

Once the music started he changed completely. He danced so lightly, wearing black patent leather shoes the like of which Ida had never seen before, and with his hand in the small of her back she felt confident as he guided her around the floor.

Yes, she liked him, she admitted as she sat down in her armchair and plumped up a cushion to put behind her back. He was a gentle man.

Next morning, being Sunday, Ida hadn't bothered to get out of bed as soon as she woke up. She had lain there reading; there was nothing important for her to get up for. In fact Sunday was the worse day of the week for her. It was the day that she felt loneliness the most.

It didn't have to be like that. Any one of her family would be only too pleased to have her for the day but she felt she shouldn't impose every week. There were times, such as today, when she had invented an excuse, telling both Jozy and Sheila that she was going out.

She closed her book and looked at the clock on her bedside table. Half past nine. She was becoming a lazy old woman, she told herself as she got out of bed.

An hour later, she had bathed and dressed, opened all the windows, put a duster around the furniture in the front room, and eaten her breakfast: a pot full of tea, toast and marmalade.

Sitting over her third cup of tea and reading the paper which had been delivered probably before seven that morning, she heard a car draw up outside. There was not time for her to wonder who it was, for at that moment she heard her front gate open, footsteps on the path and then the doorbell ringing insistently.

She heaved herself out of her chair and walking along her hallway called out, 'All right, all right, I'm coming, give me 'alf a chance.'

Pulling open her front door her eyes widened in amazement as she saw Jack Dawson and his son Danny standing there.

'Well, well, well, I am 'onoured.'

Jack gathered her into his strong arms and lifted her until her feet cleared the ground. Planting a kiss on her cheek he whispered, 'Ida, dear, you'll never know how much I've missed you. How are you? What have you been doing with yourself?'

Danny grabbed his father by the arm and practically pulled him and Ida apart. 'Give my Nan a chance, all those questions, can't you wait till we get inside?'

Ida's face had lost most of its colour and her hands were visibly shaking as she stared at Danny. He was gorgeous. Grown taller than his father, still with those enormous twinkling brown eyes and dazzling teeth. His tanned skin giving him that continental look. Dressed in a grey suit he was as spruce as a new pin.

Who'd have thought he would turn out like this?

'Come here,' Danny said, pulling Ida towards him. He kissed her cheek, then her forehead, brushed her hair over with one hand, while still holding her tight with his other hand.

Ida laughed despite the fact that she was getting worried because they were still standing on her front path for all the street to see. 'Let's get you inside,' she pleaded.

'Not before I tell you that I still think you are bloody lovely and that I'm lucky to have you for my Nan.'

Jack grinned at her and said in his best imitation of a posh voice, 'There you are, Ida. You have to agree that private schooling has done a good job on my son. Taught him to swear lovely.'

All three laughed together loudly; Ida's laugh telling them how thrilled she was to see them both.

She turned back to Jack, kissed him and said seriously, 'Thanks, luv, for bringing him 'ere today. Now will you please come indoors and let me sort out something for your dinners?'

They entered the house and as Ida opened the door to the front room, Danny spoke. 'You aren't getting anyone anything, Nan. All you're going to do is go upstairs put on your Sunday best, and me and Dad are taking you out for the day. We are having lunch at a river-side hotel. How does that sound?'

By the time they arrived in Kingston, the Griffin Hotel was filling up with guests for Sunday lunch.

'We'll have a drink first,' Jack decided, 'there's no need to hurry, our table is booked for one o'clock.'

Jack went to the bar and Danny took Ida's arm and led her out to sit in the large conservatory. The view, for Ida, was fantastic.

Kingston upon Thames was fairly close to Tooting but it was very rarely that Ida had been here: once or twice to the open market, never to sit beside the Thames and watch the river steamers glide by on their way to Windsor.

'Nan, Dad is signalling, what would you like to drink? Gin and orange or gin and lime?'

'I'd rather have a whisky and dry ginger, if you don't mind.'

'Nan, you could ask for the earth and I would try and get it for you. I won't be a moment.'

Left alone, Ida started to dream. The sloping lawn gleamed with the September sunshine; clouds of midges danced above the dark river. The whole place was alive with people out to enjoy themselves, have a nice lunch, share good company. It was a real treat for her to be part of all this.

'Here we are.' Jack set a glass down in front of her. 'Do you want some olives?'

Ida shook her head. 'No thanks. Is the dining room very grand?'

Jack looked at Danny and they both grinned.

'Not nearly grand enough for you, Nan. Besides, the old man worked here at one time, didn't you Dad? So it can't be that good. By the way, Dad still gets preferential treatment so you can ask for whatever you like.'

'I think we'd best be going in.' Jack took the empty glass out of her hand and set it down on the table. 'Ready?'

Ida hesitated at the entrance to the large dining room, then the head waiter came towards them with a flourish.

'Good afternoon. Mrs Wilcox, isn't it? Jack told me when he booked a table. I've put you by the window, thought you'd like the view. I'll bring you the menu.' To Jack he added, 'Tony will bring the bottles you ordered, Jack.'

When he had gone, Ida sat back in her chair and looked about her in amazement.

Danny, watching her face, was grinning broadly.

'What treatment,' Ida breathed. 'Does your father always get looked after like this?'

'Usually, in places where he is known. I remember you saying once that people either loved my dad or they hated him on sight. In the hotel trade I've found that he is greatly respected. Mind you, Nan, it's got a lot to do with the fact that when all the guests have gone, being head chef he will emerge from the kitchen with a bottle of brandy, and he and a few of the top staff will sit drinking into the small hours, putting the world to rights.'

'Watch it, son, don't run me down to your Nan, she knows how much I love her and always will.'

Ida felt herself blush. She knew Jack wasn't giving her a load of flattery – he meant what he said.

It was Jack that ordered for the three of them. Course after course. Each one delicious. Waiters whisking away their empty plates. Other waiters poured their wine.

Jack raised his glass 'Your good health, Ida. We don't see enough of you.'

The wine was light and cool and fresh. Ida had thought she wouldn't like it, but she was enjoying it very much.

It was half past two before they finally left the dining room and Danny, putting his arm around Ida's shoulders said, 'I have to go, Nan, I'm working tonight.' He looked at his watch. 'A mate of mine is picking me up in Market Square in about twenty minutes.'

'Oh,' Ida touched his cheek with her fingers. 'I'm so proud of you, luv.'

'And I'm proud of you, Nan. I often think of when you and I told each other that we were bloody lovely.'

'Oh, Danny! Fancy you remembering that! Do you bear any grudges?'

'None what so ever, Nan. After all, I've always had my Dad. Poor Ruby was left with no one. Now I'm not leaving you with that long face, so smile and give me a few kisses.'

'First, young man, tell me what you do for a living.'

'I told you when I last saw you I was at catering college. Well, since then I suppose you could say I've ridden on Dad's back. I am a chef too. Thanks to the old man, I've worked at some of the top places.'

'Good for you, son.' Ida said with great feeling. 'Don't leave it so long before you visit me again.'

'I won't, Nan. Sorry I have to dash.' He hugged her close, kissed her twice and said, 'I love you. Take care, God bless.'

And then he was gone.

Ida walked into the conservatory and sat down, Tears blurring her vision. She found herself feeling so sad. She thought about Danny for a bit.

He hadn't been happy as a small child and certainly not in the time that he lived with Ruby. Jack had been so involved in his job that the little lad had scarcely seen him. She felt such a stirring of pity inside her and her tears came trickling down her cheeks.

Poor Ruby, she had done her best. She had schemed and caused a lot of mischief in her time but it had all been geared towards one end: giving her own little boys what she considered to be a good life. She hadn't been asking for too much. Just enough to eat, new shoes and good, proper-fitting clothes on their backs. Not any old rubbish bought for pennies from a jumble sale. It also meant that Ruby didn't want their birthdays to pass by without them getting presents.

Ida sighed heavily. If perhaps Ruby had met Jack earlier in life. If her first boyfriend, Andy Morris, hadn't emigrated with his parents. If she had never got tangled up with Brian Brookshaw. If, if, if. If wishes were horses, beggars would fly.

Sometimes, in this life, things were forced on you, and the consequences could be quite horrendous.

Ida came back to the present with a start as Jack placed his hand on her shoulder.

'I've ordered coffee, it won't be long.'

Him just being there filled her heart with joy. The fact that he had always kept in touch went a long way to healing the wound that Ruby hadn't loved Danny as much as she should have done.

'Well, what do you think of him?'

'Jack, he's a credit to you. Like peas in a pod you and him are, and yet there is something so different about him.'

Jack laughed loudly, then bent his head and whispered, 'What you're saying, Ida, is that Danny has nice manners, that he's not an ignorant bastard like me.'

Now Ida laughed, 'Stop fishing for compliments! You are you, Jack Dawson, and nothing or no one in this world is ever going to change you.'

'Would you want them too? Don't you love me as I am?'

'There you go again, vain as they come, you know I think the world of you – for all your bigheadedness, I wouldn't 'ave you any other way. And Jack, today has been smashing, thank you for coming to see me and especially for bringing Danny.'

'Ida, it's been my pleasure. And as for Danny, wild horses wouldn't have kept him away.'

They drank their coffee and afterwards took a stroll along the towpath.

Now Ida was seated in the front passenger seat of Jack's car and he was driving her home. It was as if each of them knew that the subject which they'd been skirting around finally had to be broached. They both spoke at the same time.

'Ida—'

'Jack—'

'You first,' Jack insisted.

'All right. Tell me about your new wife. Are you happy?'

'Her name is Marion, and yes, I suppose you could say we are happy.'

'You don't sound too sure.' Ida was curious. 'Does Marion have any children?'

'No, no children. Marion works, she is a career lady.'

'And you don't mind?'

'I've accepted it now. We've a nice home, we share a lot of interests.'

'And Danny?'

'Danny has hardly ever lived at home. At first he went to boarding school, then catering college, now he has his own flat.'

'Don't you see much of him then?'

'Oh yes, don't get me wrong, Ida. Marion makes him very welcome. He often drops in with his friends. But most of the time there is just the two of us.'

Ida had suddenly gone very quiet. She hadn't altogether liked what she had been told.

'My turn is it now?' Jack had drawn up at a set of traffic lights that were showing red. He took one hand from the steering wheel and placed it over Ida's. 'D'you mind if I ask you about Ruby?'

'No. I knew you would.'

'Well?'

'Rough for her at first, as I've told you before, now I feel she is coping much better. She's no longer an air hostess.'

The lights changed and Jack drove on, concentrating on the traffic for a few minutes.

'Why did she change her job? Or doesn't she go to work now?'

Ida smiled. 'Jack, I can read you like a book. What you're really asking me is, has Ruby got married again, and the answer is No. She lives and works up in Scotland now. Don't look so flabbergasted, it was a shock to me too.'

'Phew! I just can't picture our Ruby shut away in the wilds of Scotland.'

Ida laughed this time. 'Me neither to begin with, but she seems to have taken to the life well an' truly. She sounds really happy when she telephones me.'

'I'm glad. I really am. What does she talk about?'

'Lots of things.'

'Did you tell her about me and Danny?'

'Yes.'

'What did you tell her?'

'That you live in the West Country, that you'd remarried, that Danny had been to catering college. I also told her that you had offered to come to London and take me back to have a holiday with you.'

Jack sighed softly. 'What was her reaction to that?'

'She told me I should have accepted the invitation.'

'Did she?'

'Yes.'

'Life was rotten to Ruby, wasn't it? I hope she does find happiness. She didn't deserve what happened to her.'

Ida could sense the sympathy and understanding in Jack's voice and she knew there was nothing else left for either of them to say.

Then before she realised what was happening, they were driving through Wimbledon and she was nearly home.

They got out of the car, to stand facing each other by her front gate.

'I don't know when I'll be able to get up to see you again, Ida.'

'Aren't you coming in for a cup of tea?'

'Afraid not, much as I'd like to. I'm driving home tonight, don't want to leave it too late.'

'All right, lad. I think of you often, living within the sight and sound of the sea. Give me a ring when you get a moment.'

Jack didn't answer; he merely took Ida into his arms and held her close. Then seconds later he very gently kissed her, got back into his car, raised his hand in a salute and moved off.

Just think, she told herself, Jack could so easily have been my son-in-law.

She shook her head as she put her key into the lock. God certainly worked in a mysterious way. There were times when this life was impossible for anyone to fathom out.

Chapter Twenty-one

IAN MCKENZIE WAS BACK in Scotland and Muir House had come alive again. Even the dogs had taken to coming in to the great hall and flopping down in readiness to go walking with their master.

It was the beginning of November and the weather had changed dramatically. First off, it had rained a steady downpour for three whole days. Now, thank God, it was dry but the wind was bitter, nevertheless Ruby was determined to get out of the house and to get some fresh air into her lungs.

Since Ian had returned he had seemed different. When they met for meals it was as if he was shy, but how could that be? He was the Laird, master of all he surveyed. He was friendly, talkative at times, always making sure that he stood until both she and Catherine Patterson were seated. Praise for the meal was always offered to Catherine. Mainly, Ruby told herself, it was his upright, soldierly appearance that was off-putting.

Ruby stood at the window, watching Ian leave the house

and set out walking, his stick in his hand, his dogs at his heels. Suddenly he stopped in his tracks and she saw, rather than heard, Ian order the dogs to drop and stay where they were. The dogs whined and then lay quietly as their master walked back towards the house.

Ruby, thinking that Ian had forgotten to tell her something that he wanted done, walked to the front door and stood waiting for him.

'Did you forget something?' she asked.

'No. Would you like to join me? It's not a bad day, we could go over the moors or down to the beach.'

Ruby hesitated but he gave her a smile and it was a smile that lit up his features.

'You'll need to give me ten minutes,' Ruby said.

'I haven't a mortal thing to do this morning except please myself. And the dogs,' he laughed and nodded to where they lay.

Ruby turned and almost ran upstairs to wrap herself up warm.

The beach at Queensferry was deserted. It was high tide and what with the roar of the sea and the whine of the wind it was impossible for them to carry on a conversation.

Ian was wearing what he always wore when walking his dogs, heavy corded trousers, a thick top coat and a high polo neck jersey.

Ruby's outfit was colourful and Ian McKenzie was telling himself that she looked no more than a young lassie. Ruby's choice of clothes, the ones she had bought since coming to Scotland, were vastly different to those which she had worn in London.

Today she had on her favourite tweed suit; her hat, scarf and gloves had all been made for her by Catherine.

Colourful was putting it mildly. Worked in a clever pattern of Fair Isle, Catherine had used every bright colour of the rainbow.

The bobble hat was pulled well down over her ears and the long scarf wound twice around her neck. Brogue shoes and thick stockings completed the outfit.

Even Ruby had to sometimes smile when she viewed herself in the mirror. Not exactly Tooting attire, she would murmur to her reflection.

Heads down they struggled across the sand, the dogs frolicking well ahead. The sea was rough, rollers were crashing in, wheeling seagulls added to the noise and Ian had to make signs to let her know that if they continued they would be cut off by the tide.

Turning round they were now head-on to the wind and soon Ruby was beginning to flag. By the time they reached the dunes she was glad to clutch hold of the clumps of coarse grass and that way help to pull herself up. When they finally came across a sheltered hollow Ruby was absolutely gasping for breath and she was thankful to sink down on her bottom and get away from the worst of the wind.

Ian lay back on his elbows and after a bit he put his hand in his pocket and pulled out a thick bar of chocolate. He broke it in half, handing one piece to Ruby.

'We'll be glad of a hot drink when we get back, meanwhile that will help to sustain us.'

Ruby smiled her thanks and bit greedily into the chocolate.

If anything the wind was worse, truly a gale was blowing now, as they trudged back to Muir House. They were met at the entrance by Catherine Patterson.

Catherine's looks never altered. All her clothes were

classics. Ageless. She stood watching them approach, her hands folded across her stomach, looking as if she was part and parcel of the building – which to Ruby she was.

Without Catherine for company she never would have stayed, but she was awfully glad that she had. This place, Muir House and its large estate had taken hold of her and held her fast. She loved it with a passion beyond reason, seeing that she had been born in smoky south London.

She dreaded to think of the day that, for whatever reason, she would have to pack her case and leave this wonderful place. There were days when she would take a tour through the rooms, astonished always at the high ceilings and great old fireplaces, the huge windows which looked over the estate with its colourful heathers and wild bracken. Sadly most of the reception rooms were not used now.

'Get yourselves indoors, a body could be swept away out there,' Catherine ordered when they were still yards away. 'I've banked up the fire, I'll bring you hot soup as soon as you get out of those coats and boots.'

Ruby didn't sit in a chair, she sank down on the hearthrug in front of the roaring fire, grateful to get the weight off her feet.

Looking up at Ian she said, 'Are you staying here? You must be ready for something hot.'

For a moment she thought he was going to shake his head, but he took off his heavy coat. Then he reached for an armchair and a round table, dragging them both nearer the fire, and settled himself down.

Catherine came back, setting a tray down onto the table. In front of Ian she placed a big bowl of steaming soup, telling him to help himself to a hot roll and the butter in the brown dish. She gave a smaller bowl to Ruby and told her the same. Then she bustled away saying over her shoulder that she had a batch of bread rising that needed to be got into the oven.

They ate in silence until their bowls were empty and they were both feeling much warmer.

'Are you glad you're going home for Christmas?'

The question came totally out of the blue and took Ruby by surprise.

'I'm not sure. Can't make up my mind,' she told him.

'You will come back?'

'Yes, but I don't know how long I will be gone.'

'You'll be here for Hogmanay?'

He was very close to her. Ruby lowered her eyes and he could see her thick, fair lashes. Then he heard her whisper, 'I've got to get through Christmas first.'

He made no answer and after a while she looked up at him. He thought her eyes were like those of a frightened child.

He had no idea as to what was distressing her. Why should Christmas be such a sad occasion? Because that was what it was going to be for Ruby. He could tell just by looking at her face that sad memories were flooding back.

He never quite knew how it happened. He stood up, took hold of her hands and gently pulled her to her feet, then slowly he wrapped his arms around her slim body and drew her close.

Ruby resisted, but only for a moment. He was holding her, no longer sitting a couple of yards away, but really close, so close that she could hear the thumping of his heart. Her face was pressed into his shoulder, she could smell the salt of the sea on his jersey and suddenly she felt safe.

'Oh Ruby . . .' It was a whisper, nothing more.

Several minutes ticked by and neither of them moved. Ruby was saying to herself, I never knew, I never even thought I was capable of having so much feeling for anyone, not like this, not since the twins died.

She would have been very surprised had she been able to read Ian McKenzie's thoughts at that moment, for they were very much like her own.

Gently Ian put her from him. He pulled another chair up to the hearth and guided her into it, and only then did he settle himself back down opposite to her.

The look they gave each other spoke volumes.

'A trouble shared,' Ian ventured, 'I am a very good listener and it breaks my heart to see you looking so sad.'

The urge to tell him came strongly to Ruby. If only she could bring herself to do so. To share with another person the horror of having seen her Joey and Lenny struck down by that lorry that lovely sunny day in August, when she and her mother were going to give them ice-cream and then take them up onto the common and let them have a boat out on the lake.

She had stood there, on the opposite side of the road, and watched it happen. The screams that wouldn't come out of her throat had almost choked her. Joey hadn't been killed outright. She'd held him in her arms, covered in his blood. She prayed to God to let him live, but no. Lenny had died instantly, but that wasn't enough. God had taken both of them.

This was the nightmare she had lived with for so long.

From the day after they had buried them – the day that she had walked out of her mother's house and made her way through life entirely on her own – she had discussed Lenny and Joey's deaths with no one. Not a living soul. Except her mother.

Funny, she'd got on so very much better with her mum since she'd left London. It had started with just letters. Then she had been brave and started to use the telephone. Confiding, talking for ages, telling her fears, explaining her guilt. Suddenly the twins were no longer a taboo subject, not between her mother and herself.

It eased her heartache to hear Ida tell her how she, and yes, Maggie too, tended their grave. Would she ever have the courage to go there one day? Maybe.

Suddenly she was telling Ian why Christmas was such a painful time. Why at this time of the year she couldn't go near a toy shop. Why at Christmas she felt even more lonely. She should have a family of her own, two grown up sons. Instead for the past thirteen years she had hidden herself away. Done her best to ignore the festive season.

Only this year her mother had wrested a promise from her to go home for the holiday. She was dreading it.

Briefly she told Ian the outline of her nightmare. His lips pressed together in a thin white line but he remained silent. Two boys! Both killed on the same day!

Ian McKenzie felt an lump rise in his throat as he listened to her talk. No wonder he often caught that sad faraway look in her eyes.

Once again he couldn't have said how it happened, but he was kissing the top of her head. Holding her closer. Comforting her.

'Poor Ruby. My poor Ruby.'

She turned her face away, pressing her cheek against the sleeve of his jersey.

Minutes passed before he felt her drawing away. The moment was over. Still his heart continued to thump.

'Ruby, think of how much your family love you, of how much they will be looking forward to seeing you. How it must have hurt them that you have stayed away for so long.' Even while he was talking he was realising just how much he would miss her.

Ruby took a deep breath. 'I know. And it will be great to see all of them.'

Ian took her hand between both of his. 'Well, promise me one thing, you'll do your best not to be too sad.' Then before she had time to answer, he said, 'Oh, sorry, I need another promise.'

'What?' She hadn't understood.

'Two more, in actual fact. One, that you'll take great care of yourself and two, that you'll make sure you are back here for Hogmanay.'

For answer she returned the pressure of his hand. She wasn't so sure about the not being sad part, but she had every intention of coming back to Scotland before the old year was out. Wild horses wouldn't keep her away.

Chapter Twenty-two

'So what do you think then, Mum? Make it about three or four o'clock. Let everyone have their Christmas lunch in their own houses and then come to the club for the rest of the afternoon and evening.'

Ida looked from Alan to Norman. 'That's fine by me. I think it's good of you both to close the club that day so's the family can have a good old get-together. I'm really looking forward to it.'

Her two sons grinned, and Alan said, 'What you're so made up about, Mum, is that our Ruby is coming home.'

'Yeah, well, course I am. But I know full well the kind of do that you're planning an' I also know it must be gonna cost you a small fortune. Bert tells me you've got Father Christmas planned with loads of presents for the kids.'

Norman lit a cigarette and pulled hard on it, then, his eyes twinkling, he muttered, 'That's nothing to what we've got planned for the adults.'

His brother caught on to what he was doing. 'That's

right, Mum. For the men we've got girls coming, some in wonderful costumes and some with hardly any clothes on at all.'

'What? You'd better be joking, my lad.'

Norman took up the teasing. 'Oh, we haven't forgotten you women. Tarzan-types we thought for you lot. You know, big, brawny and wearing nothing but a spotted loincloth.'

Ida cut him off impatiently by swiping him around the head with a tea towel. 'That's enough from the pair of you.'

'All right, Mum, only teasing. We promise everyone will have a great time and no expense will be spared.'

'I know that. As sons go, you're not so bad,' she paused and now her voice changed, 'Do me one favour, keep an eye on ye sister. It's bound to be hard for her, facing everyone after all this time.'

'Everyone will watch out for her, Mum.' Alan assured her.

'It's not that,' she persisted, 'It's how's Ruby going to feel when all her nieces and nephews are running around.'

'Mum! Will you please stop meeting trouble before it's even got a foot in the door? I've spoken to Ruby on the phone. So has Alan. Maybe she was – and still is – a bit apprehensive, but she knows what's she's doing. We should have encouraged her to come home a long time ago. Still, don't let's keep raking up the past. We are all going to have a wonderful family Christmas. We'll remember lots of things from the past but we won't allow them to spoil what we have.'

Alan nodded his agreement, and then started to quietly speak. 'Mum, you've known enough poverty, so has most

278

of our relations. Now, we've got it made. So how about we all work together to make this a really good holiday for everyone?'

He was right about the poverty, Ida reflected ruefully. Many a Christmas she'd had to wait until the Fountain pub paid out its loan club before she could think about buying her three children any presents. Any big present she'd had to order well in advance, have it put by and pay off the cost at a shilling a week.

That thought jogged her memory. 'Isn't it about time for the club to come out?' she asked.

'Tomorrow night. Always three weeks before Christmas. Be a busy night up the Fountain tomorrow.'

Norman stubbed out his cigarette and winked at his brother. 'I think our Mum isn't at all well. We'd best be making a move, bruv.'

'What d'ye mean, Norman? There's nothing wrong with me. I'm as fit as a fiddle.'

'Perhaps you're just tired, is that it?'

'Look 'ere, son, if you've got something to say then come straight out with it 'cos I ain't got a clue as t'what you're on about.'

Norman grinned. 'We've been here now for just over an hour and you haven't even put the kettle on, let alone offered to feed us.'

'Perhaps she's in love,' ventured Alan, 'Did you know, Norm, our Mum's got a serious dancing partner? Told my kids a while back that she's gonna be on the telly.'

'Stop it.' protested Ida. 'I don't know what I could 'ave been thinking about. Well, that's not true 'cos I do. All I've 'ad on me mind for ages is our Ruby coming 'ome. I'll get the frying pan out right now, I've some lovely rashers of bacon.'

'Thank God for that!' Alan pulled a face. 'You've managed to get her moving. Come on, least we can do is lay the table while our Mum prepares the feast.'

Ida pushed her hair back from her forehead as she took herself off out in to the kitchen, thinking, Oh, it is going to be a lovely Christmas this year. All her three children would be around her, plus her grandchildren, John and Joanna, Anne, Roy and Garry, not to mention all the rest of the brood.

Please God, don't let anything go wrong, she prayed as she stabbed at the sausages with a fork and put tomatoes under the grill.

Fancy her forgetting to offer to feed her sons! It wasn't often she had the chance to cook for anyone other than herself.

''Ave you laid that table?' she called out sharply, ''cos this lot is nearly ready to eat.'

Saturday and the air was full of excitement. Loans clubs all over London had paid out and folk were dead ready to spend their savings.

Jozy, Sheila and Ida had had an early breakfast and set off together, armed with long lists of what they were going to buy as presents. Much had been bought over the past two months but Christmas wouldn't be Christmas if they didn't visit the open-air markets and haggle over prices for little things to be used as stocking fillers.

The streets were dark, the sky hadn't lightened at all today, maybe snow was on its way. None of them could remember a white Christmas but they agreed the Cavalier Club, being almost on Tooting Bec Common, would be a smashing place to be in if it did snow.

Mr Hemmings had let Vera have last Saturday off to do her shopping and this Saturday it was Ida's turn.

All three of them were muffled in long coats, hats, scarves and gloves. Loaded with bags, Sheila asked, ''Ave we finished? 'Cos anyway I think it's time we rested our feet.'

'Cor, that's the best suggestion I've heard all morning; my feet are bloody freezing,' Jozy complained.

'I'm all for 'aving a bite to eat,' Ida agreed, 'where shall we go?'

'Pie an' eel shop will be packed,' Sheila moaned, 'but we could go down Selkirk Road and if we can't get in to 'Arrison's, we can go further along to Mario's. He does a fair old fry-up, if ye don't fancy Italian. What d'ye think?'

Heads tucked well into their mufflers, they all agreed and turned their footsteps towards food and warmth.

Sheila was right. The pie shop was packed to the doors and a queue had formed outside.

Pushing open the door to Mario's, the steam hit them in the face. They had to make their way right to the back of the shop before they found an empty table.

Empty wasn't the right word. Two men and a woman were just leaving, the table was a mess. Dirty plates, smeary sauce bottles and stained teacups didn't look all that inviting. All three wrinkled their noses.

'I'm coming, I will soon fix that for you.' Mario's daughter, Victoria, smiled broadly at them as she cleared the dirty crockery onto a tray and wiped vigorously at the table top with a very hot cloth.

'One moment – I dry the table. I just get a towel.'

'Doesn't she look pretty?' Sheila remarked as they

seated themselves down and stowed their bags beneath the table.

Jozy and Ida had to agree. The young girl had blue-black hair that reached half way down her back, and was tied with a thick scarlet ribbon. The overall she wore was spotless, its whiteness all the more pronounced against her dark skin.

'One thing about these Italians,' Jozy mused, 'They get the whole family involved, no relying on outside staff for them. I bet if we were to go out the back to their kitchens we'd see mother and father doing their bit.'

'Grandparents an' all, I'll be bound,' Ida told them. 'In fact, I've seen them before now.'

Once settled with larged mugs of tea they decided the wait had been worth it when Victoria placed a steak plate, that was almost as big as a meat dish, in front of them. Mixed grill and chips.

The portions had been so generous that none of them managed to eat it all but each had a jolly good try and felt a whole lot better for it.

'You like a sweet?' Victoria smiled as she took away their plates.

'Oh, we couldn't,' they sighed. 'Just another large tea each please.'

Hands clasped around a thick mug, Jozy said, 'Good pay out at the club wasn't it?'

'Yes,' Ida agreed. 'More than I expected.'

'Personally, I can never see how it works out. You know, why the amount differs each year.' Sheila said and she was quite serious.

'What! After all these years?' Jozy exclaimed in disbelief. 'You must know it's t'do with the loans. The more that is borrowed, the more interest is paid back and the club 'as more to pay out.'

'Yeah, I suppose so. But then I never 'ave a loan. I pay my five bob for ten shares every week for fifty weeks an' that's it.'

'Come off it, Sheila,' Ida cried. 'If we all just paid in twenty-five bob for each sixpenny share, that would be all we get out. Jeff must 'ave loans out.'

'Course he does, but I don't.'

Jozy and Ida burst out laughing.

'Some folk borrow the first week the club starts, to go to the January sales. Jeff borrows on your shares sometimes during the year. For every pound that is borrowed the club takes back twenty two shillings at a shilling a week. Got it now?' Ida asked.

'Yeah suppose so. Takes longer to save it than it does t'spend it though, don't it?'

Again Jozy and Ida laughed. 'Come on let's go 'ome before you 'ave us all in tears.' Jozy muttered.

The weather had got worse. It wasn't quite snowing, it was more like sleet that stung their cheeks as they made their way down Garrett Lane, battling against the high wind.

Hardly had they turned into Fountain Road when they heard the commotion. They stopped dead in their tracks, smiled at each other and in unison said, 'The Morgans are 'aving a go again.'

They quickened their steps.

'Wonder what's up with old Reggie now?' Sheila sighed as they approached the small gathering of women outside number seventeen.

Ida's face was aching with the cold and her hands were frozen. All she wanted to do was get on home and get into the warm. They had to stop as the pavement was blocked.

The Morgans were well known in the street. Nothing better to do than watch other peoples' goings on – as Ida knew only too well from when they used to waylay her when Ruby had lived locally. Jessie Morgan often found out what Ruby had been up to before Ida herself did.

There were times though when she found herself feeling sorry for Mrs Morgan. Her old man never seemed to have a job and although she knew that Jessie Morgan was about fifty-five years old she often looked nearer seventy.

The crowd parted and Sheila shouted out in horror, 'Oi, you bugger! You can't bash 'er about like that.'

Before Jozy or Ida had a chance to stop her, Sheila had thrust her shopping bags at them and was rearing up the garden path shaking her fist at Reggie Morgan and yelling for him to let go of his wife.

Sheila was well known for her loud mouth. When she was put out the whole world got to know about it.

Grabbing the old man by the front of his shirt, Sheila tutted loudly. 'Ain't anyone ever told you that it ain't nice to hit women?'

'She's been robbing me blind, not that it's got anything t'do with you, you interfering old bat.'

'You really expect me t'believe that?' Sheila pushed him in the chest with such force that he staggered backwards, falling heavily to the ground.

Mrs Morgan screamed, a high pitched scream that could have been heard a mile away. She bent down to help her husband up.

It was her undoing. He lashed out with his foot, his heavy boot catching her cheekbone and gashing it open, causing the blood to spurt out and run down her face.

What happened next was anyone's guess. Sheila's arms were flaying. Men had come to the rescue, picking Mr Morgan up, not very gently, it had to be said. Mrs Morgan was being led away by the neighbour from next door.

'I'll kill him,' Sheila shouted. 'You, don't stand in front of 'im. Shielding 'im ain't gonna help. He's just clouted me one and I'm gonna make mincemeat out of him.'

It was ages before it all got sorted and they were safely inside Sheila's house. Ida was bathing Sheila's face with cotton wool soaked in warm water and Dettol.

'You'll be lucky if you don't end up with a black eye for Christmas,' Ida told her, her voice full of sympathy. 'I wonder what it was all about.'

Jozy came through the door at that moment. 'Funny enough it was about the club money, as it turns out,' she said.

''Ow did you get t'find that out?' Sheila demanded of her sister-in-law.

'The missus of the Fountain is over at the Morgan's now. Said her an' her old man feel partly responsible for the fight. Going to try an' make some kind of amends, apparently.

'What 'appened was, Mrs Morgan got some loans from the club way back, and only paid the first repayment. No one bothered to tell Reggie. When it came t'the pay out, he didn't get anywhere near what he was expecting. They only gave 'im what he'd paid in. No extras. Money don't 'alf cause some problems, don't it?' Jozy finished.

'Don't know about money,' Sheila shouted, taking the pad away from her face. 'He's bloody fist ain't done my eye much good.'

Jozy couldn't look at Ida. If she had they would have both burst out laughing.

Perhaps that just might stop Sheila from rushing in both feet first in future, they thought, though it was doubtful.

Ida was praying that Sheila wouldn't end up with a black eye. Hopefully they would have plenty of things to smile about over the Christmas, without that.

After the long months of separation, Ruby was coming home.

Ida took her time over her breakfast, feeling relaxed, smiling with contentment and anticipating with pleasure the day that lay ahead.

Although Alan had asked her to go to the airport with him to meet Ruby, she had decided she would rather he went on his own. Give him a chance to have a talk with his sister.

By twelve o'clock she no longer felt relaxed. Backwards and forwards to the window, opening the front door and staring up the road, she couldn't settle. If she lit the gas under the wretched kettle just one more time the ruddy thing would boil dry.

Would Ruby turn her nose up at her old bedroom? After all she did live in a big house now. She was supposed to be staying for at least a week. Would she? Or would she pack up and clear off again when she found that life here in south London hadn't changed that much?

The doorbell ringing made her swear.

Wouldn't you know it! I no sooner get me knickers down because I'm bursting to spend a penny and they turn up.

Hurriedly she got herself up from the toilet, pulled the chain, shoved her fingers under the tap and flew down the stairs.

She couldn't get the blasted door open. Christ! I'm all fingers and thumbs.

At last! She stood on the step, a case at her feet and a bulging flight bag slung over one shoulder.

'Ruby.'

'Hallo Mum.'

Alan picked up the suitcase and walked past the pair of them into the house. Ida closed the door and held out her arms. Ruby went into them and gave her mother a kiss.

There was a tension between them but this was only to be expected, Ida told herself as she led the way through to the living room.

Alan was grinning. 'Doesn't she look great, Mum? And wait till she tells you all about Muir House and the responsible job she has. But all the same she's damn glad to be home.'

Ruby laughed gently, and her taut face suddenly relaxed.

'Listen, Alan, you told me you had loads of work to do today so let's see the back of you for now. Mum and I are going to sit down and talk ourselves silly.'

'Oh, got above yourself, have you? Well, I can take a hint. But just you remember I'm your older brother and that I shall be keeping me eye on you.'

'I'll make the tea,' Ida suggested.

'Not for me, Mum, truly I do have t'be on my way. Iris and I will bring the kids over later.'

Alan bent and kissed his mother and in a voice that was very soft he said, 'Everything will be fine, Mum. No need to treat her with kid gloves, she really is glad to be home.'

Seeing Ruby had brought back so many memories and although he wouldn't admit it to a soul, Alan had missed his young sister more than he could put into words.

'Bye, sis.' Alan hugged her close, kissed her cheek. At this point in time, his mum and his sister didn't need anyone else around. They just needed to be on their own.

Ida went through to the kitchen. Now she did need a cup of tea, badly. Through the open door she watched as Ruby took off her long smart coat, tweed, with a brown velvet collar.

She was thirty-four years old, still tiny, small-boned with a creamy fair complexion but there was a colour to her cheeks now and a shine to her hair that was swept up in an elegant style.

Suddenly Ruby kicked off her high-heeled shoes and said, 'Thank Gawd for that.'

Ida gasped. She had forgotten just how short her daughter was and she hadn't heard her speak like that for years.

Ruby caught her mother's eye and she giggled. 'I only wear flat-heeled shoes in Scotland, I'm glad to get those off. They were killing me. Oh, it is good to be home, Mum.'

Ida relaxed visibly. Everything *was* going to be all right.

As Ida came through with the tea tray, Ruby was rummaging in her flight bag and she pulled out a large flat parcel.

'This is for you, Mum. It isn't your Christmas present, it is something I saw and straight away I could see you wearing it.'

Ida carefully undid the paper, so as not to tear it. It was so pretty.

She opened out a skirt and waistcoat, and held them up as if they were precious garments – as indeed they were to her. The material was soft to the touch, the pattern warm tartan colours. There was also a long-sleeved jumper.

'That's cashmere, Mum,' Ruby told her as she shook the jumper out. 'Don't you just love the feel of it? That pale lavender colour I thought was right for you.'

Ida held the jumper against her cheek. 'I shall be afraid to wear it.'

'Nonsense. Tomorrow we'll go out and I shall make sure you wear the whole outfit.'

The smile and the look on Ida's face told Ruby that she had done the right thing. In the space of fifteen minutes, Ruby knew that she and her mother could now be real friends.

All the family had phoned and spoken to Ruby, told her they were very glad that she was home but that they were going to let her have this evening alone with her mother, give her a chance to settle in.

Both Ida and Ruby appreciated their thoughtfulness. By the time they had had their evening dinner and talked the hind leg off a donkey, they were both tired out and in need of a good night's sleep.

Ida poured hot milk into two glasses, added a generous amount of brandy and took them to where Ruby was dozing in front of the fire.

''Ere you are, luv, drink that up and get away to your bed.'

It was some time later before she herself tiptoed up the stairs to her own bedroom. Her heart had been overflowing with thankfulness. Her prayers had been answered.

Ruby had come home and there was no bitterness in either of them.

As she undressed, she heard a tap on the door. It was Ruby, looking like a lost little girl.

'You've still got your big double bed, Mum. Can I get in with you?'

Ida smiled in wonder. 'Of course you can, pet. That's what you always used to do when you were little.'

Ruby scrambled in between the covers and snuggled down. Ida got into the other side of the bed.

'Mum, I know we've been talking for hours but I still feel the urge to keep talking. Do you mind?'

'Course I don't.'

She plumped up her pillows and propped herself into a sitting position, her tiredness forgotten, and took Ruby's hand in hers.

'Remember Mum, when I wanted to emigrate with Andy Morris? I suppose every girl thinks her first boyfriend is the love of her life. I only went with Brian Brookshaw out of bravado because Andy had left me.'

'I know, luv. And at the time I did try to tell you. It was my fault though that you married him. Never mind that you were pregnant. I worried too much about what the neighbours would say.'

Ruby squeezed her mother's hand tightly. 'It were Uncle Bert and Uncle Jeff that bulldozed the wedding along. For the best reasons, though.'

'Do you regret marrying Brian?'

'Marrying him, yes. Having the twins, no. At least I did have Lenny and Joey for five years.'

'It weren't much of a life for you at that time. Struggling to keep two little boys. And Brian and his no good father on ye back all the time.'

'I know. I often think about Brian's dad. He were a dirty old bugger but I feel sorry for him. I do, ye know. Don't know where he is or if he's still alive, but he must have felt it when Brian dropped dead, just like that.'

'Don't think about things like that, Ruby, just think about the nice things. Do you remember when ye Dad first came 'ome from the War?'

'Yes, I do. All of us – you, Dad, Alan, Norman and me – went to Ravensbury Park and Dad bought us fishing nets and we caught tiddlers and brought them home in jam jars. Dad was nice, kind; he used to call me his girl and he made me laugh.'

Ida swallowed hard and blinked away the tears that were stinging the backs of her eyelids. 'Pity he died, he might have kept you out of some of the mischief you got yourself into. Remember when you worked for Mrs Morley and you gave a customer a raincoat without charging her for it?'

Ruby put her hand up to her head and groaned. 'Oh, Mum, you're not going to bring that all up again, are you? Mrs Morley had plenty of money and that woman's little boy badly needed a coat.'

Ida raised her eyebrows. 'So you felt you had to play the lady bountiful, even though the goods you were giving away didn't belong to you?'

Ruby looked at her mum and smiled saucily. 'Suppose I did have a bit of a cheek when you look at it like that.'

When they had both stopped laughing, Ida looked at her daughter, with sudden concern showing in her face.

'Ruby, I am so proud of you. You've battled your way through life. Mostly all on your own. Look at the way you live and dress now. But sometimes when I think about some of the capers you got up to, I wonder that you never ended up in Holloway Prison. All I'd really like to know is, are you happy?'

'Yes I am, Mum, and to answer the question that you're obviously afraid to ask, I am still a bit bitter over the way the twins were killed. I can't help it. I hear them cry out sometimes, I often hear them laugh.

'I picture them when I see families, little boys running to their mother when they've fallen down. I watch the mothers pick them up, fuss over them, kiss them better. I couldn't pick mine up. They were dead.'

Ruby's voice was so sad now that Ida didn't know what to do. She kissed Ruby's cheek and said, 'Try and remember all the nice times.'

Ida's kindness was her undoing. Leaning against her, Ruby began to cry, a soft sobbing sound that wrenched at Ida's heart. Ida put her arms around her, rocking her gently.

She knew that it was a long time since Ruby had been able to open up her heart like this. What could she do for her? Nothing. Only hold her and let her cry herself out. She could feel her body shuddering with each breath she fought for, and she prayed as hard as she knew how.

Inside she is still only a young girl – a girl that has lived with the nightmare of seeing her two boys killed while she had stood by helpless. All these years she had been hurting inside with never a family or friend to talk to about it. God help her find peace. All those years. All that pain. All that loneliness. Surely, Dear God, she deserves some peace of mind. Some happiness.

It was Norman who came with his car to pick them up at three o'clock on Christmas Day.

Ida was holding Ruby's arm as they walked into the

Cavalier Club. She heard Ruby give a gasp of admiration before they were surrounded by most of the family, all wanting to kiss and hug Ruby.

They had hardly got their coats off before her Uncle Bert was standing in front of her holding out a crystal glass. 'Start as you mean to go on, my darling, drink some champagne. Happy Christmas.'

'The tree looks really beautiful,' Ruby told her brothers, 'it's the biggest one I've ever seen, it must have taken hours to decorate it.'

'Don't give them the credit for that,' Rose and Iris, Ruby's two sisters-in-law laughed. 'We had plenty of help from the kids but those two brothers of yours kept well out the way.'

Both Alan and Norman grinned sheepishly.

'We held the stepladders, didn't we bruv?' Alan said turning to Norman.

'Yeah, and if I remember rightly we kept shelling out for most of those presents that are lying on the floor.'

Ida stepped forward. 'Well let's 'ope there's one or two there for you, if we ever get round to opening that lot.'

Ruby's eyes burned with tears. It was so lovely to be amongst her family again. Look at them all! She felt her two big uncles watching her and she smiled at them. They hadn't altered much; she still adored them. True, they now had lines around their eyes and mouths, and their hair had a lot of grey in it, but that happened to everyone.

'Hallo my darling.'

Ruby jumped. 'Why, Maggie! Oh Maggie, it's so good to see you.' She was drawn into Maggie's arms and held tight.

Dear God, it was lovely to see this treasured friend again

293

but the very feel and smell of her brought back so many memories – not all of them happy ones.

Ruby felt a lump in her throat. Maggie had stood by her when she had been young and done some daft things. Been there to help care for the twins, held her when Brian had lost his temper and used his fists on her. A great rush of love for Maggie washed over her.

Maggie released Ruby, holding her at arm's length, her shrewd eyes scanning her from top to toe. This lass had been hurt so much. It was a wonder that she hadn't gone stark staring mad.

'Let me look at you, you look so different, quite the posh young lady now. Tom, come take a look at what used to be our little Ruby.'

Of course, Ruby reminded herself. Maggie Marshall was now Maggie Carter; she and Tom had got married and they lived in what she'd always known as the big house in Blackshaw Road.

Tom hugged her and kissed her cheek. He seemed to have shrunk a little, his hair was very wispy but his broad smile still showed a lovely set of his own teeth.

Maggie was a marvel. She must be in her late seventies, still had a nice figure and looking very spruce. Happiness. That's what did it. If you had a good companion, someone to share your life with, you'd got it made. These two certainly had. The look in their eyes as they glanced at each other was proof enough.

Sheila came towards her with her arms full of presents.

Maggie gave Ruby a quick kiss, saying, 'I mustn't keep you all to myself.'

'Aunt Sheila, you told me yesterday that all your presents were already in the club,' Ruby said.

'I know I did, luv, and they were – all the big ones that

is. These are just what Jozy and I 'ave wrapped up as prizes for when we play games after dinner tonight.'

Her Aunt Jozy, was now standing by her side. 'Confused by all the kiddies, are you, Ruby?' Jozy asked, kindness sounding in her voice.

'Not really, Auntie, I think I've got them all sorted.'

'Well, when everyone has arrived and got a drink we're all going to sit down around the tree and open up some of those parcels.'

Ruby watched her Aunt Jozy walk between a group of the youngsters. Poor Jozy. She too must have suffered a lot over the years. No grandchildren for her.

Then her eyes strayed to her cousin Terry and Peter Gower. For almost as long as she could remember those two had been together. Two lovely young men, always so happy in each other's company. Terry she had always adored, tall well-built like all the Simmonds, his hair a sandy colour just like Uncle Bert's used to be.

Look at those twin girls! Julie and Karen, daughters of Albie and Mary, they must be about ten or eleven years old by now. Two more girls ran up to the twins and Ruby placed them as her niece Joanna, seven, and Jodie, the clever one, daughter of her cousin Billy and his wife Linda.

All four Simmonds girls, with the same build, looks and mannerisms, Ruby decided. Funny about their unmistakable looks. It was even more noticeable in her nephews, Noman's two boys, Garry and Roy; and John, her brother Alan's eldest child.

Since having spent a couple of days with her mother – days when she had opened up her heart and talked to her Mum as she had never been able to do before – Ruby was finding that she could watch these children and feel lots of love for them without feeling that her heart was breaking.

That would have been impossible a few days before. Oh, she knew she would never get over the shock of seeing her own children die in such a cruel way. But she would like to think that she had gradually come to terms with it and that it hadn't turned her into a bitter selfish person.

She had certainly set out and braved the world. Led an entirely different life to what she would have had she stayed in London.

Was she happy now?

It was a question she couldn't honestly answer.

Alan carefully watched his sister as she stood chatting to her aunts. It came to him how much the years had changed her. When she'd been a young girl she had been truly lovely and so small that both he and Norman had always felt protective towards her. Now that youth had gone. Yet in its place was a really beautiful woman. At times a sad beauty, until she smiled, and then that rare smile would light up her face and her lovely blue eyes.

She seemed almost happy, far more relaxed than he had imagined she would be after all this time away from the family. Maybe she had found someone who could soothe away all her heartaches and fears. God, he hoped so!

The aunts moved away and the moment passed. Kids were crowding round her, she was petting Joanna and laughing at the antics of her nephews.

'Auntie Ruby, we're going to open our presents now. Come on, there's loads for you.'

Ruby's hands were held, her skirt was being tugged at and suddenly she was sitting on the carpet, facing the great tree that shimmered with tiny fairy lights and tinsel. All around her were her family, each and every one she loved and whom she knew loved her dearly.

Alan bent down and handed her a square flat parcel wrapped in red and gold paper. 'Open this one first, sis. It's from Mum, Norman and Rose, Iris and me.'

She opened it carefully. Inside was a silver frame which held a picture of Joey and Lenny which had been taken on their fifth birthday. Bright bubbly boys with such mischievous smiles. She did her best to swallow the lump that had risen in her throat as she gazed, remembering the occasion when Alan had taken this photograph.

There was also a long, slim, velvet box. She opened the clasp and gasped. Lying on the plush lining was a gold locket and chain. The locket was perfectly plain, just the initials L and J engraved on the front. Inside was a coloured miniature picture of her twins.

Ruby's eyes burned with tears as she fingered the beautiful locket with wonder.

No, she wouldn't cry. She could remember them with love and always have them near her.

'Open this one, Auntie Ruby.'

'No, Daddy said she could open mine next.'

Her sister-in-law Rose was fastening the chain around her neck. 'Leave your aunt be for a minute or two and open some of the presents she has bought for you.'

Ruby felt her mother's eyes on her and she smiled, leant across and touched her hand.

'Thanks, Mum,' she said, turning her gaze to Alan, Norman and their wives. She smiled at them all. 'How can I thank you enough?'

'Have a good Christmas,' they chorused.

Blinking back the tears she said, 'I will, oh yes, I will.'

And she meant it.

Why had she left it so long to come home? What had she been so afraid of?

This was a better Christmas than she had ever dreamt it would be.

Chapter Twenty-three

To wake up in Scotland was still unbelievable to Ruby. No noise, no traffic, no hustle or bustle. Just wonderful clean sharp air that smelt of peat and pine. Moorland, heather, horses, cattle and deer in the distance.

It seemed that in the six months Ruby had been back from having spent Christmas in London she had tried unsuccessfully to fathom out what Ian McKenzie was thinking half the time.

Hogmanay had been an experience! One she would never forget. Ruby's impression was that it had carried on for days and days. Three in actual fact.

Ian had seemed very pleased to have her back. Had himself met her at the airport.

They hadn't celebrated at Muir House as Ruby had been expecting. Two single rooms Ian had booked in an Edinburgh Hotel and there, when the festivities had begun, it had been a constant social whirl of visiting Ian's friends and what few elderly relatives he still had.

Although Ian didn't have a dark head of hair he had still

been in great demand as a first-footer and it had been the early hours of the morning before they had retired to bed.

Ruby often looked back at those three days with wonder and a great deal of pleasure. If she had drunk even half the 'wee drams' that had been pressed on her she would have ended up too drunk to walk.

Her drowsiness had gone, replaced by her usual boundless energy. She was fully awake now and raring to go. She sat up, threw back the covers, got out of bed. She pushed her feet into slippers and reached for her cotton dressing gown, pulled it on and tied the belt around her narrow waist.

Drawing open the curtains she saw that it promised to be a perfect summer's day. The sky was a clear blue, not a cloud in sight, and the rays of the sun were already bright and very warm. She crossed the hall to the bathroom, sniffing the air as she went.

Catherine, as usual, had beaten her to it. The smells drifting upstairs were of freshly baked bread and she knew that the table for breakfast would already have been laid.

Hearing footsteps below she looked down over the bannister rail and watched Ian sorting through the morning mail. He stretched his arms above his head and flexed every muscle in his strong body. Then he went with long strides towards the dining room, so tall, the wide set of his shoulders, the lift of his chin, the way he smiled.

Yesterday he had returned home having been away from the estate for two days. It appeared as if he badly wanted to tell her something as they had gone through the accounts together. Their fingers had touched, he had let his hand cover hers for a long minute; her heart had missed a beat and now, observing him without being seen, the same thing happened.

She made herself move into the bathroom, closed the door and leant against it. She took deep breaths. Her racing heart settled down.

Oh, she could cheerfully kill Ian McKenzie. He was the most unpredictable man that God ever put breath into. She never knew where she was with him. Did she want him to spell it out for her? Half of her screamed, Yes. The other half was apprehensive.

Whatever he had to say to her would almost certainly change the situation and the way things were between them now at Muir House. Did she want change? Not if it meant she had to leave here. Not if it meant that she would never again see Ian McKenzie!

There! She had admitted it to herself at last.

She couldn't analyse her feelings for this man. It had been so long since she had allowed herself to really feel anything deeply. What she did know was that her days were made brighter when he was around. His Scottish accent was like music to her ears. His touch, accidently or otherwise, sent shivers running through her. His dry sense of humour often made her smile and yes, it was exactly as Catherine Patterson was fond of saying, 'When the Laird is no around, the house is only half alive.'

Catherine and Ian had already started their breakfast when Ruby joined them. Ian stayed for only a little while, long enough to drink his cup of coffee. After that, he got to his feet, looked at Ruby and smiled.

'It's such a beautiful morning, I thought we'd give the office a miss, go for a long walk. Perhaps if I give you till eleven o'clock, you would come with me.'

'Of course, I'd love to.'

'Thank you.' He left them, stepping out through the french doors into the sunshine, whistling as he went.

Ruby's heart thumped against her ribs as she did her hair, pinning it tight so that the breeze wouldn't blow it all over the place. She chose a light-weight cardigan to drape around the shoulders of her floral summer dress and changed her sandals for a pair of lace-up canvas shoes which were a sight better because she never knew which direction Ian would take and some of the going could be a bit rough.

'My, you look right bonnie,' Catherine told her as she came down the stairs. 'Ian is ready, he's waiting for you outside.

'Thanks Catherine, you will have a rest yourself, won't you? Sit out in the garden, find a shady spot.'

'Go on with you, lass. Stop ye fussing over me. Make the most of a day like this yeself.'

'All right. Bye.'

Catherine watched them set off with conscious pleasure. Those two could be so good for each other, she mumbled as she went off to finish the coffee that no one had seemed to want that morning. Trouble is they both of them needed a push in the right direction. If they each waited for the other to make the first move they would still be dilly-dallying come doomsday.

They walked slowly, savouring the scents and sounds, pausing once for Ian to speak to one of his gillies. An hour or more had passed and it was as if they had left civilisation behind.

'Shall we have a rest?'

The sound of Ian's voice broke into her daydreaming. Not a word had passed between them for ages. Being alone with Ian gave her a safe peaceful feeling. There was no need for words.

Nodding towards a clump of thick bushes Ian said, 'That's about all the shade we shall find out here.'

Ruby nodded. She settled herself down, bare legs stretched out to the sun.

Ian took the pack from his shoulder. 'It's a safe bet to assume that Catherine has put a cold drink in here for us.'

'Among many other things.' Ruby laughed.

He rummaged, taking out glasses and a flask. 'Yes, that's right, two sandwich boxes as well. Are you hungry?'

'No – not yet anyway.'

'Here, this should be nice and refreshing.' He handed her a glass and sat down beside her.

They drank and Ruby sighed with contentment.

'Ian?'

'Hm . . .'

'Why do you never talk to me?'

He looked up sharply, and for a dreadful instant she thought she had overstepped the mark.

'Is there anything in particular that you want me to tell you?'

'No, it's just that – well, last year, before you left for India, you told me you had been divorced when you were twenty-five and that it had been a shattering experience. In all the time since, you've never broached the subject again. Each time things from the past are mentioned, the conversation is changed.'

Ian sighed heavily. 'There is a reason for that.'

'Am I allowed to ask what that reason is?'

'It's simple. Many tragic things happened in my life

303

after the divorce – things that I felt partly to blame for and also things that I'm not very proud of. There was a time when I had every intention of telling you, it just became impossible for me to do so.'

'You imagine I would think badly of you?'

'Yes and no. But more than that, I decided you'd had enough hurt in your own life without having to cope with my sadness.'

'Oh, I see. My telling you about the twins and how they died influenced your decision.'

'Yes.'

'Oh, Ian, I had no idea . . .' She shrugged her shoulders, at a loss for words.

'Ruby, I have tried so many times to tell you. I want to tell you.'

'Try telling me now.'

He hesitated, searching for the right words. 'We were both so young. Our families had wanted the match. Rosalind had been very ill but the doctors said she was better and we were married when she was just eighteen and I was twenty-one. We had a baby – a boy – born within the year. Our parents were delighted.

'We named him Jeffrey after Rosalind's father. Something was wrong. We couldn't find out what. Every specialist we took him too did tests. There was nothing to be done. He was deaf. Rosalind wouldn't accept it. She couldn't cope.

'She went back to live with her parents taking Jeffrey with her. It was a bitter separation. So much animosity. Rosalind took to drinking. We were divorced but before the decree nisi was made absolute Rosalind died.'

His words hung in silence between them. Only the sound of a bee buzzing nearby could be heard. Ruby felt that Ian badly needed reassurance, she took a deep breath before turning to him. 'I'm glad you've told me. Where is your son now?'

He leaned forward and placed his hand over her own and, for the first time since he had started to speak, he smiled. 'He's fine now. He's working in the Scilly Isles, has been for about eight months since the *Torrey Canyon* ran aground near Land's End. Do you remember? The oil pollution up and down the coast was an absolute disaster.'

Ruby nodded.

'Jeffrey is with the Royal Society for the Protection of Birds. So much wild life was damaged by the tons of oil that escaped into the sea. They need all the volunteers they can get.'

Ian paused. Ruby wondered if he was going to tell her more.

The silence lengthened until Ruby spoke. 'You must be very proud of him.'

Ian threw back his head and roared out laughing. 'I am now but it wasn't always so. When he was growing up he was the bane of my life. He was thrown out of two schools because of his disruptive behaviour. He is now well-versed in sign language and he seems to have found a niche that suits him. He will be eighteen years old in a couple of months time.'

Ruby swallowed hard. One year younger than her boys would have been. She wouldn't let that thought upset her. Ian had suffered in some ways as much as she had. Live for the present, she told herself.

She gazed at his tanned face. His eyes were closed against the glare of the sun and suddenly she was filled with love for him and now she could freely admit it. Were she to have to leave Muir House it would be the hardest thing she had ever had to do. She thought about living in London again. Tried to imagine a day when she wouldn't see him, a life without him being part of it. Impossible. It didn't bear thinking about.

Ian opened his eyes, looked into hers and instinctively knew what she had been thinking. He lifted her hand and held it against his cheek. 'You know I love you, don't you?'

'Oh, Ian.'

'I love you,' he repeated. 'I think I fell in love with you the moment you walked into my office in Manchester. You were so tiny even with your high-heels and I had an urge to ask you to take your shoes off so that I could see just how tall you were. I knew I couldn't let you go. That's why I asked you to have lunch with me.'

'I didn't know – I really didn't know . . .'

'You looked so smart, so confident and yet so sad. I wanted to comfort you, since then I always have wanted to. I've never been able to get you out of my mind. And looking back, I don't think I have tried very hard.'

He moved to sit closer to her. His arms were round her, holding her so close that she could hear the thudding of his heart. She pressed her face into his shoulder.

Was she dreaming this? She prayed that she wasn't. She drew away, her face tilted up to his, and they kissed for the very first time.

It was the same for each of them. No indecisions. The world was far away, they were floating, safe, nothing and nobody mattered except themselves.

Finally, after what seemed an age, Ian broke the silence. 'Ruby, do you love me?'

'Yes, Ian, I love you.'

He sighed and drew her closer to his side.

'I'm sorry I took so long to bring things out into the open, I was so afraid . . .' His voice faltered. 'I want you to know just how much you mean to me. Not a day has gone by since you came to Muir House but you've been on my mind. You have to believe that, Ruby.'

Ruby squeezed his hand tight. 'You've told me now, Ian. We're here together, that's enough for me.'

'For the moment maybe, but I want more. Oh Ruby, I want so much more. I want you to say that you will marry me. I want you to be with me wherever I am and wherever I go. I want to wake up and find you beside me. I want to spend every day of the rest of my life with you.'

His words were thick with emotion and for long minutes they held onto each other.

Eventually Ruby pulled her face from his jacket, but stayed leaning against his shoulder, breathing in his smell and feeling the strength of his body.

He had said he wanted to marry her! When they had left the house this morning she had been feeling very vulnerable. Now, held safe in his arms, how did she feel?

There weren't words to describe her feelings. The emotions that were running through her were too tangled and complex for her to define, so intense was this moment. It was the same for both of them.

Smiling, he said, 'I am going to get to know everything that there is to know about you. That way I shall be able to tell what will make you happy and I will do everything possible to see that you never spend a day that isn't a happy day ever again.'

Something in his voice, in those words spoken so lovingly and kindly, was just too much for Ruby.

She, a rough-edged girl from London, being asked by

Ian McKenzie to be his wife. To know the security of living at Muir House, being loved by such a man as he, spending the rest of her life with him, loving him and being loved by him. Tears sprung from her eyes and blurred her vision.

Sensing she was crying, Ian pulled her round to face him and began to kiss her, first her face then her neck, finally his lips sought hers and slowly, haltingly, their kisses grew more passionate.

When they drew apart Ruby saw Ian looking at her with such love and tenderness in his eyes, and she suddenly began to realise that what was happening was meant to be and that was good enough for her.

It was late afternoon before they turned their footsteps towards home.

'Ruby, do you want to tell me about your husband?'

Ruby looked up quickly. 'Do you want to hear about him? It was all a bit sordid.'

'Well, I've known you, what is it, nearly two years now, and in all that time you've never voluntarily mentioned him. It was the same with me and Rosalind. Perhaps we were both doing our best to blot out the past.'

Ruby knew the time had come to be honest. 'I haven't talked about Brian because that episode of my life is something I'm not very proud of. I don't come out of it very well.'

'I've told you before I am a good listener.'

'Oh, Ian, you haven't the slightest idea of the way that I lived then. You've never known poverty, probably never seen it. I'm not ashamed of having been poor, but the things I sometimes did just to get by would appal you. The couple of rooms in which Brian and I lived with our two boys, well, let's just say that your horses are housed a great deal better.'

'Did you love him?'

Ruby strove for the truth. 'I thought I did at one time. I was flattered that he picked me. He was a big good-looking lad that any girl in our school would have given her right arm to go out with. I was pregnant by him when I was barely sixteen.'

'At least he did the honourable thing.'

'To be honest, I didn't want to marry him. My uncles saw to it that I did. Neighbours and their opinions matter a lot when you live in a street of terraced houses.

'It never worked, not once the twins were born. Too much responsibility, not enough money coming in. Brian left me. Went off to work in Wales. He dropped down dead, playing football after having had far too much to drink.'

They were both silent, each busy with their own thoughts. Ian was thinking it was uncanny the similarity in the stories each of them had to tell. With all the privileges he and Rosalind had been given they had fared no better than Ruby and the young lad who had got her pregnant before they were scarcely out of school.

He sighed. Wisdom only came with age. All of them far too young to cope with their problems. There would be many a day in the future when he could open up his heart to Ruby, tell her of his escapades, how he had come close to hating his own son at one point in his life. How Rosalind had drunk herself to death.

Ruby's thoughts were also running away with her. Would all these revelations cause a rift between them? Time would tell. Should she tell Ian about Jack Dawson? And about little Danny?

At sometime, she decided, she would. Not yet. Not today. Today was a day that would be stamped on her memory for the rest of time. Today was incredible! Nothing must be allowed to spoil it.

Ruby managed a bright smile. 'Have I shocked you?'

'Oh, my darling.' He stopped walking. 'Of course you haven't shocked me. Nothing you could say or do would shock me. It all only makes me even more determined to take such good care of you and to see that you never again want for anything.'

'Catherine told me both your parents died abroad, but what about your friends? Have you given a thought to them? Will they accept me?'

'Dear God! Why do women always have to raise difficulties. Don't start worrying about silly things.' Ian felt it was important to reassure her. 'None of my friends are like that.'

Suddenly he threw back his head and roared out laughing. 'You know who your best ally in all this will be?'

'No. Am I going to need one then?'

'You've had one, almost from the moment you walked through the front door of Muir House. There isn't a force that could better Catherine Patterson. She loves you and she's been praying for me to find the courage to tell you that I love you.'

'Really? I know she and I have a love for each other but . . .' Her voice trailed off.

'I have no memory of my life without Catherine being in it,' Ian said. 'She was here before I was born. My parents travelled a lot. The estate was left in the capable hands of Jock Dunbar and the house was run by Catherine. I love her dearly. When I came home from school for the holidays I spent a lot of time with Catherine, she knows everything there is to know about me. She witnessed the madness of my marriage. She's always been there for me. Her loyalty knows no bounds. Tell you what. Let's go mad. Let's run. Burst in on her and let her be the first to hear that you have agreed to be my wife.'

Holding hands they ran like the wind. Out of breath, beads of perspiration glistening on their foreheads, they arrived at Muir House.

The front door was open wide as if the house was expecting them. Welcoming them. Waiting to be told their news.

'Catherine!' Their voices mingled ringing out loud and clear.

She came towards them. One look and she stood still. Her face broke into a broad beaming smile as she spread her arms wide and said, 'Ruby, I thank God I've lived to see this day.'

Ruby went to her and they held each other close. Ian stepped forward, his arms went around the pair of them and like three children they stayed like that for several minutes.

The sun shone through the open door. Outside the pebbled driveway was bordered by tubs of bright geraniums and colourful petunias; the lawns and terraces that led down to the stables were neat and green. Beyond were narrow paths that led through the heather covered moors and further still to where the grass was unkempt and yellow with drifts of hardy shrubs.

Scotland today was beautiful. Happiness abounded when the sun shone. But there would, from today onwards, be no less happiness for the residents of Muir House whatever the weather. The snow would come, the winds and storms would make the sea cruel but Ruby knew that she would be safe and loved from this day forth.

Sunday evening and Ida was staring at her brothers and their wives as if she were afraid they were going to fade away.

'Mum? Are you there, Mum?'

Ida settled the telephone closer to her ear. 'Yes, luv, I'm still 'ere.'

'Mum, did you hear what I told you? I want you to understand, Mum. Ian – he's the only man I've really ever loved.'

Ida let a deep breath out slowly. Ruby sounded so young and naïve. 'I can't take it all in, not in one go. Will you write me a long letter? I might be able to believe it then, if I see it down on paper.'

'Are you on your own, Mum?'

'No. No, I'm all right. Auntie Sheila and Auntie Jozy are 'ere and ye uncles. We're gonna 'ave a game of cards, or at least, we were, till you rang.'

Ruby's laughter sounded down the line. 'It's not bad news, Mother. You're suppose to be thrilled for me. Tell me aunts and me uncles, they will all be getting invitations to the wedding. Ian insists that we do everything right. Bye, Mum, you'll have your letter before the week is out.'

'Bye, luv. God bless you.'

Ida was stunned. She replaced the telephone receiver and stood staring at the wall, lost in dreams.

Jozy got to her feet and broke the spell. 'Ida?'

'Yes, I'm coming.' She walked in a daze and took her seat around the table.

'Are you all right, sis?' Bert looked so worried that Ida found herself smiling.

'Course I am. But listen to this. Christ, I don't know now whether or not she's 'aving me on.'

Sheila grinned. 'Our Ruby been getting up t'some of 'er old tricks, 'as she?'

'Oh no, Sheila, nothing like that. Ian McKenzie has asked 'er t'marry 'im!'

Ida couldn't help it. She had a sneaking feeling of triumph when she saw the look on the faces of her sisters-in-law. 'She said I've got t'tell you that you'll all be getting invitations t'the wedding.'

'You sure you got it right, sis?' It was the first time that Jeff had opened his mouth.

Ida turned to face her brother. 'Jeff, I'm not sure of anything at the moment. I'm only telling you what my Ruby 'as just told me. I wanted to ask her so many things. Like why was the wedding gonna be in Scotland an' 'ow the 'ell she thought we were all going t'get there. If it does come off, that is.'

Bert got to his feet. 'I'm going to pop over 'ome. Get the glasses out, Jozy. I'll fetch a bottle, if this don't call for a drink I don't know what does.'

'Can you see it?' Ida's voice made the men pause and the women to stare at her.

Ida looked at them all with a grin on her chubby face. 'Wait till I tell the boys their sister is gonna be married in Scotland, to a Laird.' Suddenly her voice took on a serious note. 'Can one of you tell me what that will make my Ruby?'

Bert look at his brother Jeff and they both burst out laughing. It was Jeff, the quiet one, that answered Ida. 'Sis, in my opinion, that makes our Ruby a very lucky young lady. Very lucky indeed.'

Everyone in the room laughed.

Ida was thinking to herself. Well, all I hope is that it will make her a very happy young lady and one thing I do know, all the trappings that money can buy won't mean a thing if she's not happy. If this Ian McKenzie is a good man, the right one for her Ruby to settle down with, then she would be the first one to thank the good Lord for that.

Chapter Twenty-four

IDA CLOSED HER FRONT door at ten minutes to ten. Crikey, she thought, last Monday she had been calling Mike Moffett all the names she could lay her tongue to and now here she was all dressed up like a dog's dinner because he was going to take her out for the day.

Two weeks running he hadn't come to the dance club. The atmosphere hadn't been the same without him for her partner.

As she had said to Vera and Fred, surely her and Mike had become good friends, good enough for him to have dropped her a postcard if he were ill or for whatever reason it was that had stopped him from coming.

Wednesday morning the letter had arrived.

She knew it off by heart. Not that there was much to remember. Three lines: *Sorry, will explain when I see you. Pick you up ten o'clock Saturday morning and we'll have a run down to Kent. If that's all right with you.*

All the same if it wasn't. There was no return address.

She smiled to herself, Mike must know her by now.

Curiosity if nothing else had spurred her on. She had taken great pains getting herself ready. She wanted to look good for Mike.

She glanced at her watch. It was turned ten. Her anxious eyes followed every car that came down the street. He hadn't been having her on, had he?

She was wearing her best clothes. A straight camel skirt which was a fashionable calf-length, and beneath the fitted matching jacket she wore a pretty cream blouse that had a wide lace collar. She was wearing brown sensible low-heeled shoes and carrying her best leather handbag. No hat, but she'd had her hair trimmed, washed and set at the shop.

She opened her gate and stepped out on to the pavement. Then she paced up and down, back and forth.

Suddenly a car drew up to the kerb and Mike was smiling at her through the open window. It was that smile that had first attracted her to him.

He made rather a formidable sight, a broad man with a mass of greying hair, and those deep-set brown eyes that seemed to see right through a person.

'I thought you said ten o'clock, it's nearly ten past. Where've you been?' Ida said.

He leaned across, and his long thick fingers opened the door for her. He was laughing fit to bust. 'A woman ready on time? Well, that 'as to be something new! The traffic was a bit much, sorry to 'ave kept you waiting, madam.'

Ida had been about to get into the car. ''Old on, Mike,' she said, 'are you taking the mickey? And there's another thing I'd like t'know. Where are we going and why do you want me along?'

'Get in the car, Ida, and let's get going. I 'ave t'go down

to Kent t'day an' I sort of fancied a bit of company. Your company, to be exact. All right?'

A ghost of a smile came to Ida's lips. 'Oh well, in that case I 'ope we 'ave a nice day. Drive on.'

'Yes, ma'am.' Mike was grinning again.

They drove along in comfortable silence. Ida was happy. It was a lovely day; they had left the towns behind and were driving through beautiful scenery. Everywhere looked so green, the trees full blown with leaves of so many different shades.

Ida liked being with him and sitting close to him in the car, their arms touching. She really felt they were good friends and was glad that he had asked her to join him.

'We'll stop just up here,' Mike's voice broke into her thoughts. 'It's an old farmhouse. They do a great cup of coffee.'

Ida found Mike to be in great form as they sat eating hot scones and drinking their coffee, and soon she was fascinated by what he was telling her.

'You mean to tell me you saw that unemployment was going to come as long ago as 1960?'

'Not all of it, Ida. I didn't have a glass ball. It was just a matter of common sense to see that the manual work in the docks was coming to an end. There was almost no end to the variety of new machinery that was being brought into the docks. Severance was bound to come.'

'So when did you buy this land down in Kent?'

'About eight or nine years ago.'

Ida's little grin appeared. 'You're a dark horse, Mike Moffett. You know that, don't you?'

'Yeah, well, perhaps I'd better begin at the beginning. Would you be interested?'

'I'd say I would.' Ida reached for his cup, filled it with

fresh coffee from the large pot and pushed the cream jug towards him. 'I'm all ears.'

'Even when I was a coal porter on the docks, I had another interest. Me and the wife – Rose her name was – we ran a café in Osprey Street, that's in Rotherhithe, the East End of London. Whenever we could find the time we went down to Kent, Rose loved to see the hop fields.

'That's how I came to buy me land. Then, with the help of a few bricklayers that I knew, I spent four years building my own bungalow. The pity was my Rose died before I had it finished. It has some handsome mahogany wood panelling,' he finished proudly.

''Ow marvellous,' Ida breathed.

'Well, we hadn't better sit around 'ere any longer or best of the day will be gone, time we get down to East Hill.'

'You're a bit quiet,' Mike said, when they were once more on their way.

'I'm thinking about 'ow clever you are.'

'There's a whole lot more for me t'tell you yet. Just so long as I ain't boring you.'

''Onest?' Ida asked. 'Bored? Never. I think it's great. Tell me about the café. Did Rose do all the cooking?'

'Till she died she did. It was a proper working-man's café. Very popular among Surrey dockers and stevedores.'

'Go on then. Tell me what else you've been up to.'

'I've made plans to be a chicken farmer.'

She turned her head and stared at him in disbelief. This hunk of a man, a docker, going to spend the rest of his life looking after chickens!

''Ow many chickens?' she asked, the laughter coming through in her voice.

'I'll start off with about three 'undred an' fifty but I'm aiming t'ave about two thousand.'

'Do what? You are joking?'

'I'm deadly serious. I've already excavated and laid the foundations for the chicken houses; all I've got t'do now is buy the prefabricated equipment and cages and I'll be ready to go into business.'

They both went silent as Mike pulled the car right in against the hedge of a narrow lane in order to let another car pass. They were driving through hop country now. Each side of the road the tall vines twisted their stalks up the frames held straight by long canes. As far as the eye could see the bitter catkin-like clusters used for flavouring beer hung in abundance.

'Another few weeks and these lanes will be swarming with Londoners come down to pick the hops,' Mike told her, adding, 'and a jolly good 'oliday it is for them an' all.'

Soon Mike was turning the car off the beaten track, climbing high into the hills. They passed a signpost that said Kemsing and minutes later Mike stopped the car and got out to open great wooden gates. Then they were bowling along a neat gravel path that led up to a bungalow that on first sight had Ida gasping at just how lovely it looked.

'It certainly does you credit,' Ida told him as she walked, open mouthed, from room to room.

The inside of the bungalow had been decorated beautifully. There was little furniture in the front room, only two armchairs, one each side of the tiled fireplace, and a square oak table which had four high-backed matching chairs. One bedroom had what looked like a large camp bed and a chest of drawers; the other room was unfurnished.

'Bless you, Ida, I'm glad you like it,' Mike said. 'I brought some things with me for our lunch, I'll bring them in from the car in a minute. Meanwhile, 'ow about a cup of tea? There's tea and loads of other things in that cupboard over the sink, china's in that cabinet over there. I'll fill the kettle an' put it on shall I? I did remember to bring milk.'

'Oh, good on ye, Mike,' she said, breathless with excitement. 'A cup of tea sounds just what the doctor ordered.'

Soon they were sitting out in the sunshine, in comfortable cane chairs that had the prettiest cushions that Ida had ever seen. The cane table had a glass top and Mike had carried the whole set out from one of the large sheds. He must be a very tidy man, Ida was thinking, to have everything stored away so carefully.

And that house! Proper little palace. Fancy having a place like this tucked away up in the hills miles away from London.

They started on the pork pies and sandwiches and drank the hot tea. Mike had also brought plenty of fresh fruit for them to have for their afters.

'Mike, I can understand why you bought the ground, even why you worked so hard to build your own place, but . . .' Her voice faltered, would he think she was being too nosy?

Mike laughed, 'I know what you're going to say, my son asked the same question when he first found out what I was up to. You want t'know whatever gave me the idea of having chickens.'

'Yes,' agreed Ida, eyes gleaming with amusement.

'Well, it started when I was a boy of about fifteen. My Dad had a bungalow at Ashen Grove and so did George Baker, a well-known man on the river who had a wharf where he used to break up old wooden barges. He used that wood to build chicken houses and he used to do all right with the eggs. I used to ride me bike all the way to see old George an' me dad at weekends, it was about twenty-one miles. They used to let me take eggs round to 'ouses asking the people if they wanted to buy some. Some Saturdays I'd earn as much as a shilling if I sold a lot.'

'So, you always were a clever clogs then?' Ida said, smiling with pleasure because Mike had taken hold of her hand.

'I dunno about that, Ida, but I wasn't so daft when I cottoned on to you. I 'aven't felt so lonely since I've been seeing you once a week at the dance school.'

Me neither, was what Ida wanted to say, but she didn't because he had taken her by surprise and she wasn't sure that he actually meant what he'd just said.

While Mike went on talking, Ida was thinking and she was finding it hard to contain her excitement. Funny how circumstances crop up and suddenly life could have a whole new look to it.

All of a sudden so many things were happening. Her Ruby was going to get married. Live permanently in Scotland. And here was Mike Moffett, whom she hadn't seen for three weeks, turning up, bringing her down to Kent for the day to see this smashing bungalow which he had built himself and going on about his plans for the future.

'Ida, will you come down here with me again another time? It won't be cold, not indoors, even in the winter. I've a whole stack of logs stored up in the shed and it won't take long t'get a fire going.'

'Oh, I most certainly will!' she promised. 'And if you forget to invite me I shall invite meself.'

The afternoon went quickly as Mike showed her all over

his land and then took her for a walk round the lanes. He was still full of plans, he hadn't completed half the things that he had in mind to do.

It was half-past eight when Mike drew the car up outside of Ida's house.

'Won't you come in?' Ida asked.

'Not if you don't mind. I'll see you on Monday at Peggy Spencer's.'

Now he took her hand between his own two and gently squeezed; a warm feeling came over her. A little wry smile came to her lips as she wondered whether or not he was going to kiss her.

He didn't, and she felt disappointed as she stood alone and watched him drive away. Was this the beginning of more than just friendship? she asked herself. Her answer had to be, We'll see!

After all, she decided, I'm too long in the tooth to let me heart rule me head.

While Ida had been getting to know more about Mike Moffett, much the same thing had been happening to Ruby, far away in Scotland.

Ruby was thinking that during the whole time that she had been at Muir House she couldn't recall such a sudden change in the weather. The rain was lashing down and the wind was so strong that the noise was almost deafening.

She was well up to date in her office work and she wasn't sure where Ian was. He hadn't appeared at breakfast that morning and Catherine said she had heard him go out before she was up.

Ruby seemed to be seeing Muir House in a different light since Ian had told her that he loved her. Now she knew that it was to be her future home, the feeling of being loved and secure was so wonderful that half the time she was choked up as though she were crying, not laughing.

'Oh, Ian, I love you,' she said out loud. 'I do, I love you,' she repeated.

She walked around the main sitting room, a room that was rarely used, seeing everything as if for the first time and the thought came to her. It was strange that amongst all the family photographs there appeared to be no picture of Ian's wife.

Catherine Patterson stood in the doorway and as Ruby felt her presence she turned and smiled. 'I was going through all these photographs seeing if I can pick out the persons I have met. I recognise Ian's two aunts, I met them when we were celebrating Hogmanay. Is this Jeffrey?'

'Yes, it is.' Catherine's voice was gentle as she took the silver frame from Ruby's hands. 'He's a real nice lad. Life just hasn't seen fit to smile on him.'

Together they stared at the laughing face of a teenage lad, bright eyes and a bushy head of unruly hair just like his father except that it was red, a dark shade of auburn.

'Where did the auburn hair come from?' Ruby laughed.

'That,' said Catherine, 'was more than half the trouble. Jeffrey hated it. His mother's father had the same colour hair. He knew when people remarked on it but he wasn't able to answer back. Frustration was beastly for him.'

'Did he never speak?'

'Not a word. He learned sign language when he was quite small and I took the trouble to learn it as well, which is more than I can say for some.'

'You mean, Ian? He never mastered it?'

'No. Indeed I am not referring to Ian.' Ruby had never heard Catherine speak so sharply before.

'Ian would have mastered walking on water if it were

possible to help that boy. Jeffrey loves his father, he never fails to keep in touch with him, no matter where he is. I hope he will come home for your wedding.'

She continued to gaze at the picture for a while, lost in the past and hopeful of the future.

'There isn't a picture of his mother here?' Ruby phrased it as a question not an observation.

Catherine shook her head. She couldn't bring herself to tell Ruby that Ian had burned every reminder of Rosalind after she had smacked Jeffrey so hard when he was still only a toddler that it had been touch and go as to whether the tiny lad had lived or died. Catherine was remembering, though, remembering how often Rosalind had taken far too much drink, and her eyes welled up with tears. After a while, she murmured, 'I hope you take to Jeffrey and he to you. It would make such a difference for Ian.'

Ruby felt uncomfortable. 'I feel as if I am intruding, being in this room,' she apologised.

A glimmer of a smile crossed Catherine's lined face. 'I think you'll find you have to admire Jeffrey when you meet him, and if anyone can win him round I know you can. But we'll see. Now come out of here, the kitchen is the best place on a day like this and it's time we put the kettle on.'

Ruby was feeling uneasy as she pondered on Catherine's remarks. Would she and Jeffrey get along?

After all, if things went according to plan she would be his stepmother. It was going to be difficult for both of them. An eighteen year old lad. She must not make the mistake of comparing him with what her own two sons might have been like. She hoped and prayed that Jeffrey would take a liking to her and she to him.

She followed Catherine from the room with a very similar thought to that which had been in her mother's mind, We'll have to wait and see!

Chapter Twenty-five

'VERA, IT WAS GOOD of you to sit some of the dances out and let your Fred partner me.'

'Aw, go on with you. I was glad to give me feet a rest, 'sides I knew 'ow put out you were 'cos Mike didn't turn up again. I thought you said he was definitely coming tonight.'

Ida shrugged her shoulders and pushed her arm into the sleeve of her coat. Then she watched with miserable envy as couples called their goodbyes before going out into the night together.

It was the same when Fred dropped her off outside her house. She watched him and Vera drive away together, and as usual she went indoors alone.

During the following days, apart from going to do her morning shift at Hemmings' the bakers, Ida remained inside the house, venturing out only to collect the milk from the doorstep and to go to the corner shop for any odds and ends that she needed. She felt so let down. After that lovely day spent with Mike, he hadn't turned up on

Monday at the dance club. Not so much as a word had she heard from him and she felt right down in the dumps. She wasn't good company for anyone, not the way she was feeling at the moment.

'Best keep myself to myself for a while, she thought. I've been a proper dope thinking that anything could come of being friendly with Mike in the first place. I know better now.

Her thoughts flew in another direction. Wonder what he's like, this Ian McKenzie.

Up until now she had felt that he was a good man for Ruby to be working for. Now, with Ruby having telephoned to say she was going to be married to the man who when all was said and done was still her boss, she wasn't so sure.

Oh leave it out, she chided herself. You can't be her minder for ever. She's thirty-five years old. Able to take care of herself. Or was she? She'd been so trusting when she were young. Had she learnt more about life? About how to cope with the knocks, even about herself?

Ida shook her head in frustration. She was desperately concerned for Ruby. The worse time had been when she had left home after the funeral of her two boys. Just walked away, her only daughter, had gone off into the unknown, and she had stood at the window, watching, and let her go. Day after day she had worried herself sick thinking about Ruby out there on her own. Bowed down with grief and no one to share the sorrow with. So much heartache in such a young life!

Ruby hadn't deserved it. Oh, she hadn't been a saint by any means. Got up to more mischief than a barrow load of monkeys, but there had never been any real harm in her.

I did try to be a good mother to her. Honest to God,

I did try. In her heart, though, Ida was convinced that there must have been something more that she could have done. Kept a stricter eye on her when she was a teenager, perhaps? Not allowed her uncles to steamroll her into marrying that waster Brian. Listened to her more. Been more understanding. Brought her and the twins home to live with her the very first time she found out that Brian was knocking her about.

Oh, it was easy to be so wise after the event. Brian had died, and the twins had been killed. It was a wonder that her poor Ruby hadn't gone mad.

Even though Ida wasn't much of a one for going to church, she always said her prayers. Especially at times like now when she was feeling so low. Clasping her hands together she sat down in the armchair and quietly began to pray.

First she thanked God for the way that Ruby had shown such courage through all her heartaches. Secondly she asked that this chance, this whole new way of life that was being offered to her daughter, would truly be a happy one. Please Dear God, she prayed. This time, please, let fate be kind to my Ruby.

Getting to her feet she began to clear away the remains of her breakfast. If she were to set to and give the place a jolly good cleaning she might end up feeling a whole lot better.

It had turned one o'clock when she heard her front door open and Jozy's voice sail down the passage. 'Ida! 'Ave you got the plague or something? We've not seen 'ide nor 'air of you for days, been using the back way in an' out 'ave you?'

Half laughing, Ida open the living room door. 'It's you,' she said, ushering her sister-in-law in.

'Course it's me!' Jozy replied, making her way into the room. 'What the 'ell's the matter with you? Never a day 'ardly goes by that you don't pop into Sheila's or into me for a cuppa and a natter, now all of a sudden you've been 'iding yerself. What's up? You ain't worrying about Ruby and 'er news, are you?'

Ida smiled, evading the question. 'Kettle's just come to the boil, I'll make a pot of tea.'

When she came back into the room carrying two cups of piping hot tea, she said, 'I'm sorry if you've all been worried about me. I just 'aven't felt like company, been a bit down like.'

Giving one of the cups to Jozy she sat herself down on a chair opposite. Meanwhile Jozy had been staring through the back window. The clothesline was full. Blowing in the wind were the sheets from Ida's bed, towels, tea cloths, pillow cases, not to mention her underwear and woolly jumpers. Looking round the room she could see the linoleum round the edges of the floor had been polished until it shone, the big centre carpet had been hoovered, even the fire gate had been cleaned and a huge green pot fern had been stood in the hearth.

'Good Lord, you must 'ave been up at the crack of dawn,' she remarked.

'Not really, I just didn't know what t'do with meself so I set to and went through the 'ouse like a dose of salts.'

Jozy laughed. 'Well, if you 'aven't got it all out of ye system yet you can always come over to my place and give that a good doing.'

When Ida made no reply, Jozy took a few sips of her tea then set the cup back down on her saucer, before quietly saying, 'Tell me to mind me own business if you like, but they do say a friend in need is a friend indeed an' if we ain't friends after all these years then I don't know who the 'ell is.'

'I'm all right really, it's just that I 'aven't slept properly these last few nights. What with one thing an' another I seem t'be all at sixes and sevens.'

'So try telling me about it.'

'Well, for one thing, Mike Moffett didn't turn up at the dance last week and I keep wondering if I did anything to upset 'im when he took me down to Kent, and for another my Alan 'ad a right old go at me.' Ida's face said it all. She really was feeling glum.

'I know what's upsetting Alan. It turned out he and Norman had a drink with Bert the other night and the pair of them made it quite plain that they didn't think Ruby's wedding should be taking place up in Scotland.'

'And what did Bert 'ave to say on the matter?' Ida asked.

'Well, luv, you may as well 'ear it from me. Both Bert and Jeff agreed with them. Said it wasn't right nor proper.'

'Oh! 'Ad a family conference did they? Well I'll soon set them straight. I ain't 'aving them taking over like they did when Ruby got married the first time. Neither me or her got a say in the matter then.'

Punching the air with her fist, Jozy cried, 'Oh come off it, Ida. What your brothers did then they did for the best. Anyway that's what they thought at the time. Ain't their fault that things turned out so rotten. Christ, you ain't been blaming them all these years, 'ave you?'

Ida had the grace to look shamefaced. 'Sorry Jozy, I just don't know 'ow I'm gonna tell my Ruby that none of you want to go up there to see her get married. She's sounds so 'appy, you ought t'read her letter. Like a dog with two tails she is.'

Jozy gave a loud chuckle. 'Oh, Ida! You silly blooming fool. Nobody's said they don't want to see Ruby get wed. Everyone is thrilled for her. It's just that her brothers are not paupers, as well you know. They both feel badly about the way their sister went off and coped all that time on her own. But they were young themselves in those days. Now it's different. They're in the position to see that Ruby gets a real good sendoff. Think about it, luv. Can you imagine a better setting than your boys' club for a wedding?'

'Jesus!' Ida's breath came out in a rush, and her smile was one of relief. 'Is that what they're planning?'

'Not before they've spoken to Ruby. They want to get her thoughts on the idea. See if that's what she would like.' Jozy's voice was suddenly very solemn.

'They're aiming to telephone her tonight and then they're going to come and tell you what's been decided. So perhaps you'd do me a favour an' not let on that we've 'ad this conversation.'

Ida nodded. 'Of course, I won't say a word. But thanks for telling me.' Ida's bright face showed her real feelings. She was so much happier now. 'Wouldn't it be lovely? Ruby's wedding at the Cavalier! I would 'ave felt ever so much out of place if we'd had to go up to Scotland. Do you think Ruby will go for it? And God 'elp us, we're forgetting about Ian McKenzie! What if he won't agree?'

Jozy made as if to slosh her one. 'You, Ida Wilcox, must be the biggest pessimist that God ever put breath into. Why don't you try looking on the bright side for a change?'

'Why? Do you really believe that Ruby would prefer to be married down here, amongst all her own family?'

'I don't see why not. In fact I think she might be over

the moon that the boys are offering. I'll go so far as to take a bet on it.'

'We'll see then, won't we?' Ida said, smiling now. 'I won't take that bet though, 'cos I'll tell you 'ere an' now, Jozy, it would be one bet that I would really 'ope to lose.'

'Thank God for that,' Jozy exclaimed as Ida's smile broadened. 'Now, what about this Mike? It sounded as if you two were really made up when you told us about him taking you down to see the bungalow that he'd built.'

'That's what I thought at the time. 'Aven't seen him nor 'eard from him since.'

'Well, it ain't been a month of Sundays, has it?'

'No,' Ida agreed reluctantly. 'It's just that when he drove off on Saturday his last words were see you on Monday.'

''Ave you tried giving him a ring?'

'That's just it. I ain't got a clue where he lives let alone a phone number. In fact there's not a lot I do know about him. Only that for years he's worked in the Surrey Dockyard. Oh, and he did tell me that when his wife was alive they ran a café in Rotherhithe. Since then he and a lot more like him 'ave been laid off the docks. At least I think he's been laid off.'

'So where does he live now?'

'Jozy, will ye believe me when I say you've got me there? You'd better, 'cos it's true. All I know is that he comes to Crystal Palace with his sister an' her 'usband. May, his sister's name is. She told me she was glad when he met me 'cos he's always been a bit of a loner. Chucked 'imself into work when his wife died 'cos he missed her so much. D'you know, Jozy, there wasn't even any address on the letter he wrote t'me.'

Jozy couldn't help herself, she actually laughed out

loud. 'Stop playing the drama queen,' she implored Ida. 'He'll turn up, I'd lay me life on it. Blokes don't take a woman out for the day and show them all the work they've done on a place they've bought if they ain't interested in her.' She got to her feet. 'Anyway I've got t'go. For Christ's sake snap out of ye black mood an' come over this afternoon. I'll tell Sheila you're coming, get her to come in.'

She grabbed hold of Ida and placing a sloppy kiss on her cheek she said slyly, 'Before I go, 'ere's my prediction for this coming weekend. First your boys will come bursting in 'ere to tell you that they are gonna lay on all the trimmings for Ruby at their club 'cos she's delighted with the idea.' She paused, took a breath, 'And . . .'

Ida was really grinning by now. 'And?' she queried, dying to hear what else Jozy was going to come out with.

'And Mike Moffett is going to turn up 'ere, flowers in his 'and, all apologies, ready to sweep you off your feet.'

'Oh, go on, you daft fool.' Now it was Ida's turn to laugh loudly. 'You know what you ought t'be doing Jozy, you ought t'be writing fairy stories.'

'That's as may be. But just you wait and see,' Jozy told her as they walked to the front door together.

Ida wanted to believe her. No one would ever know how much she wanted both of Jozy's prophecies to come true.

Well, Ida smiled to herself, half of Jozy's forecast had come true and for that she would be eternally grateful. The boys had told her that Ruby hadn't needed any persuading. She had jumped at the chance to come home and be married amongst all her own family. Ruby had also rung her mother to say that Ian McKenzie hadn't any objections, whatever pleased Ruby and her relations was all right by him.

Norman had fetched his mother yesterday and taken her to his house in Streatham for the day. And a very nice day it had turned out to be. By tea time most of the family had turned up. With Alan and Iris living only a few doors away in the same road there hadn't been many members missing.

Dear Rose, Ida was thinking, as she recalled the spread that Rose had set out for Sunday tea. Another family discussion had soon got underway and for once the decision made by Alan and Norman had been greeted with cheers.

All Ruby's nieces were demanding to be bridesmaids.

'It isn't going to be that kind of a wedding.' Their parents had done their best to explain.

'Why not?' Jodie being the eldest of the children was demanding to be the chief bridesmaid.

'You, Jodie, may be the the bright one, but just listen for once to what I'm going to tell you,' Billy, her father, had said somewhat sharply. 'Before you were all born Ruby was married, she was very young when she had two little boys, twins. First her husband died and you've all heard about Lenny and Joey, how sadly they were killed in a terrible accident.'

Billy and his wife Linda looked round at the faces of the children seated at the table and it was Linda that took up the story. 'It was all a long time ago. Last Christmas you all met Ruby, didn't you?'

'Yes,' they chorused.

'And she told you about the estate in Scotland where she worked. Well, she is now going to marry the gentleman that she works for and everyone of us hopes that she is going to be very happy. It won't be a white wedding because it isn't a first marriage, but you girls can all be flower girls in the church if you like and you boys are old enough, I think, to act as ushers.'

Ida had felt such a rush of gratitude for all the love that her family were showing for Ruby that she had been close to tears.

It had been when Norman had brought her home last night that she had been even more touched.

'Give us your key, mother,' he said, getting out of the car. 'Though I wouldn't be a bit surprised if I don't need it. Suppose you've still got a key on a bit of string behind the letter box?'

Ida hadn't bothered to answer him. How else would her sisters-in-law and friends get in if she wasn't well? Norman had gone ahead of her, switching on lights as he went.

Once inside the living room, he watched as his mother took off her best coat and what she called her Sunday hat. 'You'll be all right now then, will you Mum?'

'Course I will, son, and thanks for a lovely day. Lot of work for Rose though, wasn't it?'

'Get on with you, don't let it worry you. Rose loves to have all the family round. You should know that by now.'

He bent his head and kissed his Mum. 'You are happy about the wedding being at the Cavalier?'

'More than I know 'ow t'tell you. It's a great chance for our Ruby, isn't it?'

'It is that, Mum. And this time it will work out. You'll see. She will be settled and as happy as the rest of us.'

'I only 'ope you're right, son. Anyway you and Alan are certainly doing ye best t'see she gets a great send-off.'

336

'We sure are, Mum. So get yeself to bed and stop your worrying. Goodnight. Alan and I will be over during the week, but if you want us we're only on the end of your phone.'

'I know, luv. Goodnight. God bless you, take care.'

She had gone up to bed feeling a whole lot happier but still a bit lonely as she climbed into her big double bed on her own.

Monday morning had brought her a wonderful surprise.

She was doing the afternoon shift at the bakers this week and hardly had she set foot downstairs than the telephone had rung. Picking up the receiver, she hadn't even had time to say hallo before the unmistakable deep voice of Mike Moffett had said, 'Ida, don't ring off on me. Not that I would blame you if you did.'

She had gasped in surprise. He was the last person that she had expected to be on the end of the line.

'I am sorry, Ida, that I 'aven't been in touch. I have an awful lot to tell you. I've managed to get hold of a heap of material from a demolished building. I'm going to build a swimming pool down at East Hill, it's gonna be glassed in an' all.'

Ida was standing there open-mouthed. This bloke was full of surprises. Was there no end to his ambitions? Talk about get up and go!

'Ida, did you hear what I said? Ida, are you still there?'

Ida slowly let out her breath. 'Yes I'm still 'ere,' she said.

'I was wondering, can you get this Saturday off? If not, it doesn't matter, we'll make it Sunday. What I want is for you t'say you're not mad at me for letting you down an' that you'll come down to Kent with me again.'

A great surge of happiness swelled up inside of her. She was sorry for all the bad names she had called him. Oh, he was a lovely man. He wanted to see her again. Wanted to take her back to visit his lovely bungalow again. Wonder if he's got any chickens yet? She grinned to herself. Course he hadn't. He'd been too busy arranging to build a swimming pool. A swimming pool! I ask you!

'Ida, say something, please. Will you come? Which day shall I pick you up?'

Will I go? Let anyone try stopping me, she was thinking. She said, 'I 'ave to work on Saturday, do you mind making it Sunday? I could be ready ever so early. By the way, shall I bring the lunch this time?'

'That's great, Ida. Sunday will be fine. As to the food, you'll do no such thing. You just leave the arrangements to me. I won't be able to get to the dance club tonight, sorry about that, but I'll pick you up on Sunday about nine. Bye for now.'

She stood there holding the receiver against her cheek. She wouldn't have cared if he had said he was coming for her at four o'clock in the morning, she would have been ready and waiting.

Suddenly everything was getting sorted. Things were looking up. She was still chuckling as she made her way across the road to tell Jozy that she hadn't been right about Mike turning up with a bunch of flowers, but that everything else in her life was coming together very nicely, thank you.

Chapter Twenty-six

IAN MCKENZIE SAT ON the edge of his desk, looking splendid in his well-tailored suit and with his sandy coloured hair neatly brushed back for once. His happy smile as always was a joy to see and his grey eyes sparkled with pleasure. Ruby couldn't help but tell herself how lucky she was that this wonderful man loved her as much as she loved him.

'You still haven't given me an answer to any of my questions.' Ian chided her. His smile was gone and in its place was a look of expectation.

'There's so much to think about. It won't be easy. It is going to take a lot of sorting out.' Ruby was shocked to hear herself making excuses. Now it had been settled between her, Ian and her family that their wedding was to take place in Tooting she was having second thoughts.

'You're not trying to put me off the idea, are you?' Ian was smiling again.

'Oh no, I wouldn't do that,' Ruby answered truthfully.

'Good. Because we do have to settle on the date. I

want a whole month free of any commitments once we are married. I intend to devote the whole of my time to my wife.' He took her in his arms and they kissed long and passionately.

'Oh Ruby, you haven't any idea what you are doing to me,' he said softly. He shook his head and sat down. 'Shall we agree on the first Saturday in November? I thought you could go home to your mother at the end of September, spend a month doing all the things that brides-to-be make such a fuss about and then I shall be there to claim you for my own for ever more.'

'Oh, so you're willing to let me out of your sight for a whole month,' she answered him mischievously.

'Will you please agree the date?' he pleaded, half afraid that she was reluctant. 'We have so many plans to make. And this will be the last chance I shall really get to talk to you for a couple of days.' He looked at his watch. 'Gracious, I'm cutting it fine, I have to be in Edinburgh for this wretched meeting in two hours.'

'Wish I could come with you.'

He laughed and gently kissed her. 'I won't disappear, I promise. You mustn't be so afraid. You mustn't have doubts. As soon as we are married we shall spend the rest of our lives together. Think about that. Lots of laughter. Lots of time for each other. Lots of love.'

Ruby did not reply. She just stood there, lovingly gazing at him. Since he had told her how he felt about her, something seemed to have happened. Things seemed different, every moment was precious. Between them there was complete trust, a warm glorious contentment that even in her wildest dreams she had never imagined. And, even as she was thinking these thoughts, he took her into his arms again.

'I love you, Ruby,' he murmured, 'I shall love you for as long as I live.'

'And I love you, Ian,' she said.

With Ian gone to his business meeting, Ruby felt at a loss and had decided to walk as far as the village. Only very seldomly had she ventured down to the fishing village of Queensferry. The local people had made her welcome enough but their curiosity regarding herself was always apparent and it made her feel uncomfortable. An outsider.

As she walked a breeze stirred the trees on the wooded slopes and disturbed the wild tufts of grass. She was grateful because the sun was high on this July day. Old stone walls flanked each side of the road and separated the fields, some cultivated, some just wild heather and rough grass. The distant hills were still capped with snow even in mid summer.

As she neared the village, Queensferry showed many signs of its industry. Small crafts of all sorts were moored in the harbour and the low cottages looked picturesque, some even quaint, with slate walls and roofs set among the winding streets.

What dominated Queensferry as a whole was the unmistakable sight of the two Forth Bridges which spanned the Firth of Forth.

Ruby stood still. Her arms crossed around her waist she hugged herself in sheer joyful anticipation. She would be crossing one of those bridges on her way to spend her honeymoon. Whether it would be the Forth Bridge or the Forth Road Bridge she had no idea.

'Have you given any thought as to where you would like us to spend our honeymoon?' Ian had generously asked her.

Her reply had made him laugh. 'None at all, but you obviously have!'

And she had been right.

'In my opinion, you have been in Scotland far too long without knowing the first thing about it. We shall take our time, head across the Forth Bridge and make our way to wherever takes our fancy. One thing is for certain, we shall end up in the Highlands, the magnificent beauty of which will take your breath away.'

Who could argue with that?

She bought some stamps in the small post office shop, posted her letters – the main one telling her mother that she was coming home at the end of September to prepare for her wedding.

She grinned to herself as she pictured her mum reading her instructions. Get a good pair of walking shoes, she had ordered, because you and I are going to tour the shops of London. No expense will be spared!

How would her mother react to that? Poor old Mum! Much more used to watching and counting every penny. Both her brothers had insisted that there was no need for their mother to go out to work. They were both of them more than willing to give her a bigger allowance. But no! Mum would never alter. Independent until the day she died.

Ian McKenzie nodded his thanks to Catherine as she handed him a tray which was laid for breakfast. He made his way across the hall and up the stairs.

It was the first day of September and already it felt like there was no warmth left in the sun. In two days' time Ruby was leaving Muir House and by the time she returned she would be his wife and log fires would be burning in the hearths. In fact, the entire house would have undergone a great change. The large room at the back where the huge glass doors led out to the walled-in garden he was having completely refurbished. It was Ruby's favourite room and one where they would be able to relax at the end of the day.

Most important were the plans he'd had drawn up for the outbuildings near to the stables to be turned into a comfortable self-contained flat.

Jeffrey was coming home today in order to meet Ruby before she left for London. Who knows, he had asked himself, whether or not Jeffrey would one day want to make Muir House his permanent home? He wanted him to feel that not only was he perfectly entitled but that he was more than welcome. Those outbuildings were dark and dingy having been neglected for far too long.

Jock Dunbar had put forward the idea that there was more than enough room on the estate for a proper self-contained dwelling place to be made available to Jeffrey, saying, 'After all, he is a man now and should have a place of his own that he could look upon as home.'

Catherine had been very keen on the idea, she too insisting that it was only right and proper that Jeffrey should have a permanent place on the estate to which he could come and go as he pleased.

She had, however, stood steadfast when Ian had suggested that the kitchen be remodelled. He hadn't fought her too hard. The big black fire range was still a beauty, and the large oak furniture both attractive and very serviceable. Ruby herself had cried out in protest when he had proposed that the huge dresser that reached almost to the ceiling and held a great display of wonderful china should be ripped out.

Reaching the landing Ian carefully balanced the tray on one hand and knocked on the door, calling out, 'I've brought you your breakfast.'

Ruby was up and dressed, sitting at her dressing table doing her hair. She had drawn the curtains back and the sunshine touched her long fair hair as the brush stroked through it making it look like spun gold.

Ian set the tray down on the side table and came to stand behind her. 'You look so beautiful,' he breathed.

She was wearing a tweed skirt and the palest blue silk blouse that had an embroidered collar. Part of her hair lay forward across one shoulder and Ian picked up the strands and let them slowly run through his fingers.

'I can't wait until the day I wake up with you beside me,' he murmured so low that she hardly caught the words. He shook his head as if to bring himself back to the present. 'I have to leave in a short while if I'm to be at the station when Jeffrey arrives.'

'You shouldn't have bothered to bring my breakfast up.'

'I wanted to. Catherine has wrapped the toast in a cloth to keep it hot. How did you sleep?'

'How do I look is more to the point? Considering we sat up talking until three in the morning I actually feel great, though I can't help wondering how Jeffrey is going to react to me.'

'He'll behave, I promise you.'

'Behave?' She sounded as if she were suddenly afraid.

Ian pulled up a chair and sat down by her side, his long legs stretched out in front of him and his arms folded. 'Sorry, wrong word. Now why don't you make a start on your breakfast and stop worrying about Jeffrey?'

Ruby eyed her tray without any enthusiasm. 'I don't feel

very hungry but I'm dying for a cup of tea.' She reached for the pot and smiled, grateful that Catherine hadn't sent her up coffee.

'Are you frightened of meeting Jeffrey?'

'Not exactly frightened,' she said faintly.

'My poor Ruby.' Ian watched as she sipped her tea. Of course she was wary and the sooner Jeffrey was here and introductions made, the better it would be for all of them. He could only imagine what Ruby must be feeling. If fate hadn't dealt her such an awful blow she would have two sons alive today, both of them near enough to being the same age as his own son Jeffrey.

He thanked God that Ruby Wilcox had applied for a job in answer to his advertisement. He hadn't been lying when he said that he had fallen in love with her at that very first meeting. Had she been sent to him as some kind of recompense and he to her? God alone knew that both of them were due for some happiness in this life. They had each been dealt enough knocks when they were young.

Ian watched Ruby's face. She was doing her best to make him believe that she truly wanted to meet his son. Perhaps they would take to each other straight away. God! He prayed that it might be so.

He only knew that nothing should be allowed to come between Ruby and himself. The frigid reserve that he had built up around himself after Rosalind had died had given way at last and he had found the courage to tell Ruby just how much he loved her.

He stood up.

'Where are you going?' she asked him.

'To get ready to go and meet Jeffrey. You aren't looking forward to him being here, are you?'

'I wish I could say that you are wrong in assuming that,

but truthfully I can't. I wouldn't blame him if he treated me as an intruder.' She paused and sighed before adding, 'I will do my best, my very best, to like him and hope that in return he will do the same for me.'

'That's all I ask. Now, please, Ruby, stop meeting trouble more than halfway. Eat your breakfast and I'll see you when I get back from the station.'

He walked across the room, opened the door and then turned round to look at her and said, 'I love you much more than you realise and come what may I intend to spend the rest of my life with you.' Very quietly he closed the door behind him.

Now Ruby wandered around the room, breakfast forgotten, feeling incredibly lonely.

It seemed in no time at all she heard the car draw up. Catherine was standing at the sink peeling potatoes and she made no move to go and meet Ian and his son.

Ruby had been giving herself a stern lecture. You're just a jealous horrible person, who instead of thinking how lucky you are that such a man as Ian has fallen in love with you, you have to start imagining trouble where so far none exists. You want him all for yourself, don't you? The answer she gave herself was Yes.

Yet in her heart the last thing she wanted was to hurt this lad. If half of what she had learned about him was true he hadn't had a fair crack of the whip in his life any more than she had.

For one awful moment her thoughts flew back to Jack Dawson and his son Danny! She hadn't come out of that relationship with flying colours, had she?

For once in your life, try learning by your mistakes. A whole lot can be forgiven when one is young and if you are given another chance at happiness only a fool would let it slip away. Now, Ruby Wilcox, she berated herself, you've got an old head on your shoulders and hopefully it is a much wiser one, so for God's sake use it.

With that thought foremost in her mind she went out to meet her future husband and what would be her stepson. She stood in the porch and watched them come towards her. Then, when they were only a few yards away, she gasped in amazement.

Jeffrey was tall, square-jawed and manly, his face so remarkably like his father's that she thought they looked liked two peas from the same pod. Only his bouncy thick hair was a different colour. As she had seen from the photograph it was a burnished copper.

Ruby met his glance and felt embarrassed to be caught staring. She turned her glance to Ian and it was left to him to break the silence. Father and son's eyes were on a level for Jeffrey was as tall as Ian. Suddenly hands were flying and fingers were tapping arms and chests and Ruby felt at that moment that she would have given a lot to be able to understand sign language.

Ian came close to Ruby. 'Darling, this is Jeffrey my son and he has asked me to tell you that he is very pleased to meet you.'

Jeffrey's eyes travelled over Ruby, however she did not find it unnerving, quite the reverse, and when suddenly the young man thrust out his hand to her and smiled, she visibly relaxed. The smile lit up his whole face and showed his astonishingly light, clear, blue eyes.

He was a handsome lad and no mistake, Ruby was thinking as he took her hand in his.

Ian let out a great sigh of relief, the sound of which was so loud it had Ruby turning quickly to face him. Jeffrey felt her jerk away and he too faced his father. Instinct told this big lad what had happened, he looked to Ruby, she raised her eyebrows and nodded at Ian's reddening cheeks. Hesitantly they all smiled and then their smiles turned to laughter.

Jeffrey linked his hand through the crook of Ruby's elbow and Ian did the same on the other side. Thus, walking three abreast, they entered the house.

Catherine Patterson, who had been watching from the window, also smiled as she sent up a silent prayer of thanks.

Jeffrey almost ran to Catherine and, as a small boy might, he put his arms around her waist, bent his head, kissed her cheek, then pulling her close he hugged her to his chest. She, in turn, patted his back.

When Jeffrey released her, she stood back, her face wreathed in smiles and nodded towards where Ruby and Ian were standing holding hands.

Then, speaking very softly, Catherine Patterson made a statement that was to set the seal for the future. 'Och, it's good to see you all together, smiles and laughter is what this old house has been missing for years. Laughter turns a house into a home.'

As Jeffrey and Catherine made their way into the sitting room Ian lingered, then placing his arm around Ruby's shoulders he looked down into her eyes and asked, 'Are you all right?'

'Yes, very much so.'

He smiled at her, a smile of grateful love. 'Jeffrey likes you.'

'I like him, too.'

He kissed her softly on her cheek. 'It makes me happy to hear you say that. I didn't want anything to spoil the love we have for each other. We'll all get along fine, won't we?'

She was filled with love for him. 'I'm sure we shall,' she answered. And she truly meant it.

Chapter Twenty-seven

'LET ME LOOK AT you, Ruby.' Ida gazed at her daughter, and her pride was so strong it was like a physical hurt inside.

'My goodness! You look so beautiful. Each outfit you buy seems to have been made for you. You'd better go upstairs, take it off and hang it up with all the other dresses.'

'Yes, Mum!' Ruby teased her mother.

'And don't forget to cover the hanger with one of those clean sheets I've laid out on the spare bed,' Ida called up the stairs.

'Mum, you know what you are? You're a blooming old bossy boots.'

During this past month Ida hadn't been to her job at Hemmings'. They had been kindness itself when she had explained that her daughter was here for a month with her, getting ready for her wedding. It had been some of the happiest weeks of Ida's life. She couldn't remember when she had laughed so much or enjoyed each day more. Shopping! They had shopped till they dropped.

They had also visited each and every relation. Old friends. Especially Maggie and Tom Carter. Ruby's first port of call every morning was the big house in Blackshaw Road. Now turned into three flats with Tom and Maggie happy in the ground floor garden flat and a nice income coming in from their tenants' rents, they told Ruby that they had got it made.

No more than they deserve, had been Ruby's first thought. Many's the time I don't know how I would have coped if it hadn't been for Maggie. A friend indeed she was and always had been to a young silly girl that hadn't had the sense to know when she was well off. But that was all behind her now.

Everyday she realised how thoughtful Ian had been in suggesting that she spend time with her mother before the wedding. The relationship between them now was so close that sometimes when she looked at her mother and thought about the heartaches she had caused her when she had been young and so silly, it made her want to cry.

'Tea's all ready, sit yeself down,' Ida called from the kitchen as Ruby came back downstairs.

'Mum, there was a letter for you on the mat when we came in, I never saw you open it. What did you do with it?'

'Nosey, ain't you?' Ida said, the colour rising in her cheeks.

'Not nosey, just interested,' Ruby laughed. 'Was it from your gentleman friend?'

Ida blinked, she felt embarrassed. 'He's not a gentleman.'

Mother and daughter stared at each other, then they both burst out laughing.

'Not a gentleman, eh? I'll have to have a talk with my big brothers about this friend of yours that takes you off to his hideaway in Kent and let them know that he's no gentleman.'

'You're asking for a clip round the ear, my girl, and don't think you're too big for me t'do it. You know very well what I meant.'

'Course I did, Mum.' Ruby stopped her teasing. 'Tell me what he had to say in the letter.'

'Well, if you must know, Miss Nosey Parker, it was in answer to one that I wrote to him. He's living permanently down in Kent now.'

'What, on his own?'

''Ow should I know?'

'Playing it pretty close to your chest, aren't you, Mum?'

'No, I'm not! And even if I were it's nothing t'do with you or ye brothers.'

Ruby's head went back and again she roared with laughter. 'Bit long in the tooth to be so coy about this friend of yours. Have the pair of you got dark secrets?'

'I ought t'tan your backside for that remark, young lady.'

'I know,' Ruby giggled. 'Seriously though, Mum, you shouldn't stop seeing him, or going to your dance club simply because I'm here with you.'

Tutting, Ida shook her head. 'Don't talk such rot. I'm enjoying every minute I'm spending with you, and it's not before time either. Once you're married an' settled an' gone back to live in Scotland again, well, there'll be all the time in the world for me t'do other things. Not now, though.'

Ida's voice had ended on a very quiet note and Ruby had a jolly good idea of what her mother was thinking. And she was right.

Ida was looking forward to the wedding. Oh yes! With all her heart she wanted this to work. For her Ruby to be settled and live happy ever after was what she had dreamed of and prayed for. It was what would come after the wedding that she dreaded thinking about. She would be alone in this three bedroomed house once again. With long days and even longer nights.

Suddenly she heard Ruby chuckle, 'Gone all morbid on me, have you? And forgetful?'

Ida looked at her and she had to ask, 'What you on about an' what the 'ell is so funny all of a sudden?'

Ruby picked up her knife and fork, gazed down at her empty place mat and then up at her mother, raising her eyebrows and saying, 'You did call me and said that our tea was ready!'

'Oh blimey!' Ida's hand flew to cover her mouth and she ran towards the kitchen, saying over her shoulder, 'I grilled us two lovely Dover soles and I put them in the oven while I cut the bread and mixed the salad.'

She came back at a trot, a thick kitchen towel wrapped round her hands, and placed the two meals down on the table. 'Mind, the plates are bloody hot.'

Ruby shook her head and she couldn't help but laugh. 'Well they should be, shouldn't they?'

They were both grinning as they started on their meal, for to tell the truth they were both thoroughly enjoying themselves. In fact, they felt more relaxed in each other's company than they had for a very long time.

It was barely six o'clock in the morning on the first Saturday in November 1968. Ruby sat by the banked up fire in her mother's terraced house in Fountain Road. As she looked around the small living room, with its old, well-polished furniture, floral curtains at the window and crisp white nets, she was filled with remorse.

'I haven't been a model daughter to you,' she told her mother, who was seated opposite. 'I'm just so glad we've had this month together. I'll miss you.'

'No, you won't,' Ida declared, forcing her voice to sound bright. 'You've got a busy and an interesting life ahead of you and with a good man, if everything I hear about him is true.'

Ruby lowered her eyes. 'I'm sorry I was such a trial to you when I was growing up,' she said softly.

'Don't, Ruby. Let's not go over old ground, that's all in the past.' Reaching out she touched her daughter's hand. 'Do you love Ian?'

'Mum, until I met Ian I didn't know what love was.' She met her mother's eyes honestly.

Ida smiled, but it was a sad smile. The thought of Ruby going back to live in Scotland hurt. Scotland was such a long way away.

'That's all I wanted to hear.'

As if reading her thoughts, Ruby quickly said, 'I'll not be on the other side of the world, Mum. I shall still ring you every week and it was Ian himself that has insisted you come and stay with us as soon as we get back from our honeymoon.' Ruby's blue eyes shone brightly and there wasn't a shadow of doubt there.

Ida didn't know how to answer. Ruby was thirty-five years old and she had never seen her look so happy and that was more than enough for her. 'You'd better go and have your bath while I make us some toast. You don't want to be late and twelve o'clock will soon come round.'

*   *   *

Alan Wilcox and his brother Norman were on edge.

'Daft, when you think about it, bruv,' Alan said as he once more swept the room with his eyes.

'Yeah, I know exactly what you mean,' Norman answered with a small sigh.

'Still, it is pleasing our mum, us laying all this on for our Ruby's wedding, and after all, there ain't much she allows us t'do for her.'

'You're dead right,' Alan agreed, 'Mum can be right stubborn. But you know something? I'm more chuffed t'be doing it all for our Ruby. There's times when I feel right guilty about her.'

'Me too,' Norman admitted, 'Turned out for the best though, our little sister got on with her life and we got on with ours. Remember, Alan, when I told our Mum I was giving up my job with the Post Office and going into business with you?'

'Don't I just! Thought at the time she was going to kill me. "Never was any good, end up in the gutter you will, and drag poor Norman with you!" I can still hear her saying it.'

'Get on with you. She never meant a word of it. You were always her favourite.'

They laughed together and agreed, 'We haven't done too badly have we?' Their thoughts were running along the same lines. The Cavalier was the perfect club south of the Thames, the place they had dreamed about. Day in, day out, the phones rang, restaurant bookings were always steady, and so many conference enquiries there were times when they had to turn them away. It was an exciting life, a great feeling and the Wilcox brothers enjoyed it to the full

Today, however, the club was closed. It was being used solely for their sister's wedding reception.

The building was old and elegant, very stately. The interior decorator they had employed had been a genius. Even though the whole place had been newly done it had retained the warmth of age. Alan had searched the shops for good furniture to substantiate that feeling.

The entrance hall and the lounge looked marvellous. They had been in close contact with Ian McKenzie about the arrangements. Even the pictures on the wall struck the right note. The frames were draped with tartan ribbon. The McKenzie tartan of navy blue, dark green and white.

The dining room was the *pièce de résistance*. Sparkling white tablecloths, the serviettes and menus each bearing a tiny tartan ribbon. Name places were in the form of a small scroll, the edging again inscribed with the tartan.

On a round table, the laced-edged cloth reaching to the floor, a silver stand held the three tier wedding cake.

'Our chefs really went to town on that cake, don't you think, Norm?'

'Most certainly do. The figures on the top should raise a smile or two.'

Alan grinned. The sugar bride was attired in a white crinoline dress, the groom wore a kilt. 'Marvellous how they managed to mix the exact colours,' Alan commented.

'I agree, but come on, can't do anything more now, let's leave it to the staff.' Norman said over his shoulder as he made for the entrance.

Alan looked at his watch. He hoped Iris had their daughter, Anne, and their two boys, Garry and Roy, all ready spruced up. It would take her long enough to get herself ready, and he wondered why it was that women did take so long. He had been tempted to use the flat at

357

the top of the club and to go to the church from there but had thought better of it. After all, he was giving his sister away and he wanted his wife's help in tying his tie.

Both Alan and Norman lived in Streatham and they had visited their local vicar, who, on hearing the whole story, he had declared that he would be most happy for their sister's wedding to take place in his church.

By midday all friends and family were in St Leonard's Church waiting for Ruby to arrive.

Ian McKenzie stood at the altar, a handsome sight in his morning suit; his tall son looking no less splendid by his side, for he was acting as best man to his father.

Suddenly the air was rent by a sound so unfamiliar to the people of south London that the heads of all the congregation twitched round.

Ian looked at Jeffrey and they both straightened up. The bride had arrived.

Ian had arranged for a piper to be waiting and he was now piping Ruby, who was walking on the arm of her eldest brother, from the car to the doorway of the church.

A gasp went up! 'Oh, doesn't she look beautiful?'

Dressed in a long dress of pale cream chiffon, a tiny hat with a veil on her head, Ruby wasn't carrying a bouquet of flowers. In her hand was a nosegay of both white and purple heather, fashioned for her by Catherine Patterson. The note that had come with it had said *To bring you luck. Not that you will need it.*

The ceremony was simple. Ruby Wilcox was now Ruby McKenzie.

The whole day was a happy one, and when it was time for Ruby and Ian to leave for the airport that would take them back to Scotland to start their honeymoon, there was a moment that clinched the day for Ida.

Ian's son's eyes were twinkling merrily as he used his fingers to speak to his father. Ruby guessed rather than knew that Jeffrey had remarked about her and she was even more convinced when Ian threw back his head and laughed.

'Share the joke with me,' Ruby implored as Jeffrey took her in his arms and kissed her first on one cheek and then on the other.

'Do you really want to know what your son has just said about you?' Ian teased.

'I'll not move from here until you tell me,' Ruby smiled, looking from one to the other of these tall men that were now her very own family.

Jeffrey's fingers again moved swiftly.

'All right son,' Ian said, as he turned to Ruby. 'Jeffrey said I am to tell you that he thinks his father is a very lucky man because you are a lovely lady and—' Jeffrey shoved his father in the back. 'All right!' Ian laughed, 'And the rest of it was you're a bit of alright.'

Ruby burst out laughing, threw her arms around her new son and hugged him close. Then she pointed to his chest and held up two fingers. 'You too,' she mouthed and Jeffrey had no trouble in understanding her.

Ida had seen and heard it all. She quickly brushed away a tear. Sometimes God does answer prayers and today he certainly had. Her Ruby had a husband who adored her and there was no doubt that Ruby was in love with him. And they had a lad that was every inch a son to be proud of.

Chapter Twenty-eight

RUBY HAD BEEN MARRIED for almost six months and so far Ida hadn't been able to settle down into her old routine. She only worked at the bakers now for two mornings a week. Torrential rain was falling when she finished her Tuesday morning shift at Hemmings' on Tooting Broadway.

She turned up the collar of her mackintosh and made a dash for the bus stop. Her ride was only a couple of stops along Garrett Lane and her house only a very short walk from where she got off the bus. Nevertheless she was soaking wet by the time she got indoors. She closed the front door firmly behind her and made for the warmth of the kitchen.

Talk about April showers! This rain had been falling on and off for three days now and it was enough to give anyone the hump.

She missed Ruby, more than she would admit to anyone. Having had her for twenty-four hours of every day for a whole month had only served to make her own life seem even more lonely once she had gone.

There were still times when she couldn't quite believe what had happened to her Ruby. All girls when they are little believe in fairytales, that a handsome prince is going to come riding on a white charger and carry them off to live happily ever after. Even grown women who read a lot, especially Mills and Boon stories, still cling to the hope that love will change their lives. Her daughter had proved that sometimes it comes true.

Personally she was thrilled for Ruby, and extremely proud of her. Her journey from south London to Edinburgh had not been a happy ride, indeed it must have been a terribly lonely one. But it had happened. She had moved from one world to another. From her way of speaking, her clothes and her manner, no one would guess it was the same girl that had grown up here in Tooting. From having lived with her for those few weeks before the wedding Ida felt sure that Ruby would cope very well as Mrs Ian McKenzie. She won't feel remotely out of place, she often comforted herself.

Not a lot had changed in her own life. She did see Mike Moffett on a more regular basis. Having moved down to live permanently in Kent, Mike had set up a pattern in which he had involved her. It had been agreed that he would only come to the dance club once a month but that he would come to London once every week on a Wednesday.

Ida rubbed hard with the towel in an effort to dry her hair, puzzling over the fact that she had rushed out of the house this morning without a hat or a scarf over her head. She shook the towel hard and hung it over the back of a chair to dry.

The reason that Mike came up from Kent every Wednesday still amused her. Only a man like him would have thought of it. There was no end to Mike's enterprises – he'd never starve, that's for sure! Mike's property in East Hill was now known as a thriving chicken farm. He freely admitted that he missed his old workmates and it was for that reason that he had hit upon the idea of delivering eggs. Not only locally in and around the districts of Kent but also in London. Everybody in the East End of London knew him and he bumped into several of his old mates when he came up on Wednesdays delivering eggs to butchers' and grocers' shops.

Mike called Wednesday his day off. Through Ida he had half a dozen customers in Fountain Road and when he'd finished his visit to his dockland friends he always made Tooting his last port of call. Ida made a point of having a good dinner ready for him because she not only enjoyed having someone other than just herself to cook for, she also looked forward to having his company on that one evening every week.

Ida was still thinking about Mike as she set a tray out for her lunch.

'Time you and Mike settled things with a proper understanding,' Alan had told her.

Her answer had been swift and to the point. 'You've all met Mike. You've told me he is a good bloke, so let's leave it at that. We're good friends, as they say, and it suits us both to keep it that way.'

Mike had asked her to go and stay at his bungalow for a weekend, so far she had refused, not saying anything to her sons, not even to Jozy or Sheila. She wanted first to settle in her own mind just how serious this friendship was before she opened her heart to her family.

The kettle had just come to the boil when the phone rang. 'Hello, me old darlin',' Mike said.

'Mike, what's up? You don't usually ring when you're coming up tomorrow.'

'That's the reason, luv, I won't be able to make it tomorrow. I've phoned around, let me customers know I won't be delivering this week till Friday. Will you pass the word your end?' He sounded cheerful and healthy.

'So why the change of plans?' she asked, trying to hide her disappointment.

'I've got a couple of mates 'ere with me now. We're putting the finishing touches to the swimming pool. Hope to get the glass surround in place tomorrow.'

'Oh, that's nice,' Ida endeavoured to sound as if she was pleased.

'What I was thinking was, Ida, the place will still be in a bit of a mess come the weekend, but 'ow about coming back with me Friday night? You could stay a few days. I'll bring you back on the Wednesday.'

It was ages since Ida had been down to the bungalow and the first thought that came into her head was whether the second bedroom had any furniture in it yet!

'Do I 'ave to decide now?' asked Ida, in a voice as cool as she could manage.

'No, course ye don't,' said Mike casually. 'I'll see you Friday afternoon. Take care.'

The line went dead and Ida sighed softly as she replaced the receiver.

Friday afternoon was fine, if a little windy. Fluffy white clouds sailed across the sky leaving huge patches of bright blue for which Ida was very grateful. She had made up her mind to go back with Mike today and the visit would be all the better now that the rain had stopped and the forecast for the weekend was promising.

It was just on three o'clock when Mike arrived and the first thing she noticed was that the collar of his shirt was crumpled and that his face had lost that nice ruddy look.

'You've been working too hard,' she told him before he had hardly set foot in the house.

'Yeah, you're right,' he said in an absent-minded way. 'I feel really knackered.'

'Come on, sit yeself down. I've got a lovely hot-pot in the oven, been in since ten o'clock this morning so the meat should be well tender and the gravy will stick t'yer ribs.'

'Thanks Ida, you're a queen,' Mike said, as he dropped gratefully down into an armchair.

'Well, well, nobody's ever called me a queen before,' Ida retorted, realising then how much she had been looking forward to seeing him and how great it was to have him sitting here and her about to dish up dinner for the two of them.

She watched as Mike's eyes closed and she decided to leave him be while she dropped the dumplings into the casserole, they would take about twenty minutes to cook so may as well let him have a snooze. He really did look dead beat. What he needs is someone to take care of him.

Ida blushed at the thought! Anyone would think if she'd voiced that out loud that she was volunteering for the job! You better watch your mouth, she told herself, and mind that tongue of yours don't get you into something that you can't handle.

She laid the table and brought the dishes from the oven. The fire had burnt low and it would be some time yet before they left the house so she threw two logs onto the embers. Being dry they caught straight away, the flames leapt and crackled, the glass vases on the sideboard gleamed with the reflection; everything looked so cosy. It was just as the start to a weekend should be, the man home from his work, having a few minutes shut-eye before the woman of the house dished up a hot meal.

Ida set hot plates down on the table and took the lid off the casserole. The aroma that rose from it was enough to make Mike stir.

'Come and sit up,' Ida invited, 'you'll feel better with some of this inside you.'

Holding a plate with a serving cloth she ladled the braised steak, moist and nicely brown, carrots, baby onions, mushrooms, peas and tomatoes until the plate was almost full. 'There's mashed potatoes in that dish and leeks and swede in the other one. Help yourself, there's plenty more meat when you've eaten that.'

Minutes passed before Mike uttered his first comment. 'How can anyone have let you stay single all these years when you can cook like this?'

'Oh goodness! Here comes the flattery,' she teased. 'Is that a way of saying you would like some more?'

'No it isn't. I'm not 'alfway through this lot yet. Talk about eat hearty.'

'Well I've made a whacking great rice pudding for afters, seeing as how the oven was going I thought I might as well. If we 'aven't got room for it we shall 'ave to take it with us. Don't want to waste it, do we?'

Mike stopped with his fork halfway to his mouth. 'Take it with us? Does that mean you're gonna come back with me tonight?'

'Yes,' she said, laughter sounding in her voice. 'All I've 'eard you go on about for weeks now is the amount of work you've done, so, I think you're right. It is time I came down and saw for myself.'

'Oh Ida, you won't regret it. And you'll be amazed at the difference in the place. You mark my words.'

He was right an' all! Ida was amazed. It was dark by the time they arrived at the bungalow and Mike said they would have to leave the tour of inspection until the morning.

'Here's the key, you go and open the door. I'll bring your case in,' he said.

Ida's hand felt along the wall and found two switches which she clicked on. One illuminated the outside of the building the other lit up the hallway which smelt of fresh paint.

'Crikey, ain't you done it up posh, Mike?' said Ida as she stepped inside.

'Well, don't know about posh, but it's all nice an' clean now. I was hoping you would like it.'

'Like it? I think it's grand,' she cried, taking note of the gleaming doors with their brass handles and the brand new red figured carpet on the floor.

Both bedrooms were well furnished, Ida noted with a smile, and the bed in each room was made up.

The bathroom too was a joy to behold and there were large and small towels laid out. A pile of blue ones neatly stacked on a cork-topped stool. A pile of pink ones set on a pretty Lloyd-Loom chair. Imagine that. Was Mike trying to tell her something?

'I've put your case in your bedroom,' Mike called out.

Ida told herself to be grateful and to keep her mouth shut. If Mike wasn't going to comment on the sleeping arrangements then neither was she.

They were both up by seven thirty next morning and Ida couldn't wait to see the outside. The front garden had been overgrown when she had last seen it. Now neatly turned earth lay ready for the summer bedding plants and daffodils bloomed in great clumps at the side of the driveway.

Ida stood back and regarded the bungalow. All newly painted in white, she thought its new black front door with its brass knocker and letter box made it look quite grand. Its windows shone but the curtains weren't all they should be. Needs a woman's touch, she decided, then quickly took herself to task. It wasn't up to her to find fault. If Mike had done all this on his own then he deserved a medal.

'Can you believe the sun is actually shining?' asked Mike. 'We'll go back in and 'ave our breakfast and then you can help me feed the chickens.'

They were in the parlour after their evening meal. They had done the washing up together, in fact they had spent the whole day doing things together.

Ida was very impressed by everything that Mike had shown her, the sight of all those chickens, Rhode Island Reds, he said they were.

Fascinating, was how Ida would have described the job of collecting the eggs. With a straw-filled trog on one arm, she had gone from nest to nest gently picking up the warm brown eggs. Once she had stopped, turning round to see what Mike was doing. He had a chicken in his hands, tenderly spreading the feathers of its wing, making sure that it was all right. She had to smile, he didn't look at all like that sort of a man. Broad shouldered, brawny and rugged would be a good description. Old corduroy trousers, a well worn zip fronted cardigan and a battered trilby hat tilted to the back of his head, he still looked more like a docker than a chicken farmer. He had felt her eyes on him, looked up and they had smiled at each other. An easy smile between good companions.

The glass-surrounded swimming pool had to be seen to be believed.

'All this is the result of your own sweat and toil?' she had timidly asked him.

'Sure is, except a bit of help now an' again from me mates. Be some time yet though before I can get it filled with water. I want to tile the inside first.'

Jesus! No wonder he looked washed out.

'If it's a nice day tomorrow, 'ow d'you fancy a trip to the coast? We could go to Romney or St Mary's Bay, there's plenty of real nice old-fashioned pubs round those parts where we'd get a decent Sunday lunch.' Mike had broken into her thoughts and she took a second or two to answer.

'Whatever you say, Mike. I'm quite happy here where I am. I think the whole place is a credit to you.'

Kent was a beautiful place. No wonder folk referred to it as the Garden of England.

Before they came to the sea Mike drove through narrow country lanes.

'Spring time must be the best time of the year to see all this,' Ida remarked as they bowled along.

Farmlands, crops just bursting through the earth, orchards with rows upon rows of trees heavy with sweet-smelling blossom. In the fields sheep for as far as the eye could see. Through the summer months, the beaches would be crowded for there were several caravan sites to be seen. This Kent coast line was also well patronised by the casual day-tripper. But now with it being only the second week in April there were only a few cars on the road, people like themselves, out for a nice run and Sunday lunch somewhere.

Mike turned the car into the almost empty car park which was right opposite the beach at St Mary's Bay. He opened the door, put his head out, turning his face up to the sun.

'Not really very warm,' he told Ida, 'but there doesn't seem to be any wind and the tide is out. D'you feel like a walk along the sands?'

'Course I do,' Ida answered, at the same time getting out of the other door.

They crossed the road, scrambled over the pebbles and Mike led the way down to the sea. The early spring sunshine was pleasant as the tiny ripples of water lapped at the sand. Far out the sea was calm, glittering and brilliantly blue.

Ida gazed at everything around her, trying to decide how she could best say thank you to Mike for these lovely few days. She turned her head to look at him, he was way up further along the sand. He wasn't wearing a hat and his thick greying hair was ruffled. Otherwise he was smartly turned out today in navy blue trousers and a grey checked jacket.

She wondered where he was taking her for lunch and was glad that she had dressed herself with care. The classic grey suit that Ruby had insisted she buy when they had been on one of their shopping sprees was standing her in good stead. And so it should, she told herself, it cost the earth. Beneath the jacket of the suit she was wearing a navy blue blouse and a three-quarter coat of the same shade of navy completed her outfit.

'I suggest that we see about finding a place for lunch now,' Mike called as he came near. 'Don't know about you, Ida, luv, but I'm starving.'

The pub they ended up in wasn't at all what Ida was used to. It was the sort of luxury that she'd only read about in books and the food had her drooling. The roast beef had been carved at their table by a white-coated chef, the Yorkshire pudding light and fluffy.

Ida was all set to say that she couldn't manage any sweet when Mike ordered steamed treacle pudding and custard for himself. But she hadn't reckoned on the waitress bringing her the sweet trolley. Fresh cream delights in all shapes and forms. Mike laughed as Ida yielded to temptation.

But Sunday evening, perhaps was the best of all.

With the lovely day behind them, the curtains drawn and a fire blazing, they listened to music, the sort of music that had been played at Peggy Spencer's dance club when they had first met in 1967.

Outside the wind had got up, rattling against the windows as if to say that summer had not yet arrived. All that only made Ida feel more secure as she sat back and enjoyed the comfort, and most of all, Mike's company. She spent too many evenings on her own not to appreciate him being there.

Ida was lost in dreams when Mike spoke and broke the spell. 'Ida?'

'Yes.'

'I want to ask you something.'

She smiled. 'Fire away then.'

'Will you be glad to go home?'

'What kind of a question is that?' asked Ida.

'What I really meant to say is will you miss me?'

'Bless you, Mike,' she murmured, 'How could I not miss you after the lovely way you've looked after me?'

'Never mind what I've done for you, how about me as a person? Tell me, will you miss me?'

'Well, of course I shall.' She did her best to make her smile affectionate.

'Ida, I shall miss you,' he said with great feeling.

Ida knew then that Mike was asking her more than he was actually saying, but it had to come from him. These few days she had come alive. She lived each hour as it came, not looking further ahead, not wanting too. She'd felt at home here with Mike. It seemed natural that they should be together. Though at this moment her heart was pounding, she felt confused but surprisingly happy.

'Ida, would you –' he stammered, 'Would you consider taking me on – permanent like? What I mean is – will you come and live 'ere with me? No – that's not exactly what I mean, I'm trying to ask you, please, will you marry me?'

'Oh,' she said.

They were sitting so close together that she could feel his warm breath on her cheek. He swayed towards her, his arms were around her. And then he was kissing her.

Nothing else mattered. Tooting was another world.

Ida had no idea how long they stayed in one another's arms. She never wanted to move again. But at last Mike broke the silence. 'I love you, Ida, don't you know that?'

'Well, I wasn't sure.'

'I'm telling you now then, I love you very much. And I promise I will look after you.'

'You, Mike Moffett?' Ida was trying to joke. 'You can't even look after yourself.'

'Please believe me,' Mike said, looking straight at her.

'We'll look after each other.' And by the sound of his voice Ida knew it was a promise.

She didn't know what to say so she said nothing. Suddenly she was back in his arms and he was kissing her again, gentle soft kisses that showed her how much he did care for her.

'I love you, Ida,' he said as they drew apart. 'Put me out of my misery and say that you will marry me, please.'

Ida eyes were sparkling. 'Oh yes, I'd like that. Yes, Mike, yes, I will.'

Suddenly she was laughing and crying all at the same time. She was to have a partner, someone of her own to share the rest of her life with.

Mike's face was beaming. He took her hand in his and held it. 'Ida, I'll do my best to make you happy. Whatever we do from now on, we'll do it together. Is that all right by you?'

She gave him a wide smile. 'I want your promise on that.'

'You've got it, lass. I mean every word. You will be my reason for living. We're going to enjoy life. Have a lot of fun. Life is going to be good for both of us. I know it.'

'Oh crickey!' Ida Suddenly cried out breathlessly, 'Does that mean that we'll be living 'ere? In this beautiful bungalow?'

'Course it does, you daft woman! Or would you rather I sold it all and we both lived in your house?'

'Definitely not!' she quickly told him.

'Well then. Just remember that you an' me are right for each other and from now on that's the way it's going to be. And that's a promise.'

Broad as he was, she fitted into his arms just right. Oh it felt so good to be held that close. Would it really be as he said? She looked anxious and Mike lowered his lips to cover hers. She felt the shivers run through her whole body. She hadn't dreamt that it could be like this. She might be coming up to being sixty and Mike had probably turned sixty but life wasn't over for either of them. They weren't on the way out. A new life was just starting, for heaven's sake!

'Let's just start to look forward,' Mike urged as he gently held her close to his side.

Oh she would. She would look forward to each and every day for the rest of her life.

'I could stay like this forever,' she sighed.

'Oh no you couldn't,' Mike declared, 'you're going to shift right now and make us both a night cap.'

'Why you old slave driver! This is a side to you I 'aven't seen before.'

He pulled her to her feet and together they went into the kitchen. 'I've got something I want to ask you,' Mike said.

'Not another proposal,' she teased.

'No,' he said, filling the kettle at the sink. 'How are you at raking out chicken muck?'

He hadn't expected the quick way in which she reacted and he had to duck as she repeatedly flicked the teacloth around his head.

'Finished?' Mike asked, tears of laughter running down his cheeks.

'Finished? I've 'ardly started. I've got t'let you know, Mike Moffett, that I'm no wilting lily. You've met your match in me, my lad.'

'Suffering cats,' said Mike, laughing fit to bust as he set the cups and saucers out.

Ida decided that all in all it had been a lovely weekend. And by God, she'd sell her soul rather than lose Mike now.

Chapter Twenty-nine

IDA MOFFETT, AS SHE was now, was a picture of health. Looking at her nowadays it would be hard to believe she had been born and bred in London, or her husband Mike, for that matter. The pair of them appeared to be proper country bumpkins.

Ida hadn't grown any taller, just plumper. Like one of his broody chickens, Mike teased her. Her cheeks were like two rosy apples, her eyes danced with merriment and these days her voice always held a note of laughter.

And so it should. What a life she and Mike led! She had never been happier. There wasn't enough hours in the day for all the things that they wanted to do.

'It's funny how things turn out,' Ida remarked to her husband, as she steadily shucked peas into a bowl. 'If anyone had told me five years ago I'd be living in a place like this an' doing all the things we do, I'd never've believed them.'

'What are you on about?' Mike called out from the doorway of the packing shed.

'Just thinking aloud,' Ida answered, getting up from the wooden bench and making for the house. 'I'm gonna make us a sandwich. D'ye want a beer or just a shandy?'

'Whatever you're 'aving. I'm almost finished. I'll put the umbrella up if we're eating out 'ere, I think it's hotter than ever today.'

Ida smiled as she busied herself setting out the loaf on the breadboard and going to the fridge to decide what she could put into the sandwiches for their lunch. It made a nice change for her and Mike to be on their own. All through the long hot days of that summer they'd had more relations coming down to visit them than they had bargained for.

Sometimes Ida felt guilty because so many of the visitors were members of her family. Mike only had the one son, Dave, married to Brenda, and they didn't have any children. The good thing was that both Dave and his wife were down here almost every weekend and they fitted in well with the Wilcox and the Simmonds families, which was great for Mike. Who could blame any of them? London must be stifling in this hot weather. Weekends there were always some of their relations here and the swimming pool rang to the sound of youngsters enjoying themselves.

Ida still hadn't got over the fact that they owned a swimming pool! At such times all the cooking was done out of doors, Mike insisting that he was in charge. Blue and white butcher's apron, tall chef's hat, he did everything with a flourish much to the amusement of the teenagers.

By the end of the first year of being married to Mike, there wasn't a trace of the old Ida left. And she would be the first to admit that was the truth. Nothing worried her now. Mike sorted everything. He made her laugh, he made her happy and she loved him more than she would have believed possible.

Together they threw caution to the wind and lived their lives to the full. Mondays they went to a club they had joined in the village. Tuesdays they had a stall at the big open-air market where they sold eggs and sometimes chickens. Wednesday was still Mike's day off. London day. Mostly Ida went with him, but not always. If she gave an excuse as to why she should remain at the bungalow, Mike would tease her unmercifully.

'It will all be here when we get back,' he would tell her.

All the same, she didn't like leaving what to her was her happy home. Tooting was still grand. Her welcome from Jozy, Sheila and dear old Maggie still assured. It was when Mike took her into the East End that she became alarmed.

London wasn't at all as she remembered. Parliament Square and Whitehall with the wonderful Cenotaph were still the same, and all the pigeons on Nelson's Column in Trafalgar Square. But the traffic was murder!

Where were all the flower sellers? The barrow boys and costermongers that she had grown up with? Even in Fountain Road you didn't get the rag and bone man or the totters shouting their wares any more.

Still, she did like to go up to the city. Sometimes.

Thursday was chicken shed day. Mucking out and making everything nice and sweet again for the birds. Friday sequel dancing, of course! They wouldn't miss their dancing for the world.

As partners they had become very good, their speciality being Latin American. Who would have believed it, she often asked herself. More so when she and Mike were asked to demonstrate a particularly difficult dance.

Come Saturday it was a safe bet that as soon as breakfast was over some visitors would start to arrive.

Ida washed some spring onions under the tap and laid them on the tray with the ham sandwiches and a bowl of tomatoes.

'God, I've a lot t'be grateful for,' she said out loud as she went back outside to have her lunch with Mike in the sunshine. 'Mike come on, wash your hands and come and sit down,' she called.

They were halfway through their lunch when Ida brought the letter out of her apron pocket. 'You got time to read this now?' Ida asked, with a smile on her face.

'Of course I 'ave,' he said reaching across and taking the envelope from her.

It was a long letter from Ruby because it was the first they had received for a month. Ruby and Ian had been touring the Continent, celebrating the fact that they had been married for six years. It was all very informative as to where they had been and the sights they had seen, but it was the last page that interested Ida the most. Impatiently she watched as Mike came to it at last.

'Oh that's a bit of good news, don't you think?' he grinned, folding the letter carefully and passing it back to Ida.

'Course I do. Jeffrey getting married is wonderful. Catherine had already written to tell me it was on the cards and that she was sure we would like the girl very much. It's great that we're being asked to the wedding, don't you think? I don't want to fly, though. I know when Ruby and Ian come down they always fly, but we can go by train, can't we?'

Mike looked at her long and hard then he threw back his head and roared out laughing. 'Ida, my luv, you really do take the biscuit. The date hasn't even been set for Jeffrey's wedding and you're going on about how we're going to get there. Scotland isn't the other side of the world. Though I suppose it is t'you. You've refused all Ian's previous invitations to go up there.'

'Yeah, well, this is different. We'll go this time, won't we?'

'Yes, we most certainly will,' Mike approved.

Ida poured more lemonade into their glasses and Mike topped them up with beer.

'Cheers luv,' he said, raising his glass to his mouth and taking a long drink. 'We won't do anything else today, we'll 'ave a rest for about an hour an' then shall we go for a walk before we start on our dinner?'

'Yeah, suits me fine. I'll just take the tray indoors and fetch my library book. Will you put a deck chair under the shade for me?'

'What kind of a wedding d'you think it will be?' Ida wondered aloud, as she settled herself down to read her book.

Mike grinned to himself before answering. 'Get on the phone to Ruby tonight – she'll be able to tell you better than me.'

A few minutes passed in silence and then out of the blue Mike asked, 'Ida, d'you think you got a good bargain when you took me on?'

Ida was puzzled for a moment. She laid her book down on her knees and twisted round to face him and was surprised to find that he was looking very serious.

'Better than I ever dreamed of,' her soft voice trembled a little.

It was a perfect answer.

'You amaze me more as each day goes by,' he said,

putting out a hand to stroke her cheek. 'I reckon I'm a very lucky man.'

Ida laughed. 'That's not what you say when half of the population of Tooting turn up 'ere of a weekend.'

Still being serious, Mike leaned forward. 'I just thought it was about time that I reminded you just how dear you are to me.'

'Oh Mike!'

Her dear loving Mike, who worked so hard and looked after her so well and made every day a happy one just by being with her. She sighed contentedly, reached out for his hand. 'You know what they say, Mike, life begins at forty. Well, it was a bit late in coming for me but you, my luv, were well worth waiting for.'

'That's all right then,' Mike grinned, ''cos I'm well satisfied an' all.' He squeezed her hand tightly. 'In fact I think I got the best of the bargain.'

Those words were music to Ida's ears.